A LIFE NA̅

To: Elizabeth.

Hope you enjoy the book.

Huychn,

Haydn H. Watson 2020

All rights reserved, including the right to reproduce this book, or portions thereof in any form. No part of this text may be reproduced, transmitted, downloaded, decompiled, reverse engineered, or stored, in any form or introduced into any information storage and retrieval system, in any form or by any means, whether electronic or mechanical without the express written permission of the author.

This is a work of fiction. Names and characters are the product of the author's imagination and any resemblance to actual persons, living or dead, is entirely coincidental.

The views expressed in this work are solely those of the author and do not necessarily reflect the views of the publisher, and the publisher hereby disclaims any responsibility for them.

pbl Print, Phoenix House, Angel Park,
Chester le Street, County Durham, DH2 1AQ

A LIFE NAVIGATED

Haydn Watson

*In memory of a dear friend
Michael Norman Rushton*

Our children carry our hopes, our dreams and our spirit for Layla, Emma, Geoff, Adam and Philippa

ACKNOWLEDGEMENTS

I am eternally grateful to the people and organisations who are listed in this acquiesce. In particular to family and friends who have encouraged and supported me with this book. My gratitude to a wonderful family and to Christine who has shown great patience and understanding throughout. This book would not have been possible without the valuable insight of Lynn Davidson and The Memoir Club. In addition, I would like thank Kris Makuch for his excellent jacket design for the book.

CHAPTER ONE

The night sky is clear with a full moon shining high above the peaks that skirt the Azow River, a tributary of the Farah River in western Afghanistan. A snow leopard lies motionless in the sagebrush just below the snowline. She has two cub's safe in a nearby cave, but she must be patient and wait for her prey to pass within striking distance. She must eat soon to sustain her own strength and in doing so, provide milk for her cubs.

Some 1000 metres below at latitude of 33 degrees north, a new born baby gives its first cry in the remote village of Azaw. It is 8.15pm, October 15th 1918 and the child is a brother for Hakim Adur Rahman. Hakim sits with his father Muhammad Fazlur Rahman outside their home waiting to be invited in to see his new brother. Muhammad has named his son Abdel Malik Rahman and as he gets up to enter his home; a cry of another kind alerts his gaze up the mountain. The snow leopard will eat again this night.

Muhammad Fazlur Rahman was also born in this village and he is the sole teacher in the village school. Education in this remote area of Afghanistan involves the teachings of the Noble Qur'an, based upon the Sunni doctrine. Sunni Muslims make up 85% of the population in Afghanistan and Muhammad's family belong to the Pashtun ethnic group which dominates the country in terms of numbers. Pashtuns comprise some 40% of the total population in Afghanistan. The country has also been hailed as the '*Land of the Pashtuns.*'

In the village, the temperature is just above freezing and Muhammad greets his son with a prayer, thanking God for his safe delivery. One thousand metres up the mountain the mother Snow Leopard is quickly consuming as much meat from the carcass of the Markhor (*small goat*), before other interested carnivores make themselves known. Often leopards lose their kills to jackals and wolves, who work in teams to steal the prey. She also has her cubs to consider, as they also often fall prey to wolves, who seek to limit the competition.

The new born Abdel is healthy and quickly begins to suckle his mother, underneath a swathe of warm sheepskin. Abdel's brother Hakim has assisted in the birth of his brother by ensuring that hot water is made available to his Aunt, who with the help of Abdel's Grandmother, delivered the baby. The house or '*Qala*' as it is better known was built by Muhammad some seven years earlier. His previous home was his Father's house, but after the death of his father he needed a larger dwelling, to house his growing family. Hakim had just been born within a week of his Grandfather's demise and the need for a bigger living space was required. Abdel's mother is called Fatima, a common name for women as it was the name of the daughter of the prophet Muhammad.

After her baby had taken his first drink of his mother's milk both Fatima and child fell asleep. She had been in labour for some 8 hours and there had been some concern as to the outcome for both mother and child. Infant mortality was very high in Afghanistan in 1918, one in three babies never survived childbirth.

The Rahman house was made form a combination of stone and clay and it has a small grazing area at the rear where six goats are tethered. Adjacent to that is a small plot of land that has been cultivated for crops including wheat, barley, almonds, mulberries and stone fruit. At harvest time Muhammad, would travel to Farah, to sell his produce in return for cooking utensils and fabrics. The return journey was 130 miles and so this would take some four days to complete. Other villages are closer with Zamaki being the nearest, some 2 miles along the valley.

In order to educate the children in the village, Muhammad had built an annex to his house. This was the school and there were seven children in the village whom attended, Hakim being one. Along with the teachings of the Qur'an, simple Mathematics and Writing were taught to the children.

At seven years of age Hakim played a vital role in the family. He looked after the animals and helped cultivate the crops. He would also accompany his father to local villages to buy and sell various produce. When he was only 5 years old, he witnessed a sight that very few people ever saw. He was tending the families small flock of goats higher up the valley, when a Caspian Tiger sprang from behind a rocky outcrop and pounced on one of the goats. The goat was killed in an instant, succumbing to a lethal bite to the neck. When he told his father of this, Muhammad fell on his knees and thanked God for saving his only son. From that day on, Hakim never ventured farther than the outskirts of the village to tend the goats.

The Caspian Tiger was a rare sight, as they were generally thought to be on the verge of extinction. They were often talked about by the village elders, but only one villager had ever seen one and that had been in 1898. That observation had occurred on the upper reaches of the Hari – Rud River near Herat, in western Afghanistan. Herat is 175 miles to the west of Hakim's village and to encounter one so far east was indeed a rarity.

Afghanistan is a historical conundrum. For centuries, it has been a land of tribal and civil conflict. It has been part of numerous empires and it has been subjected to countless invasions. It has been occupied by Alexander the Great, Genghis Khan, Tamerlane, Great Britain, the USA and Russia. Long before Britain tried to establish some form of order, it was a lawless country.

Rival tribes were constantly at war and ethnic violence was a regular problem. The violence was often extremely brutal, with punishments that included hanging, castration, mutilation or the unfortunate victim being flayed alive. This gruesome act involved the person having all of his or her skin removed and then pegged out lying in the sun to die. And finally, eaten by all manner of animals and birds.

A punishment was meted out only six months earlier in the village of Neeh, when a young man had raped a 14-year-old girl. He was heavily beaten, castrated and finally hung from a tree by his feet. Thankfully, the village of Azaw did not witness any such violence and disputes although very rare, were dealt with amicably.

The village sits in the mountain range called the *Paropamisus*, which stretches from Herat in the west and merges with the Hindu Kush in the east. In 1918, Afghanistan is bordered by Russia, India, Persia and China.

The political climate in Afghanistan in 1918 was a fragmented constitution of tribal autonomy. In 1881 a distant ancestor Abdur Rahman became the new Amir. He quickly dissolved the regional governmental system, which gave local tribes a good degree of freedom from the authority of Kabul. He chose to wage war on any rivals and created a doctorial dynasty that lasted some 48 years. He gained power as a result of the failed second Anglo – Afghan War. His appetite for swift retribution led to many tribal regions being brutally suppressed and he ordered the forced migration of many families into the Hindu Kush and beyond. In 1901 Abdur Rahman's son Habibullah was crowned the Amir after his father's death.

All of this political change had little effect on the villages on the Farah river until four months after the birth of Abdel. Then, in February 1919 after a reign of 18 years, Habibullah was murdered while he slept in his bed. By May of that year, Afghanistan was at war again with the British. The dynasty, now led by Habibullah's son Amanullah declared a *jihad* on the British. In the end, the hostilities lasted barely a month and peace was agreed.

Abdel Rahman was oblivious to all this political intrigue and thrived within the village community. That life changed in 1920, when his mother Fatima died giving birth to her third son; who also did not survive the birth. Muhammad had to consider the future for his two sons. Hakim was now nine years old and Muhammad decided that he would send his oldest son to Karachi, in North West India. He had a cousin who had a Chandlers business near the port. Muhammad was not in good health and at the age of 47 he had succumbed to a serious breathing disorder that restricted his duties to teaching in the village school.

Trips to Farah to buy and sell provisions were now out of the question. He and his family must now be self-sufficient and also rely on the generosity of the village elders to sustain a living. Movement in and out of the region was always on foot. Hakim would be accompanied by a village elder to Farah and there he would join the camel train that would pass through Qandahar, Spinboldak, Chaman, Quetta and the final destination of Karachi. In total Hakim, would walk some 885 miles (1424km). This trek would take him some 35 days, through some of the most inhospitable country.

Being a part of the camel train offered some degree of security and against all the odds Hakim arrived in Karachi and sought out his uncle to begin a new chapter in his life. It was March 20th 1920 and, on this day, the first ever flight from London to South Africa was completed, it took 6 weeks.

CHAPTER TWO

Life in Azaw continued much the same as always, with Muhammad doing what he could around the house and still educating the children three days every week. Abdel began to help around the house supervised by his Aunt and he took particular pleasure in herding the goats in the small paddock behind the house. Muhammad received a message from his brother in Karachi, saying that Hakim had arrived safely; some 12 weeks after his departure. The message arrived with a village elder who had been visiting relatives in Karachi. In the message, his brother had said that Hakim was terrified when he saw his first motor car trundling down Elphinstone Street and he thought it looked like a giant goat with wheels.

The years rolled on and Muhammad's health got increasingly worse. By 1928 he had given up teaching the village children and spent most of his time sitting doing menial chores like repairing utensils and preparing food. His breathing became much worse and he found it very difficult to sleep lying down. On January 11th 1929, he finally succumbed to his failing health and died in his sleep aged 56. Two days earlier he had told Abdel that he would be soon joining his mother as was Gods wish and he instructed him to follow in his brother's footsteps and go to Karachi. Abdel was 11 years old and later that day he and his Aunt laid his father to rest in the village graveyard.

Now it was Abdel who joined the camel train to Karachi and on March 13th, like his brother before him he joined the trek at Farah for the long journey. He would never return to his home village of Azaw and never again see the Snow Leopard skirting the rocky ledges of the Paropamisus searching for an unsuspecting *markhor.*

His journey to Karachi began with a raid by bandits after three days travel. This was a common occurrence in the south of Afghanistan. Thankfully the bandits were repelled after a fierce fight which resulted in two of the bandits being captured and beheaded. The leader of the caravan was Mohammed and he had travelled on this route many times, he knew the terrain and he was ruthless when dealing with those that would seek to kill or steal. Three years earlier his son was murdered by bandits, as he guarded the camels while camped near Delaram. The weather in the early days of the journey was particularly bleak with regular snowfall and very low overnight temperatures of – 10 degrees centigrade.

Abdel was a strong 11-year-old and he had good warm goatskin to protect him against the elements. His 'bakes' (*knapsack*) contained all his possessions including his goatskin tent and a plentiful supply of food for the early part of the journey, which consisted of dried goat meat, almonds, rice and apples.

The camel caravan arrived in Qandahar on March 20th; he had now walked some 300 miles (480km). The caravan then moved south to Spinboldak and as they approached the town, a *Buzkashi* tournament was in progress. This local sport consisted of two teams of men on horseback that used a goat's carcase. At the start, the carcase is placed in a pit. Then riders of both teams try and seize the carcase and gallop to a goal post and circle it to gain a point. The horsemen were highly skilled and the sport was played at a very fast pace. Abdel was fascinated and watched the competition with great interest. Having rested, the caravan carried on into the town to replenish their supplies of food and water.

After they left Spinboldak, they came upon a camp of *"Kuchi."* These were Pashtun nomads and for thousands of years they have travelled across Afghanistan and northern India with their flocks of sheep and goats. Being nomads, they carried their worldly possessions with them. Their camels were laden with all manner of goods including; goat skin tents, cooking utensils and babies too young to walk. As an added security deterrent, they also had dogs. These canines were fearsome, very big and trained to attack anything or anyone that trespassed into the camp. The *Kuchi* moved with the seasons to seek good pasture for their livestock; They would trek north in the spring and south in the autumn. They kept themselves to themselves and never associated with outsiders, unless it was to barter for goods or provisions.

Abdel's caravan decided to rest for the night, a safe distance from the *Kuchi* camp, so as not to intimidate and incur their wrath. However, a young teenage member of the caravan made a serious error of judgement that night, when he decided to visit the *Kuchi* camp. He was attacked by two dogs and was mauled to death. The nomads would not tolerate interference and as a consequence they suffered persecution for their principles. In turn, they would mete out severe retribution to anyone who stole or presented a threat to their way of life. They had a reputation for inflicting gruesome outcomes to those who were caught stealing or abusing their animals. The punishment was swift; Hands, eyes and tongues would be removed for anyone found guilty in this regard. This was Afghanistan in 1929, but it could have been 1029; the world to the *Kuchi* had not changed and they had no intention of joining the twentieth century.

Having given the unfortunate teenager a decent burial the caravan continued its journey south to Chaman in India some 79 miles north west of Quetta. The distance to Karachi was now some 505 miles and Abdel's feet were now heavily blistered and he had to wear sheepskin slippers to ease the discomfort. These were made for him by a wife of one of his fellow travellers. This part of the trek would take Abdel through small villages that survived on a meagre existence of basic crops of rice, corn and fruit, supplemented with meat from sheep and goats.

The caravan stopped at just such a village called Yellah. Their arrival coincided with a tribal gathering that was in the process of deciding on punishment for a villager who had stolen a goat. The caravan had to wait for the outcome before they would be invited to stay overnight and enjoy the hospitality of the village. The accused, a man of around 30 years sat alone while the village elders discussed his punishment. As he sat, he was subjected to constant berating from the women in the village.

After some twenty minutes of deliberation, the elders appeared from a *Qala* and administered a common retribution for stealing, and as two elders held the man down, another sliced off his right hand with a large sabre. His fingers were still twitching as his hand lay in the dust. To add to the pain, the man's bleeding stump was held over the hot embers of an open fire, to cauterise the wound. His cries of anguish could be heard for miles. After some ten minutes, he was escorted from the village by two women and set on the road, forever banished. At no time during his trial and punishment was he allowed to speak or defend himself.

Once the man had gone, the caravan was welcomed and provided with food and refreshment. Like Abdel, the villagers were from the dominant *Pashtun* ethnic sect and were Sunni Muslims. As the evening stole the afternoon the villagers invited their guests to join them around the camp fire and entertained their guests with singing and dancing. In the morning they provided the caravan with provisions of dried meat and fruit for the journey south into India.

Abdel had witnessed many new experiences in such a short time and though somewhat concerned, he was also excited about what the future had in store for him. During the trek to Chaman, one of the camels was attacked and killed by a pack of wolves. The wolves were dispersed, but the camel died of its injuries. Abdel joined in the butchering of the carcase, something he had learned from his father and brother. After completing another 70 miles from Qandahar they arrived in Chaman, Northern India, and latitude *of 30 degrees N.* It was now March 28th and Abdel has walked some 370 miles in fifteen days.

Afghanistan was in a state of political turmoil. Tribal unrest and the uncertainty within the Kabul government led to civil war. Nadir Khan and his brothers, Hashim Khan and Shah Wali Khan sought to overthrow Bacha-i-Saqao. The Bacha had instilled a firm religious doctrine in Kabul and had

A LIFE NAVIGATED

placed religious leaders in charge of justice and education. He embarked on a systematic purge of people of wealth and was responsible for numerous murders. Nadir Khan would eventually succeed in his quest for control later in the year.

Abdel was ignorant of all this political upheaval and was now looking forward to joining his brother Hakim in Karachi, still another 500 miles to his destination. The following day the camel train moved on their next stop Kuchlak, another village that sat in the shadow of the Brahui Mountains; some 50 miles further south. Abdel's feet were now in a poor condition; his shoes were in need of repair and he sought help from a fellow traveller, who persuaded his wife to strengthen his footwear with goat hide. The terrain was very unforgiving, with steep ridges, narrow tracks and dry river beds. They arrived in Bostam three days later on April 1st and rested for another day.

They took the opportunity to stock up with essential provisions like water, rice, nuts and fruit. While camped, another tragedy befell the entourage; when a young boy four years old, wandered off and was bitten by a King Cobra, he was dead within an hour and laid to rest in the village burial site.

The caravan was only 10 miles from the city of Quetta and another 420 miles to Karachi. Quetta is surrounded by a natural fortification in shape of four imposing hills and rises to a height of 5.500 feet above sea level. It is known as the 'fruit garden' and it has a plethora of orchards. Over 30% of the population speak *Pashto,* Abdel's native tongue.

It was a bright warm morning as the caravan entered the northern outskirts of Quetta. What took Abdel by surprise was the noise and activity that illuminated the city. The sight of people moving around in an energetic and chaotic way was strange and yet he was excited by it all. To watch men with overladen hand carts, full of fruit, vegetables, rice, live chickens and all manner of spices, scurrying through the streets and narrow alleyways, captivated him. Not that this form of labour was restricted to men. Both women and boys were just as active in this metropolis of activity. Women would be transporting goods in wicker boxes on their heads containing wheat, barley, maize, nuts and chickens; while boys would be employed in running errands, herding sheep and goats and unloading produce from carts. Then came a sound that troubled him, which seemed to get louder and louder. Then he saw it as it turned a corner and approached him some 50 yards ahead. Fear gripped him, he stood motionless in its path, until a boy had the presence of mind to grab his arm and pull him to the side of the road. As the monster rumbled past Abdel covered his ears to shut out the deafening noise. Once it had passed out of sight he turned to his rescuer and said, "What is that?"

The boy replied, "That is a motor truck and it is owned by Abdul Mahawi, who is a wealthy man in Quetta, he employs many people. My name is Moshan, I am 10 years old and I have just saved your life my friend."

Still in a state of shock, Abdel thanked Moshan and said, "You speak my language," and noticed that the boy's left ear was badly injured. He asked, "How did you injure your ear Moshan?"

"I was attacked by a mad dog, when I was 4 years old. And yes, I speak your language and in Quetta you must learn many language's including English, French, Urdu and Arabic. Where are you going?" he asked.

"I am on my way to be with my brother in Karachi."

"So, you must be with that caravan that has just arrived, where have you come from?"

"I was born in Azaw, which is high in the mountains and when my father died, I joined the caravan at Farah."

"Have you got work in Karachi, with your brother then?"

"Yes, my uncle has a chandler's store in the port and he has promised me employment." The two boys sat at the edge of the road and watched the comings and goings of all kinds of traders, shoppers, beggars, livestock and the occasional motorised vehicle. Mohammed the caravan leader had stopped the caravan for tea and some food and was now ready to move on. Much to the annoyance of two camels, who did not want to proceed and they had to be forcibly reminded with a few lashes of a cedar branch.

Abdel bid farewell to Moshan and said, "thank you for saving me from that monster and if you ever come to Karachi, you must visit my uncles store, his name is Ahmad Ali Rahman."

"May God be with you," said Abdel.

"God with you also Abdel," replied Moshan.

Quetta left an indelible impression on Abdel and he wondered what Karachi would be like. The next village on the journey would be Mastung, some 30 miles away. All kinds of thoughts were spiralling in Abdel's mind and his wonderment had been fuelled by the city of Quetta. Six miles out of Quetta the caravan came upon another tribe of *Kuchi* moving their flock of sheep to better pasture, along with their fearsome dogs.

Both the *Kuchi* and the caravan were oblivious to the politics in India at that time. Since 1911 the Indian government had been actively engaged in reconciling the Hindu – Muslim population. In 1928, Pandit Jawaharlal Nehru had his report published which was initially accepted by the All India

Muslim League. However, Mohammed Ali Jinnah the new leader of the AIML proposed a more radical approach which gave Muslims a one third representation in the central assembly of India. In addition, Muslim majority should be sustained in Bengal and the Punjab for ten years. His requests were rejected, but the seed had been sown for a new Muslim ideology within the north western provinces.

The caravan had stopped at a mountain stream to bathe, wash and set up camp about 15 miles from Mastung. Abdel had kept himself to himself for most of the journey, but had been friendly with a family who had helped him with both food and the repair of footwear. The husband was called Nabul Nadir Karim who had a wife called Haneer and one daughter named Shakira, she was 5 years old. They were also going to Karachi, where Nabul's brother had a haberdashery store. The brother's business had expanded and he needed more employees to maintain the progress gained.

Sitting at the camp fire after eating and evening prayers, Nabul had offered Abdel a position in this new venture. He respectfully declined the offer, saying he had another posting with his uncle and thanked him for his kindness. Nabul suggested that Abdel will find he has to quickly adapt to the change in culture when he gets to Karachi, not least the many different ethnic languages he will need to learn fast, if he is to be successful.

This added to the excitement for Abdel and his enthusiasm for the challenge grew with every passing hour. He slept well that night, under a clear starry night, bathed by a full moon providing a delicate twilight and dreamed of a great odyssey and asked God to protect him in this quest for a new life.

He was woken by the disparaging sounds of the camels that were being loaded up for more travelling, it was dawn and breakfast would be eaten on the move. The caravan had been reduced in number after it reached Quetta, with the remaining cohort of ten families and six camels.

Having travelled a further five miles, the caravan was subjected to an attack by two bandits. One of the bandits had a revolver which he subsequently discharged into a camel. Sadly, for him, the revolver jammed and he could not get off another shot before Mohammed felled him with a large rock. He then dragged him to the nearest tree, tied him to the trunk and despite pleading for his life, Mohammed severed both his arms at the elbow.

His accomplice made a swift getaway, a wise decision considering he was not in possession of a firearm. Mohammed had to cut the throat of the injured camel and the unfortunate animal was butchered for meat. What added to his displeasure was that it was one of his own camels that succumbed to the gunshot.

As the caravan left the scene, the bandit had died, still tied to the tree and Mohammed said, "Well, the wild animals must also eat, it is God's wish."

The brutality of the punishment handed out to the bandit troubled Abdel and it remained in his thoughts for some time. The tribal ways within the mountain regions had not changed and punishment was swift and severe, for those that chose to inflict injury and despair on others. That night he prayed as his father had taught him and asked God for his help on his journey and he remembered what his father would often say in prayer,

"Be grateful and God will give you more."

It was now April 4th and the caravan arrived in Mastung as the sun burned in a cloudless sky. Again, great activity was in abundance and people were going about their daily business. They rested and took on more water and supplies for their continuing trek to Kalat, Surab and Khuzdar; a total of some 170 miles. Abdel was now in a state of impatience and wanted to be in Karachi to start his new life and to see his brother Hakim, who he had not seen for nine years. After another 8 days the caravan arrived in Khuzdar, tired and hungry. Mohammed decided that a longer rest was needed before the caravan embarked on its next part of the journey and 2 days were set aside for rest and recuperation.

Having rested and enhanced their supplies this small gathering of humanity set off for on their journey. Their trek took them between the Central Makran Range and Kirthar Range of mountains of Baluchistan. After another nine days of hard energy sapping travel they entered the town of Bela, some 90 miles north of Karachi at a latitude of 26 degrees north. As they arrived, Abdel noticed a strange obelisk with long tentacles that reached out into the distance to another obelisk.

He asked Mohammed what was this strange sight. Mohammed laughed at Abdel's curiosity and said, "Well Abdel that is a very powerful thing that stands before you. It is an electricity pylon, which carries power to the city that allows people to switch a light on, heat a stove or run a machine. It is also dangerous; you must never climb such a beast. It will burn you and you will die."

Abdel wondered what other strange sights he would be seeing as Karachi drew nearer by the day. That night, he lay gazing through the opening of his small tent into a sky festooned with stars and drew imaginary faces of his mother and father, using the sky as his canvass. He felt sadness that they could not share his excitement, but content that God had protected him in their absence.

As the sun rose Abdel was woken by the sound of Mohammad cajoling his camels using his cedar branch as a reminder. Abdel helped himself to some dried fruit and walnuts from his knapsack to sustain him on the next leg of his epic journey.

The penultimate village before Karachi was Uthal, another 30 miles south and a further 60 miles to Karachi, it was now April 23rd. All being well, the caravan should reach their destination in 5 days.

Uthal was a small settlement with a number of qala's owned by farmers who cultivated crops such as wheat, barley, pistachios, apples, apricots, pears and plums. On arrival the village elder welcomed the caravan and set aside a qala for sleeping and promised a camp fire feast in the evening. As the travellers laid out their beds and belongings, a hunting party arrived carrying the carcases of wild deer, wild goats and pheasants. They were accompanied by their hounds, the *tazi* (Afghan hound). Abdel had heard of these dogs, but until now, had never seen one. They were very tall and slender animals and used for hunting fast moving animals such as Ibex and Gazelle's. The evening banquet would be a fine one.

Abdel sat and marvelled at the sight before him and thought of his own village and how much easier it would be to hunt near his own village of Azaw, with such magnificent hounds. Nabul, Haneer and their daughter Shakira joined him to gaze upon the spectacle and were offered pistachios, walnuts and pears by one of the village women, who said, "Welcome travellers, please have some."

"Thank you, we are grateful," they replied.

That night after prayers, a wonderful feast was prepared and there was singing and dancing accompanied by the music of a dhol (*drum*) and a reed pipe. Abdel felt excited about his future and finally meeting up with his brother Hakim again, as he sat and soaked up the atmosphere of the festivities.

Abdel woke up to the sound of rain bouncing on the roof of the qala. As with most rain showers, it did not last that long and they were soon on their way. The local villagers had provided them with provisions for the journey. Dried meat, nuts and fruit were loaded up on the five remaining camels, along with some new blankets and furs.

The camel train moved south again and having travelled 10 miles they came upon the Siranda Lake, an expanse of fresh water some 8 miles in length west of the Khurlera Plain. This was a bleak, flat and barren landscape. The caravan stopped and took the opportunity to bathe and rest for a few hours. The sun was burning brightly and the temperature was around 30 degrees C as Abdel found a shaded spot under a walnut tree to rest.

Abdel was now in a state of *joie de vivre* and began to imagine what he would encounter on his arrival in Karachi. After 4 days they reached the north west of the city.

Mohammad had enlightened all those who wished to listen, that this area of the city was known as *"white town"* as this was where the British had invested in an infrastructure and culture that included buildings such as the Law Courts, Governors House, a Masonic Lodge and Frere Hall. These were all situated within the Civil Lines Quarter, which also has the Saddar Bazaar and the Empress Market. As the name suggested this area was widely populated by white people and was a consequence of British rule and a more affluent district of the city.

To improve the trade and commerce of India, Karachi was embarking on a programme of modernisation. A major part of that involved the expansion of the port and a public works development that included; sanitation, transportation links and a number of grand buildings. Prominent buildings such as the Port Trust, Jehangir Kothari Parade and Frere Hall were built to satisfy the influx of Europeans now making a living within the commercial sector of the city.

Karachi was now becoming a melting pot of many cultures and communities that included Jews, Africans, Lebanese, Malays, Armenians, Arabs and Catholics from Goa. In 1929 Karachi was the largest grain exporting port of the British Empire. Its population was around 180.000 at this time and increasing as the city began to prosper. The caravan arrived on a fine warm morning on April 28th, having trekked some 885 miles over difficult terra firma lasting a total of 46 days. Excluding three full days of rest, they had averaged some 20 miles each day. Having lost two members of the caravan, Mohammad's best camel and survived two bandit attacks, they were all overjoyed to reach their final destination.

Abdel must now find his brother Hakim. His father had given him a letter for his uncle with an address of Rahman's Chandlers. Bunder Road. Karachi. Having befriended Nabul and his family he decided to ask him for advice on how to get to his uncles Chandler's store.

"This is good Abdel; we are also going to Bunder Road. That is where my brother's Haberdashers is located. We will all go together," said Nabul. Nabul spoke to Mohammed and he advised them to stay together, for the children's sake. There were criminal gangs operating and snatching children for slavery. Nabul was thankful to Mohammad and bid him farewell and said, "God be with you and may he guide and protect you all."

CHAPTER THREE

Nabul estimated that from where they were, it would be another hour before they found Bunder Road, which extends down to the port. Abdel was now excited and walked with a purpose along with Nabul, Haneer and Shakira.

As they walked Abdel was fascinated by the noise, smell and activity that grew in abundance. This was his life now, the constant movement of people going about their lives. Everyone seemed to be in a hurry to get somewhere. They passed street sellers and beggars in equal measure and people transporting all manner of goods on camels, donkeys and carts being pulled by cattle along dusty roads that were overlooked by huge buildings that rose up like giant sculptured mountains. As they turned into Bunder Road, a Tram hurtled past them carrying people to another part of the city.

There were wooden posts with a multitude of cables extending to the many buildings and stores and his curiosity got the better of him and he asked Nabul, "What is this?" pointing to the tall wooden post.

"This is electricity Abdel; it gives us light and power. My brother told me all about it in his letter, when he asked me to come to Karachi."

Abdel was still confused, but there was much to take in as they sought his uncle's store. Then a young man riding a bicycle came flying out of a side street and nearly knocked him over. As he passed, he looked at Abdel and recognised him immediately and turned his bicycle around and shouted, "Abdel, it is me Hakim."

Abdel was overjoyed to see Hakim and threw himself at his brother, causing the both of them to fall on top of his bicycle in great excitement.

Nabul, Haneer and Shakira all laughed at the site before them and Nabul suggested they get off the road before they suffer a similar fate under the wheels of a not too distant motor car.

Hakim looked at his little brother and said "You will need to eat well and grow fast Abdel; the work is hard and you will learn to sleep when you can."

"Do I have to have one of those things?" pointing to Hakims mode of transport.

"Oh no brother, only when you have earned it first," he replied.

"Earned it," said Abdel.

"Yes, earned it. You have to prove that you are a good honest worker before you get a bicycle Abdel. You will be a *runner* at first, taking messages and orders from ship to store and back again," replied Hakim.

At this point Nabul introduced himself and his family and Hakim expressed his thanks for helping Abdel find his destination. Nabul wished them both well and indicated that his brothers Haberdashery was not too far away.

On hearing what Nabul was searching for, Hakim laughed and said, "My friend, we deal with your brother Abdullah Nadir Karim all the time. His store is just up the road on the right next door to Mohammed Shah's gent's hairdressers." Nabul expressed his thanks and they all set off.

Abdel stood gazing at Hakim and said, "You have changed Hakim; you have face hair like our father and you have his eyes."

"I am 18 years old now Abdel and you were only 2 years old when I left our village. We have both changed and who knows where we will be in ten years' time. We must now go and meet our uncle and give him the good news that you are here and in good health."

Ahmad Ali Rahman had left Afghanistan some 40 years ago at the age of ten along with his cousin Syed Ali Rahman, who was sixteen. They moved to India after Ahmad's father and mother had been killed in a tribal skirmish near their village of Mydan. They had set up their business in a bizarre off the Bunder Road from meagre beginnings, selling pots, pans and other domestic hardware.

The business quickly expanded due to the development of the port and Ahmad's sagacity at spotting an opportunity. Within two years he had gained a premises on Bunder Road and had established a strong economic presence. Hakim continued to play an important role in the business, acting as his agent in dealing with his main customer, the East India Shipping Company. Along with his brother and his own son Abdullah, he had a reputation as a reliable businessman in Karachi.

Abdel and Hakim arrived at the store to find Ahmad scolding his son Abdullah for failing to greet a Purser from a ship that had recently docked at the wharf. This was a serious error and Ahmad made his son aware of this in no uncertain way, by giving him a whack across his back with a leather strap and said, "this is our livelihood Abdullah; you must be there on time to greet and take the Purser's requisition for goods. Now one of our competitors has claimed our customer."

Abdullah was apologetic and asked his father's forgiveness and said, "I am sorry father, I stopped to talk to my friend Mojan and I was late getting to the wharf. It will not happen again."

Ahmad replied with;

> "Guide us to the straight way, in the name God. The most gracious, the most merciful."

Hakim poured some water on the fire and said, "I will help Abdullah with his bicycle Ahmad."

Ahmad turned to Abdel and said, "You must be Abdel; you have your brother's face. Are you a good worker?"

"I am, I tended sheep when I was 5 years old," replied Abdel.

Ahmad smiled and put his large hand on Abdel's small shoulder and said, "You will not need to tend sheep around here, but you must work hard and if you do you will be rewarded. But remember business is business and turning his gaze toward his son he added, you must be reliable."

"I promised my father that I will follow his guidance and the word of God," replied Abdel.

Ahmad then told Hakim to show Abdel where he would be sleeping and then to take him for a walk around the dock area.

Before they left, Ahmad said, "Remember our motto Abdel;

Rahman's Chandlers keep you supplied, night and day."

Hakim revealed Abdel's sleeping quarters, in a room above the store, which he shared with Hakim and Syed, Ahmad's cousin.

They ventured out and Hakim took him to the docks and various other important places including Elphinstone Street, the Empress Market, Frere Hall, the Port Trust Building, the Governors House and Napier Market.

Abdel felt so small in this metropolis of humanity and soaked up all the information he could, before they returned to the store and helped Abdullah repair his bicycle.

As they worked on Abdullah's bicycle, Abdel asked Hakim if Syed had any children. He was told that it was something that was never spoken about. This was because his chosen wife had died from cholera before they could be married and Syed accepted that it was God's wish and he would not benefit from marriage and as a consequence, not have a family.

During that first week Abdel shadowed Hakim as he carried out his duties. This was hard work and required Abdel to act as a runner in support of Hakim, who had the advantage of a bicycle. They were up at 6am every day and finally ended the working day at around 10pm. The main duties involved transporting goods to ships anchored at the wharf and taking requisition orders from the ships Purser. His reward, regular food and a bed for the night. Hakim also revealed that if Ahmad is pleased with you after six months, he would start to deposit a wage for you, in a personal bank account at the Imperial Bank of India.

Abdel was impressed with Hakim's infinite knowledge of his surroundings and hoped he would quickly validate his late father's confidence in him. As they turned a corner to arrive back on the Bunder Road, Hakim pointed to a parked vehicle and said, "You see that truck Abdel?"

Abdel nodded in recognition.

"That is owned by one of our most important customers, it belongs to

James Finley & Company. They are a big supplier of cotton and jute and they export their goods all over the world. They have cotton mills here in Karachi and we supply many provisions to the mills." Here in Karachi you can buy just about anything; chickens, donkeys, cigars, beds, flour and furniture. But now, it is time to eat."

They returned to Rahman's to eat. Syed had prepared the food; chicken biryani served with bread and water. After the meal, Hakim had one errand to complete in Tariq Road. He was to deliver an order to Shah Jenhang's fruit and vegetable store, who would fill a cart of various produce for transport to a ship of the East India Company, recently docked at the wharf.

Syed retired to his room to prey and suggested Abdel should do the same, saying, "God awaits your deliverance and we must provide you with your own prayer mat Abdel. However, you must visit the mosque and introduce yourself to the Imam."

Abdel nodded in agreement and said, "I pray that God will walk with me and protect me."

The room which he shared with Syed and Hakim was just big enough to accommodate three singe beds. On the walls around Syed's bed were shelves occupied with all manner of books. Once they had finished their prayers, Abdel asked Syed, "what are all the books about? "

"They are about all manner of things, from history, literature, travel and religion. As I have time on my hands, I want to know of all things about the world we live in Abdel." Syed was around six feet tall, muscular and looked younger than his fifty-six years. He had a thick black beard and he had fire in his big brown eyes, especially when he spoke of life and prayer.

"Can I look at them?" asked Abdel.

"Yes, you are welcome to look and read. But you will find that many of them are not written in Pashto. Many are written in English, a language you must learn Abdel. We are part of the British Empire and English is a language spoken throughout the world. I learnt English from a great Ostaz (*teacher*) called Benjamin Holt, he was from a place in England called Canterbury. I could not pay for my schooling and so I went to his house three evenings every week and he taught me many things including reading, writing and mathematics. As payment I would work for him cleaning his house and tending his garden. Sometimes he asked me to look after his two children. That was 25 years ago and he is now back home in England. He was a Director of the British East India Company. When he left, he gave me this book." Syed handed the book to Abdel. On opening the book, Abdel noticed a written note on the inside cover and asked Syed what it meant.

Syed took the book and read the note;

"To a trusted and loyal friend Syed Ali Rahman. I hope you find this book a source of encouragement as your life continues. May God be with you and I wish you good health and happiness. You're friend, Benjamin Holt."

"What is the book about?" asked Abdel.

"*The* book is a story of a man who is shipwrecked and relies on his own strength and willpower to survive. It is called *Robinson Crusoe* and it was written by a man called Daniel Defoe over 200 hundred years ago."

"If you would like to read it one day, I will teach you to read in English Abdel."

"I would be most grateful Syed, my father once told me to embrace all forms of learning and this would make me a stronger man."

"Your father was a wise man Abdel and you are the apple of his eye. We will begin your teaching tomorrow evening."

India was suffering an economic slowdown and the country was finding it hard to break this austere transition. Imports and exports were decreasing and as a consequence international trade began to fall. To add to this, India was expected to still pay out the '*home charges*' that were a legacy of British rule. These charges were related to costs for maintaining the army, war expenses and other charges regarding pensions to retired British officers.

National fervour was beginning to sweep the country and the talk of independence, was gaining momentum. Three men were the catalyst for change in India at this time, *Mahatma Gandhi, Muhammed Jinnah* and *Jawaharial Nehru*. Indian nationals had very little say in the governance of their homeland and as a result they had limited influence on policy or decision making. India was still regarded as the '*Jewel in the Crown*' of the British Empire and the British government resisted any change that might promote self-determination. In 1919 the British decided to make a concession to India and introduced the Government of India Act.

This was installed to try and placate the harbingers of independence, but in reality, it just enhanced the escalation in frustration. By giving 5 million of the wealthiest Indians a right to vote in a National Parliament of two houses, the British government naively believed this would satisfy any inclination for self-rule. Back in Britain, many MP's within the Tory party were vehemently against an idea that would give any form of self-rule to India. Their argument being that it would mean the end of the British Empire. One man who was strongly against any form of self-rule was Lord Birkenhead, the Secretary of State for India from 1924 – 1928. His continued opposition proved to be a major stumbling block for Indian independence.

Despite the opposition to independence Gandhi, Nehru and Jinnah continued their programme of reform and began a radical movement of non-conformity, through strikes and the non-payment of taxes. This in turn resulted in violent clashes and riots throughout India.

Although it seemed that India was in the process re-inventing itself, life in Karachi continued to exhibit an ephemeral perspective. The port was still the hub of commerce, but the military played a large part in sustaining an economical foothold, with its reliance on goods and services. However, the worldwide depression of 1929 extended to India and both imports and exports were dramatically reduced. Local businesses had to tighten their belts to ride out the economic storm. To add insult to injury the Indian Government under the British Raj, created the Salt Tax.

This increased the financial burden on the majority of Indians and led to the Salt March (Satyagraha) on April 5th 1930, led by Mahatma Gandhi. This in turn galvanised the Indian people and the Indian National Congress began its Civil Disobedience Movement.

Life for Hakim and Abdel became a greater challenge, but they worked hard for Rahman's Chandlers and they enjoyed a reasonably adequate existence. Ahmad did create a bank account for Abdel and after six months of running errands, he became the proud owner of a Raleigh dynamo powered bicycle, complete with front and rear lights. Abdullah had not satisfied his father that he had enhanced his standing enough to acquire a bicycle and continued to hone his people skills within the company on foot.

Throughout the city there were many tea houses. These establishments were not just for the avid tea drinkers. They became meeting places for all kinds of activities including gambling, clandestine gatherings, soliciting, racketeering and on occasion, drinking tea. Many tea houses were equipped with upstairs rooms, which afforded a degree of privacy for certain romantic liaisons to take place.

Abdel was intrigued by these places and asked Hakim about their profitability within the community. Hakim offered Abdel a little advice and said, "those tea rooms are not for the likes of you and I Abdel. This is where big deals are discussed and we are not yet schooled in high finance, but one day I hope to have my own company and then I will sit among the important people, smoke cigars and meet the desirable ladies."

Abdel continued his evening studies under the tuition of Syed. Although age was now catching up with Syed, his attention to his student was constant and he began to expand Abdel's vocabulary in English, which Abdel seemed to master very quickly. Syed would sit on his mat, wearing his yellow turban and his whites, (pants and overshirt) and test Abdel on his progress in spelling and grammar, while sitting on his prayer mat that Syed had given him. He encouraged Abdel to read and when he came upon a word he did not recognise; to look it up in his Oxford Dictionary.

Syed also encouraged Abdel to go to the local cinema and on his first visit, he saw the Jazz singer starring Al Jolson. Coincidently this was the first 'talkie' released in 1927. Abdel was in awe of this and expected the performers on film to appear from behind the screen. He found it a most incredible sight.

Most of the dialogue was lost on Abdel, although a Pashto translation did appear on the bottom of the screen. Abdel could not concentrate on the sub titles, due to his bewilderment at the spectacle before him.

On his return to his room that night, he spoke in excited terms of the experience of the cinema to Hakim and Syed, who laughed at Abdel's naivety and said, "You will witness many things in this world Abdel and I pray to God that you learn all that you can, to keep you safe. As it is written;

"Dear believers, seek help through resilience and prayer. Indeed, God is with the resilient."

As time passed, Abdel gained new friends within the community and he formed a strong friendship with Osman Ali Khan, who he met one evening at prayer.

Osman was born in Mersin, Turkey; his parents emigrated to India when he was 11 years old. After only a year in his new country, tragedy struck and both his parents were killed in 1928 when a local tram on Elphinstone Street slipped it's track and collided with a number of pedestrians. He was taken in as an orphan by a local family, Shah Ali Khan and his wife, who had their own son Zahir, aged 9.

Abdel and Osman would often spend Sunday's at the port and wander around looking at the ships docked at the wharf. They would talk to merchant sailors from many different lands and listen to their tales and adventures. Abdel quickly realised that many used the English language to communicate and Abdel became Osman's interpreter during these encounters. As a result, Abdel's proficiency in English was greatly enhanced.

One particular merchant seaman that Abdel gained friendship and respect for was a Yorkshireman, called Jack Rowley. He was the Chief Engineer on a cargo ship called The City of Venice. The ship brought imports of machinery, farm vehicles, paint and household goods from Britain. She weighed 8762 tons and had a top speed of 13.5 knots. Jack often regaled about his many sea travels around the world and this fascinated Abdel.

Jack would often take Abdel and Osman on board the ship and educate them on the turbo electric engines that propelled the ship. On occasion, they might sit and eat with some of the crew in the mess room.

Abdel's interest in all things to do with seafaring grew rapidly, he and Osman would walk the jetty and talk to the fishermen about their boats. The local fishermen used *Dhow's, Hody's or Ulak's* to cast their nets from.

On rare occasions the skippers would agree to take them on short fishing trips out into Sonmiani Bay to fish for Green Turtles, Dorado and Bluestripe Snapper. Osman often succumbed to sea sickness and would decline an invitation if there was a heavy swell out in the bay.

In March 1931, Jack Rowley invited Abdel on a voyage to the Persian Gulf, where his ship would be taking a cargo of jute, rice and tea. The cargo on the voyage back to Karachi included; oil, timber and fruit.

Ahmad had to sign papers allowing Abdel to go on this trip, which he did reluctantly, mindful that he was losing an important member of his workforce. Abdel was now 13 years of age and on November 12th he boarded the City of Venice with his prayer mat and a change of clothes. He would join the ship's crew as an engineer's mate.

Their destination was the port of Ad Dawhah and the voyage would take 4 days at a speed of 11 knots, sailing some 933 nautical miles. After a further 2 days in port, the return voyage would mean a total of 1866 nautical miles sailing through the Arabian Sea.

As the ship weighed anchor and left her moorings, Abdel was filled with wonder as he waved to Osman and Hakim standing at the wharf. Standing at the bow of the ship, he knew almost at once that he was destined to sail the seas and begin of a new life. This was a world away from herding goats, back in his homeland in the foothills of the Paropamisus Mountains.

Abdel's proficiency in the English language had enabled him to communicate with most of the crew on board, but not all. There were crew members from Italy, Mexico, Portugal and the Philippines, who had a smattering of English that was sufficient to get through the day.

Jack allowed Abdel to familiarise himself with the ship on the first day and went through the rules for sailing on the high sea. The Captain was John T. Westley; a Cornish man some 6' 4" in height, with a well-groomed ginger beard. The crew numbered 20 men and Jack as Chief Engineer was in command of seven seamen, plus Abdel. His Second Engineer was a Scotsman called Rory McDonald and his Engineering Officer was Bill Hawkins who hailed from London. In addition,

Jack had five Engine Ratings, Tom, Sidney, Norman, Bob and Alan. These would be Abdel's companions during the voyage and they would all work, eat and sleep as an entity.

CHAPTER FOUR

While Jack was explaining the workings of the ship and where everything happened, he asked Abdel a question and said, "Who is the most important person on the ship then Abdel?"

Abdel thought this through and replied, "It must be the Captain of course Mr Jack."

"Oh no, who will feed you Abdel?"

Abdel looked perplexed and Jack said, "It's the Chief Cook, never forget that my son and remember to compliment him on his cooking."

The Deck Ratings were Vito the Italian, Chino from Portugal, Raul from Mexico, Larry from Ireland and Tico from the Philippines. Harry Johnson from Newcastle was the steward and he assisted the exalted one; Chief Cook Richard Adams, who hailed from Lancaster.

In addition to the crew, the ship was carrying six passengers bound for Riyadh in Saudi Arabia. The ships voyage through the Arabian Sea, the Gulf of Oman and into the Persian Gulf would generally be a pleasant and trouble-free trip. However, the weather report for the first two days indicted that a cyclone was moving North West of the Maldives.

The cyclone appeared on the third day of the voyage and measures were taken to maintain a safe speed, without compromising the safety of ship and crew. The cyclone passed without too much disruption and moved onto landfall at Gavater in Persia. As with most cyclones, having reached land it decreased rapidly; but no doubt the local population had to endure some element of damage and suffering as a consequence.

The sea returned to a steady rolling swell as the ship entered the Gulf of Oman and their destination of Ad Dawhah in the Trucial State of Qatar. After four days at sea the ship dropped anchor. Abdel was told not to leave the ship after docking at the wharf. He would be given some time on shore, but only in the company of either Jack or the second engineer Rory. But first, he must help the engineering crew to carry out essential maintenance in the engine room.

Having completed the required maintenance checks and repairs, the crew were given time on shore. Abdel accompanied Rory on this excursion and found the experience somewhat different to that of Karachi. It was a good deal hotter and life seemed to be taken at a leisurely pace.

This was not lost on Rory who was less than impressed with the performance of the stevedores when he said, "these buggers are too slow to catch cold. We will be here for a fuckin week getting the ship loaded up."

Abdel knew that Rory was unhappy due to his bad language, which he often used to express his disdain. Syed had warned Abdel that he would encounter such profanities as he travelled and met people and he had heard a number of *"new"* English words, since he had been working for his uncle in Karachi.

Rory and Abdel walked around the port and the local market where Rory bought some new shirts, which cost him 3 riyals, after some heated bargaining.

The locals had a friendly disposition and Abdel was gifted pomegranates and almonds as he wandered around the market. He took some back to the crew who had decided to stay on board.

Rory's concerns relating to the time spent taking on board the cargo, proved to be reasonably accurate. The ship left the port after a longer than expected stay of 4 days, much to the Captains annoyance. The ship also had to wait three hours for a family who were joining the ship for the return voyage to Karachi.

Abdel's first thought was that his uncle would be worried that he had not returned on the scheduled date and relayed this to Jack saying, "I will not get back to Karachi on time Mr Jack, what will my uncle think?"

Jack allayed his fears and replied, "Don't worry son, I will get the Captain to send a wire to the Harbour Master at Karachi, to let your uncle know we will be later than expected. Just give me his name and his address and I will pass it onto the Captain."

When the ship had sailed beyond the Strait of Hormuz, Abdel witnessed a sight that would stay with him all his life. He was on deck soaking up the sun and gazing out to sea when there seemed to be a number of birds circling an area some distance from the ship. Vito the deck rating was close by and Abdel shouted over to him to take a look. When Vito saw the commotion, he looked excited and said, "You are going to see something you will never ever see again, watch carefully." Then from beneath the waves rose a Blue Whale in all its majesty, some 80 feet in length and probably weighing 100 tons.

Abdel was awe struck and could not speak, eventually he said, "It will sink our ship Vito."

Vito laughed and replied, "No Abdel, it is only interested in that shoal of krill, it will not harm the ship."

Crew members Chino and Raul came to watch and take in the spectacle, which lasted no more than ten minutes. After breeching a number of times, the leviathan sank beneath the waves and was never seen again.

Abdel was still in a state of shock and said, "It will swallow ten men at once."

Vito once again laughed at Abdel's ignorance and added, "It is good to know that the Blue Whale is a friend of man Abdel. He is not interested in us; he collects small sea animals and fish in his big mouth and swallows them. The Blue Whale is the biggest animal on the planet."

"How do you know all this asked Chino?"

"I read books Chino; you should do the same," replied Vito.

"Reading books do not pay me my wages," said Chino.

Vito looked at Chino and shook his head and said to Abdel, "Do you read books Abdel?"

"I do, Syed is teaching me to read English books. I want to read *Robinson Crusoe* one day Vito."

"Who is Syed?"

"He is my uncle's cousin and he has lots of books," replied Abdel.

"You will do well to follow his teaching; the world is full of knowledge and you will be rewarded for your efforts Abdel," added Vito.

That night Abdel dreamt of sea monsters and giant birds, as his imagination spiralled out of control as he lay sleeping in his bunk. In the morning, he spoke of the Blue Whale to Tom and Sid in the engine room. They were more concerned with the smooth running of the ship and his excitement was quickly extinguished when Tom said, "Never mind that bollocks Abdel, go and grease those nipples on those engine bearings."

Abdel duly obliged, but the sight of the Blue Whale left a lasting impression on him.

The ship docked at Karachi laden with nuts, fruit, oil and machinery on November 26th at 5pm. Abdel's first voyage at sea was over and he loved every minute.

Before leaving the ship, he thanked the Captain, Jack, Rory and Vito for all their help and promised he would be back one day.

Jack walked Abdel along the jetty and shook his hand and said, "Well Abdel, you now have your sea legs."

Abdel looked down at his legs and gave Jack a puzzled frown.

Jack grinned and said, "It means you are a worthy seaman; you don't get sea – sick and you have been a boon companion on this voyage."

Abdel smiled and said, "You have been a good friend Mr Jack; may God be with you."

"I hope he will Abdel, you have been a sound shipmate," added Jack and he turned and walked back to the City of Venice.

Abdel ran all the way back to Rahman's Chandlers and spent the remains of the day talking to anyone who would listen, about his sailing adventure on the high sea.

Hakim listened intently to Abdel as they sat down with Syed to eat after evening prayer and asked Abdel if this was what he wanted to do. Abdel nodded and said, "Yes Hakim, it is a life I want," and turned to Syed saying, "What do you think Syed?"

Syed looked at Abdel and said, "If this is what you want, then you must do it Abdel. I would say this to you, we must give you all we can to help you. That means more knowledge and understanding of men and the world. You must be skilled in many things; only then will you be ready and God will watch over you. God is great."

Hakim then spoke of how Rahman's Chandlers had become a modern business and said, "We have a telephone Abdel."

Abdel had seen these talking machines at the big hotels and the Harbour Master's office and could not understand how they worked.

"This will increase our customers; we will be rich Abdel."

Syed looked across at Abdel and smiled and said, "It will give us other clients, that is the hope. But as I am the only one who can speak reasonably well in English. It will be me who must spend more time talking into this machine."

Syed did not seem to be too keen on this change in his working conditions.

"It is wonderful Abdel; our number is Karachi 2654 and we can talk to someone in Calcutta," added Hakim.

"Who do we know in Calcutta then Hakim?"

Hakim was left somewhat bereft of ideas and said, "It will happen, my father said we must expand."

Again, Syed looked at Abdel and just smiled.

That night Abdel and Syed sat and talked about many things. Abdel was intrigued with all the books Syed had and he asked him why people read books? Syed expanded on the subject of reading and said, "It is for you to understand Abdel, learning comes from many things, observing, listening and doing. Reading gives you knowledge of many things like history, religion, mathematics, geography, medicine, literature and trade skills, like seamanship and business. What you must do, is look to learn all you can and this will make you a stronger person. Knowledge is wealth Abdel and you must embrace it.

"Your reading is now good and before you went on your voyage with Mr Jack, I said that one day you could read *Robinson Crusoe*. Now you are able to read, I will give you this book. If you see words that you do not understand you must use the dictionary and it will give you there meaning."

Abdel thanked Syed and took the book from the shelf, which was sandwiched between John Bunyan's Pilgrim's Progress and Jonathan

Swift's Gulliver's Travels. He opened the book and began to read out loud: *I was born in the year 1632, in the city of York…"*
Syed raised his hand and said, "Abdel, you must now read to yourself in silence and if you find a word you do not understand, then you must ask. If I am not here to help you, then underline the word with this pencil," and he threw a pencil to Abdel, "Then use the dictionary."

"Thank you Syed, I will do as you ask."

Within two minutes Abdel was asking Syed what was meant by *"a foreigner of Bremen?"*

"Foreigner means a person from another land and Bremen is a city in Germany," replied Syed. Who feared this would be the longest ever reading of Daniel Defoe's classic?

The next morning Abdel was given a special job. He was to go to Jacob Levi's jewellers' shop on Bunder Road. On arrival, he was to collect a package for delivery to the Captain of a ship called the *Amra* owned by the British India Steam Company, docked at the wharf.

The Captains name was Jack Talbot and Abdel must ensure that he alone must receive the package in person. If that could not be done, then the package must be returned to Jacob Levi.

Jacob Levi had arrived in Karachi in 1881, along with his father, mother and his three sisters; Martha, Deborah and Rachel. They left Linkuva, a small town in Lithuania to escape the *Pogrom* that was being carried out in Eastern Russia. Many thousands had been murdered or driven from their homes, in an anti-Semitic purge. By the time they arrived in Karachi, they had travelled some 4000 miles through Russia, Turkey, Iraq, Persia and India.

Abdul duly arrived at Levi's shop and parked his bicycle outside and went into the shop. As he pushed the door open a crescendo of noise overwhelmed the atmosphere from the bells hanging on the inside of the door. Jacob Levi appeared from the back of the shop, looked at Abdel and said, *"shalom, boker tov."*

Abdel stood somewhat confused and was none the wiser after Mr Levi had spoken. Mr Levi spoke again and said in English, "That was Hebrew for hello and good morning, what is your name and what do you want?"

Abdel was reassured and replied, "My name is Abdel Rahman and I have been sent by my uncle Ahmad Ali Rahman to collect a package for delivery to Captain Jack W Talbot of the Amra, which is docked at the wharf."

"Well, you have explained yourself very well young Abdel, your English is very good. Perhaps you need to learn Hebrew, it will help you. Are you Urdu or Pashto?"

"I am Pashto," replied Abdel.

Jacob Levi was a small man of around 60 years old, with a long grey beard and a kind face. A blue silk yarmulke was pinned to what was left of his hairline and as he smiled, he revealed a limited number of teeth, three of which were encased in gold.

"Where have you learned your English Abdel?" he asked.

"From Syed Ali Rahman," replied Abdel.

"Ah yes, I am familiar with your family now, they have a thriving business I hear."

"Thriving business, what do you mean?" asked Abdel.

"It means it is doing well and making lots of money."

"Oh yes, we are getting a telephone soon and we will have lots of customers," said Abdel.

Jacob Levi smiled and said, "Yes, I am sure you will."

He then produced a package that was securely wrapped in thick hessian cloth, which he then placed into a leather bag which included a strap for carrying.

"Here is the package for Captain Talbot, please make sure you give it to him in person. The ship has a black funnel with two white bands and it is called the Amar."

Abdel took the bag and said, "How will I know the Captain?"

"That is a very good question Abdel. Well, when you meet him, you must ask him this simple question; which only he knows the answer - What is the first name of my third son?"

Abdel said his thanks, turned and began to walk to the door.

"Wait, I have not given you the name of my third son."

Abdel turned back in embarrassment, grinned and said, "You must think me a fool now."

"Well, lets us just say that you are of a mind to get the job done. My third son's name is Moshe. You will remember that I hope."

"Yes, I will and I know to return the package if I cannot find Captain Talbot," replied Abdel.

"Very good, God be with you," said Mr Levi as Abdel left the shop and placed the strap of the leather bag over his head and mounted his bicycle to carry out his job.

The journey to the wharf took only 10 minutes and there were 3 ships tied up. The first was the Amra. Abdel went first to the Dock Office to seek permission to board the vessel and was told that the Captain Talbot was indeed on board.

The Amra was a passenger and general cargo vessel, recently arrived from London. Its latest human cargo included a regiment of Irish Guards on route to the North - West Frontier, sent to maintain stability. The ship was one of the first ships the British East India Company that had been fitted with diesel propulsion and she had a gross weight of some 8314 tons and a length of 461 feet.

Abdel ascended the ships gangplank and scampered on board, where he was met by a rating who directed him to the Captains quarters.

On arrival, he knocked on the door and heard a voice say, "Yes, what is it? I hope it's not you Smith, telling me we are not going to sail tomorrow you bastard."

"No Captain, it is me, with a package from Jacob Levy," replied a nervous Abdel.

The door swung open and giant of a man stood glaring at Abdel.

"Now then, shiver me timbers what have we got here then?" he bellowed.

"I am Abdel Rahman and I must ask you a question, which you must answer if you are to get this package," he replied.

"You had better come in then; I hope it is not a difficult question you wish to ask. I am only a simple sea dog," and he motioned Abdel into his cabin.

Abdel felt a little overawed and said, "If you cannot answer the question correctly, I must return to Mr Levy with the package."

The Captain roared with laughter and said, "My word, you are a fine one; I should make you my Deck Officer. Right then, what is this very important question you must ask me Abdel Rahman?"

"You must give me the name of Jacob Levy's third son," replied Abdel.

"Now that is a hard question shipmate, because Jacob Levi has only two son's Abraham and Shimon," said the Captain, with a wry smile on his face.

Abdel was now in a state of turmoil, and not knowing how to extricate himself from this dilemma. After some deliberation, he finally said, "then I must take this package back to Mr Levi."

The Captain was now laughing and said, "You are a very good negotiator Abdel and you would be right to go back to Jacob with this package; however, Jacob and I planned this little muster. On receiving my package, I am to write you a note saying I have accepted the package, inspected it and I am happy with its contents. I must also give you a sovereign for your troubles."

"What is a negotiator?" asked Abdel.

"It is someone who discusses terms; bargains or barters with others in order to get a deal," replied the Captain and went on, "I must also add that your use of English is very good, where have you learned this?"

Abdel started to feel at ease for the first time and said, "I have been taught by Syed Ali Rahman and I am reading about Robinson Crusoe."

"Now there was a sailor who was dealt a raw deal indeed."

The Captain took the leather bag from Abdel and opened the hessian cloth. Inside was a beautiful gold ring mounted with a sparkling gemstone. The Captain lifted the ring up so he could examine the clarity of the stone and said, "Jacob has done me proud, this a magnificent piece of workmanship, is it not Abdel?"

Abdel was dumbstruck and just gazed at the ring in amazement.

"You might be wondering who this ring is for Abdel. Well, I have commissioned this ring as a gift for my dear wife who sits at our home in London nursing our baby son Harold. She will receive this when I return home, on route to our final destination of Hamburg."

The Captain then penned a note and handed it to Abdel to read.

Abdel looked at the note and began to read silently. The Captain stopped him and said, "You must read out aloud, then I will know that you have read it correctly Abdel."

Abdel started again;

"I, Captain Jack William Talbot, Master of the ship The Amra have received this gold and sapphire ring provided by my good friend Mr Jacob Levi. I must commend him on his craftsmanship and my grateful thanks for his discretion in this venture. My thanks to Abdel Rahman for his part in this transaction and as agreed I have rewarded him with a sovereign. Your grateful friend, Captain J. W. Talbot."

Abdel asked what the words discretion, commend and transaction meant and the Captain happily explained their meaning.

As Abdel left the cabin the Captain said, "You are most welcome to return anytime Abdel and I wish you fine weather and clear passage in your life. Don't forget to take this note back to Mr Levi."

"Thank you, Captain, I will do so now," replied Abdel and he left the ship, collected his bicycle and set off for Mr Levi's shop on Bunder Road.

He parked his bicycle outside the shop and entered again and created another cacophony of noise from the bell ringing as the door was pushed open.

"Ah Gods messenger has returned, so what have you for me Abdel Rahman?"

"You did not tell me the truth Mr Levy; you have no third son," replied Abdel.

"You are correct and I make my humble apologies to God and you Abdel. But there is good reason behind this falsehood. I had to be sure that you would carry out my wishes with honesty. Have you a note for me from the Captain?"

"Yes, I have Mr Levi," and he handed Jacob the note.

He read the note and looked up and said, "You must call me Jacob from this day Abdel; you have proved to be a trustworthy man and I thank you for your virtue in this matter. As we say in Hebrew;

"Ba – ruch hag – ge ver, a – sher yiv – tach Yah – weh, and in English that means; Blessed is the man who trusts in the Lord."

Jacob went on to say, "You were prepared to come back with the package until the Captain explained the situation, were you not?"

"Yes Mr Levi, I was."

"From the note it seems you have a sovereign from the Captain as reward."

Abdel produced the sovereign and Jacob gave him another and said, "Now you have two, for your good work, I will have other tasks for you Abdel if you would be in my employment."

Abdel nodded and said, "I would like to work for you when you need me Mr, I mean Jacob and I thank you for this sovereign."

"You are most welcome, Shalom Abdel," he replied.

Abdel smiled and said, "shalom to you Jacob," and left the shop very satisfied with the day's efforts. As he rode his bicycle back to his uncle's store, it crossed his mind that no money had been exchanged for the ring that had been given to the Captain. Jacob Levi must be a rich man indeed if he can make such treasures without any reward, he thought.

It was now early August 1932 and the weather had been extremely hot and dry for some weeks. The large British presence in Karachi was feeling the effects of this, especially the families of the officials working in the government departments.

British schools were closed for the holidays and leisure time at the beach resorts like Clifton and Paradise Point was limited, due to the strong sea currents that prevailed at this time of year.

It was a warm Sunday morning when Osman suggested that he and Abdel should go fishing for turtles and snappers of Manora Island. Osman's father Shah Ali Khan had recently acquired a Sloop fitted with a staysail and mizzen spanker, which was moored at the wharf. Osman was determined to overcome his sea sickness and he had learned to "roll with the movement of the boat" when he went fishing with his father.

It was 9am and the sea was reasonably calm as they set off from the wharf. Osman took the rudder while Abdel managed the sails. It took some time before these novice sailors mastered the conditions and at times steering a straight course was troublesome. They were helped by a *Soldier's Wind*, which resulted in very little *tack* being employed. However, they persevered and after an hour and a half they reached Manora Island.

They dropped anchor some 200 yards from the beach and lowered the sails. Abdel was a keen swimmer and said, "I will slip over the side and have a swim Osman."

"Be careful Abdel, there are sharks in this depth, as well as sea snakes," replied Osman

"You are here to warn me Osman, so be watchful my friend."

While Abdel enjoyed his swim, Osman prepared his nets for fishing. Within minutes gulls and frigate birds began to circle their small craft in anticipation of an easy meal. As Osman was securing the rudder bar, he noticed a large shadow just ahead of the bow of the boat. His first thought was that it was a shoal of Bluestripe Snappers and alerted Abdel saying, "Abdel it's time to cast our net, be quick and get aboard."

Abdel was about 20 feet from the boat, when he saw it. A shark fin out of the water between him and the boat. Osman spotted it and quickly grabbed an oar and began to thrash the sea from the sloop.

Abdel had to tread water until he thought it was safe to make a swim for the boat. Osman was thrashing and shouting to scare off the shark as Abdel managed to reach the grab lines and haul himself aboard, nearly capsizing the sloop in the process.

The shark continued to circle the boat for some ten minutes, before giving up on an easy meal. It was a big Blue Shark, probably around 12 feet in length and well known for harassing swimmers and often causing fatalities in these waters.

Abdel was still in a state of shock and Osman said, "Did it attack you Abdel?"

Taking large breaths and finally recovering enough to speak he said, "It was a very big fish Osman; God was with me today."

"I thought it was a big shoal of snappers when I saw the shadow just under the bow of the boat."

"Well, lets us cast our nets and hope our shark does not return," added Abdel.

They cast a net on both port and seaward sides of the sloop. They were virtually becalmed at this point and sat and talked about all manner of things for over an hour. Osman then decided that enough time had been spent on this fishing trip and said, "Let us reel in our nets Abdel, the wind has strengthened and we should be thinking of getting back to the wharf."

Abdel agreed and they hauled in the nets. The port side net only produced a few flying fish and a green turtle. The seaward side net produced a much better result with at least 12 flying fish, 3 snappers, 3 green turtles and much to their surprise a sea snake. Osman was concerned about the sea snake and said, "We must be careful with that sea snake; it might not be dead and if it bites one of us our family will have to put us in the ground."

They carefully separated the fish from the snake and Abdel gave it a crushing blow with the oar, which resulted in the snake being decapitated. The head and the body were returned to the sea, only for a gull to quickly scoop the carcase up and fly off.

The voyage back to Clifton Wharf took less than fifty minutes, thanks to a good tail wind. On arrival at around three in the afternoon Abdel and Osman unloaded their catch and hired a rickshaw to take their haul back to Rahman's Chandlers for gutting and filleting.

They then took their haul to Faroods Fisheries on Elphinstone Street, where they were paid 30 rupees for their labours.

Abdel's reading was generating much praise within Rahman's Chandlers and he became a focal point for learning. Uncle Ahmad had asked Abdel to teach his son Abdullah to read and for a commission of 5 rupees a week he agreed. He had finished reading Defoe's *Robinson Crusoe* and was now embroiled in *Kipps* by H.G. Wells. He found this book difficult to understand and would regularly have a plethora of words and quotes for Syed to decipher. After some three weeks of interpretation Syed suggested that Abdel should put the book aside and select another book that he would find easier to comprehend. Abdel agreed and chose another seafaring tale in Robert Louis Stevenson's *Treasure Island*.

Hakim had found an interest in cricket and had become talented in the sport, which he would play on Saturday's at the Karachi Grammar School. Cricket was generally a sport the British played, with teams from the British Army, the Port Authority and the Government Offices. The locals were afforded spectator status, but soon the popularity began to produce talented young men, who on occasion were allowed to take part in domestic games.

In 1926 the MCC toured India and as a result of this ground breaking event, cricket grew in popularity. Hakim hoped he would play for his adopted homeland one day. Abdel would join Hakim sometimes, but did not have the passion or the aptitude to excel in cricket and at times found it boring in the extreme.

Despite the depression, Rahman's Chandlers survived and enhanced its standing within the local business community. Procurement of contracts for goods and services at the newly built Aerodrome and a steady expansion within the port trade resulted in Ahmad Ali Rahman employing two more workers to embellish the workforce. Abdel was an important employee of Rahman's and he had acquired a sound reputation as an essential provider of new ventures.

In October 1933, he persuaded his uncle to open a tea house in Tariq Road, which he would devote half of his working time to. Unlike many tea houses in Karachi, Rahman's was in business to only sell and serve quality tea, coffee and non-alcoholic beverages. To help Abdel in this new business enterprise, Ahmad gave him one of the employees to assist him, his name was Kaleb Mahgreb.

Kaleb was born in Hermel, Lebanon and left with his father and mother when he was 5 years old. His father opened a Leather Goods Store in Karachi, but Kaleb was not too enamoured with this work and his father had asked Ahmad if he had a job for his son at Rahman's.

So, Rahman's new Tea House opened on November 24th. The two young men there to head this new project were Abdel Rahman aged 15 and Kaleb Mahgreb aged 16 years old. In order to keep a watchful eye on his new business, Ahmad asked Syed to make regular appearances to ensure everything was running smoothly. Much to Syed's chagrin, who felt the Tea House was an unnecessary burden.

The following years went by without much change in the lives of those within the confines of Rahman's Chandlers. Abdel would still go fishing with Osman, sometimes Kaleb would tag along. Hakim had given up on becoming a cricketer and devoted his time to the business. The Tea House was a success and profits were burgeoning.

The world in 1934 was becoming a troubled place. Adolf Hitler had ordered the purge on the National Socialists and on June 30th the SS carried out the *"Night of the Long Knives,"* executing Ernst Röhm and his senior officials, thus clearing the way for political domination in Germany. Joseph Stalin was also instrumental in purging the Soviet Union of so-called dissidents and political opponents, through a campaign of mass murder.

CHAPTER FIVE

The Great Depression was showing signs of recovery and constraints on imports and exports were being lifted.
Rudyard Kipling is awarded the Gothenburg Prize for Poetry along with William Butler Yeats. Gangsters Bonnie and Clyde are killed by police in Bienville Parish, Louisiana.
Afghanistan joins the League of Nations and Persia becomes Iran. Gaston Doumergue forms a new government in France and fears of another war in Europe begin to develop.
Then on May 31st 1935 an earthquake struck Quetta and the effects were felt as far away as Karachi and Agra in the east. In total some 10.000 people lost their lives in Quetta and the surrounding villages including Mastung and Kalat. Abdel was asleep as the earthquake struck at 2.30am in the morning. He awoke to see Syed's bookshelf tumbling down on Hakim's bed, resulting in screams and obscenities from Hakim.
Syed tried to calm the situation and said, "stay where you are and try to hold onto your bed Abdel, I will see to Hakim, it will not last long."
Three minutes is an eternity in an earthquake and the buildings on Bunder Road suffered some internal damage, but nothing catastrophic. The previous year another earthquake had occurred 6 miles south of Mount Everest at latitude of 26 degrees N and the tremors had been felt in Karachi, Bombay and Calcutta. More than 7.000 people had died that day.
The following day a survey of the damage was carried out and apart from some items of furniture and windows devoid of glass, the repair cost would be minimal. Abdel had experienced "God's anger," as his father had once said, back home in Azaw; but nothing like this.
As they cleared up the mess in the morning, Syed said to Abdel, "This is a message Abdel."
Abdel looked confused and replied, "A message Syed, I don't understand, a message from who?"
"From God Abdel, it is time you left us and begin a new chapter in your life."
Hakim overheard the comment, laughed and added, "Yes Abdel, you are a bad omen. Go and sail the high seas and leave us in safety."
"I hope Kaleb is alright down at the Tea House. I must go and see," and he quickly dashed out of the door and ran to Tariq Road. He was there in 4 minutes and saw Kaleb sitting outside on the porch nursing cuts to his arms.
"I am glad to see you Kaleb, but you are hurt my friend. You must go to the Doctor on Tariq Road. I will take you now."
Kaleb turned to look at the damage to the Tea House and said, "No tea

today Abdel."

"Don't worry we can clean the place up later, first you must see the Doctor."

They walked back to Tariq Road and Doctor Urban's surgery, only to find a long line of people waiting for treatment. Kaleb's cuts were not serious so Abdel brought him back to Rahman's and Syed bathed and dressed the wounds.

Ahmad's house had only suffered some exterior damage to his porch and he said to concentrate on the store and look to get the windows replaced in both the store and the Tea House. He had already commissioned the glazier Mr Salmi to do the work.

"That was quick Ahmad," said Syed.

Grinning from ear to ear Ahmad said, "Ah well, Mr Salmi and I have an understanding."

In 1936 Ahmad's health deteriorated and after seeking medical advice, he was informed that he had contracted malaria. He was 57 years old and his decline was rapid; on June 26th he succumbed to the disease. Prior to his demise he had left instructions that his son Abdullah Ali Rahman, Hakim and Abdel would carry on the business.

Within a month of his uncle's death Abdel had made a conscious decision to leave the business and join the Merchant Navy with the British East India Company. Before informing Abdullah and Hakim, he sought the advice of Syed one morning before he set of for the Tea House.

"I am going to leave Rahman's, Syed."

Syed looked surprised and said,

"This is not because of the earthquake is it Abdel? Anyway, you have not read any Shakespeare yet."

Abdel seemed perplexed and was struggling to see the link, then replied, "But Syed, how will Shakespeare make such a difference?"

"I am making fun of you Abdel; I have known for some time that this day would come. I can see it in your eyes and in your heart. You have been a great servant to Rahman's Chandlers and you have learned so much, about many things. Ever since the death of my brother Ahmad, I have seen a change in you Abdel and with God's guidance I am sure you will prosper in life. You must tell Abdullah and Hakim soon as they will need to employ more staff. I am 63 years old now and my work in the store is concerned with the administration paperwork and answering that annoying telephone."

"You will still have time to read your books," added Abdel, with a smile.

"I shall indeed, if God wills it Abdel," he replied.

"I will now go to the Tea House and talk to Kaleb about my plans and then I will speak with Abdullah and Hakim tonight, after evening prayer at the Mosque."

As he left, Syed said, "You will need many books when you are at sea Abdel, I will put a small collection together for you."

Abdel left Syed and made his way to the Tea House and gave Kaleb his news.

"But what will I do Abdel? I am alone here," said Kaleb, with an expectant look on his face.

"Do not worry Kaleb; I have not left you yet. I will find a new employee for the Tea House and it will be a month before I have my papers to sail," replied Abdel.

Over the course of the following seven days Abdel had found a new worker for Kaleb, carried out repairs to both the store and the Tea House and secured papers to join the British India Steam Navigation Company. On his papers were the details of his employment, which read as follows:

Name: Abdel Malik Rahman Home Address: Rahman's Chandlers. Bunder Rd. Karachi.
Date of Birth: October 15th 1918 Age: 17

You will be employed as a Deck Rating for the British India Steam Navigation Co Ltd and you have been appointed a crew member of the ship Domelia, a passenger/general cargo vessel of 8.444 tons. The Domelia is 460 feet in length and a breadth of 58 feet, with a service speed of 12 knots. She was built in 1921 by Barclay, Curle & Co Ltd, Whiteinch, Glasgow.

For identification purposes the ships funnel colours are: - Black with two White Bands separated by a thin Black Band.

The ship will dock at the Clifton Wharf, Karachi, India on Saturday, September 21st 1936 at a time allocated by the Harbour Master.

You must report to the ships Purser, Mr J.H. Cawthorne at 11.00am on September 26th.
The Domelia will be carrying passengers and cargo to Bombay, Colombo and Calcutta departing on September 26th 1936.

Details of Pay and conditions will be availed to you, once on board the ship. Please remember to bring along two testimonials and a recent photograph, which must be handed to the Purser once on board.

*Issued by Company Superintendent: Mr T. E. Dalrymple. Date: September 3rd 1936.
The British India Steam Navigation Co Ltd. 122 Leadenhall Street. London. EC3.*

Abdel asked Syed to explain what some of the information on his papers related to and in particular his likely pay as a Deck Rating. Syed relayed the information and reminded Abdel that he must report to the Purser once on board. Then he would be told about his pay and conditions. Syed clarified what a testimonial was and said he would provide one, but he must find another.

Abdel was at a loss as to who he could ask and then he said, "What about Captain Jack Talbot of the Amra?

I still have the sovereign he gave me for delivering his wife's ring made by Jacob Levi."

"Well, the problem with that is, the Captain is on his way to Hamburg remember."

"Oh yes, I forgot," replied Abdel

Jacob Levi would be a good man to ask for a testimonial, he is a respected businessman in Karachi," added Syed.

"Yes, that is a very good idea Syed, but will he agree?"

"You can only ask him Abdel; he is a good honest man," said Syed.

"Yes, I will visit him tomorrow," he replied.

With the opening of the airport in Karachi in 1924, trade was enhanced and Ahmad quickly seized the initiative and established a contract with the airport authorities in supplying various commodities, such as tea, coffee, sugar, bread and hardware items including brushes, cleaning materials and toiletries. In order to receive these products, the airport authority had to use their own transport and make the trip to Bunder Road to collect their orders. Syed was aware that the truck drivers were of the opinion that Rahman's should be delivering the orders directly to the airport. The use of rickshaws and carts were fine for the port, but the airport was some 10 miles out of town. A decision had to be made and so Syed drew up a contract with Mr Singh's Motor Vehicles on Tariq Road to supply a 5-ton truck to Rahman's. The agreement on finance for the vehicle involved a deposit of 2.000 Rupees and 12 monthly payments of 300 Rupees. The cost of the vehicle would be 5.600 Rupees with an additional 5% added for interest, leaving a total figure of 5.880 Rupees (£452).

At 10.00am Monday, September 8th 1936, Mr Singh collected a Morris Truck, newly arrived on a ship from London and drove the vehicle to Rahman's on Bunder Road. Both Hakim and Abdel looked in amazement as the truck trundled up to the store, with an excited Mr Singh shouting and waving from the driver's seat.

"Syed what have you done?" asked a bemused Hakim.

"This is called expanding the business Hakim. We must look to improve our reputation and provide a personal service and that requires us to deliver our goods. It will also allow us to be noticed and advertise our business."

Abdel was shocked but excited about this new development, but asked a very important question when he said, "Who will drive it then?"

Mr Singh looked at Syed, he looked at Hakim and Hakim looked at Abdel.

"Oh no, it cannot be me, I am joining the merchant navy," said an exasperated Abdel.

Syed laughed and calmed all those in attendance and said, "Do not worry; I have employed a driver called Mr Najibullah Daoud. He has been recommended to me by Mr Khan who works for James Finley & Co Ltd. I have employed Mr Nawaz to paint our name and address on the truck and he is on his way as we speak, thanks to the miracle of the telephone."

Abdel had some free time on Sunday afternoon and went walking along the wharf. He picked an old packing crate to sit on as he watched the various activities of loading and unloading cargo from the ships currently docked.

He was thinking of Mr Jack Rowley and where he might be on the City of Venice and Captain Talbot on the Amra. Had he given his gift to his wife yet?

As he sat and contemplated his future, a young girl about the same age as Abdel stopped smiled and said, "Are you lost?"

"No, I am not lost. I am just sitting here watching the ships being loaded up for their next voyage."

"Do you work here?" she asked.

"No, I work for Rahman's Chandlers on the Bunder Road," he replied.

She was about the same height as Abdel with long black hair that swept across her face from the warm inshore breeze sweeping off the wharf. Abdel was quite smitten by her pretty face and that infectious smile and said, "Do you live near the port then?"

"No, I live in Zeburissa Street, my father has a printing business and my name is Maheera Sardar and I am 17 years old."

At this point she sat down next to Abdel and said, "so what is your name?"

"I am Abdel Malik Rahman and I am 18 years old. I work for my uncle, but in 17 days' time I am going to join the Merchant Navy and work for the British India Steam Navigation Company."

"That sounds very exciting, are you not afraid Abdel?"

He felt a warmth and understanding as she spoke his name and answered, "Oh no, I have already sailed with Jack Rowley, who is an Engineer on board the City of Venice. I thought it was wonderful and I plan to sail around the world, like some of the great explorers such as Columbus, Magellan and Cabot."

"What school did you go to in Karachi Abdel?"

"I have not had schooling in Karachi, I was taught by my Father until I was 11 years old. When my father died, I moved to Karachi to join my brother Hakim. He also works for Rahman's Chandlers. Syed, my uncle's cousin has taught me how to read English books and I have read *Robinson Crusoe* by Daniel Defoe; I am now reading *War of the Worlds* by H.G. Wells, have you read these books Maheera?"

"No, I must concentrate on my studies in the Koran, Mathematics, Science and Cookery at the Mama Parsi Girls School. I can write and read in English; can you write in English Abdel?"

"Yes, but Syed has said that I need to check my spellings with my dictionary, because I make too many mistakes."

"Is it a good school Maheera?" asked Abdel.

"It is hard work from 7.30 in the morning until 5.30 at night, but we do get one hour for lunch and breaks at 10 o'clock in the morning and 3 o'clock in the afternoon. Our school motto is 'Let humility, charity, faith and labour light our path.'"

At that point Maheera's father called to her from the port office and she said, "I must go now Abdel, it has been very nice talking to you and I hope you prosper in your new job, goodbye."

"Thank you Maheera, may God guide you through your studies, goodbye."

She then walked to meet her Father and as Abdel looked on; her father appeared to be admonishing her for wandering off. They then climbed onto a motorised rickshaw and drove off.

Abdel hoped he would see her again someday, so he could regale her with his adventures on the high seas.

The following day Abdel went to see his friend Jacob Levi to ask him for a testimonial to present to the British India Steam Company.

The door chime seemed louder than normal as he stepped into Jacob's jewellery shop.

"Shalom Abdel, so good to see again, how are your family?" asked Jacob.

"Shalom Jacob, well since my uncle died, we have been working very hard."

"So, I hear, and you now have a Tea House as well. I paid it a visit last week and enjoyed a cup of very good Darjeeling. The proprietor Kaleb is a fine young fellow and we talked for some time about Rahman's."

"Your door bell seems very loud today Jacob," added Abdel.

"Yes, this is because we had a robber last week who managed to get into my shop and steel some coins that were on display. He somehow got in by silencing the bell, how I don't know."

"But with my hearing not what it used to be; I have had a louder bell-hang fitted. Mr Bashir my neighbour saw him running out of my shop and he came to tell me. I was in the back of my shop at the time. I hope he uses his ill-gotten gains to good use Abdel."

"Have you told the police Jacob?"

"Oh yes, but I do not have much faith in them, I am just a Jew who has much in privilege and the money to replenish any loss. Now what I can I do for you today?"

"I am here today to ask of you a great favour Jacob. I am joining the Merchant Navy and I am going to work for the British India Steam Navigation Company. To gain a job with them I need two testimonials, one I already have from Syed and could I ask you to supply me with another."

"This is truly an honour Abdel; I would be very pleased to provide you with a testimonial. Who would think it, a Jew with little importance been given such valued task? I have a typewriter in the back of my shop and I will do the testimonial tonight. When will you be leaving us to sail the seven seas then Abdel?"

"I have to report at the wharf on September 26th with my papers and board the *Domelia* taking up my post as a deck rating. We sail the next day Jacob."

"I am sure you will make us all proud Abdel and as we say in Latin; *Sit Deus in requiem tibi improvide tempestatis unda.* Which means, May God steer you through troubled waters."

"Where did you learn Latin Jacob?"

"From books Abdel, from books. I see Rahman's have now got a truck; the business must be growing Abdel."

"Yes Jacob, Syed said we had to expand our customers and provide transport for our provisions to and from the airport."

"Ah yes, the airport with those flying metal seagulls. Times are changing Abdel. Sometimes I think I am too old for all this change."

"I must leave you now Jacob, I have many chores to do. Can I collect the testimonial tomorrow at around 5 o'clock in the afternoon?"

"Yes, that will be fine."

Abdel then went to see Kaleb at the Tea House and then back to Rahman's to join Najibullah on a trip out to the airport delivering cotton for a flight to Aden.

The next day at 5 o'clock he arrived at Jacob Levi's shop, and opened the door to a crescendo of ringing from the door-bell. Jacob was sat behind his counter working on a watch.

"Shalom, I will attend to you very soon Abdel, but I must repair this pocket watch for Doctor Smithson who has a practice in the Civil Lines Quarter near Frere Hall, please sit on that chair."

Abdel looked on as Jacob concentrated on his task, carefully tinkering with the workings of the pocket watch.

"That's it, back to full working order," said Jacob, holding the watch in his hands admiring his handiwork.

"Now then Abdel, take a look at this timepiece," and he handed the watch to Abdel.

"It is beautiful Jacob."

"Yes, it is Abdel and one day you might own a watch like this yourself. It is a 14kt Gold Omega Grand Prix Paris Chronometer Pocket Watch, made in 1896."

"I have no watch yet Jacob, but it is my intention to buy one as soon as I have enough money," he replied.

Jacob then put his hand under the counter and produced an unsealed envelope.

"Here is your testimonial Abdel. You can read it now, but then you must seal it. In this way your employer will assume you have not seen it. However, I will not change anything that I have written. Now give me the name of the man who will open this envelope and I will write his monocle on the front of the envelope. His name is Mr J H Cawthorne. Purser, I have his name written here on this slip of paper," and he handed it to Jacob.

Jacob removed the testimonial from the envelope and handed it to Abdel. It read as follows:

This is testimonial for Abdel Malik Rahman of Bunder Road. Karachi. India.

Dated this day of September 10th 1936.

I have had the pleasure of knowing Abdel for these past three years and I have found him to be an honest and reliable young man. As a businessman I have to ensure that my business is both profitable and also meets the requirements of my customers. I am aware of the excellent reputation that Rahman's Chandlers have maintained in their own business and Abdel has played a major role in their success. Abdel has chosen to seek his future in the merchant navy and I have no doubt he will continue to show a high degree of enthusiasm and loyalty in this regard. I have no hesitation in recommending Abdel Malik Rahman for employment with the British India Steam Navigation Company and wish him prosperity and good fortune in this new venture.

Your humble servant, Jacob Levi.
Levi's Jewellers
Bunder Road. Karachi.
Signed: Jacob Levi Date: September 10th 1936.

Abdel read his testimonial and with a tear in his eye said, "Is this who I am Jacob? Some of these words I do not understand, but I can see that you have faith in me. I hope I can be as good and honourable as you. I must thank you for this very good testimonial my friend and I will now seal it."

Jacob asked Abdel to have a look at his recently arrived SBR Bakelite & Wood Radio and brought it out and put it on the counter. It had just arrived from Belgium and the radio was the new entertainment medium that had gained in popularity in the United States.

He plugged it in and fiddled with a dial on the front. It suddenly crackled into life, but Abdel was a little wary of it.

"It is alright Abdel; I am just starting to get used to it."

He finally he managed to locate a transmission in English. It was the BBC World service.

"I listen to the world service and it keeps me informed of world events Abdel "

The speaker was announcing that Spain was in the midst of a civil war and the fascists were also growing in strength in Germany and Italy.

"These are troubling times; fascism is an evil that concerns me Abdel."

Abdel could only understand some of the dialogue from the radio, but he could see it troubled Jacob and he said, "I am reading *War of the Worlds* by H.G. Wells and it talks about other beings from the stars in the sky. Syed tells me it is just fiction anyway. What do you think Jacob?"

"Well, I have not read this book, but we need to make sure we live in peace in this world Abdel and that is fact."

"You do not need to worry Jacob; watches will always need repairing and your jewellery shop will make you a rich man in a peaceful Karachi."

As Jacob seemed pre-occupied with his new radio set, Abdel took the opportunity to say goodbye and set off for Rahman's. As he strolled past a stationary tram that was letting passengers disembark, he recognised Maheera. She was with her father, he tried not to look too interested, but Maheera had other ideas. She stopped in front of him and said, "Abdel, it is very nice to see you again. Father, this is the boy I was talking to on the wharf."

Her father seemed disinterested, but said, "Oh is that so, my daughter tells me you have a Chandlers Store, is that correct?"

"Yes Sir, that is correct."

Maheera had a cunning smile on her face and she winked at Abdel.

"She also tells me that you are going to join the British India Steam Navigation Company."

Maheera was now staring at Abdel with an exaggerated smile.

"Yes Sir, that is also correct," and then he said, "if you would allow it, I would like to send your daughter post cards from places where my ship docks."

The smile on Maheera's face quickly disappeared and took on a look of disbelief.

"That is a matter for discussion with my family, but may I wish you a safe journey on board your vessel; come along Maheera, we must be going."

Before Abdel could say goodbye, they were gone, but the look over her shoulder from Maheera suggested his request might be considered.

Having arrived back at the store he ate with Abdullah, Hakim and Syed, before going to evening prayer at the mosque. When he returned, he gave Syed his testimonial to keep safe and said, "Have you written my testimonial yet Syed?"

"Yes, I have done so and I will give you it when you go to join your ship."

Abdel pondered this for a little while then said, "Have you hand written it Syed?"

"Yes, why do you ask this?"

"Jacob Levi used his typewriter."

"How do you know this, it is sealed."

Abdel very nearly fell for the bait, but he diffused the situation when he said, "Jacob told me and showed me his typewriter and his new radio from Belgium."

Syed just gave Abdel that knowing smile and added, "That Jew must be rich to have a telephone, a typewriter and a radio."

Syed asked how Abdel's reading and writing was progressing. He also asked Abdel if there were any more of his own books that he would like to take with him. Abdel spent the next hour combing through all Syed's books on the shelves and selected 5 books. They were; Shakespeare's *Hamlet*, Bunyan's *Pilgrims Progress*, Conan Doyle's *A Study in Scarlet*, the Readers Digest World Atlas and the Oxford English Dictionary.

"That is an interesting selection of books Abdel. But most of all, do not forget The Noble Qur'an. I will box them up along with *The War of the Worlds* for you; ready for your departure."

That night, as he lay pondering how his life was about to change forever, he still saw Maheera walking away and looking over her shoulder.

There were now only two weeks left before Abdel would clamber aboard the *Domelia* and begin a new chapter in his life.

Those two weeks seemed an eternity and on September 24th Syed organised a farewell dinner for Abdel at the Tea House.

A banquet was laid on with all manner of food; there was chicken biryani, blue snapper, bottis, tikka, fresh fruit, rice, nuts and breads. In attendance was, Syed, Hakim, Abdullah, Kaleb and Abdel. As they sat down Kaleb said, "There are many chairs here Syed, there are only five of us."

"We must wait for our guests to arrive before we can enjoy this farewell dinner for Abdel," replied Syed.

Everyone looked a little puzzled.

Hakim said, "But everyone is here Syed."

Before Syed could respond in walked Osman, closely followed by Najibullah.

"Can we eat now asked Kaleb?"

Syed shot Kaleb a look of disdain and replied, "No we will not, we have other important guests yet to arrive."

Abdel was quite bewildered by this and the next guest brought a sense of happiness to the occasion as Jacob Levi strolled into the Tea House saying, 'shalom, I am here for my good friend Abdel Malik Rahman. I here he is leaving us."

Abdel rose to his feet and embraced Jacob and said, "this is truly a happy moment for me, welcome Jacob. I am honoured to be invited to this farewell dinner. I hope all this food is kosher," and smiled at Syed.

"Please sit Jacob, we are still awaiting others guests," said Syed.

Other guests, who could they be? Thought Abdel.

As if on cue Jack Rowley appeared, closely followed by Maheera's father.

Abdel looked at Syed in amazement but Syed just grinned, rose to his feet and said, "Now it is time to introduce everyone that is present here today."

After all the introductions both Syed and Jacob said a prayer for safe passage for Abdel on his maiden voyage. Abdel could not hide his astonishment and asked Syed how he managed to get everyone here together without his knowledge.

"By the miracle of telephone Abdel."

This generated much laughter and Jacob added, "You see Abdel, there are times when the telephone brings people together."

Maheera's father Mr Sardar rose from his chair and announced, "I have given my permission for Abdel and my daughter Maheera to exchange letters during his travels as a merchant seaman."

Syed gave Abdel a nod and raised his eyes to prompt him to respond to this gesture.

Abdel rose and said, "May I give my thanks to Mr Sardar and I will be forever in his debt for his wisdom and charity. May God bless him and his family."

Then another arrival, a small smartly dressed man wearing wire rimmed spectacles, who was carrying a knapsack.

Syed introduced him as Mr Ali who has a photographic business in the Empress Market and added, "I have asked him to take some photographs of this gathering and he has promised that he will have them ready before Abdel sets sail tomorrow, is that not so Mr Ali?"

"Yes, that is so Mr Rahman."

Mr Ali then set about positioning everyone for a series of photographs that lasted some twenty minutes.

"Will you not join us Mr Ali?" asked Hakim.

"You are very kind, but I must get back to my shop to develop these in time for tomorrow," he replied.

Then the feasting began and for some three hours many subjects were discussed including how Karachi was slowly gaining momentum as a thriving port again after the great depression. The hope being that this would further enhance business opportunities. Abdel could see that Syed was using the gathering as an opportunity to promote Rahman's. However, he was outshone by Jacob Levi who used all his business acumen to gain some notable business with Mr Sardar.

With the feast drawing to a close, Jacob rose to his feet and expressed his grateful thanks for being invited along to wish Abdel well on his new life. He then produced a small leather-bound box from his pocket and said, "I would like to honour this occasion by giving Abdel this small gift that I am sure he will have very good use for." He handed the gift to Abdel saying, "The box has a small hidden catch Abdel. If you just press just under the lid, it will open."

Abdel activated the catch and on opening, was stunned to see a Gold 14kt Omega Grand Prix Paris Chronometer Pocket Watch.

"If you take it out and flip the lid, you will see that it is unique Abdel."

Abdel was in a state euphoria and flipped the lid, which had been engraved on the inside. He read the inscription to everyone;

"To my dear friend Abdel Malik Rahman. A man of unquestionable honesty and loyalty. Dated this day of September 10th 1936."

Abdel was overcome with emotion and with tears in his eyes, embraced Jacob Levi saying, "You are so kind Jacob; I will try and live up to your faith in me." Then after regaining his composure he asked, "What does unquestionable mean?"

At that everyone laughed, and Jacob said, "It means that you can be trusted to do the right thing Abdel."

As he gazed at his watch, it suddenly dawned on him that this was the watch that Jacob was working on when he last saw him in his shop.

"But that was for Doctor Smithson near the Frere Hall."

Jacob smiled and said, "there is no Doctor Smithson Abdel, may God forgive me for that untruth. I will leave you with this thought Abdel."

"The beat of your heart will rise and fall with the actions you take."

All those present shook the hand of Jacob Levi and thanked him for Abdel's wonderful gift. Then Syed announced that he too had a gift for Abdel and handed him a parcel wrapped in brown paper.

Jack Rowley offered Abdel some advice and said, "ships can be lonely places Abdel, you must quickly learn that hard work will be rewarded and selecting friends on board is important. The Deck Officer on The *Domelia* is Mr Macintyre; he is a good friend of mine."

"I have asked him to keep a watchful eye on you."

"That is very kind of you Mr Rowley; I am in your debt for doing such a thing," replied Syed.

Abdel unwrapped the parcel to find a copy of Jonathan Swifts Gulliver's Travels.

When he opened the book, he found $50 and £50.

He embraced Syed saying, "I hope to make you proud of me Syed."

"You have already done so Abdel."

The guests then said their farewells and left the Tea House for Kaleb to tidy and close up. Syed, Abdel, Abdullah and Hakim all returned to Rahman's and retired for the night. As they lied in their beds Hakim said,

"Well Syed, there will be much more space in hear when my dear brother has set sail."

"Yes, that is true Hakim, because you will be sleeping with Abdullah in his room. I want some peace and quiet."

Abdel laughed and said, "I will still need a bed when I come home Syed."

"That is fine, you do not snore as badly as your older brother," he replied.

Hakim's silence spoke volumes.

The weather in Karachi was still hot with cloudless skies, temperatures not falling below 80 degrees Fahrenheit. From May to October the temperature had little variation from day to day. Rain falls, but very sparingly throughout the year. The prevailing wind tends to blow from south to north at this time of the year.

CHAPTER SIX

Abdel woke up to the sound of movement downstairs; he bathed and got dressed to find Hakim preparing a breakfast of bread, pancakes and tea.

"Where is Syed?" He asked.

"He has gone to the mosque to prey."

"It's early, he would normally go after breakfast," replied Abdel.

"He will soon be back no doubt."

Within ten minutes Syed had returned, holding a parcel, which he gave to Abdel and said, "this must go with you at all times Abdel."

Abdel opened the parcel to find a new edition of the Noble Qur'an. He thanked Syed for his kindness and they all sat and ate a hearty breakfast. Nearing the end of their breakfast, Mr Ali arrived and presented Syed with his photographs.

"How much do I owe you Mr Ali?" asked Syed.

"For you a special rate Mr Rahman, its 40 rupees."

Syed looked through all 10 photographs and said, "You have great skills Mr Ali; I look much younger," and smiled displaying his four remaining teeth.

Syed paid Mr Ali 50 rupees and thanked him for his prompt service.

Syed laid out the photographs on the table and asked Abdel to choose one that he could take with him to present to the Purser. Abdel chose a group photograph along with his self-portrait. Hakim did the same.

"Where is Abdullah?" asked Syed.

"Still in his bed," replied Hakim.

"Remind me, what time you have to board your ship Abdel?"

"I have to board and present myself to the Purser at 11am, with all my papers."

"Well, it is now 9am and I think we should assemble your possessions and walk to the wharf and see your ship the *Domelia*."

Abdel was now in a state of wonderment, a new life, new friends and a new home. All this only hours away. How would he feel when the ship sets sail? He will miss Syed, Hakim, Abdullah, Jacob, Osman and Kaleb. He will miss fishing with Osman, the truck ride to the airport and what about Maheera? Then he realised that he did not have Maheera's address.

"Syed where is the address for Maheera's house?"

Syed smiled and said, "You have it in your pocket, another copy in your knapsack and a further copy in your memory."

"Oh yes, I am nervous and yet I am excited Syed."

When they had gathered everything, they left the store and walked along Bunder Road. They had only walked a hundred yards when Abdel stopped and said, "But I have not said goodbye to Hakim, Abdullah, Jacob, Osman or Kaleb."

"Calm yourself, they will all be at the wharf before you board. I have used the telephone to let them all know. Now let us go into the mosque to pray together."

After prayers Syed sat with Abdel and spoke of what he should be wary of and how to behave in the company of men and their coarseness saying, "You are going to work and live with men who perhaps have no regard for you or what you believe. Be wary of their roughness and do not follow in their unkind ways. Do not seek the bed of women who would take away your soul for money. You will have a heavy heart when men insult you by calling you a coolly or wog. You must have strength and look to God and seek the kinship of honest men Abdel.

"It is written in the Noble Qur'an that many prophets have exalted their passion for God, including Moses, Abraham and Jesus. The world has many ways to worship God Abdel. You will meet Jews, Seeks, Hindu's, Buddhists, Christians and non-believers. You must carry the thoughts of the prophet Mohammed with you all your life Abdel Malik Rahman. You start this new life as a boy, but when you return you will be a man. Remember your father, he was a devout man and you have many of his qualities."

"I know I will face these test's Syed, but I am strong and I am determined to make this new life a success and I thank you for your guidance and teaching, since I have been with Rahman's."

They arrived at the wharf at 9.45am. The ship was being loaded with cargo and a few passengers were milling around the port office. As they stood and took in all the activity Abdel's concentration was interrupted by a tap on his shoulder. He turned to find Hakim, Abdullah, Kaleb and Osman standing laughing.

"Did you think we were not coming?" said Kaleb.

Abdel smiled and then caught site of Maheera and her father standing near the port office. His heart jumped and he felt overwhelmed that she was here to wave him off.

It was now 10.45am and Syed said, "I think it is time you said goodbye Abdel, it will take five minutes to walk up that gangplank."

Abdel embraced them all, said goodbye and carried his burgeoning knapsack and prayer mat toward the gangplank. Passengers were boarding ahead of him and as he stepped on the first rung, he felt light headed and stopped to look round to see his family and friends all waving and to his great joy saw Maheera waving both her hands in the air, only to be halted by her father.

Once on board he was directed to the Purser's cabin by a rough looking man who wore a cloth cap and whose arms were heavily tattooed. He had a deep scar that ran from his left eye down to his chin. The deck ratings were employed in getting the ship ready to weigh anchor and leave the wharf.

Abdel found the Purser's cabin and knocked on the door.

"Yes, who is it?" said a voice from within.

"It is I Abdel Malik Rahman, I am the new Deck Rating sir."

"Come in then, Abdel Malik Rahman" the voice replied.

Abdel opened the cabin door and stepped over the 6-inch plinth, slipped and fell full length at the feet of the Purser.

"Well, that is some introduction young Abdel. Now be quick and get to your feet and let's see the make of you. I am not a God; you need not fall to your knees in worship. But I am reminded that many souls have commended me for my temperance and fortitude."

Abdel could not understand what he was saying, so he composed himself stood up straight and extended his hand to the Purser.

This was ignored and the Purser said, "Indeed, I like the cut of your jib and calling me sir will certainly help your cause. Have you got your papers Abdel?"

Abdel presented his testimonials and photograph to the Purser.

Taking the papers, he said, "I am Jack H Cawthorne, Purser of this fine vessel the *Domelia*. I have here your Pink Card, which you must keep safe at all times. It has your date of birth, your rating and your details pertaining to your height, hair and eye colour. I addition it has your own personal registration number. Now I must measure you for your height, stand against that chart behind you."

Abdel turned to see a measurement chart on the wall.

"Stand still with your head resting against the chart and do not move. I expect that you may well grow in the next few years, so I will measure you again in a years' time. Providing you have not fallen overboard or succumbed to some fatal attack while on shore."

"Your height young Abdel is 5' 7". Tell me your date of birth and I will complete your registration."

"It is October 15th 1918 sir."

The Purser looked closely at Abdel and said, "Your eyes are brown like ebony and your hair is as black as night." He then presented Abdel with his Card and added; "You have not told me how long you are signing up for young man."

"I want to be a seaman for ever sir."

"That is very commendable, but this life is not for everyone. You can sign up for 3 or 10 years. You can buy yourself out of course, but that is an expensive outlay for one so young. Which is it to be then?"

Abdel had his first important decision to make and after some thought said, "I will sign up for 3 years sir."

"Very good, please sign this document" and handed Abdel a pen.

"What do I do sir?"

"Just write your name in this place," and he pointed to the line marked signature.

"You can write your name?"

"Oh yes sir and I can read also."

"Well reading this won't make any sense to you. I am surprised you can read, there are not many wogs on this boat who can."

Syed's words of caution echoed in Abdel's head when talking of men who would look to denounce you.

This was something he would have to live with, but the Purser had been friendly and helpful. Jack Cawthorne then wrote down Abdel's name on the back of the photograph and stamped both the photograph and pink card saying, "You are now Deck Rating Abdel Malik Rahman of the *Domelia* and I wish you good health and fortune as a merchant seaman with British India Steam Navigation Company. Your pay will be £20 every month. Your food and bunk are free, but if you break ship rules you will be fined and it will be docked from your pay. You will also be supplied with the required garments and fatigues needed to complete your duties. Do you have any questions?"

Abdel did not have a question and replied; "No sir, I am happy to be here."

"Alright not so able seaman Rahman, report to Mr Bob Macintyre who is the Deck Officer. He will give you your duties and show you where your quarters are."

Armed with his papers and with a spring in his step, Abdel left the Purser's cabin in search of Mr Macintyre. The ship was now a hive of activity and the crew were employed in all manner of duties as Abdel navigated his way to Mr Macintyre's quarters. He then happened upon another seaman and asked where Mr Macintyre would be.

The man said, "He is on the foc'sle checking the cable holders."

This meant absolutely nothing to Abdel and the look on his face spoke volumes.

The man pointed to the bows of the ship and said, "That's him with the Officers Cap on, with the thick black beard and I am Bobby Khan, what is your name?"

"I am Abdel Malik Rahman. The new Deck Rating sir."

"You need not call me sir Abdel; I am a Deck Rating just like you."

Bobby was tall and slender and had thick black hair that sat under a cloth cap. He also had a good growth of facial hair, which suggested that he was a little older than Abdel.

"I will take you to meet Mr Mac, come with me."

They moved on and approached Mr Macintyre as he was inspecting the cable holders on the deck. Mr Macintyre turned to face the seamen and said, "Now then Bobby, these cable holders need more grease on them. Get your finger out your arse and look lively."

"Yes, Mr Mac sorry I will do it now."

Bobby quickly departed leaving Abdel standing, waiting for a chance to speak, as Mr Macintyre turned back to inspect another cable holder. Without turning around, he said, "So you are our new Deck Rating is that so?"

"Yes sir, I am Abdel Malik Rahman."

Having inspected the cable holder; he turned, faced Abdel and said, "Do you think this holder is well greased then Abdel?"

Abdel closely examined the holder, and then said, "I think it is sir."

"You would be right there Abdel Rackman," he replied.

"My name is Rahman sir," added Abdel.

"Oh yes, a good friend of mine has recommended you and I hope Jack is accurate in his opinion of you young man."

"Yes sir," replied Abdel.

"First of all, you do not need to call me sir, Mr Mac will do fine. Have you got all your papers and belongings?"

"Yes, Mr Mac."

"Then come with me and I will show you your quarters."

Abdel followed Mr Mac into the belly of the ship to a seaman's mess and indicated where he would be billeted. He was given bunk number six and was told to lay his knapsack on his bunk and accompany Mr Mac to the store where he would be furnished with his fatigues.

After this Mr Mac took Abdel to his cabin and gave him a talk on the work he would be employed in on board. Having covered all the rules and requirements he gave Abdel a pocket book produced for the British India Steam Navigation Company and said, "This is your sailors bible; I am informed that you can read; is that so?"

"Yes, I can read Mr Mac."

"Good, this will help you then. Not many of your brethren on this ship can read. They have learned by doing and instruction. Now, tell me about yourself; where you come from and why you chose to become a merchant seaman."

Abdel talked for some twenty minutes, Mr Mac listened and took a genuine interest in what Abdel was saying and when he had finished, he said, "I now have a little potted history of you Abdel, this helps me make judgements and informed decisions on you and how best to accommodate you on this ship. What I am saying to you is this; carry out your duties correctly and obey the rules of the ship. You can set aside time to follow your religion, but it must not interfere with the safe running of this vessel, do you understand?"

Having listened and understood most of what Mr Mac had said he replied; "Yes, I think I understand Mr Mac, so I can use my prayer mat and pray?"

"Yes, as long as you are not on watch" he added.

"Thank you, Mr Mac."

"Well, it's time to leave Karachi Abdel. I want you to team up with Bobby, who you have met, I think. I want you to stand with him at his station as we cast off the jetty and watch and learn."

"Yes, Mr Mac."

Abdel returned to the foc'sle and joined Bobby. A cry of "singled up" was sounded and then "let go, aft" followed by "all gone aft" and "all clear aft." Then the order to "let go the spring" with a response of "all gone," then "let go forward." Again, the response of "all gone forward" and as the ship slowly cleared the jetty a shout of "all clear forward" was given.

Then Mr Mack ordered "all hands at your stations," and the deck ratings apart from Abdel and Bobby, set about securing ropes, wires and all gear for sea. Within fifteen minutes, the ship had turned and left the harbour heading south east on a course for Bombay. On board were 32 passengers and a cargo of jute, timber and oil with a crew of 20.

The weather was good with a light prevailing wind and a cloudless sky. Abdel turned to Bobby and asked;

"Why are you called Bobby?"

"This is my name on board ship Abdel, when I first joined Mr Mac gave me this name because he used to shout *"Khan, where are you now"* and I would lift my head up and shout "here *Mr Mac."* He said it reminded him of a seal bobbing up and down in the sea, so he named me Bobby, my true name is Abdullah Mazar Khan."

Bobby went onto tell Abdel of his other shipmates, who were Deck Ratings; "As well as us, there is Spike Rafferty, Pablo Cortez the Spaniard, Jim Shearer and George Hollcroft. You have already met Spike I think; he was the big guy with the tattoo's and the big scar on his face. He is an

Irishman from Cork and he is a good man to have alongside you when you are on shore Abdel."

Before Abdel could react, a shout was heard and Mr Mac appeared alongside saying, "Bobby get your carcass in gear for a fire drill and take Abdel with you and run those fire hoses out."

"Yes Mr Mac, let's go Abdel," replied Bobby and they scurried off to locate the fire hoses.

The deck was awash with men carrying out drills and securing equipment for deployment. The drill took some twenty minutes to complete, under the watchful eye of the ships Master; Captain George Hepplewhite who observed the activity from the bridge. Mr Mac then ordered all ratings to muster on the foc'sle.

Mr Mac addressed those gathered and said,

"Alright gentlemen a few words from me and to tell you want I want from each and every one you. Firstly, we are bound for Bombay with a cargo of diesel oil, jute and timber. We also have 32 passengers on board."

"I want duties to be carried out without delay and you will arrive for your watch on time. Anyone late for their watch will lose a day's pay. Secondly, we have a new Deck Rating who has joined the ship today: step forward Abdel." Abdel stepped forward. "This is Abdel; he will be paired up with Bobby until he is ready to carry out duties. I don't want him sent for any stupid items from the store like; a bucket of steam or a long stand and unlike some of you buggers, he can read and speak English very well. Are there any questions?"

Big Spike spoke up and said, "Will we get shore leave in Bombay?"

"Yes, we will be in port for two days, with one day for shore leave; but avoid the brothels, they are rife with syphilis."

"Any more questions?"

No response was forthcoming and Mr Mac dismissed his charges and climbed up to the bridge.

Bobby took Abdel and familiarised him with the duties he would eventually need to master and where his watch would be.

As they moved around the deck, Abdel noticed a *Dhow* sailing west with two lateen sails fully deployed. This design afforded a great deal of manoeuvrability when sailing close to the wind.

These dhows had been using these waters for centuries transporting spices, jute, silk, rice, wheat and all manner of exotic fruits. The weather was warm with a moderate prevailing wind. After an hour of training, Bobby and Abdel found a quiet corner behind a lifeboat station and sat and chatted about all sorts of things.

Abdel was somewhat perplexed by Mr Mac's advice about Bombay and said, "What is this syphilis Bobby?"

"You have not been to a brothel yet Abdel?"

"No, I have not Bobby, is it a store of some kind?"

"Oh yes, but what you buy in this store is big trouble Abdel."

Bobby went on to inform Abdel of the potential dangers involved and the subsequent health issues associated with syphilis. Abdel realised that in Karachi they were the special 't*ea Houses*' off Bunder Road.

Once again Mr Mac's voice could be heard and both Abdel and Bobby leapt to their feet and returned to the fo'csle. On seeing them Mr Mac said, "Abdel, the Captain wants to see you now. Bobby take him to the Captains quarters and be quick about it."

Bobby took Abdel to see the Captain and left him outside the door saying, "The Captain always meet's his new sailors when they arrive, do not be afraid he is a good man."

George C Hepplewhite was a small but stocky fellow with a full head of hair that swept across his brow. He sported a *"full set"* and his appearance belied his fifty-two years, with no apparent grey visible. He had been the ship's master for five years. He had been in employment of the British East India Company for 18 years. He had served in the Royal Navy during the Great War and was a Petty Officer on board the Destroyer *the Shark* at the Battle of Jutland on May 31st 1916, when it was sunk in battle with the loss of 86 crew. He was one of only six survivors that day; having clung to a piece of decking, until he was rescued. Jutland was the largest naval battle of World War I, with a total causality list of 6.784 and the loss of 14 ships.

Abdel knocked on the door.

"Who is it?"

"It is Abdel Malik Rahman Captain."

Abdel stood as footsteps approached and the door was swung open.

"Ah, our new Deck Rating, come in young man and sit in that not too comfortable chair."

Abdel did as he was instructed and found that the chair was well secured to the floor.

Expectations can sometimes be misjudged and Abdel was a little surprised to see that the Captain was only slightly taller than himself. This was not lost on the Captain, who recognised Abdel's observation and said,

"Were you expecting a big six-footer with the bluster of a dockyard labourer?"

Abdel could not quite interpret what was said and responded with; "Yes, I mean I don't know Captain."

"Relax sailor, I am testing your nerve. I always see my new crew members as soon as I can. I like to know what makes them tick. "

"Like a clock Captain," replied Abdel.

The Captain laughed and said, "Yes like a clock, because this ship must be run just like a clock. With every minute used effectively. You have been recommended by another Officer I hear. However, this will count for nothing if you fail in your duties. I am also told that you can read and write English. You will be valuable to your shipmates in this regard, I am sure. Now, tell me about your life and why you have chosen the British East India Navigation Company to expand your career?"

Abdel understood most of what the Captain had said and then embarked on a monologue of his short life history. The Captain listened intently and on occasion had to ask for clarity with some elements of the soliloquy.

When Abdel had finished, the Captain said, "Well, you have had an eventful 18 years. You have seen violence and death. You have travelled many miles for one so young. You also have sound testimonials, which the Purser has shown me. But remember this sailor, you are part of the crew and this ship will only run smoothly if one and all perform their duties to the letter. So, work hard, stick to the rules and stay loyal to your shipmates. You have left your loved ones behind and now this ship is your home and all those on it are your family. You will get homesick, every sailor does. But you must overcome this, if you are to serve this vessel to the best of your ability. Do you understand Deck Rating Abdel Malik Rahman?"

Abdel felt that he understood most of what the Captain had said. "I will try hard to carry out my duties Captain and I hope that God will guide me at all times."

"Let us hope that God guides us both sailor."

Abdel had noticed that the Captain had a bookcase on one wall of his cabin full of books and asked; "Have you read all of these books Captain?"

"No not all, some are for reference, they are rules and regulations and others for navigation. I have read a number of them. If you spot one you would like to read, then just ask," he replied.

"I am reading *War of The Worlds* by H.G. Wells Captain"

"Now there is a fanciful tale, if ever there was one. Let us hope this fiction never turns into fact."

The Captain rose to his feet and gestured for Abdel to leave his cabin. Abdel got up and as he walked through the door he said, "Thank you Captain, God be with you."

Abdel made his way along the corridor to the sailor's mess for dinner.

The *Domelia* was doing 12 knots and making good headway as she sailed into in a calm light wind, with a reading of 1 on the Beaufort scale. Abdel was sitting with Bobby, Spike and Pablo enjoying his first meal of scrambled egg on toast. Spike took the opportunity to question the ship's new rating and turned to Abdel and said, "So, you are the new coolie on board, hard work is the Captain's watchword on this fucking tub my son."

Bobby spoke for Abdel and said, "He has already sailed on a merchantman; the City of Venice and he has had a talk from the Captain. So, he knows what he has signed up for Spike."

"You never know what you have signed up for Bobby, so let that be a reminder. Anyway, good luck to you son, just be wary of that bastard the Mate."

"Who is the Mate?" asked Abdel.

"He is the Chief Officer Mr Robert Sanderson, when on board he is known as the Mate," added Bobby.

"He will have you doing double watch's that one, if he don't like the look of you," added Spike.

As Spike took a drink of his tea, Abdel stood up and said, "I am not a coolie Spike; I am Pashto and I will work hard and I will expect thanks only from God and no one else." He then sat back down as his audience looked somewhat shocked at his short riposte.

"I like this young fellow, he has spirit. Welcome to the *Domelia* young Abdel, stand and shake my hand," said Spike.

Abdel rose and took Spike's giant shovel of a hand. Spikes grip was powerful yet reassuring and Abdel said, "I think you have a strong will Spike and I am sure God has guided you well."

"I don't know about that, but I don't suffer fools gladly shipmate."

Pablo joined in the conversation and added; "This man Spike, he has been good friend to me since I joined the ship at Lisbon."

At that moment Mr Mac arrived and told all present of their watch duties for the week. He informed Abdel that his first watch would be shared with Bobby, so he could be familiar with the duty. They would be on watch at 4am until 8am, and then Abdel would have the watch thereafter.

It was now 3pm on a warm humid September afternoon as the *Domelia* made its way to Bombay, some 450 nautical miles and 2 days away.

The Captain had informed his officers, that once docked and unloaded of cargo and passengers, some of the crew would be allowed shore leave; but not Abdel. He had much training to do under the tutorage of Mr Mac. In addition, Pablo, Jim Shearer, Engine Ratings Tom Gardener, Harry Billings and all the Officers, would remain on board.

Abdel was given an hour to set up his bunk and store his possessions in his locker. With some help from Pablo he completed the task and stored his pocket watch, clothes, books and Maheera's home address, which he used as a bookmark for War of The Worlds.

He was provided with a key to the locker, fastened to a cord that had to be worn around the neck at all times. At 5pm Abdel was given instruction on knot tying by Jim Shearer, who was considered to be the best at this craft.

During the months that followed the *Domelia* sailed around the coast of India and spent time in the ports of Bombay, Madras, Calcutta and Colombo and Jaffna in Ceylon. As the end of 1936 drew near, a worrying shift in world politics began. Two years had passed since Adolf Hitler had gained the position of Supreme Ruler (*Fuhrer*) of Germany and the Spanish Civil War had started earlier in the year. Hitler's purge on the Jews was gaining momentum and Germany was establishing a powerful military presence.

Abdel took the time to write letters to Maheera and posted the letters while they were docked in Madras, Calcutta and Ceylon. The work on board ship was tiring and he found that he spent less time reading and more time sleeping. He was gaining skills in knot tying, map reading and general maintenance.

He had a keen eye for watch duty and was able to identify sea changes and weather patterns. He enjoyed the spectacle of dolphins swimming across the bows of the ship and he was beginning to recognise the various types of fish often visible from his watch. After some 14 weeks at sea, the *Domelia* returned to Karachi to take on a cargo of rice, jute and machinery, bound for Rangoon in Burma. On his first day back in Karachi he spent time with Osman and regaled him with his tales on the high seas.

On his second day ashore, he went to see Maheera, only to be told by her father that she was not available. When he returned to Rahman's' he asked Syed if he had any news of Maheera.

Syed was expecting this to happen and said to Abdel, "Sit down Abdel, I have made some sweet tea and we will talk of Maheera."

Abdel was confused and pondered what Syed had to say.

Syed handed Abdel his cup of sweet tea and sat down.

"I have news of Maheera Abdel, but it is not happy news that I have to give you."

"Why, what has happened to her Syed?"

Syed took a sip of his tea and said, "Maheera has been chosen as a wife for another man Abdel."

Abdel took some time to register the news and looked at Syed; "This cannot be true Syed; I have written her letters saying how much I favoured her."

"Have you had her replies Abdel?"

This hit Abdel in the pit of his stomach and the realisation that he had not received any letters dawned on him. He started to think of excuses why she had not replied and said, "Perhaps she did not send them to the correct ship Syed."

Syed just looked at Abdel with soulful eyes and added; "God has willed this Abdel; she has been promised to another man by her father and she must agree or her family will be shamed. She is to be given in marriage to the son of a prosperous businessman called Mr Ahmed bin Abdullah. He owns a transport company in Karachi."

This information fell on deaf ears and Abdel made no response. He sat and felt lost. He had a feeling of abject loneliness and nothing Syed could say would make a difference. He spent the rest of the day wandering around the wharf in the hope she would appear, she never did.

In that short stay back at Rahman's, Abdel had noticed that Syed's health had deteriorated and he was spending more time at the Mosque. Before he returned to the *Domelia* he discussed Syed's health with Hakim.

Hakim also told Abdel of his plans to leave India and hand over the business solely to Abdullah. He would then seek his fortune in South Africa. He would open up a Rahman's Chandlers in Durban. He believed it was a country with more opportunities.

On returning to his ship Abdel was informed that they would be sailing to the Persian Gulf with a cargo of rice, barley, cotton and 16 passengers. The ship would be visiting Muscat and Sharjah and from there sailing to Bandar Abbas in Persia to pick up a cargo of oil and fruit bound for Port Sudan on the Red Sea.

As the *Domelia* sailed on to the Red Sea the Captain, the Chief Officer Robert Sanderson and both Deck Officers, Bob Macintyre and Norman Baker gathered for a meeting in the Captain's cabin. Topics discussed included the growing threat from Germany, the weather, cargo, destination and the crew.

The captain asked for a full breakdown of the crew and comments from those present.

Robert Sanderson began by having his reservations as to the competence of Spike Rafferty and said, "Rafferty is a liability skipper; he is workshy and nothing but trouble when he gets ashore. In my honest opinion he has the IQ of a cable holder. He is also a bad influence on the crew; he stirs up discontent too much for my liking. If it is trouble you want, he is the man you're looking for."

"Strong words Robert, do the rest of you share this opinion?" asked the captain.

Both Deck Officers Norman and Bob responded in unison with; "No skipper."

Their riposte angered the Chief Officer, who added; "Come on you both know he is crackers and it's only a matter of time before he ends up in clink. He is always seen with the crimps in port and how he hasn't caught syphilis amazes me."

"Well, a fool and his money soon go separate ways," added the captain.

"I agree he is a bit of an arse at times, but he never misses a watch and he is always on his mark with duties," added Bob.

"I will ask the Purser about his financial situation as regards the crimps, but I tend to agree that despite his shortcomings; he seems to get on with his work," replied the captain.

The captain moved the meeting on by asking about the crew, in particular the new deck rating Abdel Rahman and said, "Our new lascar seems an interesting young man, how is he doing Bob?"

"He has some promise skipper; he picks things up pretty quick. He seems good at spotting changes in weather patterns and he is a good man to have on watch."

"He can read and write you know," added the Captain.

"That will do him no good on this ship," said the Chief Officer.

"Alright Robert what the hell is up with you today? You have not got a good word for anyone."

"Knowledge is dangerous for the likes of him," replied the Chief Officer.

"I think he is a good man to have if we get into a spot," added Norman.

The captain went on to issue plans for docking, pilotage and unloading cargo in Muscat. He also suggested getting in touch with the Seaman's Mission and look to get Spike Rafferty involved with other more worthwhile activities like trips, film shows and organised dances, when he gets shore leave.

"Good luck with that skipper," said the Chief Officer.

"Have faith Robert, the good lord works in mysterious ways," added the captain. They then discussed the threat of war. The captain began by saying, "It looks increasingly likely that war is inevitable gentlemen. I have a communication from the company that preparations are already in place that will result in many merchant vessels being commissioned to assist the Royal Navy in supplying vital cargo in various ports in Europe, North Africa and the Middle East."

"We will be refitted then?" asked Norman.

"Yes, to what degree is unknown Norman, but it will mean some form of armament and perhaps some strengthening of the bulkheads," replied the captain.

"I would expect we will get a 3-inch Anti-Aircraft Gun mounted on the deck," added Bob.

"We shall see, but in the meantime, this is strictly hush hush. No word of this to the crew, I will inform the Officers," said the captain. After a brief discussion about the weather the meeting came to a conclusion with a prayer read by the captain. As the officers left the cabin the captain asked Bob to send for the Purser to join him in his cabin as soon as possible.

As the officers walked off along the middle deck Norman said, "He always says that."

"What?" asked Bob.

"The good lord works in mysterious ways," replied Norman.

"The good lord won't help that swine Rafferty," said a disgruntled Robert Sanderson.

"Robert shut your gob about Rafferty, it's getting monotonous," barked Bob.

The voyage to Muscat was accomplished with the help of good weather enhanced by coastal breezes that are common in this environment on the Tropic of Cancer. Abdel had now gained some respect from those around him, not least from Bob Macintyre.

Abdel was now gaining respect not just with the officers, but also the crew. He listened to what the crew would say and speak only when he had something, he thought was valuable to add. One such occasion occurred after dinner in the mess.

Spike was setting out plans for his excursion in Muscat, when he went ashore. He was asking other crew members if they would be joining him on this trip and said, "Well, who is up for some fun in Muscat then?"

The response was somewhat muted and Bobby said, "Not me Spike, I am saving my money for other things."

"Money is like spit in the rain; it just disappears young Bobby. No matter what you spend it on," replied Spike.

"That is a load of bollocks Spike; you would find trouble on the surface of the moon. None of us want to spend time in an Arab clink thank you," added Jim Shearer.

"I'm on duty anyway, I won't be going ashore," said George Hollcroft.

"Ah well, suit yourselves you miserable swine's. I will be on the loose and partaking of some company with the dusky maidens, that's for sure," quipped Spike.

"Watch you don't get 'snotty cock' then," joked Jim.

Abdel had a puzzled look on his face and it did not go unnoticed by George who said, "Abdel, I don't think you know what that means do you my son?"

"No, I do not George, what is snotty cock?"

Amid the laughter Pablo joined in by saying, "This is what you get when you go with unclean women Abdel."

A day before they docked in Muscat, the captain informed Spike that he would only be allowed shore leave on the condition he attended the Seaman's Mission when he left the ship. This was not greeted with any degree of satisfaction by Spike, but he reluctantly agreed. The prospect of disciplinary action which could mean suspension of all shore leave was too grave a consequence for Spike.

The ships course took a northerly sailing up to Bushehr in Persia, then a return sailing to Doha. From Doha, the *Domelia* sailed back through the Straits of Hormuz to Karachi, arriving on January 14th 1937.

When Abdel arrived back at Rahman's he sensed something was not right. The store was quiet and Abdullah and Hakim were not there. When Abdel went upstairs, he found Syed in bed sleeping. He looked very ill and he had lost a lot of weight. As he stood and looked at his mentor and he hoped he would wake and he could tell him of his latest adventure. After some twenty minutes both Abdullah and Hakim arrived with Doctor Salman.

The Doctor had arrived in Karachi in 1927 with the Red Cross and decided to stay. He created a "pay as you will" practice on the Bunder Road.

Abdel quietly asked Hakim why did Syed look so unwell. Hakim looked at the Doctor, who gestured to them to come out of the bedroom. He quietly closed the door and said, "I am afraid Syed has not long to go before he dies; his body is shutting down and I would say that it is only a matter of days now. His heart is very weak and he may not wake up at all."

Abdel was shocked and tears began to fall down his cheeks. Hakim and Abdullah both folded their arms around Abdel and Hakim said, "He will soon be in paradise; it is Gods wish. We must now tell all his friends they must come to prey and give thanks to God for his life."

"I will go to the mosque and tell the Imam that Syed will soon be following the path of the prophet."

As they stood in embrace, the Doctor went back into the bedroom and carefully listened to Syed's heart and checked his pulse. He then left the room to re-join Abdel, Hakim and Abdullah and said, "He is not in pain, but his breathing is very weak. You might want to say your farewells to him."

Then suddenly a noise came from the bedroom. They all rushed in and were amazed to see Syed awake and gesturing to them to come closer. The doctor joined them and stood at the end of the bed.

Syed's speech was barely audible and so Abdel leaned close to Syed.

"I am so glad to see you all. God will have my soul soon and I will join both of your fathers in heaven." Then he looked at Abdel and said, "The man who is silent and keeps his council before his God, will have the power over the unbelievers." He then asked if all would say a prayer with him for his journey into heaven.

The doctor said the Lord's Prayer as Syed, Abdel, Hakim and Abdullah said the following;

> *"In the name of Allah, the Most Kind, the Most Merciful.*
> *O Allah, change my fear in my grave to love. Oh, Allah have mercy on me in the name of The Great Qur'an and make it for me a guide and light and guidance and mercy.*
> *O Allah, make me remember what of it I have forgotten, make me know of it that which I have become ignorant of and make me recite it in the hours of the night and day and make it an argument for me. O Lord of all the worlds. Ameen."*

They all left Syed to sleep and the doctor said he would return in the morning. As they sat down to a meal of chicken saffron and rice, Hakim informed Abdullah and Abdel of his desire to go to South Africa and seek his fortune. Abdullah was not so sure of Hakim's plans and said, "You know of no one in South Africa Hakim, how will you start a business?"

"I have made contacts and I have many testimonials to my name Abdullah. Mr Roberts of the East India Company has provided very good references for me. Besides, many Indians have gone to South Africa and are doing very well."

"Where will you live"? Asked Abdel.

"I have an allowance that my father left me and property is cheap Abdel," replied Hakim.

Abdel turned his attention to Abdullah and said,

"How will you manage Rahman's Chandlers Abdullah?"

"Do not worry Abdel, I have Kaleb and Mr Ali's son Naeem who has agreed to work for me. Business is good and we now have the truck that Mr Singh has rented to me at a very low cost. I am to buy it soon, once I have enough funds saved."

Two days later Syed succumbed to his illness and passed away in his sleep. This was a major turning point in Abdel's life and now he felt alone and bound for a future filled with uncertainty. In three days', time he would return to his ship and he somehow felt that he would never return to Karachi.

With this thought in his mind, he had two things he must do before he rejoined his ship.

Within an hour he was standing outside Maheera's fathers printers' shop. He plucked up the courage to go in. Mr Sardar was working on a printing press in the back shop and he heard the ringing of the doorbell as Abdel entered.

"How may I help you sir," he asked.

It was evident that he did not recognise Abdel and Abdel said, "It is me Mr Sardar, Abdel Malik Rahman."

The realisation suddenly dawned on Mr Sardar and a look of panic began to show and he said, "Oh, you should not be here. My daughter is to be married soon; this is most uncomfortable Mr Rahman. My family is in preparation for this important day. You must leave before my daughter returns."

"I only wish to give her my best wishes Mr Sardar," replied Abdel.

"No no, this cannot happen, I must ask you to go please."

As if by God's Grace the door opened and in walked Maheera. At first, she did not realise who stood before her, but then she gasped and said,

"Abdel, why are you here?"

She felt so pleased to see him, but she knew that she could not show it and continued; "Have you heard that I am to be married soon?"

Abdel was so pleased to see her and replied; "Yes, I know this and I do not know what to say Maheera."

His heart was pumping and his thoughts were spiralling then suddenly she grabbed him by the hand and they both rushed out the door. Her father was now in a state of high anxiety and shouted; "Maheera where are you going, you shame me and your family, come back."

She turned and said, "It will be alright father. I will return soon."

They walked to the wharf and sat at the same bench they sat on the first time they met. Maheera thanked Abdel for the letters and said she will always keep them. She wanted to reply to them, but her father had forbidden it. This man she will marry will make the family prosper and she must agree to it or be banished from her family forever. Abdel felt that she had been very honest and he began to understand her reasoning. They talked about many things and Abdel talked about his future as a merchant seaman and the adventures that he would experience. She wished him good fortune and they parted in the knowledge they may never see each other again.

He now had one more important thing to do and within ten minutes he was walking through the door of Jacob Levy's jewellers' shop. The old Jew was sitting working on another watch when the doorbell swung into action. Having got to his feet he looked up to see Abdel.

His face beamed and he said, "God be praised Abdel, let me look at you." He hugged Abdel and beckoned him into the back of his shop and with a gleam in his eye he said, "Now tell me all about your life on the high seas."

They drank sweet tea and talked for over an hour. Abdel gave him his news, about the death of Syed, his crew mates, Maheera and Hakim's plans to go to South Africa. Abdel could not help thinking that the old man looked frail and tired and Jacob did divulge his day's working in the shop may be nearing the end. He had grown weary of the work and he was thinking of selling the business to a young Jew whose business was thriving in Quetta.

"I am 67 years old now Abdel and both my sons are abroad. Shimon is in Ceylon and Abraham is in Germany. They are both doing well, Shimon has a business as a tailor in Colombo and Abraham is in Berlin. I am worried for him there; he has a store dealing in electrical goods. He has sent letters saying the National Socialists are targeting the Jewish community. He said he may immigrate to the United States with his wife and children."

"Anyway, Abdel have you still got your watch?"

"Oh yes Jacob, I carry it with me all the time," and he pulled it from his pocket and gave it to Jacob.

The old man carefully examined the watch and said, "It could do with a clean I suspect, let me do that for you tonight."

"That would very kind of you, but I must report to my ship at the wharf in two days' time Jacob."

"Do not worry; I will have it ready for you tomorrow Abdel," he replied.

That night Abdel struggled to sleep. His thoughts were spiralling and he drifted from one thing to another. He thought of Maheera and how her life would change. He remembered Syed and all the things he would say, where is he now? He would know what to say, he always did. He eventually fell asleep and was woken by a crashing sound from downstairs. He rushed down the stairs to see Abdullah mopping the floor and cursing.

"Syed would not be happy with you Abdullah, using that foul language," said Abdel.

"God will forgive me Abdel; this was our soup for breakfast," replied Abdullah.

Abdel helped him clean up and they sat, drank tea and talked of the future. Abdel wanted to stay in the store and see all the regular customers. It was a kind of farewell to his past and he enjoyed meeting old faces and sharing his adventures with anyone who would listen. After lunch he went back to see Jacob and collect his watch. True to his word Jacob had the watch ready and it looked very new.

"Is it a new watch Jacob?" asked Abdel.

"No, it is not, but look at the cloth I used to clean it," he replied.

The soft cotton was filthy and Abdel was shocked.

"I knew it would need cleaning. Even a small piece like this attracts dust and chemicals from the air Abdel."

"I am sorry Jacob; I will take better care of it from now."

"Do not blame yourself, you cannot prevent it. However, you must get it cleaned regularly to keep it in pristine condition."

"What is this word pristine Jacob?"

"It means keep it as clean as you can Abdel."

"I promise I will Jacob, thank you my friend."

They talked of many things and Jacob seemed troubled by the news from Germany. He had been listening to his radio and he was very concerned for his son Abraham and his family.

"I will pray for them tonight and hope God guides them in this difficult time," he said.

"I will also pray for them Jacob" and went on; "When I was a young boy, my father told me of a story about Ibrahim, who was unsure of God and he knew of people who worshipped false idols and *shirk* is the worst sin in Islam. But Ibrahim was a strong Muslim and God gave him the strength to cast these false idols. God gave Ibrahim the wisdom to see that we should not copy those who have become non-believers. God is merciful Jacob."

"I agree Abdel and I only hope that those who would do harm on my faith, will seek a more peaceful resolution to their concerns. I fear for my brethren."

After their long talk, Abdel said goodbye and promised he would be back soon to spend more time talking of many things.

The next day Abdel walked up the gangplank of the *Domelia* and made his way to his billet where Pablo and Bobby were relaxing.

"Well, what news have you for us?" asked Bobby.

"My uncle Syed has died and Maheera has been promised to another man," said a soulful Abdel. "This is sad news about Syed, but he will be in paradise now Abdel," added Bobby.

"Have you spoken with Maheera; will she not favour you over this man?" asked Pablo.

"No, she must take him for her husband, it has been decided by both families," replied Abdel.

As they sat and waited for someone to break the silence, in walked Spike full of bluster and said, "Come on then what tales have you got for me; I have had the bastard mission chaplain dragging me around the bloody town on charity work. I haven't had a drink across my fucking lips in three days. It'll be the work of that bastard Sanderson the Chief Officer I'll wager; he hates my guts that one."

As they sat and listened to Spikes protestations, the captain and the chief officers were discussing their next voyage to Calcutta, in the captain's quarters.

"Now gentlemen, I have our new orders from the company and we are bound for Calcutta with a dry cargo of rice, barley and machinery. We also have eight passengers on board bound for Madras. On arrival, we will pick up another six passengers bound for our final destination."

"What's the latest news on our possible involvement in any conflict with Germany?" asked Stanley Hope the Engineering Officer.

"Well Stan, I am still in the dark on that one. As soon as I know, you will know."

"I have it on good authority that some merchantmen could be fitted with catapults on the foredeck to take spitfires skipper. They used this in the first world war," said Stan.

"We are not long enough for that," added Norman.

"That's a fact, we are only 460feet long," added Stan.

"It is all conjecture anyway; I will keep you informed gentlemen. Remember; say nothing of this to the crew. We don't want anyone jumping ship on this trip. Anyway, I am sure the politicians will sort it all out. Nobody wants another war," said the captain.

After discussing the cargo, passengers, pilotage, watch duty and engineering the meeting came to a close.

Back below deck, Spike was still bemoaning his treatment from the Chief Officer Sanderson and continued his tirade.

"I am going to get of this barge the first chance I get. A mate of mine is on a ship of the Bank Line, the pay is better and they are moving oil and petrol from Philadelphia to Mexico, Brazil and South Africa."

Abdel listened to the conversation and his mind began to wander at the thought of these distant places. He knew that Hakim would be soon in South Africa and the opportunity to see him would be wonderful. Bobby had noticed that Abdel was somewhere else and he suspected that he was imagining all kinds of possibilities and said, "Well we are happy here on the *Domelia*, are we not Abdel?"

Abdel heard his name and gathered his thoughts and replied; "What did you say Bobby?"

"I said, we are both very happy here on board the *Domelia* Abdel."

"Oh yes very happy Bobby," he replied.

The *Domelia* sailed onto Madras then Calcutta returning to Karachi in March 1937. After docking at the Wharfe Abdel made his way to Rahman's Chandlers and learned that Hakim had left Karachi a week earlier on a tramp steamer. Abdullah gave him a letter that Hakim had written before sailing. Abdel opened the envelope and read.

"My brother, I am sorry I could not say goodbye. I am on my way to Durban in South Africa. I have bought a property near the port and I will open it up as another Rahman's Chandlers. I hope you can come to Durban soon. I hope God will guide you and I pray that we will be together very soon, may peace be upon you Abdel."

Hakim included his address in Durban as;12 West Street, Port Natal, Durban, South Africa.

Reading the letter gave Abdel a sense of loss. Not just Hakim's absence, but he now knew that he may not consider Karachi his home anymore and though this made him sad, he was convinced his life had changed and his future lay elsewhere.

With that in his mind, he went to see Jacob Levy. When he arrived, the shop was closed. On the inside of the front door was a sign saying, "Many apologies, but I will not be open again until Monday."

Abdel wondered what would cause such an event, Jacob never closed his shop even over the sabbath. As he stood pondering what to do, a man approached and said, "Do you want the Jew, Jacob Levi?"

"Yes, is he unwell?"

"Not him, but his wife died yesterday and she is being buried today."

Abdel felt a sense of guilt; he had never met Jacob's wife Rebecca. She was always upstairs and Jacob never spoke of her in any great detail. He returned to Rahman's and sat in his old room he shared with Sayed and Hakim.

He pulled out his pocket watch and his latest book Pilgrims Progress. He was finding this story somewhat confusing and found the narrative difficult to understand at times. When on board he considered asking the captain to explain some of the content, but felt he would not have the time or inclination to advise him.

He then heard voices in the shop downstairs and he immediately recognised the voice of Osman. He put down his book and raced downstairs.

"Osman where have you been, it has been so long since I saw you my fisherman friend."

Osman laughed and embraced his good friend and said, "You are a sailor of the seas now Abdel, but it is wonderful to see you."

"Have you seen any sharks lately of Clifton Beach?" Abdel asked.

"Oh no, I have not done much fishing Abdel. I am thinking of joining the Indian Army. They had a recruitment day last week on Elphinstone Street and I signed up. I have to have a medical next week and if that is fine, I sign up for 5 years."

"There is talk of a war soon and if you sign up, you will fight for the British, Osman," said Abdullah.

"Who will be at war then?" asked Abdel.

"Germany of course, have you not been listening to the BBC Abdel?" added Osman.

"Oh yes, Jacob Levi was telling me about his son in Berlin. He is being threatened by the national socialists," said Abdel.

"India is part of the commonwealth, so we will be at war with Germany Abdel," said Abdullah.

"I have heard of this commonwealth and I have heard many people say we should be independent and have home rule. Mahatma Gandhi has campaigned for independence for some time now," added Osman.

"Will you be able to kill a man Osman?" asked Abdel.

"I must, or be killed myself Abdel."

They discussed the prospect of war and when if ever it would begin and end. There talk lasted for a good hour before a familiar face entered the shop. It was Spike, he was drunk and staggered into the shop, knocking over a set of pots and pans.

Abdullah was not pleased and before he could speak Abdel grabbed a chair and said to Spike; "Spike, this is our family business, you should not be drunk in here. Please sit down."

Spike was somewhat surprised to see Abdel and said as he slumped into the chair.

"So, this is your tea house then young Abdel, how about a drink for your old shipmate?"

"This is not a tea house; it is a chandlers and you are not welcome in here," said Abdullah.

Abdel waved his hand at Abdullah and said, "Osman will you get a drink of water for him please."

"It's not water I want, its whisky I need," grunted Spike.

"You will be in trouble again with Mr Sanderson," said Abdel.

"To hell with him, he will be going overboard if I have my way," replied Spike.

Osman returned with a glass of water, but Spike was having none of it and rose to his feet and stumbled out of Rahman's into the street.

Thankfully, Jim Shearer and George Hollcroft were just passing and persuaded Spike to join them on route back to the Wharfe.

"This man should not be a friend of yours Abdel," said Abdullah.

"He is a shipmate Abdullah; I work with him; but I do not call him a friend," replied Abdel.

"Are all your shipmates like this?" asked Osman.

"No, this man has a good heart, but he is prone to take alcohol and seeks the company of lustful women," replied Abdel.

"God will punish him for this affliction," added Abdullah.

"He will no doubt have to answer to God one day," said Osman.

They returned to the shop and picked up the pots and pans that had crashed to the floor and Osman said, "Before we pray at the mosque, we should eat."

So, they closed the shop and enjoyed a hearty meal of spiced chicken and rice.

The next day Abdel made his way to Jacob's shop and to his surprise it was open for business. He walked in to see Jacob cleaning yet another watch.

"Well, I am I glad that God has returned you safe and well Abdel Malik Rahman."

Abdel was unsure how to react to Jacobs pleasant demeanour and was a little speechless.

"I know you have heard of my sad loss of my dear wife Rebecca Abdel. Do not be saddened, she lived a good life and God chose the moment when she had to go and the hard part of this was having to telephone my sons with news of her death. I will miss her Abdel and it may be, that the time to join her will not be that long."

"How did she die Jacob?"

"I found her asleep in her chair upstairs, but the Lord had taken her. The Doctor who examined her said she most likely died from heart failure."

They talked for some two hours about everything from sea travel to the threat of war and both agreed that the future was filled with uncertainty. Jacob was deeply concerned for his son in Berlin.

Reprisals had increased and his son was hoping to get to America, if he can afford a passage aboard a ship for him and his family. He wanted to send his son money, but the German postal authorities were intercepting mail to Jews.

Abdel promised to look in on Jacob every time he returned to Karachi and they both said prayers for their friends and families. Abdel left the old Jew and hoped he would somehow have faith in God and his life would be a happier one.

After two more days ashore, it was time for Abdel to return to his home the *Domelia*, ready for her next voyage. The captain asked all the officers to muster in his quarters at noon to divulge their next passage, prior to their sailing at 5pm.

All were present and the captain thanked all present for their punctuality and asked for any reports relating to the crew while ashore.

Chief Officer Sanderson was the first to respond and said, "Well, as usual Spike Rafferty got himself drunk again and had to be helped aboard by Shearer and Hollcroft, no doubt suffering from whisky remorse."

"Has he created any trouble ashore?" asked the captain.

"Not that I am aware of," added Bob Macintyre the Deck Officer.

"Good, any other issues then," he replied.

"It appears not," said the Purser Mr Cawthorne.

"Alright let's get down to business. I have the details of our next trip. The company want us to sail to Cyprus, with a cargo dry goods including; rice, barley, mango's, cotton, steel and timber. We will also have 20 passengers bound for Jedda and another 6 passengers bound for Alexandria. We will hopefully dock at Jedda on April 5th and all being well Alexandria on the 7th. Our final destination will be Famagusta, Cyprus around April 10th. Our return trip takes us back through the Suez Canal docking at Aden and Mogadishu in East Africa. We will be carrying fruit, wheat, salt, olive oil and maize. We have no passengers on the return journey. Any questions?"

"The Suez Canal can be a pain in the arse skipper, depending upon the number of ships are sailing at any given time," said Norman Baker.

"Yes, that is the card we are dealt sometimes Norman."

"How are things in your engine room Mr Graham?" asked the captain.

"Fine skipper, but Harry Billings has gout again. He is suffering at the minute," replied Phil Graham.

"Is he off the beer then Phil?"

"Oh yes, he has had enough this trip and we might have to sign him off and send him home skipper. His right foot is the size of a diver's boot."

"Right I will ask the company to get him a ship from Cyprus back to blighty. We will get a new engine rating in Famagusta."

"Any more news on Germany skipper, it seems this Adolf Hitler is bent on confrontation. Reports indicate that they have embarked on a substantial naval and military manufacturing programme," said Stanley Hope.

"Yes, it does not look good and we only hope that Mr Chamberlin can use his negotiating skills and calm the waters, so to speak. I will keep you in the picture gentleman and when I have any further information you will know about it. However, I must stress that these discussions should not be repeated in front of the crew. I am I clear on this?"

All present nodded in agreement.

Chief Steward Mike Harris asked; "Can we acquire some new bedding for the passengers for our next trip after this one skipper. It is looking a little tired now."

"I am sure the company can afford this, am I right Mr Cawthorne?"

"Yes, I will organise this when we get to Famagusta skipper," replied the Purser.

"Excellent, now anything else men?"

Those in attendance remained silent and the captain then said a prayer.

"We pray for good weather and safe passage to our destination and for our loved ones back home, Amen."

CHAPTER SEVEN

The voyage from Karachi to the Gulf of Aden was achieved without any notable problems. The Red Sea on the other hand posed many issues in relation to safe navigation. The central channel is littered with coral reefs and shelves and is shallow for nearly half the distance.

Yet for centuries many have sailed in and out of the Red Sea. The ancient Egyptians, Alexander the Great, Zheng He, Ibn Majid and Joao de Castro have used it as a gateway to both the Mediterranean and Indian Ocean.

Consequently, the captain spent a great deal of time on the bridge to ensure navigation was performed without incident. Winds constantly blow from the north-west and steerage must be meticulous in order to maintain a safe passage.

The *Domelia* docked at Jedda on April 5th as planned, but the ship was delayed for 24 hours due to problems with the diesel-generators. All engineering officers and ratings (except Harry Billings) had to work round the clock to get the ship ready to sail. Shore leave was not granted and the rest of the crew were given extra duties.

A quick turnaround in Alexandria made up for some lost time and the *Domelia* docked in Cyprus at 5pm on April 10th. Shore leave was granted for some crew members including Abdel, Bobby, Pablo, Jim Shearer and Officers Norman Baker and Robert Sanderson.

Norman Baker had a particular interest in ancient history and had planned to visit the site of the tomb of St Barnabus. Abdel and Bobby decided to join him on this trip, much to the surprise of Norman; having told them it was a Christian shrine. Norman managed to procure a taxi for the short trip to the monastery and shrine. On the short trip from Famagusta Norman gave Abdel and Bobby a short history lesson on St Barnabas; stating that he was in fact a Jew who had been converted to Christianity by the apostle Paul and later he was made the Patron Saint of Cyprus.

Bobby seemed confused and asked Norman; "How can it be that he gave up Judaism and then worshipped Christianity? They believe in the same God, as I believe in God."

"Yes, but remember that Judaism is based on the Torah and the Old Testament, whereas Christianity is based on the New Testament and the Gospels. And yet both Moses and Jesus are named in the noble Qur'an are they not Bobby?" added Norman.

"Yes, the noble Qur'an names Isa (Jesus), Musa (Moses) and Ibrahim (Abraham) but Allah has said they have taken the wrong road and they will be judged on the Day of Resurrection," replied Bobby.

"That may be the case Bobby, but the most important thing is that you follow your path to God and believe."

Abdel sat and listened; he was amazed how Bobby could speak with so much passion.

They arrived at the Monastery and visited the tomb, which was very small and it had a number of icons fixed to the wall. Abdel felt it had a serene and illuminating presence and it reminded him of what his father had said to him when he was a boy;

> *"If it is only once in your life Abdel, you must go the Holy City of Mecca and worship at the Hajj."*

He knew this would be something he must do. When he has the opportunity, he will pilgrimage to Mecca and worship at the Kaaba. He might even kiss the Black Stone, as did the Prophet Mohammed.

Having returned to his ship, Abdel went about his duties and before bedding down for the night, he wrote a letter to Hakim.; wishing him good fortune in South Africa and promised to visit him as soon as he can.

Harry Billings was put on a ship back to Liverpool and a new engine rating an Italian, called Vincenzo joined the ship.

The *Domelia* set sail for Aden, back through the Red Sea and from there onward to Mogadishu in East Africa. In 1936, this part of East Africa was under the control the Italian Empire or as Mussolini called it the "*Africa Orientale Italiana.*" This included Abyssinia, Eritrea and Somaliland. Fascism had spread and Mussolini could see the geographical advantages of occupying these strategic colonies.

The Captain had informed the crew that shore leave would not be granted, due to the volatile climate of the area. The ship arrived back at Clifton Wharfe, Karachi on April 16th. After a week back in Karachi, Abdel returned to the *Domelia* for duties.

The Captain summoned all his officers to his quarters at 2pm that same day and informed them of the next trip. He began with the itinerary relating to the ports of call and said, "The voyage will take in Muscat, Palestine, Malta and Italy. The cargo to Muscat is timber, rice and cotton. From there the ship will sail onto Haifa with a cargo of oil, dates and spices. Then onto Malta and the port of Valetta, followed by the final leg of the voyage to Naples, any questions so far?"

Robert Sanderson made the first comment when he said, "Well, Valletta may be a problem if Spike gets shore leave, he will make a point of getting to the Gut and Strait Street."

"There will be no shore leave in Valetta gentlemen, Naples yes, but not Valletta."

"What are we hauling back to Karachi skipper?" asked Bob Macintyre.

"That, I am unsure of at the moment Bob. The company will let me know when we get to Muscat," replied the Captain.

"How are things in engineering Phil and how is the new engine rating settling in?"

"All's well skipper, we have used the electric oil pump to push through the cold lubricating oil through the engine bearings to warm and de-aerate the oil. This has done the trick, so we are fully operational. The new man Vincenzo is fine, he speaks decent English, which is always a blessing," said the Chief Engineer.

"Splendid, now how are the deck ratings Bob?"

"They are starting to work as a team now skipper, Abdel, Pablo, Bobby, Jim, George and even Spike," replied Bob.

"Good, do you think we need another rating Bob?"

"At the moment, I would say no skipper."

"Right then, has anybody else got anything to add?"

"Yes, that Kedgeree was bloody lovely this morning Tom," added Norman.

"Glad you enjoyed Norman, but don't tell the crew for Christ's sake," replied the Chief Cook.

Laughter reverberated round the captain's quarters and the Steward; Mike Harris intervened."

"Oh yes, that is a perk of the job for us Officers, is that not correct skipper?"

"Only if it is deserved, Mike," said the captain and continued; "Right, now about the ongoing threat of war. If our German friend Adolf Hitler maintains his current approach, it is highly likely war will be inevitable. If that transpires, the company will be required to concentrate on supplies that are fundamental to the war effort. In turn all UK registered merchantmen currently moving cargo will be commissioned to supply vital cargo to UK and overseas destinations. Some vessels may undergo modifications to allow weapons and ordinance to be shipped. It may well be that certain ships will also be fitted with guns fore and aft, probably 20mm Oerlikons or Lewis Guns.

"If we are required to act as a support vessel and we are fitted with armaments, then the crew will be signed on as naval personnel under special articles. As a requirement some of the crew will undergo training in the deployment of any weapons,"

The officers assembled remained silent and there was a pensive ethos within the captain's quarters. Then, the Purser Jack Cawthorne said, "There may be some reluctance with some crew members for this change in their articles skipper."

"Yes, I am aware of that Jack, but we will cross that bridge when the time comes," replied the captain.

Oblivious to all this talk of war, Abdel was below decks with Bobby, Pablo, Jim and George enjoying a plate of Welsh Rarebit. Jim and George were playing dominoes and Jim said, "Hey Abdel, do you know what Welsh Rarebit is also called?"

Abdel looked at Jim somewhat confused and answered; "No, I do not know what it is called Jim, but I know it is cheese on bread."

"Yes, that it is lad, but it is also known as a Cardiff Virgin."

George laughed and added; "They are a rarity indeed Jim."

Abdel, Pablo and Bobby were a little perplexed until it was explained and Pablo said, "Cardiff, I have been there on a tramp steamer. We loaded up with coal and sailed to Gibraltar. It was a dirty ship that one."

The *Domelia* completed her voyage, returning to Karachi on May 25th with a cargo of steel and machinery. Spike managed to secure another job as a deck rating on board a ship bound for the Caribbean and he was replaced by an Indian called Ranjit Singh who was only 16 years of age.

Further trips to Cyprus, Malta, Egypt and Palestine were accomplished up to end of 1938. In January 1939, Jacob Levi suffered a stroke and sadly died on February 12th.

The stroke resulted in Jacob's inability to talk and he was severely weakened, he contracted pneumonia and passed away in his sleep. Abdel was able to attend his funeral, as the *Domelia* was being fumigated while berthed at the Wharfe.

War looked increasingly likely and despite Neville Chamberlain's *"peace in our time"* announcement in September of 1938, the threat of conflict with Germany was looking inevitable. Hitler had acquired Saarland in 1935 and added the Rhineland and the Sudetenland before the end of 1938.

After undergoing her fumigation, the *Domelia* was given a new coat of paint and the accommodation was refurbished, with the stewards wishes for new bedding finally approved.

The next sailing involved skirting round India from Karachi to Bombay, Madras, Calcutta and Chittagong, carrying cargo including oil, fruit, timber, coal, rice, maize and barley. In March 1939 the *Domelia* was requisitioned by the British government for transporting cargo from the USA across the Atlantic from Halifax to ports in the UK and its dominions in Europe. As a consequence, she would require modifications to strengthen its bulkheads and to be fitted with Anti-Aircraft weapons.

On March 21st the Captain summoned the crew on deck and informed them of the changes to the *Domelia* and where she would be heading. He addressed all the crew in the presence of Mr J. F. Holmes of The British East India Company.

"Good morning men, thank you for your prompt arrival. As you are well aware, it is very likely that Great Britain will be at war with Germany in the near future. I would hope that even at this late stage, war can be averted. However, we must be prepared for conflict and to this end the company has relinquished possession of the *Domelia* temporarily to the British government. This means that seaman employed by the British East India Company will automatically transfer their employment through articles of war. You do have the right to transfer to another ship if you so desire. However, details of routes, cargo and destinations are not available for security reasons.

"If you chose to leave the service, then it would not be beyond the realms of possibility that you may be called up by the armed forces anyway. If you stay with the *Domelia*, you will assume your current role within the crew and carry out your usual duties.

"Due to the requirements of the war office, the *Domelia* will require some modifications below decks and that will be carried out in Gibraltar. We sail in two days' time. If you have any questions can you please refer them to your Engineering or Deck Officers.

"May I thank you for your hard work and patience and I hope to see you all in two days' time. If not, then I wish you well for the future. If you would like to speak to Mr Holmes, then he is available at the port office tomorrow morning at 10 am. Thank you and God Save The King."

The captain then asked all officers to accompany him to his quarters. When all were seated, he revealed more information relating to operational procedures and the re-fitting that would be carried out in Gibraltar.

"Well gentlemen, this is a fine mess we are in. Like the rest of the crew you can choose to seek another commission if you want. But I would be very honoured if you would all stay with me on this new diversion into dangerous waters. If any of you would like to leave the *Domelia*, then you must do so now."

No one moved and Bob Macintyre said, "We are all in this skipper, to hell with it, you have to die of something."

Without prompting every officer slammed their hand on the table and said, "To hell with it."

The captain was visibly moved and a nod of appreciation was enough to generate a positive atmosphere in the room.

"To business then gentlemen, we are bound for Gib in two days' time. We will not be taking cargo and speed is of the essence. Firstly however, we must find out what sort of crew we will have in two days' time. We can sail with a skeleton crew, but I would rather not. So, Bob and Phil you must determine who is staying with the ship as soon as possible."

"Will do skipper," they both replied.

"The details of the re-fit have been transcribed from the admiralty and they are; The bulkheads are to be replaced with heavier steel plating. We will be fitted with stronger decks fore and aft. We will be fitted with two Oerlikon 20 mm Anti-Aircraft Guns, again fore and aft. On completion of the re-fit we are to sail to Liverpool and collect our orders, firefighting equipment and ammunition. Our initial destination will be Halifax, Nova Scotia and we must be there by June 25th, I know you will all have many questions. But, can they wait until we have sailed. The important thing is to establish a crew and lift morale gentlemen. I do not need to remind you that the crew need only to know that we sail in two days' time. So, please be vigilant and do not discuss any of these issues with anyone other than yourselves. Can I finally end with a prayer for us, our families and the country" and continued; "Dear God, grant us the strength to overcome the troubles we are about to face. Look to protect our families and our nation from those who wish to do us harm. Lord do not forsake us in this difficult time, Amen."

Abdel had decided to stay with the ship, along with Pablo, Bobby, Ranjit, Jim and George. Every other seaman chose to stay with the ship after meeting with respective officers. Mr Holmes of the British East India Company also informed all crew members that they would see an increase in their wages during the hostilities. The exact amount would be divulged once the ship had sailed.

Abdel wasted no time in going to Rahman's and telling Abdullah. He also sent letters to Hakim and Osman who was undergoing training with the Indian Army in Bangalore. He wanted to send a letter to Maheera, but thought better of it, as it may cause trouble for her. Before he returned to the *Domelia*, he went to the cemetery to visit the graves of Syed and Ahmad. He also visited the graves of Jacob and Rebecca Levi. On the day of departure, he went to the mosque and prayed for his life and hoped; *Allah, the Most Gracious, the Most Merciful* would guide him through all that he encounterd.

On March 23rd the *Domelia* slipped away as the sun rose, into a calm sea. The ship sailed to Bandar Abbas in Persia to pick up supplies of fresh water, then through the Suez Canal to Malta and finally onto Gibraltar, arriving on

April 2nd.

While in Gibraltar the captain asked his officers for any seaman that they could recommend to train to use the Oerlikon 20mm Guns. He needed four men to volunteer, failing that the navy would select their own gunners.

Bob asked his deck ratings and to his surprise both Jim Shearer and Pablo Cortez put their names forward. Phil asked his engineering ratings and his volunteers were Tom Gardner and Ralph Paterson.

They went through a rigorous training routine aboard the Destroyer HMS *Hamlet* for three weeks before re-joining the crew who were staying at a hotel during the re-fitting of the *Domelia*. Two more seamen were added to the crew, both lascars Abdul Rahani and Mohammed Sulieman.

During all this activity Abdel sought to keep himself fit and he would go out running and play cricket or football with the crew. Other than sports he would read. He eventually finished *Pilgrims Progress* along with *Treasure Island* and *The Time Machine*.

He also acquired skills in playing dominoes with George Hollcroft and the Chief Cook Tom Seymour.

On May 11th 1939 the *Domelia* was completed, furnished with enhanced bulkheads, decks and fitted with two Oerlikon 20mm Guns, fore and aft. Two days later she set sail for Liverpool. Abdel confided in George on a number of occasions, during their games of dominoes, about his hopes and fears for what lies ahead.

On one occasion" Abdel said, "I have never been in a war, yet I have seen violence and death. How will I know death is near George?"

George looked at him and said, "Abdel, you will know, but I guess your mind will tell you to survive no matter what. What we are going to see, no man can describe, but you will remember it till the day you die Abdel."

Before docking in Liverpool, the captain summoned the officers in his quarters for another briefing, it was 4pm on May 13th and the ship was anchored of Liverpool awaiting the Pilot to guide them into the Mersey.

"Welcome men, a few updates to discuss with you and a general resume of how we are performing. We will have the Pilot on board in about two hours and once we are alongside, I will give the crew 24 hours shore leave, they have deserved it.

"Firstly, I have the training report from Gibraltar regarding the gunnery practice on HMS *Hamlet*. The report has been produced by Lieutenant T.G. Whitchurch of the Royal Navy and it reads: Following an intensive training programme in the operational use of the 20mm Oerlikon Gun aboard HMS *Hamlet*, I have observed the following able seamen and I have produced this report.

"*Jim Shearer*: He has shown aptitude and all the required dexterity both in preparation and implementation of all safety standards in regard to the effective deployment of the 20mm Oerlikon Gun. His level of accuracy in stationary targeting was 89% and in moving targets his accuracy was 74%. He took some time to adapt to his positioning prior to firing, but he improved as the training progressed. I therefore conclude that he should be considered for deployment as an Oerlikon Gunner on board any Merchant Navy vessel for the duration of any hostilities.

"*Pablo Cortez*: Despite his limited grasp of the English language, Cortez has shown an exemplary approach to the training. He has performed exceedingly well on all aspects of the training. His levels of accuracy have been first class and his results in target accuracy are very high. For stationary targeting he gained 94% and for moving targeting he attained 91%. I therefore recommend Cortez for deployment as an Oerlikon Gunner on board any Merchant Nay Vessel for the duration of any hostilities.

"*Thomas Gardener*: Gardener found the training difficult and had problems with the operational aspect of the Gun. His sighting of targets was erratic and at times over zealous with his firing. As the training continued, he did make improvements. However, based on his levels of accuracy, I would limit his deployment. It would be appropriate if given the opportunity, he was able to get more practice, prior to any hostilities. His accuracy was 76% for stationary and 68% for moving targets.

"*Ralph Paterson*: Engine rating Paterson carried the procedures with confidence. Initially he found the target setting troublesome with regard to speed and distance, but as the training progressed, he gained in confidence. His scores for firing were satisfactory; gaining 88% for stationary and 84% for moving targets. Again, I would recommend him for gunner on the Oerlikon."

"Any comments gentlemen?" asked the captain.

"Are we likely to get able seaman from the Royal Navy as support skipper?" said Norman.

"Yes, it is likely we will be allocated two Navy able seamen, one will be a signalman," replied the captain.

"When skipper? We are under way shortly," asked Phil.

"We pick them up at Portsmouth Phil," replied the captain.

"Ah Pompey, do we have some final shore leave then skipper?" said Stan.

"No chance, we are on a timeline now Stan, here are our orders. We sail to Portsmouth and pick up our RN seaman and further supplies. So, make the most of Liverpool gentlemen, it may be some time before you get any shore leave. We get to Halifax and load up cargo to return to Liverpool. I will know what the cargo is when we get to Halifax. It could be food, military vehicles, oil, ammunition or a combination of these. We are classed as a Mac-ship and we will act as an escort merchantman within a convoy of ships, some of which will be warships including destroyers, corvettes and minesweepers. The rest will be merchant ships carrying all manner of cargo."

"These two navy boys, they will have two masters then skipper, is that correct," said Robert.

"Yes, technically they will, but they answer to me while on board this ship Robert. I am informed that they will be billeted in the passenger's quarters and they are to get a bottle of beer every day. In addition, they will get an extra shilling a week Jack."

"I hope her majesty's navy are going to provide the money for this," grumbled Jack."

"Yes, I am told this will be allocated, along with the beer," replied the captain.

"The crew will not be too happy about this skipper," added Bob.

"Dead right Bob, so I will make sure all the crew get a bottle of beer every day. As for the extra shilling, that information should not be relayed to the crew gentlemen. However, Cortez, Shearer, Paterson and Gardener will also receive an extra shilling a week as gunners."

"Any other issues gentlemen?"

The officers declined any comment and the captain closed proceedings with; "Before we set off, I want to address the whole crew on deck gentlemen, officers will man stations to cover for ratings, is that clear gentlemen?"

A nod approval all round and the meeting came to a close.

Walking back to the bridge Bob said to Norman; "No prayers this time Norman?"

"No, I reckon he knows more than he is letting on Bob," replied Norman.

The *Domelia* docked at Liverpool on May 16th and due to errors in communication, the supplies were not ready and a further six days were lost. Before leaving the dock, the captain gathered the crew on deck and informed them of their commission and details of the voyage, the beer allocation and the new crew members. The ship eventually left Liverpool on May 23rd bound for Halifax, Nova Scotia. The weather was good and being midsummer the voyage should be favourable. The estimated arrival in Halifax was some 10 days away on June 2nd. On board were the two Royal Navy seaman seconded to the *Domelia*. Able Seaman John Westlake from

Barrow and Sid Bainbridge from Inverness. Sid would support the gunners in deployment of the Oerlikon Gun and John was employed as the signalman/A.L.O. (Air Look-Out).

Abdel was only four months away from his 21st birthday and he was now a valued crew member aboard the *Domelia*. He took a keen interest in John Westlake and his skills in signalling using Morse Code and Semaphore. He quickly adapted to the use of flags and the Aldiss Lamp.

After a day at sea the new gunners were given more practice on the Oerlikon Gun without live ammunition. Pablo continued to show his prowess in this activity and Tommy Gardener slowly began to improve his levels of accuracy.

Abdel penned another letter to his brother in Durban and began reading Dickens Great Expectations, which he bought in Liverpool. He was also becoming a domino player of some excellence, much to the annoyance of his shipmates. He had accumulated a nice little financial nest egg collecting money from all comrades. Abdel never forgot to read the Qur'an every day and pray, which he did along with Bobby, Abdul and Mohammed.

The *Domelia* arrived in Halifax on June 3rd and took on cargo of fruit, flour, vegetable oil, salt, nuts, bananas, corned beef and cotton. The ship sailed out of Halifax on June 12th and arrived in Liverpool on June 22nd.

Germany had now signed the *"Pact of Steel"* with Mussolini and Hitler now had his sights on Poland, having already claimed Czechoslovakia. Appeasement was the byword across Europe and diplomatic measures were explored to try avert war. This provided Hitler with the impetus to escalate, seeing that the allies were weak and unready for any conflict.

Having docked in Liverpool, the *Domelia* took on a cargo of agricultural machinery bound for Egypt. She left Liverpool on July 1st 1939 for the destination of Port Said. The return journey to Liverpool was completed on July 10th. Further voyages to and from Egypt continued throughout August. On the last trip to Port Said, Abdel thought he may be able to do a pilgrimage to Mecca for the Hajj. He raised the issue with Bob Macintyre, who then approached the captain.

Flights to Mecca from Egypt had just started and Abdel hoped he could take in the pilgrimage to the Holy City for the Hajj on September 1st.

The captain discussed the logistics with Bob Macintyre and it could be granted on religious grounds dependent upon sailing times. The ship was due in Port Said on August 28th and would be in port for seven days, leaving for Liverpool on September 3rd.

Permission was given for Abdel to travel, but no financial assistance would be provided. A loan could be procured from the Purser, Mr

Cawthorne, which could be repaid at his discretion. Abdel was told that failure to return for the return voyage would result in a charge of desertion.

Abdel accepted this condition and went to see the Purser as the *Domelia* approached Port Said.

"Why do you people want to travel in all this heat to worship a boulder?"

"It is my faith; we are asked to visit the Hajj at least once in our life Mr Cawthorne sir."

"You will need to book a return flight, which will cost you £40. Have you got £40 Abdel?"

"No sir, but I do have £12 and if you would grant me a loan, I would be most grateful"

"Well, I think it's a waste of money, but I will sanction the loan. It will mean your wages will be forfeited for five months I am afraid. However, you won't starve on this ship."

"Thank you, sir, God be with you."

"I do hope so, there are dangerous times ahead for us all Abdel."

Having secured the loan from the Purser, Abdel went below decks to tell Bobby.

Bobby was less than impressed and said, "I will never see the Hajj Abdel."

"Never say that Bobby, the time will come when you will pilgrim to Mecca. It is Gods wish."

"I hope and pray that will happen, God is merciful and will you say prayers for me Abdel"?

"Yes, I will do that and for all my shipmates Bobby."

Abdel ventured to Mecca on August 29th and his first experience on an aeroplane terrified him. He felt so helpless so high from the ground on board a Savio-Marchetti SM 83, along with 17 other passengers. Flying at 235 mph so high above terra firma troubled him and he was glad to see the runway after 3 hours and 20 minutes.

The world was on the verge of another World War. Hitler was adamant that Poland would soon become part of the greater Germany and he had ordered his troops to ready themselves for invasion. Diplomatic moves had come to nothing and the world waited for the inevitable.

Abdel was consumed by the spectacle of the pilgrims on this holy site where Islam is worshipped and at times, he felt a sense of togetherness with the thousands gathered in prayer. It would be something he would remember all his days. He was not looking forward to his return flight, but on boarding on Friday, September 3rd all the passengers were told by the pilot, that Great Britain was at war with Germany.

This news kept Abdel preoccupied until the plane touched down on September 3rd at 3pm. He got back on board the *Domelia* at 5pm. The ship was a hive of activity and Abdel was instructed to help Bobby in general maintenance of all deck fittings, secure all rigging and coil down ropes. At 9pm the *Domelia* set sail for Liverpool with a cargo of petroleum and a crew of twenty-five souls. That same day the liner Athenia was torpedoed by a U Boat off the Hebrides with the loss of 125 souls. No warning was given and aboard were refugees including women and children on their way to America. In addition, 28 American citizens lost their lives. This was the first loss at sea and was the beginning of a relentless pursuit by German naval forces.

With the outbreak of war confirmed, further training on the Oerlikon Gun was carried out. This time live ammunition was used to create a sense of realism for what may be forthcoming. Flotsam and jetsam, along with any rubbish thrown overboard were used as targets. Birds in flight were targeted and dolphins, sharks or any creature of the sea within range, were fair game.

The *Domelia* reached the Mersey safely on September 14th without experiencing any enemy contact. When they arrived in Liverpool, the captain was summoned to a meeting with a representative of the British East India Company, Mr David Robertson and a Vice Admiral of the Home Feet T.F.H. Hoareshall. DSO. RN. The meeting was convened to provide orders for sailing within the convoy and notification of lines of communication, rules of engagement and allied air cover. In addition to these orders a decision had been made to replace one of the Oerlikon Anti-Aircraft Guns with a 4-inch gun on the Fore Deck.

The captain stressed that further training would be needed in the deployment of this Gun and was informed that the navy would be providing two DEMS (Defensively Equipped Merchant Ship) Maritime Regiment gunners to operate the gun and therefore the current navy personnel on board the *Domelia* would be relieved of their duties. Having collected his orders from the Vice Admiral he returned to the ship and asked all the officers and the ships new medic Dr Stewart Lloyd to attend a briefing in his quarters.

When all were seated, he welcomed the Doctor and introduced the officers and asked; "Have you acquainted yourself with the ships medical quarters Stewart and will they be adequate?"

"Yes, they are indeed adequate Captain," replied the Doctor.

As a result of the change in personnel Pablo and Jim Shearer were given the duty as gunners on the aft Oerlikon Gun with Ralph Patterson supporting and Tom Gardener would support the two Royal Navy seaman with the deployment of the 4-inch gun on the Fore Deck.

Robert Sanderson asked; "What are we carrying on these convoys skipper?"

"Well Robert, on the way out to Halifax, Nova Scotia not much really. We will have some machinery and a little timber for ballast. On the return voyage back to blighty, we will have ammunition, oil, military vehicles and food stuffs as cargo."

"How many ships in the convoy skipper?" said Norman.

"Good question Norman, at the moment we will be a merchant fleet of 24 ships that will include 6 Tankers. As yet I do not have exact details of the number of warships that will escort the convoy. That as you might expect, is somewhat confidential at the moment. However, it will include Destroyers, Corvettes and Minesweepers."

The ship left Liverpool on September 20th, bound for Halifax, Nova Scotia. The two new Royal Navy gunners; John Matson from Carlisle and Sam Channer from Hexham, had joined the ship two days earlier. An escort of two Corvettes accompanied the *Domelia* as far as Scapa Flow. The sailing to Halifax was uneventful and without incident, other than regular fire drills. The ship docked on September 26th and took on board oil and military vehicles for the sailing back to Liverpool.

Information relating losses of shipping was scarce and the general consensus of opinion was that the U Boat threat was in its infancy. This was little solace for the crew of the Aircraft Carrier HMS *Courageous*, which was torpedoed by a U Boat on September 17th, south west of Ireland. The ship sank after just twenty minutes, with the loss of 519 of the ships company.

CHAPTER EIGHT

While in Halifax the Captains of all the ships in the convoy met to discuss the formation of the convoy and where each ship should be placed. Merchant vessels would be deployed on a basis that cargo with important military use for the war effort, were given priority. This meant that along with other ships carrying oil, military vehicles, guns, ammunition, troops and other military materials would be offered greater protection from the U Boat threat. The convoy would adopt a rectangular formation spread over an area of 6 miles. Oil tankers and ammunition carrying vessels would be kept apart to avoid any chain reaction if a ship was hit. The centre of the convoy would contain ships with cargoes of general cargo, military hardware and troop carriers. The Royal Navy escorts would be two destroyers and four corvettes and all Captains were answerable to the Convoy Commodore. However, if the convey came under U Boat attack, then the Escort Commander would take control.

The warships were the destroyers HMS *Kelly* and HMS *Kelvin*, supported by four corvettes; HMS *Bluebell*, HMS *Allington Castle*, HMS *Violet* and HMS *Samphire*. The corvettes would hold their positions around 10.000 yards from the convoy, on port, starboard and astern, while the destroyers would circle some 5.000 yards on bearings of north west and north east of the flotilla.

As the convoy set off for Liverpool, there was a great deal of trepidation below decks on the *Domelia*. Abdel sat with Pablo and Jim and could not concentrate on his dominoes.

"What's up Abdel? You're not your usual self today my son." asked Jim.

"I am worried that we are all going to be killed in this war," he replied.

"Ah, we have a lucky skipper Abdel, have you noticed he never sails on a Friday," Jim replied.

"Why is that, Jim?" asked Pablo.

"Because it is unlucky to sail on a Friday, you land lubber," added Jim.

In the engine room Harry Billings, Ronnie Brown and the engine ratings were squeezing out as much power as they could to maintain a top speed of 15 knots. Most of the merchant vessels were doing likewise, but some were struggling to maintain their position within the convoy. Having sailed some 3 hours out into a fairly heavy Atlantic, two ships had given up trying to sustain equilibrium and fell back some 12.000 yards already.

HMS *Violet* maintained radio and visual contact, but the distance was getting greater rapidly. As the sun was setting, one of the stragglers fell to a U Boat attack and sustained a direct torpedo hit to its bow. From the deck of the *Domelia*, Abdel could see the smoke and flames which engulfed the ship some 2 miles astern. He looked on in horror as it slipped into the sea, bow first. She was gone in 4 minutes. His mouth suddenly dried up and he felt faint until a cry from Deck Officer Norman Baker shook him back to reality.

"The bastards, they have picked on a sitting duck."

"I hope one of those corvettes goes and gets any poor buggers still alive in the water," he added.

The ship that was sunk was carrying grain, sugar, fruit and cotton and a crew of 32 souls, she was the Empress of Bangustan and there were no survivors. The U Boat Wolf Pack had struck a silent but catastrophic blow and no doubt that there would be more before Liverpool was reached.

As the *Domelia* made headway keeping in a tight formation, Abdel was given watch duty. He positioned himself on the forecastle, which gave him a panoramic view ahead of the ship and good visual contact with the rest of the convoy. The *Domelia* had two other ships ahead, two aft and three on both port and starboard. He was seconded to this role as a reward for some excellent work in predicting sea movement and weather conditions. Using the ships binoculars, he was employed to spot anything unusual on the surface such as periscopes, mines or sudden sea changes.

Anything out of the ordinary, he would inform the Officer on Watch, who was Robert Sanderson on this occasion. He had a clear horizon and a full moon and he was both excited and terrified, as he peered through the binoculars and scanned the sea. As advised by the Chief Officer, he changed his perspective and used his own vision from time to time for a greater spectrum of the sea. It was on one of these instances that he spotted it. At first, he thought it was just the wind churning up a wave. When he looked through the binoculars his heart leaped. Approximately 1000 yards from the starboard bow a periscope was slicing through the waves. Due to the need for silence, he quickly a made the short distance to Robert Sanderson.

"Sir, I have seen something. Quick sir," and he led him to his watch position. Robert Sanderson grabbed the binoculars and scanned the area where Abdel had pointed.

"I can't see anything Abdel, are you sure?"

Then he saw it.

"Jesus Christ, it's a U Boat Abdel, get to the bridge tell the Captain now."

With his heart still pounding Abdel reached the bridge and told the Captain the position of the U Boat. Signals were sent to all ships and to the Commodore's destroyer, HMS *Kelvin*. Within minutes the destroyer was on a bearing to intercept. U Boats are a lot faster on the surface, but always vulnerable as a better target for guns to inflict damage. The ship had sprung into action and the two navy gunners John and Sam were in position to receive orders for engagement.

As quickly as it had appeared, the U Boat sank out of sight. HMS *Kelvin* continued the search and dropped depth charges in the hope of a kill, without success. The incident lasted no longer than 20 minutes and Abdel returned to his watch. At the end of his watch Abdel was summoned to the Captains quarters where he was given a warm reception by the Officers present and the captain said, "You may well have averted a disaster Abdel, well done young man. If we get to Liverpool in one piece, I will personally write off your loan to the ships Purser Mr Cawthorne."

All the officers shook Abdel's hand as he left the Captains quarters.

As the convoy continued across the Atlantic, sea conditions worsened and waves of some 30 feet were buffeting the ships. At 2pm on September 30th another ship was sank by a U Boat. Again torpedoed, but it took some time to fall beneath the waves. This allowed rescue to be carried out and 23 sailors were plucked from the icy sea alive. Sadly, all those in the engine room failed to get out and seven sailors were burned alive. The ship was the Oregon Star and she was carrying steel, timber and military vehicles.

The *Domelia* maintained good speed and the convoy continued on a north east bearing. They passed some 30 miles north of the Azores on October 5th when another merchant vessel was torpedoed. The Winnipeg Progress had a cargo of oil and steel and was hit midships by two torpedoes. Within minutes she was burning and bow down, she sank surrounded by burning oil and the few souls that abandoned ship were burned alive. The protection of British air cover was still some 200 miles away and the menace of more U Boat attacks were a constant threat.

The general moral within the ships company was positive, but anger and a determination not to be beaten was regularly instilled by the officers. This was reassuring for Abdel who was finding this very terrifying, yet exciting. He continued to share the watch duties and during the day he would scan the sky for German aircraft who were now within range for sorties on the convoy. On one such occasion he spotted a Heinkel 111 at 3000 feet doing 250mph on the starboard side. Luckily it passed without engaging and as it got ever closer, he could see that smoke was billowing from its undercarriage.

It eventually exploded on impact as it fell into the sea some 4000 yards to port, this produced a great cheer from those on deck.

To everyone's great relief the *Domelia* and its convoy reached Liverpool on October 12th and discharged its vital cargo. The crew were given 3 days shore leave. Abdel made one trip ashore with Bobby on his 21st birthday, but he found the experience very strange. He was awe struck by the buildings and their grandiose. He also found it difficult to understand the language, even though his English had improved, the local people spoke so quickly and he found it hard to understand a word they were saying. He and Bobby would look at each other in amazement and confusion whenever they were engaged in conversation with any of the locals.

During the lay off in Liverpool, some of the crew took the opportunity to visit their families. Jim Shearer, George Hollcroft, the cook Tom Seymour and officers Stanley Hope, Phil Graham and Norman Baker all spent a few days with their nearest and dearest. On return all the officers were summoned to the Captains quarters to hear of their next trip.

They would be loading with a cargo of coal for France, to be shipped to St-Nazaire. The *Domelia* would sail on November 4th and pick up the coal at Cardiff docks before departing on the 6th for France.

The captain informed the gathered officers of their passage and said, "We are taking a divertive voyage to Monaco with a cargo of coal gentlemen. We will be in the convoy ONS 7 and therefore we will join the convoy just south of Jersey. The rest of the convoy is sailing from the Tyne. From St-Nazaire we will then take on ballast and then in the same convoy sail across the Atlantic to Nova Scotia to pick up military vehicles and steel. I have been informed by the Royal Navy that the Germans have been laying mines in the North Sea and the English Channel."

"Christ is it not enough to be bombed and torpedoed," added Bob Macintyre.

"We lost three ships last week, 10 miles of Spurn Head Bob," replied the captain.

"I hope this convoy has not got any slow-moving tubs skipper; they are sitting ducks for these bastard U Boats," said Phil Graham.

"Steady, language Phil, remember where you are please," said the captain.

"Sorry skipper, but you know what I mean."

"Yes, I do Phil but, if there are any of these ships, they will just have to make the best of it. We must maintain good speed, it's the best defence. We cannot drop speed to maintain the formation of the convoy. As yet I do not have the list of vessels, but I expect that to be relayed to me tomorrow."

"Let's hope and pray there are no 9 knotters in the convoy," said Robert Sanderson.

"How are the two Navy boys settling in Norman?" asked the captain.

"Fine skipper, they seem like decent fellows. I think their itching to get the 4-inch gun into action."

"Well, I will be just as pleased not to see it in action," replied the captain.

"Here here to that," added The Purser, Jack Cawthorne.

"Oh, that reminds me Jack. I said I would pay off Abdel's debt for his pilgrimage to Mecca."

"Why on earth would you do that skipper?"

"Remember his efforts in spotting that U Boat. He did a grand job and I told him that I would pay his debt of if we returned safely to Liverpool. So, can you sort that for me please?"

Jack looked a little perplexed and said reluctantly, "Yes, will do skipper."

The captain went on and discussed maintenance, signalling, stores, drills, supplies, discipline, watches, safety, navigation and the moral of the crew.

"Now then gentlemen, we performed well on our recent voyage from Halifax. We maintained our position within the convoy and sustained good speed and my thanks to all concerned. Our crew, like most of us are seeing things that will have an everlasting effect. This will likely get worse, especially if we take a hit; whether it be bomb, torpedo and mine. We must act quickly if we are struck. If we can save the ship, it is my duty to inform you that we must do our utmost to prevail in this regard. If we launch boats it will be on my command and the same goes if I am convinced, we have to abandon ship. Drills are vital and the more we do, the greater chance of saving this ship and lives of everyone on board."

The room fell silent and finally Robert Sanderson said, "You have our full support skipper, if we are all honest it scares the life out of us. Being out there in the North Atlantic only minutes away from slipping into that heaving grey perilous ocean, keeps us focussed and with the help of God and our seamanship we will prevail."

All nodded in agreement and Norman added, "We must not let our guard down men, keep the crew sharp, on their toes and watch out for the weaknesses in individuals."

As if on cue, there was a knock on the captain's door.

"Come in," said the captain.

It was the steward Mike Harris and he said, "Just had a communique form the admiralty captain."

"Yes, what is it?"

"The aircraft carrier HMS *Renown* has been bombed and sunk off Gibraltar, with the loss of 764 crew with only a handful survivors captain."

The sense of loss was measurable and silence was finally broken when the captain said, "Gentlemen, this is what we have to accept and there will be more of this horror and mayhem. Let us take a minute and remember our fellow seafarers lost in this lamentable tragedy.

As those present bowed their heads in respect, the second engineer Ronald Brown said, "My younger brother is on the *Renown*."

"We pray he is a survivor Ron," said the captain.

After a minute's silence the captain adjourned the meeting and asked Ron to stay. The rest of the officers made their way to their stations. Below decks the news of the loss of HMS *Renown* was received with shock.

Jim Shearer voiced his disgust and said, "We have got to win this fucking war and put an end to this waste of life."

The next day the *Domelia* sailed out of Cardiff bound for the convey of Jersey. On November 6th the ship joined Convoy ONS 07 and set sail for St-Nazaire in France.

Late that afternoon Abdel was off duties and decided to try and catch some sleep. Abdel felt fear and foreboding and lay on his bunk wondering what the future would hold for him and his shipmates.

As he lay, his mind wandered and he thought about his father, Syed and Hakim. He wondered if Jacob Levi's son had got his family out of Germany. He thought about Maheera and eventually fell into a deep sleep. He awoke two hours later to frenzied activity below decks.

"Come on Abdel shake yourself; we have trouble again. Get your arse on deck" shouted Jim Shearer.

Abdel arrived on deck to see the Corvettes moving through the convoy on the hunt for U Boats, discharging depth charges as they made their way through a moderate sea, with waves about 4 feet high. As he scanned the sea, he could make out a burning ship at the rear of the convoy.

"They have nailed another one," said Mr Mac as he instructed Abdel to get on the port bow and look for any mines or U Boats.

Abdel took up his post and with a pair of binoculars searched the sea for anything untoward. As he scanned the sea ahead of the port bow, the ship succumbed to a tremendous shudder in her stern. The *Domelia* began to list to port and Abdel was knocked to the deck. Within a minute another torpedo struck a midships on the starboard side. As Abdel turned to look at the devastation, he saw Robert Sanderson struggling to keep his feet on deck. Then an explosion resulted in great shards of metal flying across the deck. Abdel watched in horror as one of these shards decapitated Robert Sanderson some 30 feet away. Abdel was frozen in fear, he could not move.

Then a voice cried out; "Launch the boats, abandon ship."

It was Bob McIntyre; he was directing the crew that were topside and then he spotted Abdel.

"Abdel get your carcase up off the deck and get the boats off."

The ship was listing badly and sea water was pouring over the deck from the stern. Fires were breaking out and the first torpedo had rendered the ship dead in the water. Bob McIntyre feared that it was too late to lower any boats and shouted; "Abandon the ship we are going down, every man for himself."

Abdel scanned what was left of the *Domelia*, he saw Bobby jump in the raging sea. The ship was listing badly when he heard a voice from behind him.

"Come on Abdel, we must jump now."

It was Pablo, he pushed a life jacket into Abdel's hands, which was quickly fitted and together they leapt some 20 feet into the sea.

On impact Abdel felt a huge surge of freezing cold sea engulf his body and he struggled to maintain his breathing due to the shock. Instinct kicked in and once he surfaced, he quickly began swimming away from the ship. As he swam, he heard the disturbing noise from the ship as she continued to list. What he also heard were the cries and screams of some of his shipmates who were drowning in the sea or injured and still on board the ship.

Screams of despair that included cries to God, mothers and wives as terrified seamen were drowning or being burned to death.

Abdel continued to make the distance from the sinking ship greater, as he swam for his life. With the advice of Jim Shearer ringing in his ears that; being too close to the ship would mean you would be sucked down with her when she sank.

The Corvettes were frantically trying to locate the U Boat and zig-zagged through the convoy. Abdel had now been in the water some 10 minutes and his limbs were now beginning to seize up. The *Domelia* had sunk within 6 minutes of the second torpedo striking.

As Abdel was fearing he would lose consciousness, he was suddenly pulled from his icy world and bundled into a lifeboat by Norman Baker.

Shivering uncontrollably, he fell to his knees and thanked God for his rescue. A voice then said, "It's Norman you should be thanking Abdel, he spotted you," said Bobby.

Abdel looked up to see Bobby, Pablo, George, Jim, Mr Mac, Stanley Hope and Norman sitting in the lifeboat. Bobby, Pablo and Stanley Hope were covered in oil which had leaked out the ship after the second torpedo. There were still occasional cries of desolation from the sea from the poor souls who were drowning. Abdel and his shipmates were unaware that they were the only survivors who were now sat in this lifeboat that bobbed precariously in the North Atlantic. After some 30 minutes a Corvette rescued Abdel and his shipmates. The Corvette lowered her scrambling nets and this bedraggled band of seafarers struggled up the netting. As they did so, Bob McIntyre sat in the lifeboat sobbing.

The trauma of what had transpired was too much for him. A sailor from the Corvette had to scream at him to compose himself and get to his feet and climb the netting, much to the chagrin of the Corvettes Captain. His major concern being that they were a sitting target for further U Boat attacks.

Having received medical attention for hypothermia and a few injuries, they were given tea and ham and eggs. They were also informed that they were the only survivors. They all sat silent and after what seemed like a long time, Stanley Hope said, "Gentlemen, there for the grace of God we are here to live another day. Let's us bow our heads in remembrance of our lost shipmates." He then recited the Lord's prayer.

CHAPTER NINE

No one below decks survived the attack along with the Captain who went down with the ship. In total 15 of the crew perished. The bodies of Tom Gardner, the Steward Mike Harris, the Cook Tom Seymour, both Navy Gunners John Matson, Sam Channer and the Doctor Stewart Lloyd were recovered from the sea.

As is the custom in war at sea, the bodies of those who had fallen were returned to the sea and the Captain of the Corvette, Capt. David Williams DSO gave the eulogy which included Psalm 55: 4-6.

Fear and trembling come upon me,
and horror overwhelms me.
And I say, "O that I had wings like a dove!
I would fly away and be at rest."

The convoy proceeded with no further attacks and arrived at St-Nazaire on November 11th. As the Senior Officer Norman Baker made contact with the British East India Company and relayed the loss of the *Domelia*, the survivors and those who lost their lives. The remainder of the crew were given accommodation in St-Nazaire and waited for news of their next ship.

They did not have to wait long; a telegram was sent to Norman Baker on November 14th saying that the remaining crew members would join the Merchant Vessel the *Barat Star*. A 9870-ton freighter built in 1932, with a maximum speed of 17 knots and modified with armaments including three 20mm Oerlikon Guns and two 4-inch Guns fore and aft. In addition, like the *Domelia* she had reinforced bulkheads. To enhance the fight against the U Boats a new weapon was employed and the *Barat Star* was one of the first merchant ships to have one deployed. It was nicknamed the *Hedgehog*. This was a weapon that had 24 small bombs that would be fired at a range of 250 yards in a circular pattern. They were equipped with contact fuses that would only explode when contact was made.

The crew would muster at the dock at 13.00 hours on November 16th. New papers, passports and indentures to be provided on arrival by a Mr G. S. Hamilton of the British East India Company. Officers would continue in their current positions and able seamen would assume their previous jobs.

The French authorities organised a truck to transport the men to the dock and they were given a hero's farewell from their hotel by the staff and the locals.

On arrival, Mr Hamilton was waiting and duly served the men with their papers and a month's wages. It was then that the enormity of what had occurred and that he had managed to survive, thanks to Norman Baker. It also dawned on him that he no longer had his watch given to him by Jacob Levi and his books. They were now at the bottom of the Atlantic.

The officers Bob McIntyre, Norman Baker and Stanley Hope were welcomed on board by Capt. John G. Sheed. He was a slight figure, no more than 5' 6" in height with a handlebar moustache and dark brown eyes that evoked a weary appearance. They were then escorted to the Captains quarters for a briefing with the other Officers.

Abdel, Pablo, George, Jim and Bobby were shown to their bunks by the Steward Thomas Robinson, a big man of Irish persuasion. When shown their bunks Thomas said, "Now then men, first of all; no fucking Irish jokes on this ship unless you want to lose some teeth. Do you all understand?"

All present nodded and George added; "Well, that's a welcome I have never had before."

"Look, I know you fellas have had a rough time, losing all your shipmates. However, I am here to tell you that we could all be down in Davy Jones locker this time tomorrow. We need to get on and stay focussed and pray to God that we get through it."

Once they had set up their bunks and stored what they had the Steward gave them a tour of the ship to meet the rest of the crew. The crew was a mixture of British, Spanish and Lascars.

Back in the Captain's quarters the new Officers were introduced to the current Commissioned Officers.

"Can I introduce you to the following Officers that are joining us gentlemen. Mr Bob McIntyre, Deck Officer. Mr Norman Baker, Senior Deck Officer. Mr Stanley Hope, Engineering Officer."

Those present looked at each in surprise and before anyone spoke the captain said, "Yes, I know it is normal that to have only one Deck Officer. However, I have been instructed by the company to appoint Norman as Senior Deck Officer as a reward for his outstanding work on the *Domelia*. Are there any questions on this?"

There was no response from those gathered and the Captain continued to introduce the current Officers on board.

All Officers present rose one by one and introduced themselves.

Mr Ron M. Braithwaite. Chief Engineer.

Mr Jack N. Cooper. Chief Officer.

Mr Ernie Stevenson. Purser.

Dr David F Bunyan. Medical Officer.

Mr Bill Davison. Navigation Officer.

The Captain went onto mention the steward Tom Robinson, who was currently showing the new crew members their quarters and introducing them to the current crew and added; "We also have six Royal Navy ratings on board as Gunners to operate the weapons which include the 20mm Oerlikons, 4-inch Guns and our new revolutionary Hedgehog missile launcher. You will no doubt meet them in due course. They are; Able Seamen, Ralph Smith, Nobby Calvert, Jack Henson, Bill Pattinson, Paddy O'Neill and Isaac Levinson. I now believe that our good Doctor David needs to do a '*short arm inspection"* with the new crew members. Is that not so David?"

"Indeed Captain, please excuse me gentlemen and can I express my warmest greetings to our new Officers," said the Doctor.

"Thanks again," added the Captain.

"Does our Doctor not need to be in attendance for your information regarding our voyage Captain?" asked Norman.

"Normally he would be Norman, but I have a arranged a private briefing with David in an hours' time," replied the Captain.

He continued, "Now gentlemen, firstly our destination and cargo. We leave in two days' time bound for Liverpool, with a cargo of oil and explosives."

Looks of concern traversed the room and Bob McIntyre said, "Christ, now I know why we have all this weaponry on board."

"Yes, we need to be able to offer some stern resistance if attacked Bob. We are ready though; the Navy boys have had some firing practice and there good," replied the Captain and went on; "After delivering our cargo at Gladstone Dock in Bootle, we will load up with military vehicles and aircraft parts and our destination is Valletta, Malta. Half of the Convoy will then press onto Alexandria in Egypt. Malta has only limited docking at Marsaxlokk and we will have to anchor of shore until we can get into port to discharge our cargo. We will be joining Convoy ONS 044 west of the Scilly Isles on November 26th."

The briefing continued with details of duties, maintenance reports, engineering reports, catering and watch times. Meanwhile below deck the Doctor was preparing for his *'short arm inspection.*

Having met most of the crew the steward then escorted Abdel and his shipmates to the medical room. Jim Shearer was aware of what was about to follow and said, "Well boys, it looks like we are going to get checked for snotty cock."

Pablo and Abdel looked puzzled and Bobby added; "I am clean, I do not have this disease."

"Then you will get the thumbs up then, won't you Bobby," replied Jim.

"That sounds painful, Jim," said George and laughed.

Abdel and Pablo still had confusion written all over their faces until Bobby explained what was about to happen.

One by one the Doctor invited them in and carried out the procedure of examining every man's genitals for signs of venereal disease.

Abdel was first in and felt this was very unnecessary and said to the Doctor; "I wash and bathe myself all the time Doctor and I have not been with any women. I have kept my honour sir."

"That is good to hear, but it is my duty to inspect your genitals. So, can you strip from the waist please able seaman?"

"My name is Abdel Malik Rahman sir and I will do as you ask, but I am not happy with this."

The Doctor carried out his inspection of Abdel's genitals and when finished said, "Very good Abdel Malik Rahman, you have a clean bill of health. You may go now and thank you."

Abdel felt ashamed of what had transpired and left the medical room without speaking to any of his fellow crew members. Much to Jim's hilarity, who shouted as Abdel quickly made for the crews' quarters.

"You can lose your cherry at our next port of call Abdel."

Abdel arrived at his bunk and lay and pondered his future. He thought of his fishing trips with Osman and wished he could be back on the Bunder Road. He wondered if Hakim was happy with his life in South Africa. He thought about Abdullah his cousin and how business was at Rahman's Chandlers. The events of the past few days had been traumatic and he drifted off to sleep.

The *Barat Star* sailed for Liverpool at 14.00 hours on November 19th. Being a reasonably new ship, she was able to maintain good speed at 17 knots and would reach Liverpool two days later, providing there was no further contact with the enemy.

During the course of the voyage the chat in the crew's quarters revolved around some leave in Liverpool and how best to spend the time.

George and Jim felt the need to spend a night on the town and encouraged Abdel, Pablo and Bobby to join them. After some persuasion they agreed that they would join their shipmates, once shore leave had been granted.

The *Barat Star* duly docked at Gladstone Dock at 16.00 hours and discharged her cargo. Shore leave was granted for 24 hours and most of the crew descended on Liverpool for the evening. As organised Jim, George, Pablo, Bobby and Abdel all made their way into Liverpool for an evening's entertainment.

Abdel and Bobby were somewhat wary of what might happen, bearing in mind that neither of them would being drinking alcoholic beverages.

There first port of call was a pub called the Lion Tavern on Dale Street. Jim and George ordered their drinks and Pablo got lemonade for himself, Bobby and Abdel. While Jim and George chatted with a couple of local men at the bar, their three shipmates found a table in the corner. Abdel was fascinated by the whole experience. He watched and listened to the banter; most of which he could not understand and at times he asked Bobby or Pablo to translate.

After Jim and George had drank their pints the party moved onto the Vernon Arms. Again, Jim and George ordered pints at the bar. Abdel noticed that there were many women in the pub and he asked Bobby why this was so?

"Most of the men are at war remember Abdel, in the Army, Navy or Air Force. That is why women are not with men," replied Bobby.

"Will they all be married then Bobby?" asked Abdel.

"This I do not know Abdel; you will have to ask."

Abdel thought about this and noticed two young women standing at the end of the bar.

"I will ask those two women Bobby."

Before Bobby could intervene, Abdel was out of his seat and approaching the bar.

"Good evening ladies, my name is Abdel. Can I ask if you are both married?"

The two "ladies," laughed, and one said to the other, "Well Doris, there is a chat up line, if ever there was one."

Abdel failed to grasp the predicament he was in and said,

"Are your husbands in the Army?"

Doris then said, "You know what Jean; this wog has a nerve don't you think. My Bill is next door in the bar playing darts. I should go and get him and I am sure he would belt this cheeky swine."

"Oh, he doesn't mean any harm Doris, he will be one of them lascars from one of the ships in Gladstone Dock" she replied.

Jim who was chatting with George at the other end of the bar, had picked up on the comments from the two local women and decided to intercede and walked over to join the conversation.

"Evening ladies, I hope my shipmate is not giving offence in any way. He is quite naive in matters of the fairer sex."

Jim's charm offensive worked and the situation was improved when Jim advised Abdel to return to his seat. Abdel was none too pleased to hear the term" wog" again, but remembered what Syed had warned him about. There would be those who would seek to humiliate him, because of his colour and faith. As he sat down to re-join Pablo and Bobby he said in Pashto;

Bayad tse wakrum? Ne pohezham, yam ghusa.

Pablo looked at Bobby and asked what Abdel has said?"

"Abdel is angry; he does not understand what he has to do Pablo."

Abdel sat in silence as Pablo added; "Do not be insulted by them Abdel, it is they who do not understand."

Back at the bar, George joined Jim and the pair of them eased the tension and spent the next ten minutes chatting to the two ladies, they then all moved onto another local hostelry.

They all arrived back at the ship for 10.30pm as requested by Jack Cooper, the Senior Officer. The remaining time in dock involved the loading of cargo, fuel and provisions for the voyage to Malta.

The Captain gathered the crew on the forecastle and informed them of their voyage, cargo and destination. He also said there would a Fire Drill not long after leaving Gladstone Dock and all the crew should be prepared and respond with speed and fortitude. As a reward for their endeavours so far, he also informed the crew that they would all get a tot of rum when they next had a meal on board.

The *Barat Star* left the dock at 9am on Saturday, November 25th, with the local Pilot from the Liverpool Pilotage Service on board. Having guided the *Barat Star* clear of the port, the polit Cutter arrived alongside to collect the Pilot. Once out in open sea, she was joined by the Destroyer HMS *Berwick*. She would shadow the *Barat Star* as protection, until she met the Convoy. The weather was not good and a heavy swell was developing out in the Irish Sea.

After half an hour at sea the Captain called all the Officers, to his mess for a briefing. Except Jack Cooper who had the watch on the bridge. He began by welcoming them all and congratulating them on a swift demarcation form Liverpool.

"Now then gentlemen, it would be wrong of me not to extend my concerns about this trip. It will be difficult to say the least. We have vital cargo on board and it must get to Malta. We must all be vigilant and you must instil a sense of urgency in this regard to your crew. We must look at the positives; We have a strong experienced crew and Royal Navy able seaman on board to man the weaponry. We must ensure that your men are on their mark at all times, we cannot carry any slackers. Any problems must be dealt with swiftly gentlemen. We will have a Fire Drill sometime within the next 2 hours. We are looking at a moderate sea, with waves 4-5 feet. So, we should make good time to the Scilly's. As you have no doubt seen, we have an escort. It's the Destroyer HMS *Berwick*. When we reach the Scilly's and join up with the Convoy, there will be a couple of Minesweepers in attendance."

"The Germans have been laying mines all over the English Channel. Any one of these things can send us down, so ensure your spotters are on their game, because these magnetic mines lie just below the surface."

The Captain then asked for charts from Bill Davison the Navigation Officer. He laid them out on the table and said, "Right, let's look at this. We have air cover as far as the Iberian Peninsula. From then we have nothing other than a few Sunderland Flying Boats out of Gibraltar. This is why we are carrying aircraft parts to Malta to try and extend our airborne protection of convoys in the Mediterranean. The main threat comes from the U Boats, as you might expect. However, The Germans are deploying Heinkel bombers from bases in Spain, thanks to that other bloody dictator Franco. They also have Aircraft Carriers in the Med and so expect to see Stukas on sorties. What concerns me greatly is the problem of getting into the port at Malta. The port can only take 4 ships at any one time and I am informed that 6 merchantmen will be docking in Malta. This means 2 ships will have to anchor at sea and await their turn to unload cargo. I don't want us to be one of those two ships. The two tankers will be first in I am certain of that, but we will wait and see if we get the short straw. Thankfully, we have the Oerlikons and the 4-inch guns to counteract this threat, along with two Destroyers which will remain as our escorts."

Then he went on to update the Officers with the latest news from the admiralty on ship losses. "The latest communiques are as follows gentlemen; HMS *Royal Oak*, torpedoed at Scapa Flow 833 lives lost. October 14th. British Tanker – *Regent Tiger*. Losses unknown. November 21st. HMS *Gypsy*, Sunk by Mine. Losses unknown. English Channel. November 21st. HMS *Aragonite*, Minesweeper, Sunk by Mine. Losses unknown. November 21st. Armed Merchant Cruiser, Rawalpindi sunk off Iceland. Losses unknown. November 23rd.

"This is just the start gentlemen; we have lost a total of 197 vessels since the start of the conflict. That includes 89 by U Boats and a further 108 by mines, aircraft and enemy fire from warships. Obviously, these statistics are minimal in terms of their content, but they do highlight the problems we will have to encounter. You may well know of friends or relatives serving on these vessels and I will do my best to inform you, once I have the details. Suffice to say that relatives back in blighty may well learn of any fatalities before we do and I can only give you my deepest apologies in advance. Give this information to your ratings and if they want to give you names of relatives that are serving on any of these vessels, we will see what we can do."

The mood in the room was sombre as the Captain asked for any comments. Chief Engineer Ron Braithwaite was the first to speak and said, "These bastards don't care who they send to their death. They sank the Athenia, a bloody Cruise Ship for Christ's sake."

"Yes, that is what we are dealing with Ron," replied the Captain.

"Will our Navy Gunners have a gun drill before we get to the Scilly's Captain? asked the Purser, Ernie Stevenson.

"It may not be possible Ernie; it may draw some unwanted attention. Anyway, they had that practice in the Bay of Biscay remember, before we docked at St. Nazaire."

"Oh yes, that's right Captain. I just hope they have their lamp oil in."

"How have your boys settled in Bob? asked the Captain.

"Just fine Captain, they have not had a great deal of time to think of what happened to the *Domelia* and the shipmates who we lost. But I am sure they won't let anyone down," replied Bob.

The Doctor gave his medical report on the new crew members and a general overview of the moral of the crew, which he believes is positive.

"Just to add gentlemen, we will have the Fire Drill in 20 minutes; before the weather gets any worse. I would like to borrow a phrase from Lord Collingwood before the Battle of Trafalgar when he said;

"Now, gentlemen, let us do something today which the world may talk of hereafter."

The Captain then closed the briefing with a prayer. "Let us pray gentlemen and hope that God gives us a safe passage to Malta." He then read Psalm 117 verse 2: "Th*e Lord's right hand has triumphed;*

His right hand raised me up.
I shall not die, I shall live
And recount his deeds, Amen."

The Fire Drill went as well as could be expected, other than one of the engine ratings fell off a ladder and suffered a gash to his head, which the Doctor stitched and kept him in the sick bay for 24 hours. The *Barat Star* made decent headway making 15 knots against a strong north westerly. Progress was made slower as the wind grew into a hurricane, this resulted in more loss of life, but not on the *Barat Star*. Back at Liverpool the Pilot Boat the S.S. Charles Livingston got stranded on Ainsdale Beach. The heavy sea swept away her bridge and upper deck.

Six crew members sought refuge in the fore-rigging and were rescued by the Lifeboat. Four other crew members were washed overboard, but managed to get to shore. Sadly, 23 crew were lost. Eight were Pilots and another eight were young apprentices. It seemed that mother nature took no sides in this conflict, which left families grief-stricken from the loss of loved ones.

The *Barat Star* joined the convoy early on the morning of Tuesday, November 28th. The weather was better with a Code 5 – A strong breeze and a rough sea, with waves of some 10 feet high.

The convoy would be using a 5-mile block configuration with ships in a parallel formation, some 1000 yards from port to starboard and 550 yards from stern to bow for each vessel. The convoy consisted of three troop ships, 10 tankers, and some 32 other vessels carrying raw materials, ammunition, military vehicles and aircraft. In addition, 4 Escort Destroyers would be in a central position within the convoy. The 2 Corvettes would be 8.000 yards, port and starboard of the convoy.

At 11.00 hours Convoy ONS 044 set sail for Malta. Abdel now knew what might befall him and his shipmates and it left him in a state of constant fear. He was resting below decks, but could not sleep, his next watch was 14.00 hours. What Abdel did not know was that recent hot spots for U Boat attacks had been identified by the admiralty and one of these was the Atlantic where it funnelled into the Straits of Gibraltar.

Captain Sheed was in possession of that information, along with his Senior Officer for Navigation, Bill Davison; along with every Captain within the convoy. The convoy should be approaching this 'turkey shoot" in two days' time.

The sea had relented and the headway was good with the *Barat Star* more than holding her own within the convoy. The Corvettes were in a constant state of alert and circled the convoy on the lookout for U Boats. Then, with the convoy some 125 miles due west of La Coruna in Northern Spain, five specs appeared on the horizon at 2000 feet, approaching from the north east. Heinkel 111 bombers, armed with bombs for deploying and wreaking havoc. The alarm was sounded and action stations implemented. The Royal Navy gunners sprang into action aboard the *Barat Star*. Within 5 minutes the enemy had delivered bombs without success on the targets at the perimeter of the convoy. The Destroyers were quickly into action and one Heinkel exploded at 300 feet after a direct hit.

Abdel was on watch and he stood in a state of terror as the planes plunged and released their bombs, then climbing steeply to avoid the incoming fire from the destroyers.

The *Barat Star* was 1000 yards from a tanker on her port side when a bomb made a direct hit on the tanker. The noise was tremendous and the tanker exploded a midships and burst into flames. The accuracy of the pilots of the Heinkel's was not great, with bombs missing their intended targets. Within 20 minutes the action was over with another Heinkel falling from the sky into the sea after another direct hit. This time it was shot down from the *Barat Star*. Gunner Isaac Levinson had scored a direct hit with his 4-inch gun and a great cheer went up as the plane hit the sea.

CHAPTER TEN

The Corvettes could not get close to the tanker, due to the fierce heat and were unable to find any survivors. Other ships close to the tanker had to take avoidance measures as the sea around the wreckage was burning. No attempt was made to locate any survivors of the downed aircraft. The other Heinkel's departed as quickly as they had arrived.

Abdel was still frozen by fear as Bob McIntyre shouted; "Abdel, don't just fucking stand their man, check for any damage. We are still at action stations."

Abdel then realised; he had urinated in his trousers.

He then set about searching for any damage on deck. He found no evidence and reported back to Mr Mac.

"I have not found any damage Mr Mac sir," he said.

"Very good, but you are not here watching a bloody film Abdel. This is war my son. You should be looking for any bombs that don't explode and fall into the sea or looking to help with rescue and identify survivors. There is always something to focus on shipmate, remember that," he replied.

"What do you mean focus on Mr Mac?" asked Abdel.

"This means you should help in any way you can Abdel, do you understand? he added.

"Yes sir Mr Mac, I will do that sir," he replied.

"Abdel, stop calling me sir, that is for the Captain. Mr Mac or Bob will do thanks."

"Yes sir, Mr Mac"

Bob McIntyre just shook his head and said, "Alright carry on, remember you are on watch, so watch."

The convoy continued on and reached the south of Portugal on a moonlight November 30th at 22.00 hours and set a bearing for the Straits of Gibraltar. Much to the Captains surprise, the convoy did not encounter any enemy action and reached the Mediterranean without any further losses.

Sailing south from the island of Pantelleria, which is a hundred miles north west of Malta, the escort Corvettes were very active in a U Boat search. They managed to force a U Boat to the surface after dropping a number of depth charges. Unfortunately, the U Boat managed to escape under the cover of darkness. The convoy reached Malta on December 4th at 14.00 hours.

Much to the relief of Captain Sheed, the *Barat Star* was asked to dock first, along with the two tankers and another merchantman that had a cargo of food. The need to get the military vehicles and aircraft parts ashore was essential to the war effort. The other vessel was carrying food produce including potatoes, wheat, salt, apples and nuts. Malta does not have enough arable land to cultivate crops to feed the population and as a consequence produce needs to be imported. The remainder of the convoy pressed onto Alexandria with three Destroyers and the Corvettes as escort.

Unloading took until 22.00 hours and the crew were informed that shore leave would be granted the following day from midday on Tuesday, December 5th. Pablo, Abdel and Bobby decided to stay together for their excursion in Valetta. As they sat waiting for midday in their quarters Abdel had already made his mind up to buy some books while ashore and said, "I lost everything when the *Domelia* was sunk. I must buy the Noble Qur'an and other books. I must also have a new prayer mat and some more clothes, but I cannot buy a new watch."

"Why is that Abdel?" asked Pablo.

"I do not have enough money Pablo and it would be wrong because I might lose it if we get blown up again."

"This is true," added Bobby.

"I must buy a pen, some writing paper and envelopes. I must write to my mother in Cadiz and ask her if she and my sister are well. She keeps asking me when I will come home? If I could get to Gibraltar, I could ask for leave to see them," said Pablo.

"We do not know where we are going next, even Mr Mac does not know. I asked him yesterday, but he did not know," added Bobby.

"We might go back to Liverpool or Cardiff," added Abdel.

Within two minutes Mr Mac appeared and said, "Right then, you horrible set of miscreants, you have ten hours shore leave so bugger off."

"Do you know where we are sailing to next Mr Mac?" asked Abdel

"Not a clue, but never mind that. Make sure you do not upset any of the local women Abdel. I do not want to have to fish you out of the Med tonight," he replied.

"I am not a wog or a lascar Mr Mac and I will not have my family dishonoured," said Abdel.

"Now there you go, that talk will get you a good hiding. You must learn to turn the other cheek Abdel. Remember, people who say these things are lacking in intelligence and you must show you are intelligent by choosing not to react. What you need is the company of a good women tonight. In fact, you could all do with it. So, go and make love tonight boys and find a lady on Straight Street."

As the three able seamen left the ship Abdel said to Bobby; "Mr Mac is a good man Bobby."

"Yes, he is a good man and he has been kind to us Abdel. I do not know about making love Abdel. Have you been in love?"

"I do not know about making love, but back in Karachi I met a girl called Maheera. She was very beautiful, but she was promised to another man and then I left to join the *Domelia*," replied Abdel.

As they walked out of the port Pablo said, "I have not made love to a girl, but I would like to."

The three young men stood and looked at each other and Bobby said, "We should find a beautiful girl tonight, just like Maheera and make love. Just like Mr Mac told us. It is your 21st birthday present Abdel."

"Will we share the same girl Bobby?" asked Pablo.

Again, all three looked at other and began to laugh and Abdel said, "Well, we shall see, but we must not disrespect any lady's tonight."

"We are honourable men," added Bobby.

They walked into Valetta on a warm sunny afternoon, innocent and yet happy that they had left the troubles of the war behind them for a few hours at least. They had not walked very far when the city came alive with people doing all manner of things. Street sellers with all kinds of products including food, jewellery, clothes, drinks and books. There were bars and cafés on every street and sitting outside one such café was Isaac Levinson; the Gunner form the *Barat Star*.

He noticed the three protagonists and shouted; "Hey, shipmates from the *Barat Star*," and waved his hand.

Pablo recognised him and waved back in his direction and said, "Look, there is the Gunner who shot down the plane from our ship."

They all went to join Isaac, who was pleased to see them and invited them to join him. They ordered coffee and sat and talked of the war and what might be on the horizon for the *Barat Star*.

As the conversation progressed Abdel asked why his fellow Gunners were not with him.

"Well, my Royal Navy shipmates have gone to sample the local female hospitality. I myself have not because I have a loving wife at home in Bethnal Green."

Isaac could tell by the looks of confusion around that his audience had not a clue about what he was saying and so he attempted to explain in simpler terms.

"My fellow gunners have sought to find ladies who would like to make love to them. Do you understand what that means boys?

"Oh yes sir, Mr Mac told us to go and find a beautiful woman and make love also," replied Pablo.

Isaac smiled and said,

"Did your Deck Officer say how you would do this?"

"Yes, he said we should go to Straight Street," added Abdel.

Isaac stood and pointed to a long street that stretched up for about a mile and said, "There it is boys, but I must give you some advice."

He then sat down and provided much more information on the acquisition of beautiful women who might provide the required entertainment. His monologue left the three young seamen somewhat shocked and disappointed.

"We have to give these women money as well?" asked Bobby.

"You do indeed, but you can pay less for some ladies," he replied.

"Why is that?" asked Pablo.

"It is because of their age; they might be older than your mother," said Isaac.

Pablo quickly genuflected, looked shocked and said, "God forgive me, I have sinned."

"Not yet you haven't," added Isaac.

This information had left our intrepid Romeo's in a state of flux and Isaac felt that he had ruined their day and said, "Listen, I could be of service to you if you like."

"What do you mean?" replied Bobby.

"I could try and find some girls that will give a discount. It will still cost you £2 each and your time limit will be short."

"Time limit, what is that?" asked Abdel.

"Well, you will only have 10 or 15 minutes with the girl," replied Isaac.

"Do we all have the same girl?" asked Pablo.

"Yes, the same girl," replied Isaac.

All three nodded in agreement and began to produce the required £2 for the venture.

"No, hold onto your money for the moment. Wait until I have found a girl. Just sit here until I return. Do you understand?" said Isaac.

There was sense of foreboding as the three prospective lovemakers sat and discussed what was about to transpire. Abdel suggested that it may not be a good idea and said, "We should leave now; I must buy books and a prayer mat."

"We must stay Abdel; we have given our agreement to this," replied Bobby.

After a wait of some twenty minutes Isaac returned.

"Where is the girl?" asked Bobby.

"She is working, but she will be available in an hours' time. I will take you to her address then," replied Isaac.

"What is her job?" asked Pablo.
Isaac laughed and said,
"She is a dancer."
"Is she old like my mother?" asked Pablo.
Smiling, Isaac said, "No, she is not old and she is a very good dancer."
"But I cannot dance," added Bobby.
"I am sure she will teach you a few steps of dancing," joked Isaac.
They had another coffee and then Isaac said, "Now we are ready to go."
He then rose to his feet and set off up Straight Street, followed closely by his three anxious customers.

After a five-minute walk Isaac arrived at a large wooden door. He entered and invited his shipmates in. He then opened another door to reveal a large seating area populated by many scantily clad girls. Some of which were serving men with drinks and others just sitting chatting. To his surprise, Bobby noticed that Norman Baker, the Senior Deck Officer from the *Barat Star* was sitting with a girl on his knee. He tried to hide his face but Norman had spotted all three of them as soon as they walked in.

"Well well, it's nice to see these boys are up for some fun. Fill yours boots boys."

Whereupon he disappeared with his companion, through another door.

Isaac then asked all three for their £2 and escorted them all through another door which led to a corridor that had a number of doors. Outside one door there were two chairs. He stopped at this door and went into the room with the £6 and returned within a minute and said, "Right, her name is Isabella and who is first?"

Abdel decided that this was the time to embark on something that he hoped would make him a man and said, "I will be the first" and stepped through the door.

As he stood somewhat perplexed with the situation Isabella said, "Please come in, I am here to make you happy."

She was dressed in a white lace nightdress that reached her knee. She had ample breasts and she had long brown hair that rested on her shoulders. She was around 5' 3" in height. Abdel scanned the small room that had a bed, a small sink with a large water jug and a mirrored dressing table. A small chair was positioned in front of the dressing table.

"What is your name?" asked Isabella.

Abdel was still trying to take in the environment and appeared not to hear her.

She then said, "Can you speak English?"

This evoked a response and he said, "Oh yes and my name is Abdel

Malik Rahman and I am a Deck Rating on board the *Barat Star*."

Isabella giggled. "Why do you laugh at me? asked Abdel.

She realised that her laugh had offended Abdel and added, "I do not laugh at you, I am sorry. I am here to make you happy and make love to you Abdel."

"I have never been in love," replied Abdel.

"Do you not have a sweetheart, a lady where you live?" she asked and motioned him to sit on the bed.

Abdel sat on the bed and said, "I thought I had a girl, but she was promised to someone else in Karachi."

"Oh well, I will try and be very gentle with you, we have 10 minutes to make love," and she removed her nightdress and slid into the bed.

Abdel removed his shirt, trousers and underwear and joined her. She assumed a dominant role in the lovemaking, having realised that this was Abdel's first sexual encounter. They were entwined for 15 minutes; much to the annoyance of Pablo and Bobby, who were sitting outside.

As Abdel left the room he said, "I thank you for this lovemaking Isabella, I think you have made me a man."

Bobby was next and he had to wait until Isabella invited him in, adding another 5 minutes to the wait. Abdel just sat and reflected on what had just occurred. Pablo was constantly asking questions about his experience, but Abdel felt inclined to treasure the moment alone, he smiled and said, "You will find this lovemaking very good Pablo."

After Isabella had completed her performance, the three young men walked from the brothel with an air of satisfaction and Pablo said, "I did not wash after this lovemaking; I hope I do not get snotty cock."

"Well, you will have to wash when you get back on the ship," replied Bobby.

Before returning to the ship, Abdel got his new prayer mat and bought a copy of Great Expectations along with the Noble Qur'an, using some of his money he had left.

The following day, December 6th the captain summoned his officers for a briefing at 10.00 hours on their next trip.

> "Good morning gentlemen, I hope you are all rested and in good spirits. I do hope all those that have visited the fleshpots of Valletta have seen the MO Mr Bunyan for a short arm inspection."

No response from those gathered.

"I have an update on the war and in particular U Boat activity in the Mediterranean. Firstly, how the war effort is going. In November alone, 27 merchant ships and the destroyer Blanche have been sunk by magnetic mines. The Port of London was on the brink of closure. However, it transpires that the enemy made a big mistake in dropping one of these mines into the sea off Shoeburyness and it did not sink but washed up on the mudflats. The Royal Navy are now carefully examining the mine, which is apparently avoiding detection by our minesweepers."

"Thank god we are getting some success against these tyrants," said Bill Davison.

"Yes Bill, let's hope we have an answer to this menace," added the Captain and went on; "The Germans have made Malta their priority and they are well aware of the strategic importance of the island and its proximity to Italy and North Africa. It will undoubtedly get a lot worse and the War Office is expecting a heavy assault on Malta. So, to our next destination gentlemen. We are to return to Cardiff dock and take on military vehicles, oil and ammunition. On our way back, we are to dock in Gibraltar and take on supplies of fruit and vegetables for home."

"Do we get an escort back to Gib and Cardiff skipper?" asked Norman Baker.

"I am hopeful a Corvette will be made available for the trip, but I can't guarantee it Norman, I'm afraid."

"When do we sail captain?" asked Jack Cooper.

"In two days, Jack, are we ready Ron?"

"Yes captain, just some minor engineering work to complete," he replied.

"Alright gentlemen, keep the crew on their toes. Any negativity I want dealt with swiftly, be firm but fair. One other matter, the Navy boys want to test the Hedgehog. I will give that order, only if there is a U Boat threat and we do not have an escort."

"Any questions gentlemen?"

"Yes captain, Ranjit one of my lascars is not the full shilling, he has been sleeping while on shift and stumbles around," said Ron Braithwaite

"What's wrong with him?" he replied.

"I think he is drinking Palm Wine captain."

"Christ, that stuff makes you blind," added Ernie Stevenson

"Where in God's name did he get that from?" asked the captain.

"Not sure, I think he brought it on board when we were in Freetown in August."

"Well, deal with it and find his poison and throw it overboard. Make sure he is with you when you do it and dock his wages by a third. We cannot carry anyone on this ship. When we get to Gibraltar, inform the company and get him off my ship."

"Yes captain, will do," replied Ron Braithwaite.

As the officers left the captains quarters Bob McIntyre and Jack Cooper were discussing the impending trip to Gibraltar and Bob said,

"Well, at least we will be able to make good speed without a heavy cargo. It will make it a bit harder for the U Boats to track us and get a fix on us. What do you reckon Jack?"

"Don't bank on it Bob, these bastards hunt in packs remember. If we don't get an escort, we will have to use the Hedgehog. Don't forget we are well in range of North Africa and Italy and enemy aircraft are just looking for a sitting target."

The two men parted and went to their respective posts.

Down in the aft accommodation Abdel was fastening his prayer mat to his bunk when Pablo appeared fresh from his visit to the medical officer Mr Bunyan.

"Do you have this pox then Pablo?" asked Abdel.

"The Doctor said he thinks not Abdel, but he told me that some sailors have another way of washing after they made lovemaking with a woman," he replied.

"What is that Pablo?"

"He said that some sailors wash their private parts in their own piss, he said they believed this stops any infection. But he is not sure and he said, it is better if you do not have lovemaking with these women," replied Pablo

"I think the Doctor is a good man Pablo, he is wise in these things," added Abdel.

"Yes, he is wise and we must not do any more lovemaking until we are married Abdel."

Abdel looked at Pablo and thought to himself. That would be difficult based on the pleasure he had with Isabella.

Jim Shearer, George and Bobby joined them, along with Dennis Smith and Bob Hart the engineering ratings.

"How about a game of dominoes then boys?" said George.

"Good idea," said Jim and he got his bag of dominoes form his locker.

"Do you know that these dominoes have been all over the world. I bought them in Caracas in Venezuela ten years ago," he said.

"Wait a minute, you got torpedoed on the *Domelia* and you had to jump into the briny. The dominoes would be in your locker when the ship went down," said Dennis.

"Ah well, those dominoes mean a lot to me Dennis. So, I made sure I tied them to my belt and hung them on the inside of my trousers mate."

"Well, at least they have at least one wash then," joked Bob.

Abdel was not tempted to join the domino game and instead started to read *Great Expectations*. He had learned to underline any word he did not understand and within a minute he was asking; "What does this word explicit mean?"

"It means to be exact, positive, clear or to be true, now no more questions. Just underline any words and I will explain after our domino game is over Abdel," replied George.

"This I will do George," he said.

He then proceeded to read out loud: "*So I called myself Pip and came to be called Pip. I give Pirrip as my...*

"Abdel, we don't want to hear it, so shut the hell up," added Jim.

Abdel gave Jim a look of disgust and continued reading in silence.

As they all sat playing domino's or in Abdel case reading, Bob McIntyre came into the crew's quarters and said,

"Alright you shifty band sea dogs, I have some information for you. We will be leaving for Gibraltar in two days' time. We will pick up cargo there and return to Cardiff dock. Any questions?

"Will we be in a convoy then?" asked Jim Shearer.

"No, but we might get an escort, possibly a Corvette," he replied.

"Bloody hell, we will be a sitting duck," added Bob Hart.

"Well, we will have to be bloody vigilant on watch. Thankfully, we will be sailing without heavy cargo and let us hope our speed of 17 knots is enough to gets us to Gib safely and in one piece," he replied.

"Anything else?" he asked.

"Mr Mac sir, will I see my mother if we get shore leave in Gibraltar?" said Pablo.

"I don't know Pablo; the Captain has not said anything about shore leave. If he does you will be the first to know. Anyway, where does your mother live?"

"She lives in Cadiz with my sister," he replied.

"Not sure you will get permission for a trip to Cadiz from Gibraltar, Franco is an ally of that swine Hitler remember. Travel may be impossible from a British colony. We will wait and see," replied Bob McIntyre.

Bob Hart then added; "So where is your father then Pablo?"

"My father was killed fighting for the partisans against Franco three years ago. The Fascists would not even allow my mother to claim his body. We do not know where his body is," he replied.

"I did not know this Pablo; I am sorry for your loss," said Bob McIntyre.

"Thank you, Mr Mac, this why I joined the merchant navy. Now I am fighting Fascism, is that not right Mr Mac?"

"It is indeed Pablo and when this is all over, you will get back to Cadiz I am sure," he replied.

Bob McIntyre left the crew's quarters in a sombre mood and Abdel tried to concentrate on his book. But that proved to be difficult. Pablo's story of his father was a distraction and he picked up his Holy Qur'an and he was reassured when he read;

"Fight in the way of Allah against those who fight you and do not transgress, certainly God loves not the aggressors," (2:190)

On Friday, December 8th at 13.00 hours the Barat star left Malta bound for Gibraltar. The weather was good, with a Slight sea with waves of 3 feet and good visibility. Much to the disappointment of all concerned, an escort was not provided. There was a little air cover from Malta and there would more air cover once the ship was nearing its destination of Gibraltar.

In the last officers briefing the Captain had decided not to mention the threat from the German battleship *Admiral Graf Spee*, which had been cruising in the Atlantic and had sunk six merchant ships since October. As it turned out, a telegraph from the admiralty communicated that the Graf Spee was now moving in the South Atlantic and had sunk two more ships, the *Doris Star* and the *Tairoa*. Then on December 7th another steamer the *Streonshalh* was sunk.

At 17.00 hours on Sunday, December 10th action stations was called. The watch had spotted a conning tower some 500 yards to starboard. Abdel and his shipmates donned their life jackets and moved to their respective stations. Isaac Levinson, Nobby Calvert and Jack Henson manned the Hedgehog and began firing their bombs in an oval pattern at a distance of 250 yards. In total they fired 24 bombs without any direct contact. The U Boat had acted quickly and submerged before the Hedgehog could deploy its charges.

Thankfully, no more siting's were made on the voyage to Gibraltar and the *Barat Star* docked on Thursday, December 14th. Sadly, for Pablo he could not visit his mother in Cadiz, travel permits were not granted for anyone from Gibraltar, regardless of citizenship. The ship was loaded with food produce and embarked for Cardiff on December 18th. This time it was part of a small convoy of eight merchantmen, supported by two Corvettes and a Frigate. The *Barat Star* docked in Cardiff on Saturday, December 23rd.

Abdel would spend the Christmas in Liverpool, although like Bobby and the lascars he had never celebrated the festive period, being a Muslim. The *Barat Star* was given seven days to prepare for its next trip and many crew members took the opportunity to go home to visit families for Christmas. This did not apply to Chief Engineer, Ron Braithwaite, Engineering Officer, Stanley Hope, ratings Sam Brown and the six lascars. They remained on board for essential maintenance, as did Pablo, Abdel and Bobby.

The Captain John Sheed took the opportunity to go home to his wife in Blackheath, London for four days.

Liverpool, like many cities had to act early and prepare for the worst in 1939. Children were evacuated to other towns and villages. Petrol was very quickly rationed. With a maximum of 200 miles of fuel per month at 4s 2d per gallon. All households had to have blackout curtains and neon lights were switched off. Like a number of ports and industrial centres, Liverpool expected to be targeted with heavy bombing by the Luftwaffe.

Back on board the *Barat Star*, Abdel, Bobby and Pablo were enjoying some downtime. Abdel was reading Great Expectations, while Bobby and Pablo played dominoes.

Abdel was going through Jim Shearer's written explanations of all the words he had underlined in the book and he turned to his shipmates and said, "I could be this boy called Pip, he has no mother or father and he is being raised by his sister. He has a hard life and he has been attacked by a violent man, who has said he would tear his heart and liver out."

"Who has said that they would tear your liver out then?" asked Bobby.

"Nobody yet Bobby, but I have seen many violent things as a boy and I hope that God looks favourable on me."

"Well, God has been watching over you so far Abdel," added Pablo.

The mess door opened and in walked Sam Brown the engineering rating, along with two lascars.

"Hello men, how you all doing. We are bloody bored down below; we have done our chores and we have come up here for some relaxation. These two shipmates are Amjad and Rundu."

"Welcome Sam, do you play dominos?" asked Bobby.

"Yes, and I would be keen on joining your game fellas, are yee playing for money? he replied.

"Oh no, we do not gamble with money Sam," added Pablo.

"Niver mind, I'm ganna play anyway," he said.

Abdel had found Sam's dialect strange and said, "You have another type of English Sam, you speak different."

"Whey I, that's reet young man. I am a Sandancer from the north east of England. We tark proper ye nar," he replied laughing.

Both Amjad and Rundu sat with Abdel and they were intrigued with his book. They spoke English but neither of them could read and much to the annoyance of the domino group, Abdel decided to read out loud to his new audience.

Not surprisingly, Sam won the domino game; Pablo and Bobby decided to curtail the game and instead asked Sam about his life in the merchant navy.

"I have had an arful time so far boys. I have been shot at in a brothel in Cairo, beaten senseless in a pub in Glasgow and my last ship hit a fucking mine off Ramsgate and I ended up in the sea. But I am still here to tell ye arl the tale."

"Why are you called a Sandancer Sam?" asked Bobby.

"Well, because the toon is reet on the coast and we also have a good population of lascars and other folks of your colour in the toon," he replied.

Having heard this, Abdel joined in the conversation and said, "It is not easy to dance in sand."

"It is if you are pissed my man and I am partial to a pint or three, when I am on shore leave," he replied.

"Have you a wife back home Sam?" asked Pablo.

"Whey nor, niver had the time or the inclination. It's ganna take a woman with strong willpower to take me on fellas."

Sam went on to regale his shipmates of his exploits while at sea, for the next two hours. At 8pm Abdel went on watch until midnight, leaving his fellow sailors to enjoy Sam's reminisces.

On December 30th, new orders and intended destination were revealed to the officers by the Captain.

"I trust you all have had some relaxing time off with loved ones for a few days' gentlemen. But firstly, can I thank those who remained on board over the Christmas period. Thanks to you Ron and Stan, I have a bottle of Whisky for you both. Can you give my thanks to your ratings and Tom could you see that they all get two bottles of beer?"

"Yes Captain," replied Tom.

"Right let us get down to business, firstly the Engineering Report, Ron."

"Thanks Captain, everything is on song. We ran the power and have run the main engines and the bearings are fine. All temperatures and pressures were good on the eight pistons of the main engine. We are ready to sail Captain."

"Thank you, Ron," he replied.

The Captain the asked for each officer's report before informing those gathered of their next mission.

The only item for discussion was raised by the Doctor, David Bunyan when he said, "We have a problem with one of the navy ratings Captain. Able Seaman Ralph Smith, he broke his arm this morning falling from the bridge stairwell. We will need to replace him on the gunnery rota."

The Captain pondered this for a few seconds and then said, "Hang on, don't we have a deck rating who was on the *Domelia* that was trained on the Oerlikon. Is that not true Bob?"

"Yes captain, its Jim Shearer and he is good, he did very well and achieved a first-class accuracy report during training."

"That settles it then, inform him immediately of his new duties will you Bob"?

"Yes captain."

The Purser, Ernie Stevenson joined the conversation and added; "He will need a rise in pay captain, the navy boys are on an extra £2 per week."

"That's not a problem is it Ernie?"

"No no captain, I just thought it might be problematic if he chooses not to take up the post."

"Well, increase his beer ration, that ought to clinch it," added Jack Cooper.

"Will you put that to him Bob," said the captain.

Yes captain, he replied.

The captain then informed all those present of their next mission and said,

"Our new mission gentlemen takes us back across the Atlantic to Halifax. We set sail from Liverpool's on January 2nd with a cargo of steel and minerals. In addition, we have 12 passengers, they are naval engineers who have volunteered to go and help our allies."

"They must be keen or very well paid to volunteer for this trip," added Bill Davison.

"Now then Bill, there is a war on, you know. Let's afford them the respect they deserve," replied the captain.

The captain continued; "We will be joining Convoy OSN 221 just off Malin Head. We will not be sailing south through St. Georges Channel; the Germans have been dropping mines. Instead, we will make our way out from Liverpool north west round the emerald isle. Any questions gentlemen?"

"I gather we will have a naval escort?" asked Stanley Hope.

"Yes Stan, I am informed we will have three destroyers, a minesweeper and two corvettes in attendance for the voyage," he replied.

The captain closed the meeting with a quote from Lord Blyton's The Corsair and said;

> *"O"er the glad waters of the dark blue sea,*
> *Our thoughts as boundless, and our souls as free,*
> *Far as the breeze can bear, the billows foam,*
> *Survey our empire and behold our home.*

Finally, keep your men sharp and ensure that we as officers instil a spirit of determination. Thank you once again."

The *Barat Star* completed the return voyage to Halifax and back to Liverpool without any serious enemy encounters, save for a lone Stuker that had a go at one of the tankers in the convoy without hitting its target and was then promptly blown out of the sky by a sharp-eyed gunner on board one of the destroyers.

The ship continued to sail in convoy's in both the Atlantic and the Mediterranean during 1940 and 1941, with only a few skirmishes encountered. In June 1942 U Boat activity was inflicting heavy losses to merchant shipping. A total of 700.000 tons of allied shipping was lost worldwide, a staggering 144 vessels in one month. America entered the war after the attack at Pearl Harbour in December of 1941. This allowed the USA to provide air cover from the eastern seaboard.

The effect of this was to slowly reduce the losses of ships in the Atlantic. However, the majority of shipping was lost in the Atlantic, accounting for 90% of merchantmen worldwide.

In July 1942 the *Barat Star* was involved in supplying the allied forces in North Africa and departed Toxteth Dock in Liverpool with a cargo of ammunition and military vehicles bound for Libya.

The ship was part of a small convoy that included one destroyer, one frigate and one corvette as escort. The convoy were 300 miles east of the Azores when they were attacked by a U Boat.

It was 2pm on a warm July afternoon. The weather was good with a moderate wind and visibility was good, as Abdel stood at his watch on the forecastle surveying the horizon. What he could not see was that astern of the *Barat Star*, some 5000 yards south west of the convoy, a U Boat just below the surface, was lining up two torpedoes.

A corvette had picked up the U Boats signal and was alerting all ships of its presence when the first torpedo hit the *Barat Star* on the port side below the water line of the poop deck. Abdel was thrown in the air from the impact and landed strewn on a cable holder. He was dazed but managed to get to his feet. All hell broke out with sirens sounding and actions stations called throughout the convoy. The second torpedo again hit astern, but this time it destroyed the rudder and the poop deck was severely damaged. Fire quickly erupted and boats were launched. Abdel sought refuge behind the capstan as chunks of metal started flying through the air from an explosion in the aft bulkheads. Almost immediately the ship began to settle by the stern, she was rapidly taking on water and going down. As normal, Abdel had his life jacket on and looked to see if he could locate a boat and spotted Jim, George and Pablo lowering a boat on the starboard amidships. He ran to lend a hand and climbed aboard with his shipmates. Jim was bleeding heavily from a wound from his arm, a large amount of flesh had been torn off from his elbow to his forearm.

George was swearing and cursing with words Abdel had never heard as the boat hit the water. Pablo was trying to stem the flow of blood from Jim's arm with a sleeve of his shirt he had torn off. Jim was struggling to remain conscious and George grabbed him and shouted; "It is your old mucker George, Jim stay awake you swine, you are not going to let these bastards beat you. Look at me." Then he realised that a shard of steel had embedded itself in Jim's thigh, resulting in massive blood loss. Jim never spoke but gave George the faintest of smiles before closing his eyes.

George knew Jim had passed away and stood up in the boat and with his arms outstretched and screamed; "If there is a God, why oh why has it got to be like this. Tell me why?"

He then just fell on his knees sobbing.

The scene around them was carnage, bodies in the water and cries from men drowning or being burnt alive; and to Abdel's horror his friend Bobby was one of them, what was left of his body was lying face up. There was nothing below his waist, save for his intestines which were still attached to his upper body.

On seeing this Abdel vomited over the side of the boat. Other boats were in the water but only Jack Cooper, Bob McIntyre and gunners Isaac, Paddy and Nobby were the only other survivors. Twenty-two men were lost including the Captain John Sheed. The men in the engine room died instantly from the first torpedo. Within 5 minutes the *Barat Star* was half submerged vertically, stern first. She sank amid a sea of oil and flames. They were no other survivors and the U Boat also sank a tanker and another freighter before escaping.

The survivors from the two boats clambered up the scrambling nets of a corvette and were escorted to the medic for first aid. Not a word was spoken for over an hour as they sat and drank hot tea. Jim Shearer's body was lifted aboard by three naval ratings.

Finally, George spoke and said, "I have had enough of this shit, I can't go on pretending, only luck has kept us alive. I want to go home."

He started to sob again and Isaac Levinson said, "Listen, you are alive, we are alive. We must thank the Lord our God and pray we live to see our families after all this is over."

Pablo genuflected and Abdel replied; "When will this war be over? God has saved me twice already."

"Then he will save you again, and again," added Isaac.

George looked up with tears cascading down his face and said, "No he will not, we are destined to die at the hand of these Nazi bastards, it will happen."

The room fell silent and those present sat and contemplated their lot. The Corvette remained on escort duty until the convoy approached Gibraltar, where she docked and handed over the remaining crew members of the *Barat Star* to the care of the British East India Company on July 27th 1942.

George Hollcroft was discharged of his duties on medical grounds and returned to England. Both officers Bob McIntyre and Jack Cooper asked for all survivors be kept together on their next commission, as a mark of respect for their endeavours.

This was granted along with a period of leave that would last for three weeks. Their next ship was undergoing a refit in Gibraltar and it would not be ready until August 18th. She was the Talmahna and she was being converted to a Troop Ship to be deployed in the Mediterranean. She was a coal burner with a maximum speed of 16 knots and had a gross weight of 9120 tons and could carry 2.100 troops.

CHAPTER ELEVEN

While Abdel and Pablo were waiting for their new ship to be readied a huge task force was deployed to escort a much need convoy to Malta. It was code named Operation Pedestal and involved 14 merchantmen, 2 aircraft carriers, 4 battleships, 7 cruisers and no less than 32 destroyers. The convoy suffered heavy losses to the merchant ships, along with some losses to escorts. Only five out of fourteen merchant ships made it to Malta. Warships lost included an aircraft carrier, two cruisers and a destroyer. The Germans had inflicted serious damage to the convoy. However, vital supplies did get through to the beleaguered island.

With the Americans thrown into the conflict after Peral Harbour, they embarked on a massive ship building programme never seen before. Thanks to the innovative designer Henry J. Kaiser, the Liberty Ship was born. In shipyards in California and Oregon ships were being assembled and launched in only 10 days. This would eventually tip the balance of power in the allies' favour as the war in the Atlantic progressed.

Thanks to contacts established by the company's agent in Gibraltar, Pablo managed to get to Cadiz to see his mother and had a week's furlough before returning to his new commission. All crew members were asked to report for duty aboard the Talmahna on August 16th at 11.00 hours.

This was a totally new crew for the ship and ratings were congregated in the poop deck accommodation for their initial briefing and work details. Bob McIntyre was promoted to Senior Deck Officer and Jack Cooper would be taking up his previous post as Chief Officer.

The Captain was Hamish F. McDonald a Scotsman from Falkirk, it was his third command in four years, having been bombed twice by the Luftwaffe. The remaining officers were;

Alan Wainwright - Navigation Officer.
Tom J. Halliwell – Chief Engineer.
Harry K. Morrison – Purser.
Malcolm N. Bruce – Engineering Officer.
Kenneth G. Baxter – Steward.
Dr Peter S. Davidson – Medic.

In addition to Abdel and Pablo, the deck ratings included 4 lascars and a Scotsman William Patterson.

While the ratings were getting acquainted in the poop deck, the captain was addressing his officers in his quarters. Captain McDonald was a giant of a man 6" 4" in height with a full set and thick ginger hair, which caused his cap to sit precariously upon his head. When he welcomed his officers, he shook each by the hand and smiled revealing two gold teeth. He motioned them all to sit down and began; "Welcome men, thank you for being prompt and might I add, well turned out. Firstly, I would like to be addressed as Hamish, not skipper, master or captain if you don't mind. We are all captains on this tub and masters of our responsibilities. As you are no doubt aware our cargo is of the human kind, we are first and foremost a troop ship, with a capacity for over 2000 passengers. In this regard we are a significant target for the enemy and therefore we have Royal Navy personnel aboard to man the armaments. As yet they have not arrived, but I expect them later today."

"There will be seven able seamen serving as gunners for the duration of service. They will report and take orders from myself, the Senior Deck Officer, Chief Officer and the Navigation Officer, when required. I believe all the crew have been given new Articles of Agreement under the Merchant Shipping Act. I am led to understand that we are ready for sea, is that the case Tom?"

"Yes captain, sorry Hamish, I beg your pardon," replied Tom.

"It's fine Tom, thanks. So, we are to set off for Cardiff in two days' time, where we will take on fuel and 2000 troops bound for North Africa. We will be in Convoy ONS 17 naval escorts including minesweepers, cruisers, frigates, destroyers, 2 battleships and corvettes. Air cover will be scarce once we leave the Bay of Biscay and we will be open to attack from the Luftwaffe as usual. Our convoy will include three more troop ships, tankers and an assortment of merchant vessels. Needless to say, that U Boats will be our greatest threat and I know some of you have been at the sharp end of this nightmare. We must show resolve and have a confident approach to our mission. Remember, we will have young men aboard, some of whom have not seen any action and therefore they have not experienced the horrors of war.

"When I have closed this briefing, I would like you to speak to your men and reassure them that they will be fulfilling a vital role in defeating the enemy. Do you have any questions men?"

"Do we have any cargo for the trip to Cardiff Hamish?" asked Jack Cooper.

"Well, not as such other than fuel and coal; however, we will be taking passengers in the form of troops injured in North Africa. We will have some 60 soldiers on board Jack, their injuries are not life-threatening Peter, before you ask. If there are no more questions men, I would like to draw attention to that quotation in that frame on the wall behind you. It is from the Bard of Scotland, Robbie Burns. I find it inspirational."

All present turned around to read;

Till a" the seas gang dry, my dear,
And the rocks melt wi" the sun;
I will luv thee still, my dear,
While the sands o" life shall run.

The Captain added that he wanted to speak to the crew before sailing.

Abdel was again given watch duties with an emphasis as an observational role. After Bob McIntyre had spoken to his crew members, Abdel got into a conversation with William Patterson. This proved a challenge for both Pablo and Abdel. They could barely understand what he was saying. Many times, they had to ask him what he had just said. This was dealt with pretty quickly by Billy, as he preferred to be called; when he said, "Noo then boys, I will need to slow my accent doon, do ya ken what a mean?"

This statement of intent was totally lost in translation and Pablo and Abdel just looked at each other in confusion as Billy roared with laughter.

The Royal Navy ratings arrived only three hours before the ship was due to leave, much to the annoyance of the captain. He summoned them to his quarters and gave them a real going over for their late arrival. As they were getting their dressing down. One rating made a fatal mistake when he said, "Well skip, we was stuck in a bar and we was in a bit of a punch up with some locals you see."

The captain went berserk and said, "Don't you ever call me skip again, that is a name for a fucking dog. It's captain to you Sonny Jim and don't you forget it. I have a good mind to fine the fucking lot of you. Now get your arses up on deck and I want to see those guns gleaming and good enough to eat your dinner off. Do you understand?"

In perfect unison, they all said, "Yes captain."

"Right, now fuck off," he replied.

At 14.00 hours on August 18th, the Talmahna eased out of Gibraltar and joined a small convoy of ships bound for England. As escorts they had a corvette and two frigates. The voyage was without incident and no enemy action was encountered. The ship docked in Cardiff at 1800 hours on August 22nd 1942. The following day coal and oil were taken on board, along with 2000 troops and their equipment. They spent three days in Cardiff and the captain granted shore leave for four hours on August 24th, to all except the navy gunners. Abdel was able to buy yet another prayer mat and copy a of the Holy Qur'an, his third so far.

The Talmahna set sail for North Africa on August 25th under the cover of darkness at 21.00 hours to join Convoy ONS 17 south of Mizen Head, Ireland. Three more troop ships sailed from Toxteth Dock in Liverpool to join the convoy. In total some 8000 soldiers were on route to North Africa with a heavy escort of 35 warships including 2 battleships, 5 cruisers, 12 destroyers, 7 Corvettes, 4 frigates and 5 minesweepers. Barrage balloons were trailed from many of the warships to counteract enemy aircraft. The cables would slice through aircraft fuselage and they offered a degree of protection during the early stages of the voyage.

Having made headway for some 12 hours the convoy came under attack from six Junkers 87 bombers, more commonly known as Stukas. Each plane was carrying a 1000 lb bomb and four 100 lb bombs. Abdel had spotted them on the horizon some 5000 yards south west on the port bow. Action Stations were activated and the gunners set up for deployment on the 4-inch guns and Oerlikons fore and aft. Despite heavy fire from the destroyers and the battleship two direct hits were made on one of the troop ships from Liverpool. A 1000 lb bomb hit amidships and a 100 lb bomb exploded in the bridge. Some of the troops managed to get on deck and jump into the sea before the ship heels over and sinks. It took only 6 minutes for the ship to disappear below the surface, taking some 1860 troops to a watery grave.

A small number of survivors were plucked from the sea by a corvette. The stukas continued their assault without inflicting any further serious damage to the convoy. One stuka was shot down by a destroyer as it turned to make a pass for another attack. Thankfully, there were no attacks or sightings of U Boats during the trip. The convoy completed the voyage without any further losses and docked at Benghazi, Libya on September 2nd.

The captain agreed on some much need shore leave and granted a 24-hour furlough for the crew, including the Navy Gunners.

While in Benghazi, Abdel and Pablo decided to go for a trip around the town. Some of the buildings were totally destroyed, due to the bombing which had occurred. However, they wandered around and Abdel found a mosque which he entered and prayed, while Pablo waited outside. When Abdel reappeared, they found a street café where they sat and enjoyed a coffee.

They sat and they talked of their life as merchant seamen and Pablo said, "Abdel I am weary of this life. When I saw my mother in Cadiz, she begged me not to return to the ship. Do you think we will survive? So many of our shipmates have gone and we will never see them again."

Abdel sat silent for a while and finally said, "I have prayed for their souls Pablo. I have seen many wicked things Pablo and I am always afraid that I will die. Our friends on the *Barat Star*; Bobby, Jim, Sam, Bob, Dennis and the poor lascars in the engine room have all died, this makes me angry and sad."

The two sat and talked of the things that they had witnessed and what the future might hold for them. Before they knew it, the sun was setting and it was time to get back to their home, the Talmahna.

The war was spreading throughout the globe, in Europe, Africa and Asia. After Pearl Harbour, the ally's chances of victory had strengthened with the USA now involved. However, the Japanese were proving to be a powerful adversary and since 1941 Japan had swept across South East Asia at an alarming rate.

The Talmahna left Benghazi on September 7th bound for Gibraltar. She had some 125 injured soldiers on board, for them the war was over. Further trips across the Mediterranean to Malta, Egypt and Libya were undertaken until to July 1943. The ship was in Gibraltar from July 9th for repairs and some modifications to bulkheads. Pablo got the opportunity to visit his mother again, taking five days leave.

Abdel spent some of his time writing letters to Karachi and to South Africa. He had now improved his literacy skills to write in both Pashto and English. In return, Hakim had also enhanced his communication skills and his letters to Abdel were also in English. Unlike his cousin back in Karachi. Abdullah had to get help from Osman, who wrote his reply for him in English. Rahman's was very profitable it seems, Abdullah said it was down to the war. He did say that there was revolution in the air and many influential people were calling for independence from India.

Meanwhile in South Africa, Hakim was enjoying a prosperous life, he now had three shops and he was soon to be married. He had opened two more shops, one being a Gentlemen's Barbers and the other a Haberdashery shop. His Chandlers was doing very well and he had a big house not far from the port. He said that Abdel must come and visit after the war and he would pay for his travel. This gave Abdel a sense of reason and he used this to motivate himself to look forward with hope.

As part of the maintenance duties Abdel was handed the painting job topside along with two of the new lascars, Abeid and Sardar both hailed from Chittagong in the East of India. Their English was very good and they had been together on many ships for the last ten years. Most of their trips were in the far east, travelling to China, Japan, Burma, Thailand, Australia and New Zealand. They were older than Abdel, both being 34 years old.

After their work duty all three would join the others in the poop mess and discuss what the future had in store for them.

Many such meetings involved discussions about the ship and the Captain Mr McDonald. On one such occasion one of the navy gunners Paddy White, Chalky to the rest of the crew, announced that; "That bastard the captain, will get us all killed."

Abeid asked him; "Why do you say these things Chalky? He is a good man I think."

"Listen here boy's, I know of a sailor that sailed with this guy and he said he was a mad scotch git who was more concerned about having the ship shining like a tanner on a darky's arse, than being ready for action stations," he replied.

Abdel was confused by this description of the Captain and said, "What do you mean Chalky?"

"What I am saying is, he wants the ship to look like a bleeding palace, not a merchant tub. Polishing guns and painting everything that does not move, won't matter a jot when the fucking Germans send their Stuka's and U Boats to sink us."

"Don't listen to his shite, he is always winging and moaning," added Derek Small his fellow gunner.

"Go and boil your head Derek," replied Chalky.

General banter continued as those gathered spoke of their hopes and aspirations once the war had ended. Deck rating Alan Pickering spoke of the war and how it would have a lasting effect on many when he said, "This is truly a World War and it is down to the ego of one man, Adolf Hitler. It is power that has reared its ugly head. Like Alexander the Great, Genghis Khan, Tamerlane, Ivan the Terrible and Napoleon, power is a drug which fuels fear in people. This dictator must be stopped, Mussolini and the Emperor of Japan have chosen to join this fascist despot. Many have lost their lives and many more will die, until this lunatic is defeated, but he must be eliminated."

"Damn right, Alan," said Derek.

"Will the allies win soon Alan?" asked Sardar.

"I bloody hope so and the sooner the better. I have a wife and child back home, who I have never seen. He will be two years old now," he replied.

"What is his name?" asked Abdel.

"Alan James, after his father and grandfather," said Alan.

"What family do you have Abdel?" asked Abeid.

"I have a brother Hakim in Durban in South Africa and a cousin Abdullah in Karachi in India. I hope to visit my brother after the war and also go back to Karachi to see how Abdullah is prospering with Rahman's Chandlers and the Tea House," replied Abdel.

"Alright you lot what about bringing some humour to the conversation," added Derek.

"Come on then, your first," said Alan.

"What do you say to a scouse in a suit?"

"When is the court date?" said Derek.

Blank looks from everyone except Chalky and Alan, who laughed along with Derek.

"I shouldn't be laughing, I'm from Bootle. But its bloody spot on," added Chalky.

"Right my turn now," said Alan.

"I was waiting for a bus one day and I noticed a bloke with a dog on a lead. I asked him if it bites? He said no, so I bent down to stroke it and the bastard dog bit me. I said to the bloke, I thought you said your dog doesn't bite. He said, it's not my fucking dog."

Both Derek and Chalky howled in laughter, Abdel, Abeid and Sardar joined in but out of sheer ignorance. They had no idea what was funny about being bitten by a dog.

"This lot are laughing, but they don't know why," joked Chalky.

"Now it is my turn, listen to this. I once shot an elephant in my pyjamas. How he got in my pyjamas I will never know."

Before anymore jokes could be relayed a shout from the poop hatch. It was Bob McIntyre.

"Everyone on deck pronto, the captain wants to speak to the crew," he said.

When everyone was assembled on deck a roll call was carried out by Chief Officer, Jack Cooper. Pablo's name was called and Bob McIntyre replied with; "He is on shore leave Jack."

"Thanks Bob," he replied.

He continued and called out Gupta Rawhindi, no response.

Then a voice from the back;

"He has got de sheets sir."

"Who said that, step forward," he replied.

The engineering rating Wasim appeared and said,

"It was me sir, Gupta is not well sir. He sheet all over his bunk sir."

Laughter permeated throughout the crew and Jack said

"Are you aware of this Malcolm?"

"No, I am not Jack, but he will have more than his bunk to worry about when I see him," replied Malcolm.

The captain remained stern faced throughout this amusing exercise and when the roll call was over, he began his discourse.

"It is important to see humour as a release from the worry and tension we have to contend with gentlemen. I share your concerns and I fully appreciate what you are going through in these troubled times. The war is being fought on many fronts and our mission is to support our armed forces in ultimately defeating the enemy. I know many of you have already experienced harrowing and distressful encounters and lost many friends. The threat of attack from above, the surface and below never diminishes and we must be vigilant. It is vital that we maintain high standards of efficiency and discipline.

"We are dependent on each other gentlemen and I have every confidence in your unwavering loyalty to this ship. All I ask of you is that you trust in my resolve and the steadfast determination of all the officers, as we discharge our duties. We are all shipmates and I thank you for your continued cooperation. As a measure of my gratitude, you will each receive a tot of rum and a bottle of beer when you return to the mess. For those of you who do not imbibe in alcohol, I have asked the Purser to award you an extra £1 in your pay for this week. Thank you and may God be with you all."

As the crew returned to their respective duties or rest periods, the captain called for all officers to a briefing in his quarters for details of their next voyage.

As the officers took their seats the captain said, "Well gentlemen, how did you think my chinwag with the crew went?"

"Very honest and it seemed to go down well Hamish," replied Alan Wainwright.

The officers nodded in agreement and Bob McIntyre added; "I think you touched a nerve there Hamish, it will have kept them focussed I hope."

"Yes Bob, that was my intention," he replied.

"That was funny about Gupta though Hamish, how you kept a straight face I don't know," said Jack Cooper.

"Damn right Jack, it was funny. I hope the silly sod gets well soon; we need all hands in good health," replied Hamish.

"I will give him something to dry him up Hamish," added Peter Davidson.

"Concrete might do the job," joked Malcolm Bruce.

"Right then gentlemen, our orders for the next trip. We will leave Gibraltar bound for Tunisia on August 23rd. Our refit will be completed by then. The refit and modifications to two bulkheads have been carried in order that we can take both cargo and troops."

"On arrival at the port of Tunis we will take on a cargo of military vehicles in the form of Jeeps, Staff Cars, Half Tracks, Mark III Valentine Tanks and Churchill Bridgelayers. The troops will be the 5th Battalion Sherwood Foresters. In total we will have 800 soldiers on board. The destination is Malta, we will dock in Valetta. The troops and military hardware will then be transferred to ships for landing at Salerno. This information has come direct from the admiralty and as you might have gathered this is part of a large-scale invasion of Italy.

"Both British and American forces will be advancing at various destinations on the Italian mainland and Sicily. It transpires that the Italians are on the brink of capitulation and ready to agree to an armistice. Allied forces will land in Sicily, Calabria, Anzio and Salerno. Once Salerno has been secured, we will be delivering troops and cargo straight to Salerno, any questions so far gentlemen?"

"Will we be getting grief from the Italian Navy on route to Malta then Hamish?" asked Tom Halliwell.

"I have had no details on that one Tom, but I suspect what's left of the Italian Navy, will be reluctant to engage us. We will have a massive escort of British and American warships for this, as well as air support," he replied.

"I bet the bastards have mined the harbours around Salerno though," added Bob.

"Well, that's when the minesweepers will have to do their bit Bob. Dare I say it gentlemen, that we may be seeing the beginning of the end of this war. The German army is fighting on all fronts in Europe and it looks like we might have secured North Africa. It only remains to be seen if the Japanese throw the towel in or continue alone. However, can I ask you to be economical with your information when talking to the crew, we must avoid any complacency. Have you any more questions gentlemen?"

No further questions were forthcoming and the captain stood and walked over to his cabinet and produced a bottle of rum, along with a tray of glasses. He poured each officer a drink and asked them to stand.

"Gentlemen, I would ask you to raise your glass to Great Britain, King George, the Talmahna and all who sail on her."

Back on deck Abdel was finishing his painting duties and he took a break to look out to seaward and he tried to imagine what the world would be like after this war was over.

CHAPTER TWELVE

The Talmahna left Gibraltar at 15.00 hours on August 23rd. She was joined by three other merchantmen and rendezvoused with their escorts 120 miles west of the Isle of Alboran. The escort's comprised of 2 destroyers, 2 cruisers, 1 frigate, 4 minesweepers and 2 corvettes. The Talmahna sailed into Tunis on August 26th, without encountering any enemy action during the 700-mile voyage. The ship was alongside for some seven day's while the military hardware was loaded. There was a delay in getting the troops on board and they were eventually all aboard on September 1st. A further delay, awaiting specific invasion plans meant that the ship did not leave Tunis until September 5th. During the 16-hour voyage to Malta a number of the troops relaxed on deck and got into conversation with some of the crew. Abdel sat with a few soldiers enjoying a smoke after his watch was finished.

"Well, have you been bombed yet asked one soldier?"

"Oh yes sir, I have been sunk twice and I have lost many friends," he replied.

"Yes, we have lost many friends in our regiment. I will be glad when this is all over and we can all go home," said the soldier.

"Where do live in England?" asked Abdel.

"I am Corporal James F. Peterkin of the Sherwood Foresters and I come from South Shields," he replied.

"Do you know a man called Sam Brown? He was killed on the *Barat Star*. He was from your South Shields I think," said Abdel.

"South Shields is a big place but no, I don't know him," he replied.

The two young men talked for some time about their experiences in the war. Corporal Peterkin had served in North Africa and in Belgium before his regiment were selected for this latest campaign.

"Have you a wife in South Shields?" asked Abdel.

"Yes, her name is Catherine. I also have also four sisters and another brother, who is in North Africa fighting in the western desert. Do you have family?" he said.

Abdel told him of his brother in Durban and his cousin in Karachi and his hopes of seeing them both again soon. The conversation came to an end when Bob McIntyre arrived and told Abdel to check all the winches and derricks for lubrication.

"Yes sir Mr Mac," and he bid farewell to the Corporal.

Bob asked the Corporal if he thought the war would be over soon.

"Bloody good question mate, I hope so. I have had enough now," he said.

"We have all had enough, anyway good luck in Italy," said Bob

"Thanks mate," he said.

The ship docked in Valetta and unloaded its cargo of men and machines. The captain gave the crew a 24-hour shore leave.

The Talmahna continued to ferry troops and cargo to Malta as the invasion of Italy gained momentum all through 1943. In 1944, after another refit, the ship was involved in supplying much needed aid to Greece. Although still a threat, the U Boat menace had diminished and the trips to Greece were achieved without any major incidents at sea. Abdel longed to see his brother in South Africa and his cousin in Karachi and in October, he asked Mr Mac if he would speak to the captain for an extended leave.

"Not a chance Abdel, as long as the war goes on. You won't get any long-term leave."

"So, Mr Mac I will have to wait until the war ends, I think yes," he replied.

"That is it Abdel and when it does happen you can ask the company for leave and a change of contract. That could be anywhere in the world," said Bob.

"Thank you, Mr Mac sir," he said.

"Abdel, when the hell are you going to call me Bob?"

"You will always be Mr Mac sir,"

Bob laughed and said, "Well Abdel, I have been called a lot worse over the years."

"Yes, Mr Mac but you are a good man"

"Praise indeed, now get your arse up on the forecastle. You're on watch."

As 1944 drew to a close the Talmahna sailed to and from Gibraltar to various ports in the Mediterranean including, Valetta, Alexandria, Beirut, Tunis and Famagusta. While in Gibraltar in January 1945, the ship was returned to a merchant vessel without armaments. The guns were dismantled and lifted onto the dock. The Royal Navy gunners were transferred to other ships and the bulkheads returned to their former location. On May 14th the U Boats finally surrendered, but the war in the far east continued with the Japanese holding out on remote islands and refusing to surrender.

On April 30th 1945, Adolf Hitler committed suicide in his bunker and Germany surrendered on May 7th thus ending the war in Europe. The struggle in the seas had taken a terrible toll on ships and men. In total 2.426 British Merchant ships were sunk, with a human cost of 29.180 seamen lost.

"As always, their spirit was indomitable, their professionalism unchallenged. The price they paid for their bravery and dedication was horrendous."

The end of the war brought about a change in circumstances for Abdel. On June 12th 1945 he met with the British East India Company agent Mr

Gordon Anderson in Gibraltar. He informed Abdel that the company could offer him a posting on various routes. Abdel was granted two month's leave in order to see his brother Hakim and his cousin Abdullah.

Abdel decided to wait and see how his visits to South Africa and Karachi influenced his future. While in Gibraltar, he spoke to both Hakim and Abdullah by telephone and arranged to sail to Durban first, then to Karachi. With the help of Mr Anderson he managed to get tickets for places on board two merchant vessels, one bound for Durban on June 27th and another from Durban to Karachi on July 28th, arriving in Karachi on August 4TH. The same ship would bring him back to Gibraltar from Karachi on August 18$^{th.}$ Mr Anderson only took a token sum of £15 from Abdel as mark of gratitude for his good work on the Talmahna. This left Abdel with £24 left as his emolument, he had his personal possessions with in his knapsack, which amounted to his prayer mat, the Holy Qur'an, spare clothes, a notebook and pen and a copy of The Man in The Iron Mask.

Abdel boarded the Karanpo on June 27th, only this time as a passenger not a seaman. The ship had other passengers on board, bound for Durban. The ship was built in 1931 and had accommodation for 60 passengers and a top speed of 18 knots. Once on board he located his cabin. He felt a strange sense of foreboding as he lay on his bunk and listened to other passengers entering their cabins. He had said goodbye to his shipmates before leaving and he felt alone for the first time in a long time. Pablo had stayed with the Talmahna, along with most of the crew. Both Abeid and Sardar had decided to return to Chittagong and Mr Mac left the merchant navy and went back to England. Abdel's voyage to Durban would take 15 days covering 7.000 miles.

The ship would pass through the Suez Canal, south through the Red Sea, east through the Gulf of Aden, then south down the east coast of Africa to Durban. He would arrive in Durban around July 11th. The ship had a total of 51 passengers, all bound for Durban. The cargo included, spices, wheat, barley, farm machinery and timber. At the age of 27 Abdel was now looking forward to seeing his family for the first time in nine years. He felt happy and looked forward to the next chapter in his life.

During the voyage to Durban Abdel had made acquaintances with a few other passengers. He struck up a friendship with one young man in particular. His name was Rueben Solomon a Jew, who had escaped from Poland in 1942. He was going to South Africa to work for his uncle in his jewellers' shop in Durban. Both his parents and his sister were taken from their Warsaw home when he was out looking for food, he never saw them again. He was 17 years old and somehow evaded the Germans and eventually managed to get a ship to Gibraltar from Gdansk.

They had many things in common, they had both experienced violence, hardship and sorrow and this seemed to create a bond between them. Rueben spoke good English, having attended a good school in Warsaw, which had a curriculum that encouraged foreign languages. They exchanged anecdotes of their life and spoke of their hopes for the future. On one such occasion the topic of romance was broached and Abdel asked; "Have you been with a lady yet Rueben?"

"No, I have not Abdel, before my parents were taken my father had plans for me to marry Ester Rosenzweig. She was the daughter of the shoemaker that lived near us."

"Do you know where your family was taken Rueben?"

"Many people were taken Abdel, they were sent to concentration camps such Auschwitz, Belson, Treblinka and Buchenwald. I will never see them again; I have been informed by the Jewish Council that they will have been killed. If by some chance they have survived the council have my details and I live in hope that one day I might see them again. I also have an uncle in Krakow who survived and I keep in contact with him."

"This evil man Hitler has caused so much fear and sorrow, it makes me so sad," replied Abdel. Abdel returned to the topic of romance and said, "So this girl, the daughter of the shoemaker. Why did you not marry her Rueben?"

"She was also taken on the same day as my parents and I never saw her again," he replied.

"Have you been with a lady Abdel?"

Abdel considered his answer for a few seconds and said, "I am not sure she was a lady Rueben, I had to give her money. I will tell you this, it was a very good feeling to make love."

"Where did this happen?

"It happened in Malta and her name was Isabella. She was very kind, she also made love to my friends Pablo and Bobby. I think this was her job and I was told that there are many women like this in ports around the world."

"I am twenty years old; I have lots of time to choose a wife Abdel," he replied.

They continued to meet and have their meals together as the voyage progressed. They would often stand on deck and enjoy the sights from the ship as they sailed through the Suez Canal, the Red Sea and round the horn of Africa down into the Indian Ocean to Durban.

The Karanpo docked in Durban at 3pm on July 12th. Rueben and Abdel exchanged addresses before saying goodbye on the wharf.

As Abdel turned to make his way out of the port, he heard his name being called from a throng of people near the Harbour Masters Office. Then he recognised Hakim, he rushed to him, embraced him and said, "Hakim I thought I would never ever see you again."

Abdel released his hold on his brother and Hakim said, "Little brother is not so little any more, you are a man Abdel. God be praised."

The two brothers left the wharf and made their way to a waiting motor car.

"This is my car Abdel, get in," said Hakim.

Abdel was in a state of bewilderment and said, "This is yours Hakim, you must be a wealthy man."

"Yes Abdel, I am a successful businessman in Durban. Even the whites say good morning to me," he replied.

Abdel had a puzzled look on his face and said, "Whites, I do not understand Hakim."

"There a lot of things you will not understand about South Africa Abdel, just get in my car."

Abdel climbed into the passenger seat next to Hakim and they drove away from the port. There journey had only been some ten minutes, when Hakim stopped outside a row of buildings. Hakim said, "Here we are Abdel."

Abdel got out of the car and was nearly wiped out by a car passing at some speed. He just managed to evade its side mirrors, but it was a close shave. Hakim shouted; "Always look behind you before you open the car door Abdel."

Abdel turned towards the buildings and then saw *Rahman's Chandlers.* The sign also read *"World Trader to The Maritime Industry."*

The building covered three floors and it was much larger than the Karachi shop, as Abdel stood and took in the façade Hakim said, "Well my brother what do you think?"

"It is most wonderful Hakim; you must have many customers."

"I have many customers Abdel, one is your employer The British East India Company. I am a very important businessman in Durban. I also have a big house not far from here. I will take you there soon, that is where you will stay."

"You said in your letter that you have a barbershop and a haberdashery."

"Oh yes brother, the Barbershop is on St Andrews Street and the Haberdashery is in Smith Hall Street. But first I want you to see my house on Avondale Road. Before this, you must enjoy tea and cake in Rahman's and relax after your long journey."

They went into the store and were welcomed by a young boy.

"This is Mapo Abdel, he will bring you your refreshments. He works for me as my personal assistant here in Rahman's. I have three other employees in this store called Atta, Benjamin and Mohammad. You will meet them soon."

He then asked Mapo to bring the refreshments and find Atta, Benjamin and Mohammad. Within a minute the three employees arrived and greeted Abdel with a hand shake and expressed their pleasure in meeting Hakim's brother.

Atta then asked; "Did you have a bad time in the war at sea?"

Abdel said that he had some very worrying moments and that he had lost some friends. Hakim interrupted, waved them away and said, "Go now and tend to your chores, my brother is tired from his long voyage."

All three scurried away leaving Mapo to pour the tea. As they took their seats at a table prepared with a tray of breads and cakes, Abdel said; "Hakim you said in your letter that you planned to get married."

Hakim smiled and replied; "Abdel, that is the news I want now to share with you. I am to be married next week. I have waited for you to arrive to be able to confirm this wonderful news. This means you can be present."

Abdel embraced his brother and asked; "What is her name and where is she from Hakim?"

"Her name is Rahmina Khan, she is 24 years old and her father has arranged this Nikah (wedding). He is a business friend of mine in the Coal Export Business. Their family moved here from Hyderabad twelve years ago."

"Abdel looked surprised and said, "She is ten years younger than you Hakim and remember you are *"peshtane,"* Hakim and wedding means *"wade."*

"Yes, and she is beautiful Abdel. I will always be *"pectate"* but we all follow the teachings of the Noble Qur'an. Sadly, you cannot see her until our wedding day. You will be one of my witnesses replied.

"I have no clothes for this wedding, Hakim. Abdel," he replied.

"Do not worry, I will see that you have all you need. I have arranged for both of us to go to Mr Patel's tomorrow to choose our material and jewellery."

"Do you have to pay for this wedding?" he asked.

"I have agreed to provide the *"pays sangha"* (monetary gift) and I will also pay for the *"Malatya"* (feast). I want you to give a reading from the Holy Qur'an Abdel. Will you do this?"

"I will be very happy to do this Hakim and I see you have not forgotten your native language *der she,*" he replied.

"Now I will take you to my house, back to the car and be careful when you open the door."

They arrived at Avondale Road and got out the car.

"This is my house Abdel."

Abdel gazed at the house. It was a detached building with a porch and a front garden. It had many windows where colourful drapes hung.

The door furniture included a letterbox, door knocker, handle and the number twelve made from brass. The door was painted black and a plaque was attached to the wall, as Abdel got nearer, he read the inscription: *This is property of Mr Hakim Adur Rahman. Director of Rahman's Chandlers. Built 1943*

Hakim opened the front door and they both entered. The entrance hall had hardwood floors and panelling. From the hall there was access to stairs and to the downstairs rooms. Hakim took Abdel in the front room that looked out onto the road. The room was furnished with carpets, armchairs, tables, standing lamps, a bookcase and a desk.

"This is very wonderful Hakim; you have a fine house," said Abdel.

"I have one ninth of an acre of land behind the house, some of it is garden. I can have another house built in five years' time, if I wish."

Hakim went over to the desk, opened it and brought Abdel a leather-bound case.

"This is my gift to you Abdel, I hope you use it to record your life from this day."

Abdel opened up the case to find a camera.

"This is for me?" he asked.

"Yes, my brother and I want you to take photographs of my wedding and your visit to Durban, it is a Kodak Retina 35mm. A very fine camera Abdel, instruction for its use are in the case."

"You have been very kind Hakim; I will do as you ask and I will use this camera on my travels and post you the photographs."

"Let me show you your room Abdel"

Both men climbed the stairs to the first landing. Hakim opened a bedroom door and said, "You will not have slept in a bed like this."

Abdel walked in to see a double bed with a huge headboard made from teak. It was carved with exotic birds and the sheets and pillows were also decorated with wild birds.

"I have never seen such a bed; it is very big and very beautiful Hakim."

"All the bedrooms have similar furnishings, but with different designs on the bedsheets."

The rest of the day the brothers sat and talked of their homeland, Karachi, the war and their future. Hakim asked Abdel to join him in Durban to help him with Rahman's. He did not say no to this offer, but asked for time to think about it over the next few days.

The next day the brothers went to Mr Patel's and are measured for their costumes. They would be ready in two days' time. They also had time to go to the Barbershop and the Haberdashery store and meet all the employees. Abdel had noticed that all workers in shops, stores and markets were nearly all black and as they drove back to the chandler's store, he asked Hakim; "Why are all the employees black?"

"This is South Africa Abdel, the whites are in control of the industry, business organisations, the law and the government."

"But you are not white and yet you are a wealthy man Hakim."

"I am not white, but remember I arrived here with funds to support a business venture and the government will tolerate the fact that I am not white. It means I can generate business and employment for black South African's. There is history of bloodshed between the British, the Boars and the Zulu's. The white population control everything that happens in South Africa. The blacks only live in the townships outside the city and these places are not very good places to live, the workers are poorly paid."

"But you have blacks working for you, Mapo and the others in the haberdashery are blacks Hakim."

"Yes, but I pay more than the minimum wage Abdel. I do not agree with this system Abdel and my friends in the Indian Business Organisation are trying to form a Passive Resistance Party to ask the Local Government to provide a better way of life for the local workers. There are many of us Indians in Durban and we work hard Abdel."

"You were born in Azaw in Afghanistan and you are Pashto Hakim."

"Yes Abdel, but I am now a South African, I have two passports one says that I am Indian and another says I am South African, but I will always be an Afghan and a Pashto."

On arrival back at Rahman's the brothers had some lunch and then went for a walk along the wharf and into town. Durban was a melting pot of cultures, there were Chinese, Indians, British, Dutch, German and French businesses plying their trade. Abdel felt a sense of frustration for the black workers, it was their country and yet they were slaves to the ruling oppressive establishment.

It was very evident that Hakim was a well-respected man and he was greeted and recognised by many of the proprietors and local officials as they strolled around the town.

Abdel was wrestling with Hakim's offer to join him in Durban. His offer was very tempting, but he wanted to carve his own future and the more of what he saw in Durban troubled him. His ambivalence was born out of the despondency he felt relating to the oppression of the native population. He could not function in this environment not until some kind of equality for the blacks is created in South Africa. This more than anything else was telling him that he would decline Hakim's offer. He decided that he must tell Hakim before his wedding, so that he could enjoy the happiness of the day, without it playing on his mind.

After their stroll around Durban, they returned to Rahman's and Abdel told Hakim that he wanted to return to his job as a merchant seaman, after he had visited Abdullah in Karachi.

Hakim although disappointed said, "I am sorry that you will not be joining me here in South Africa Abdel, but I except your wishes and hope that you go on and have a peaceful and happy life and I hope God the most gracious, the most merciful will guide you on your way."

The date of the wedding was set July 19th at the rising of the sun both Hakim and Abdel went to the local Mosque and prayed. The wedding itself would take place in the Mosque and the feast would be at Hakims residence in Avondale Road. The time of the wedding was 11.00am and the cleric Imam Mohammad Abu Ahmed would conduct the wedding. Both the bride and groom would have two witnesses. The bride would have her father and her sister as witnesses and Hakim would have his friend Mohsen Farzan and Abdel. Family guests of the bride and friends of Hakim would be in attendance.

Rahmina and her sister were resplendent in white and gold costume, she was indeed very beautiful. Abdel and Hakim were dressed in traditional silks and both men had their beards shaved off for the ceremony.

After the marriage ceremony was complete and vows had been exchanged, Abdel read out a prayer for the couple. He was more than a little nervous but a smile from Rahmina helped him focus as he said;

"Oh God, bless this couple with faith, love and happiness in this world and the next.
Oh God, you are loving and the merciful.
Oh God, unite the couple and their families in faith and love.
Oh God, you are the Just."

From the mosque Hakim and Rahmina were escorted to a waiting car, bedecked with flowers and ribbons. The rest of the wedding party were allocated chauffer driven cars to take them back to Hakim's house for the feast. Abdel shared a car with Mohsen and Rahmina's sister Yasmin. During the drive to his brother's house Abdel introduced himself to Yasmin and Mohsen. Yasmin thought that Abdel looked very much like his brother and said,

"If I did not know it, I would say that you are twins."

"I am the younger and I much more attractive than Hakim," Abdel joked.

"Mohsen joined in the conversation and said,

"Hakim is very lucky to have such a beautiful bride like Rahmina."

"That is very true, God has blessed him," replied Abdel.

The feast went on for some five hours. When all the guests had left Hakim and Rahmina left for their honeymoon, a five, day stay at the St Lucia Game Reserve, some 100 miles north east of Durban. Abdel was asked to look after Rahman's with Mapo, Atta, Benjamin and Mohammad until his return on July 25th.

During his temporary supervision of Rahman's, Abdel's opinion of the subjugation that the Quasi-Zulu's suffered from was abhorrent and it reinforced his belief that he wanted no part of it. He observed many instances where the native blacks were treated no better than animals.

He also took the opportunity to take many photographs with his new Kodak. He had taken many shots of the wedding and ensured that he recorded images of all the staff at Rahman's. One evening after closing up the store, and strolling down St Andrews Street, he heard the sound of music emanating from an open door. As he approached, he looked up at the sign, it read *Big Jo's Jazz Club*. His intertest was sparked and he went in. He walked into a large open area where table and chairs were scattered with people sitting drinking to a five-piece band who were playing on a small stage.

As he stood and took in spectacle, a white man got up from his chair and said, "Can you not read kaffa, this is a white's only club. It is written on the door, now go back out where you came from."

Abdel was not impressed, he was not sure what kaffa meant, but he suspected it was something to do with the colour of his skin. He could hear Syed's voice in his ear and reluctantly he turned and left, to a cheer from all those present.

He had been enticed into the club by the music and it reminded him of the Al Jolson film he saw in Karachi when he was younger. He walked back to Avondale Road and felt bitter that he had not responded to that defamatory slur in the club.

The following day, it was still playing on his mind and he told Mapo all about it.

Mapo listened to Abdel's story about Big Jo's Jazz Club and said, "You must be very careful; this is not good Abdel. Very dangerous for you, they could beat you for what you did."

"Mapo, what is a kaffa?"

"I am a kaffa Abdel, I am black and African. You are coloured, but some of the whites call all of us kaffa. They also call us wogs, niggers, darkies and coons, this is normal in South Africa."

"This is very wrong Mapo, I don't want to live like this," said Abdel.

"You will be leaving soon, I think?"

"Yes, I am going to Karachi soon to see my cousin Abdullah. Do you live in the township Mapo?"

"No, Hakim lets me stay here for six days and I go home to my shack on Sunday's to see my mother and my brothers and sisters. My father works in the tin mine and only comes home once a month. We are lucky Abdel; Hakim is a good employer and he looks after us. Sometimes he gets medicine for my mother and he does not ask for money."

Abdel told Mapo of his interest in the music he heard in the club and Mapo said, "If you like this music, Benjamin has a gramophone and he has this jazz music. I will go and get him now" and off he went.

He was back with Benjamin in less than three minutes.

"You like jazz," asked Benjamin.

"Yes, I would like to hear more of it I think," he replied.

Benjamin took Abdel into the back of the store and opened a wooden cupboard and pulled out a gramophone. He also had a number of long-playing records and put one the gramophone. It was Django Reinhardt playing guitar at the Hot Club in Paris. Abdel was smitten, he loved the sound, how the guitar stood out and the melodic passages that moved through the instrumental.

"This is wonderful Benjamin, have you seen this man?" He asked.

Atta who was putting an order up in the food store shouted; "That is big noise, not like it. I like Nelson Eddy and Jeanette McDonald."

"Listen to him, he has only seen one film' *Naughty Marietta* he knows nothing," said Benjamin.

"Back to Abdel's question," he said,

"No, I will never see this man; he is very famous Abdel. But I can hear him anytime I want to, as long as I don't forget my duties to Rahman's."

Abdel looked through Benjamin's collection of musical recordings. He had many different artists including Duke Ellington and Benny Carter.

He asked Benjamin where he got these records from.

"I have a friend who works in a music store and sometimes he lets me have old stock at a discount price. But you can hear all these musicians and bands on the BBC world service on the wireless," he replied.

"I must get a wireless if I am to listen to this jazz" he said.

"It will cost you about £15 to £20 to buy one Abdel," said Benjamin.

"That is a lot on money, I will have to save money from my pay, but I can do that," he replied.

Mapo appeared and asked Abdel to return to the front of the store, a customer wanted to see him. It was Hakim's friend Mohsen.

"Welcome Mohsen, it is good to see you. How can I help you?"

"Can we talk Abdel?" he asked.

"Please come into our office Mohsen, Mapo can you bring us some tea."

"Yes Sir," and off he went.

Abdel was a little surprised that Mapo had called him Sir, but he put that thought aside as he asked Mohsen to take a seat.

"How can we help you?" he asked Mohsen.

"It is you that can help me Abdel. I know that Hakim has asked you to be his partner here in Durban," he said.

"Yes, he has asked me, but I have said I want to go back to sea Mohsen. What do you ask of me?"

"I would be most grateful if you could speak for me to Hakim, to be a partner in Rahman's. I would like your recommendation, if you would grant such a thing," he said.

Abdel felt it was a brave thing for Mohsen to do, since he barely knew him and said, "I am honoured that you have asked me to speak for you Mohsen. Hakim has a very successful business and he has worked hard to make Rahman's a big trader in Durban," he replied.

"Yes, this very true and I would like to help him to be a big success," said Mohsen.

Abdel though that a little bit of planning was needed in order to endorse Mohsen for this position in Rahman's and said, "I will discuss Hakim's plans with him when he gets back from his honeymoon. I will not say that you have approached me, but I will mention that you would be a good choice for a partner and we will see how he feels about it. What do you say to that?"

"If you would do this thing for me, I would be very happy Abdel. My father said he would give Hakim a bursary for my training, if he would employ me," he replied.

"Well, let us see how Hakim feels about this first."

"Yes, that is good, I will say goodbye now, I know you are busy. God be with you Abdel."

"Thank you, Mohsen and God be with you."

After Mohsen had left, Abdel called Mapo from the store.

"You called Abdel."

"Ah, now I am Abdel, when that customer came in you called me Sir."

"Oh yes, when a customer is present, I must call you Sir," he replied.

"Why is this so Mapo?"

"Because I am a kaffa Abdel."

Abdel was angry and with his egalitarian patience wearing thin he said, "Mapo you are not a slave; you are not a servant. You are an employee of Rahman's and you must have respect for yourself, do you understand?"

"Yes Abdel, but I call Hakim Sir when customers are in Rahman's," he said.

"Not any more Mapo, I will speak with Hakim."

"I don't want to make trouble for Rahman's," he said.

"Mapo, you are a working man and you are employed by Rahman's. You are a valuable part of the business."

"Yes, thank you Abdel Sir," he said with a great big smile on his face.

Abdel laughed and said,

"Get on with your work Mapo."

Hakim and Rahmina arrived back in Durban on July 25th. Abdel had enjoyed the sense of responsibility it had given him, but was glad that Hakim had returned. He now knew that this life was not for him and his decision to continue in the merchant navy was the right one. The remaining three day's he had in South Africa were organised by Hakim and involved days out to the country. One such trip was a visit to the Drakensburg Mountains, the day before Abdel was due to leave.

Hakim had hired a jeep and a driver for the day. The drive out, would take three hours and Abdel chose the opportunity to discuss Mohsen's role with Rahman's.

As they sat in the back of the jeep Abdel said, "Have you thought about a partner for Rahman's yet Hakim?"

Hakim was a little surprised by the question and replied; "Why brother, does it worry you?"

"No but I think it is a good idea Hakim, it seems that the business is good and you are getting new customers all the time. It would be sensible to have a partner to share the responsibility."

"Yes, that is true, but who could fill such a role?"

Now was Abdel's chance to introduce Mohsen to the equation and he said, "Well, I have been very impressed with your new brother in law Mohsen. He seems to be a determined young man; he has experience working for his father and he is part of the family now."

"His father has already recommended him Abdel and I have been considering it. His father has also said he would provide a financial bursary to help with his training."

Abdel felt quite secure now and pressed his brother on the matter.

"I would certainly give him an opportunity to show you what he can do Hakim."

"Yes, I think I will Abdel and thank you for your advice."

Abdel sat back in the jeep, reassured in the knowledge that his little bit of politics had opened a new chapter in the history of Rahman's.

On Abdel's last day, Hakim had arranged a farewell feast for Abdel at Avondale Road. The new family were all present. In addition, Hakim had closed Rahman's for the afternoon, this meant that Mapo, Benjamin, Atta and Mohammad could also attend. During the course of the afternoon, Mohsen took the opportunity to speak to Abdel about the possibility of him being a partner and he asked if he has spoken to Hakim about it.

"Yes, I have had words with my brother and he is giving it some consideration," he replied.

Little did Mohsen know but within ten minutes of their chat, he was about to find out. Hakim asked everyone to gather round for a farewell send off for Abdel and he said "As you know my brother, who I had not seen for nine years; will be leaving us to go to Karachi later today. It has been wonderful to see him and for him to be present at my wedding to Rahmina. We wish him well in the merchant navy, he has seen lots of despair and death, but lets us hope the world will be a better place for him."

A round of applause was given for Abdel, who replied; "Thank you all very much, I have very much enjoyed my stay here in Durban and I wish you all happiness and success for the future, praise to God for he is the most gracious and merciful."

Hakim then spoke and said, "I have another announcement to make, I have decided to offer Mohsen a partnership in Rahman's Chandlers, if he would be kind to accept it."

Mohsen was visibly shocked and looked straight at Abdel, who had a smile as wide as his face.

Mohsen strode up to Hakim and embraced him saying, "It would be a great honour to join you Hakim, I thank you for your confidence in me."

Another round of applause was given and lots of shaking hands and embracing ensued.

Hakim drove Abdel to the wharf and waved him off at 6pm on July 28th. The sun was still shining brightly as the ship, the Camina eased away from the dock. Abdel took the opportunity to take a photograph of Hakim on the wharf, as he waved him off.

Abdel was sad that he was leaving his brother, but was safe in the knowledge that Hakim was happy and looking forward to having family of his own. His attention now focussed on Karachi and how Abdullah was managing the business. He also thought about Osman, Kaleb, Mr Ali, Mr Singh and Maheera.

CHAPTER THIRTEEN

The voyage from Durban to Karachi was uneventful, say for a school of bottle nosed dolphins that escorted the ship past the Comoros Islands on the second day. Abdel was one of only nine passengers on the Camina and socialising was infrequent. He used the time to enhance his photography skills taking pictures of the ship and any unsuspecting passengers or crew.

The Camina docked in Karachi at 3pm on August 4th and once the gangplank was lowered, he was off the ship and on his way to Bunder Road and Rahman's. On arrival, he walked into the store and to his surprise a woman was behind the counter. She looked up and said, "Can I help you sir?"

"Is Abdullah in the store?" he asked.

"Oh no sir, he is out at the moment, visiting a customer. Can I help?"

Abdel was a little disappointed to find Abdullah not present, he had mentioned in his last letter that he was arriving today. However, he swallowed his pride and said, "It is not a problem; I am his cousin Abdel Rahman. I have just arrived from South Africa this afternoon."

The woman was very apologetic and replied with; "Oh Mr Rahman, I am so sorry. I did not realise; Abdullah had told me you might be arriving today. He told me to make you welcome and give you some refreshment. Please come in and I will telephone him to tell him you are here."

When she returned, she introduced herself as Hafsah Bin Amjad. She has been working for Abdullah for two years and she is also studying at the University. Her father has a motor vehicle repair garage on Elphinstone Street and is a good friend of Abdullah. She then left and returned with tea, bhuna chicken, breads, cakes and fruit for Abdel.

"Will you not join me and eat Hafsah," said Abdel.

"Oh no Mr Rahman, I will work on the stock check I was busy with, when you arrived."

After some fifteen minutes, Abdullah came bounding into the store saying, "So where is my long-lost cousin? They embraced each other and Abdullah said, "God has been gracious and his mercy has kept you safe."

The cousins sat and talked of many things and discussed how business was progressing here in Karachi. Abdullah raised the issue of independence from India and went on; "There are many people who want independence Abdel, I am not sure it is a good thing."

"Who are these people Abdullah?"

"There are many including important people here in Karachi Abdel. Even Mahatma Gandhi who is a Hindu wants independence from Great Britain. He has had talks with Mohammed Ali Jinnah and the prime minister Nehru.

There have had protest marches in Faisalabad, Hyderabad, Badin, Mirpur Khas and here in Karachi."

"Would it be a good thing for the business?"

"I do not know Abdel, no one knows. It looks like independence could mean a partition of Hindu's, Sikhs and Muslim's. I fear we will be having troubled times ahead. The Hindu's as you know, own 50% of the businesses in Karachi and if the country in partitioned it is feared they will all move away from Karachi."

"Let us pray that whatever happens, it is peaceful Abdullah."

"Well, you have your own face hair and you have grown into a strong man. Your shoulders are broad now and you have your brother's nose with that curve at the top. You must be 5' 9" in height now, the merchant navy has made you a man."

"Yes, that is true; so, Abdullah tell me have you seen Osman, is he still in the Army?"

"Oh yes, and he is based in Rawalpindi for his training," he replied.

"That means he will not get to go fishing then. Have you seen Maheera?"

Abdullah knew that question was coming and said, "Abdel, you must forget her. She is married with two children now and her husband is an important man in Karachi."

"Well, I am sure she is happy."

Abdullah diverted the conversation by asking how Hakim was doing in South Africa?

Abdel spoke of Hakim's new wife and his new family. He also expressed his worries about South Africa and how the native blacks are treated. He told Abdullah about Hakims gift to him of a camera and said, "I will need to see Mr Ali, I have some film that needs to be developed into photographs. Then I can show you Hakim, his family and where he lives."

"We will go to see Mr Ali tomorrow, now tell me all about the war at sea Abdel."

Abdel was reluctant to talk about what he had seen and how it had affected him, but after a short while he recovered his composure and detailed his time in the convoys, the friends he lost and the places he has visited including his pilgrimage to the Hajj and Malta where he had his first romantic liaison with Isabella.

Abdullah listened intently as Abdel reflected on his recent past and the horror of war. When Abdel had finished his exposition, Abdullah said, "God has kept you safe Abdel Malik Rahman, God is merciful, God Is Great."

"Yes Abdullah, God has guided me and God has shown mercy, God has power over all. But remember we are still at war with Japan, who have refused to surrender."

Abdullah then talked about Rahman's and how well it was doing.

"We are thriving Abdel; I have appointed new staff here and at the tea rooms. I have also opened a hardware store in the Empress Market. We have just got a contract with the Indian Army."

"The Army, are selling guns Abdullah?"

"No, we are supplying military garments for the Indian Army. I have a manufacturer here in Karachi called Mr Abdul Zahedan, he makes the uniforms and I fly them out to Lahore from Karachi Airport. We make a good profit Abdel; we make £2 for every uniform delivered."

"How much does Mr Zahedan make?"

"He makes £1. 10 shillings, he is very happy with this arrangement."

They then decided to go for a stroll around Karachi and drop into the Tea Rooms to see Kaleb. They then visited the mosque to pray and finally sat down to eat back at Rahman's at 7pm. After eating Abdel decided to retire for the night and he climbed the stairs to his old bedroom. As he lay in bed the memories came flooding back; talking to Syed about his books, the earthquake and Syed's last day's and he fell into a deep sleep.

He rose early next morning and went downstairs at 7.30am. He was excited about getting his photographs developed at Mr Ali's. As he entered the backroom, Abdullah was just putting some rice and chicken in a bowl.

"God be praised the sailor has risen," he said.

He put the bowl on the table and said, "Eat well cousin, we have a busy day. We go to Mr Ali's first, then to the airport and show you how our enterprise is going with the Indian Army. Then I have a surprise for you in the afternoon. Is there anywhere else you would like to go Abdel?"

Abdel thought for a minute, then said, "Yes, I would like to go back to my village Azaw; but I know that is not possible Abdullah. I also do not think I will ever see Hakim again."

"Why do you say this Abdel, what are you going to do with your life? You can always stay here and hop be a wealthy businessman."

"I am going back to sea Abdullah; I like being a merchant seaman. I enjoy travelling to different parts of the world and meeting people. Ever since I was eleven years old, I have journeyed to many places and I have learned lots of things. I do not know where I will find happiness, but I am sure one day, with Gods help I will prosper."

They set off for Mr Ali's and arrived just as he was opening his shop.

"God be praised is that the skinny boy who went to sea all those years ago," said Mr Ali as he saw Abdel standing at his door.

The two embraced and Abdel said, "You have not changed Mr Ali."

"I fear your eyesight has failed you Abdel or you are just being respectful. But thank you anyway" he said.

"Come in the both of you and have some tea with me" and he locked the door behind them.

After a short resume of his life at sea, Abdel produced his camera and said, "Look at this camera I got as a gift from my brother in South Africa," and handed it to Mr Ali.

"This is a magnificent camera Abdel; very expensive, your brother must be a rich man. A 35mm Kodak Retina and it looks like the current model."

"Can you develop the film into photographs for me please," asked Abdel.

"It would be my pleasure, but it will take me a few hours," is that satisfactory for you?"

"Oh yes, that would be very good Mr Ali, thank you."

The three men chatted for an hour and Abdullah suggested he and Abdel should go to the airport to supervise a cargo of uniforms for the Indian Army.

To get there would take too long walking, so Abdullah had arranged a car from Mr Ahmed's Taxi Service, whom he used quite often for his business trips around Karachi.

As they climbed into the car Abdel asked, "Where is your car? I thought you could drive now."

"It is in the garage under repair, I hit a camel last week on my way to the airport. The car just bounced of the camel, but the damage was bad. The owner of the camel was not happy because it had an injury to its back leg. He said it was his best camel."

The taxi driver laughed and added; "They all say that."

"I had to pay him for his troubles and I have to pay for the damage to my car. That was an expensive day Abdel."

They arrived at the airport and entered the airport gates at the cargo services. Abdullah asked the taxi driver to wait, it would take some twenty minutes to inspect the cargo and oversee the loading. They walked into the cargo bay where the plane was parked and the cargo was being checked by an employee of Mr Zahedan. Abdullah recognised him and said, "Is everything in order Yusef?"

"Yes sir Mr Rahman, 2.000 complete uniforms and leather belts."

"Can I inspect one please Yusef?"

"Of course, sir and split open a carton and handed a complete uniform to Abdullah."

"You see Abdel, feel the quality" and handed him the uniform.

"It is very good quality, fit for King George himself," added Yusef.

"Yes, it is very good, but it must be very hot to wear during the day," said Abdel.

"Yes, but very warm at night also," replied Yusef.

They all watched as each carton was lifted into the plane and when all the cargo was aboard, they thanked Yusef and left and got into the taxi.

"Now that surprise Abdel, we are off to the cinema," said Abdullah.

"The cinema," replied Abdel.

"Yes, it has been modernised, it has a bigger screen and much better seats since you were last there," said Abdullah.

"What is the film?" asked Abdel.

"We are going to see two Laurel & Hardy films; they are very funny. It's called slapstick in America" he replied.

On the way to the cinema, Abdel told Abdullah about how he liked the music of Django Reinhardt. Abdullah had not heard of him but said, "We will have to go to the music shop owned by Fazur Khan, he will have his long players."

"I would like that, but do we have a gramophone?"

"No, but I think we can buy one at discount from Mr Khan," he replied

They arrived at the cinema and Abdullah paid the taxi driver his fare, they walked into the foyer of the cinema and Abdel said,

"This is very different since I was last here to see that Al Jolson film, the Jazz Singer."

"That is so my cousin, I will get our seat tickets."

"Please let me pay for this Abdullah."

"No, this is my gift for you, anyway I know the manager Mr Ranjit Singh. He uses Rahman's for many supplies," he replied.

They got to their seats and from the first minute the cousins were in raptures of laughter, along with everyone else in the cinema. The first film was *Way Out West* followed by *Block-Heads*.

As they walked of the cinema Abdel said, "It is good to laugh Abdullah; it makes you feel good."

Then Abdullah burst into song with the *Blue Ridge Mountains of Virginia*. Abdel joined him and the two of them were given some strange looks as they sauntered down the road. They were still singing when they walked into Rahman's and Hafsah broke into laughter at their appearance.

"I hope you gentlemen have not been drinking any sinful potions in that tea room of yours," she said.

"No indeed not, we have been to the cinema to see Laurel & Hardy, they are so funny," replied Abdullah.

"Mr Ali telephoned to say that the photographs are ready for collection,

Mr Rahman."

"Very good, thank you Hafsah," and he turned to Abdel and said, "Shall we go and collect them now Abdel and we could also go and see Mr Fazur Khan in his music store."

"Yes Stanley, that's another fine mess you have got me into," he replied.

With a spring in their step and in a jovial mood the cousins strolled out of Rahman's like two children full of fun. Hafsah smiled and shouted; "Don't forget, I finish at 7.30pm to do my studies."

As they walked away, Abdullah raised his hand in the air to signify he understood. The pair arrived at Mr Ali's and entered his establishment to be greeted by the man himself.

"I have developed your film Abdel; however, you need to improve your photography skills. You have a number of spoilt photographs, because you have had the sun on the lens, I am afraid. The photos of your family have all developed well, I am pleased to say," and he handed a brown envelope over to Abdel.

"How much do I pay for these?" asked Abdel.

"This time they are free of charge, as a gift from Mr Ali," he said.

"You are very kind Mr Ali, thank you very much sir."

Abdel passed the photo's to Abdullah who looked at each one and said, "Hakim's wife is very beautiful Abdel."

"Yes, she is beautiful and her sister is very pretty too," he said.

"Oh yes this must be her with her father, is it not?"

"Yes, that is so cousin, her name is Yasmine."

"Is it not time that you found a wife Abdullah," said Mr Ali.

"I am too busy with the business, perhaps I will marry one day, if God grants me it."

They left Mr Ali's shop and made the short distance to Fazur Khan's music store. The store was more than just a music shop. It was also a tea room and furniture store. The music department was upstairs on the third level. After climbing two flights of stairs they entered a world of sound. Music was being played on a gramophone and in one corner a young girl was playing a piano.

Mr Khan greeted Abdullah and said, "It is good that you have visited my store, what can I interest you in?"

"It is for my cousin here Abdel," and he introduced Abdel to Mr Khan, they shook hands and Abdel said, "I would like a gramophone to play some long-playing records on."

"I have many sir, many different models," and he escorted both of them to an area devoted to various examples.

Abdullah asked Abdel a relevant question when he said, "Abdel, will you be able to carry one of these machines in you kit bag?"

Abdel thought for a moment and replied; "Well, perhaps not they are very big Mr Khan."

Mr Khan keen on a sale of some sort, diverted Abdel away from the gramophones and onto the radio stand. A variety of Short-Wave Radios were on display.

"Hcr we have a range of radios for you to look at; we have the Garod Commander Catalin, the Philco Tranistone models 42-PT3 and 42-PT96. A Stewart Warner A72TS and two Philips Radios the BS 471A and the Bakelite 371A."

"Can I hear them please Mr Khan?"

"Of course, sir, let me plug the Philco Tranistone 42 for you," he replied.

He switched it on and found the BBC World Service, a Mozart symphony was being played. Mr Khan then did the same with another three sets until Abdel said, "I will have this one Mr Khan."

"A very good choice sir, the Transitone is a popular radio," he said.

"How much does this cost?" asked Abdel.

"It will cost £16 sir, is that alright for you sir?"

"Yes, that is fine Mr Khan."

The transaction was completed and Abdel was now in possession of his own radio. The cousins retuned to Rahman's just in time for Hafsah to go to college. Abdullah cooked a meal of lamb Balti and rice and they ended the day listening to Abdel's radio.

The following day at 8.15am the USA dropped the first Atomic Bomb on Japan at Hiroshima. The aircraft was a B-29 nicknamed the *Enola Gay* and it unleashed 15.000 tons of TNT, which killed 166.000 people. Three days later a second nuclear bomb was dropped on Nagasaki, killing another 80.000 people.

What the world did not know at the time was that the ship that carried the uranium for the bombs was torpedoed by the Japanese on July 30th near the tiny island of Tinian, north of Guam. The USS *Indianapolis* was on a secret mission and heading for the Philippines after dropping the material off, when a Japanese submarine spotted it. Only 317 sailors survived out of a total 1.197, there was not enough time to launch boats and many sailors were lost to exposure and shark attacks.

Abdel was delighted to see Osman during his second week in Karachi. Osman was on four days leave from his regiment and met up with his friend. They hired a boat and had a fishing trip at Pitiani Creek and returned and ate their catch of fish and crabs at Osman 's house.

Osman was recruited into the 155th Indian Infantry Brigade and as yet had not been used in the war, having only completing his training within the last 3 weeks. However, if the Japanese did not surrender, his regiment would be called to comb the islands around Java, the Philippines and Borneo for pockets of Japanese soldiers. Abdel gave Osman his copy of the Man in The Iron Mask and suggested he would enjoy it.

Abdel's short stay back in Karachi was drawing to a close and he began to think about his future. Abdullah had made no secret that he wanted Abdel to stay and help him with Rahman's. Abdel felt Karachi pulling him back but he had made his mind up and he wanted to see what else the world had to offer him.

On his last day in Karachi he attended the mosque for prayers with Abdullah in the morning and then a final meal along with Abdullah and Hafsah. He left Abdullah at the wharf at 1.30pm and walked up the gangway to board the Camina. In his nap sack was his copy of the Noble Qur'an, prayer mat, clothes, camera, photographs and his radio. The ship left the wharf at 2pm on August 18th and Abdullah had been joined by Mr Ali and Hafsah to wave him off. The Camina made good headway and reached Gibraltar after some 15 days at sea, docking in Gibraltar on September 2nd, the same day as Japan surrendered, thus ending World War II.

Once docked Abdel left the Camina and sought out Mr Anderson at the British East India Company Office. Mr Anderson was pleased to see him and said, "Well now seaman Rahman, how was the holiday?"

"It has been very good sir; I have seen South Africa and my brother who has just been married."

"I wondered if you were going to come back to us, after what you have been through young man. I have a number of opportunities for you and various locations in which to consider. Here is a list, have a look at it and come back to me tomorrow with your chosen destination. The posting for all Articles of Agreement under the Merchant Shipping Act and it is for a Deck Rating. I have booked you a room at the Missions to Seaman for the night."

He handed the list to Abdel and said, "See you tomorrow at 10am."

CHAPTER FOURTEEN

Abdel arrived at the company office at 9.55am. Mr Anderson was on the telephone and acknowledged Abdel's presence with a wave of his hand through the office window. Abdel waited a couple of minutes, then he was invited in by Mr Anderson.

"Good morning Able Seaman Rahman, have you slept well?"

"Yes, thank you Mr Anderson."

"So, have you looked at the list I gave you and chosen one?"

"I have, I would like to take up a job on the west coast of America."

"That is a surprise, I thought you might have gone for the Camina or the Durban Castle, as these ships keep you close to your home port," he replied.

"I know this Mr Anderson, but I want to travel in other parts of the world and the ship the Santa Rita will sail on the west coast of America and South America."

"So, be it then, I will contact Grace Line in San Francisco by telegram to inform them of your employment, do you want a three-year contract?"

"Yes, three years Mr Anderson."

"It will take me some time to write up your Articles and organise how you get to San Francisco, so can you return in about 2 hours? I might need to book you in to a hotel for a few days, depending on what ships are available for travel."

"That is very good Mr Anderson, thank you."

Abdel left the office in a state of excitement, a new adventure would soon begin.

At 12.00 midday Abdel returned to the office where Mr Anderson was just compiling Abdel's Articles of Agreement.

"Alright young man, sit down and I will go through all the paperwork with you. What I give you, must be handed over to Grace Line in San Francisco on your arrival. You will get to San Francisco around September 26th all being well, is that clear?"

"Yes sir."

"You must hand over this envelope to Mr Danilo, when you get to San Francisco. He will then contact your ship the Santa Rita. Someone will arrive and collect you from the Grace Line Office. Your posting is for a Deck Rating and your pay will be £10 a month, but you will be paid in dollars. That works out at about 40 dollars a month."

"Now this is how you will get to San Francisco. Listen carefully, I have booked you on a ship called the *Benedict* a ship of the Booth Steamship Company. It sails from Gibraltar in two days' time and it is bound for New Orleans."

"Where is that, Mr Anderson?

"It is in Louisiana; from there you will then board a train that will take you to San Francisco. Grace Line will have a train ticket with the Southern Pacific Line, waiting for you at the railway station, when you arrive. When you get to San Francisco make your way to Pier 24 where you will be collected by a Mr Felix Danilo, the Purser of the Santa Rita. Now I need a photograph of you to post to San Francisco office of Grace Line. So, stand up and look happy Abdel Malik Rahman."

Abdel did as he was told and Mr Anderson took his photograph twice. Returning to his exposition he said, "Don't worry, I have written all this down for you Abdel, you don't have to remember it verbatim."

"What is verbatim sir?"

"It means I have written it all down for you, so when you need to, just look at the information I have provided. Everything you need is in this envelope including next month's pay, which amounts to $32. I have booked you into a small hotel just outside the port here, it's called the Majestic. You are booked in for one night and it is paid for. You must report to your ship the *Benedict* at 11.00 hours on September 5th and find the Purser, Mr Gordon Ballantyne. He will be expecting you, have you any more questions?"

Abdel was somewhat overwhelmed with the information so quickly delivered and could not think of a question and said, "No sir, it is very good."

"Splendid, so now you can enjoy some relaxation in Gibraltar and you may want to get any English money you have, exchanged into dollars while you can."

"Yes sir, thank you sir," and he turned to walk out of the office.

"Able seaman, where are you going?" shouted Mr Anderson.

Abdel turned back to see Mr Anderson pointing to the large brown envelope lying on the desk.

"You will bloody need that, you daft sod."

"Oh yes sir sorry sir, thank you sir," and he picked up the envelope and left Mr Anderson who shook his head in wonderment.

Abdel spent the rest of the day getting some items for his kit bag. He bought a dictionary, to replace the one he lost when the *Domelia* was sunk. He also bought a copy of The Strange Case of Dr Jekyll & Mr Hyde, having finished The Man in The Iron Mask. He added to his literary collection with a Readers Digest Atlas. He was left with £5 which he exchanged for $20. He now had everything he needed for the trip, but getting it all into his kit bag would be a challenge. He managed to succeed in that task and on a warm sun lit September morning he walked up the gangplank of the *Benedict* at 10.50am. The ship was smaller than any of the other ships he had been on, it was 422 feet long with a top speed of 12 knots. Its hull was black with a black funnel.

The ship took only 12 passengers, but all were first class births. This was luxury for Abdel, he had never ever been in a first-class cabin, let alone sleep in one. With his kit bag well laden and clutching his brown envelope he arrived on deck and asked one of the crew where to find the Purser. He was directed by a man in overalls to where to find the Pursers cabin.

He knocked and a voice shouted; "Just hang on a minute, I will be with you soon."

Abdel waited for what seemed a long time and then the voice shouted; "Come in sailor."

Abdel opened the door and found the Purser sitting with his feet on his desk.

"Good morning, who might you be?

"I am Abdel Malik Rahman; I am a passenger on my way to New Orleans sir."

"Are you now, have you got your first-class ticket?"

The Purser was sure this guy had the wrong ship and said, "Let me see now" and he looked through Abdel's paperwork.

"Well I'll be dammed, a wog in first class, whatever next."

Abdel dropped his kit bag on the floor, stood up straight and fired back; "I am not a wog sir; I have a British passport and I am a serving able seaman in the merchant navy."

The Purser was a little perplexed and said, "So, what are you doing on board as a passenger?"

"I am on my way to America to join my ship in San Francisco," he replied.

"Oh sorry, are you the captain," he replied sarcastically.

"Abdel ignored the comment and said, "You will find that all my paperwork is in order, I think."

The Purser took his time to finger through Abdel's evidence from the brown envelope and finally said, "It seems that everything meets the requirements for a first-class passenger. I don't suppose you have any valuables you want me to hold for you during the voyage, do you?"

"I will keep everything with me in my kit bag in my cabin," he replied.

"Very well Abdul, you have cabin number 4. I am sure you will have no trouble finding it, Gooday to you."

He handed Abdel his brown envelope back and sat back without making any eye contact.

"It is Abdel not Abdul," he replied as he turned to leave.

"Whatever, mind your head as you leave my cabin," said the Purser.

As he made his way to his cabin, he could here Syed's words ringing in his ears;

"You will have a heavy heart when men insult you by calling you a coolly or wog. You must have strength and look to God."

Within an hour the *Benedict* had left the dock and she was out into the Strait of Gibraltar on her 5000-mile voyage. Abdel's, cabin was very comfortable; it even had a toilet. The wardrobe was huge and his clothes amounted to, three shirts, two pairs of trousers, one jacket and his underwear and socks. In addition, he had two pairs of shoes and a woolly hat. His cabin had a bedside cabinet with a small reading lamp perched on the top.

The *Benedict* broke out into a moderate sea with waves around 5 feet in height, a fresh breeze and number five on the Beaufort Scale. Along with the twelve passengers the ship's cargo consisted of timber, spices, bananas and coconuts. Passengers could eat alone or sit with other passengers in the dining room. For his first meal Abdel decided to eat alone and he was served dinner by a steward at 7pm. It consisted of kedgeree, chicken casserole and mixed fruit along with water to drink. That first night he stayed in his cabin and after praying he started reading *Dr Jekyll & Mr Hyde*. He was glad of his dictionary to be able to decipher some of the words he did not know. He fell asleep with the book in his hands at 10pm.

On his second day at sea, he wandered around deck and spent a little time gazing out at sea. Gone are the days of looking into the horizon for enemy ships or U Boats. It made him think of all his shipmates lost on both the *Domelia* and the *Barat Star*. He missed the companionship of Pablo, Bobby, Mr Mac, Jim Shearer, George Hollcroft and Billy Patterson. He also thought about the men he had met and wondered if they had survived. Had Isaac Levinson, Jim Peterkin and Jacob Levi" son's managed to live through this terrible war. Abdel started to feel acrimonious at the thought of so many people who had played a part in his life, were now either dead or nothing but a spectre of his past.

The character Dr Jekyll had become a man in turmoil, trying to enhance his understanding of the human mind and in doing so, failed to see the dreadful outcome. Abdel had seen many barbaric things and his expectations for the future were clouded in uncertainty. While feeling outrage at the horrors of war, the despondent and subjugated blacks in South Africa; he felt that his faith would conquer any uncertainty and navigate him to a better life. He returned to his cabin and prayed that God would guide him to this new life and asked God in his mercy to watch over his brother and his cousin.

At 7pm he decided to join the other passengers for dinner. Not all were present as there were only nine people seated when he arrived. As he took a seat at the dinner table, he was acknowledged by all, with a nod of the head and the odd "good evening" from some of those present, he said, "Good evening to you all, my name is Abdel Malik Rahman, I am very pleased to meet you."

A man sitting directly opposite him said, "Good evening to you sir, my name is Raúl Hernandez, *la sed de Aventura*."

Abdel looked confused by the final statement and said, "I am sorry sir," I do not speak Spanish."

"Please, I sometimes forget who I am speaking with. What I said was, I think you have a thirst for adventure, is that so?"

"I have seen many things both as a child and as a man. I want to see more of the world sir and I hope one day to have a family, God willing."

"I am also looking to better myself; I lost my wife when she was shot by Franco's Nationalists in February 1939. They came looking for sympathisers of the Republic in Burgos where we lived and they did house to house searches."

"They broke our door down and fired shots as they entered the house. One bullet struck my wife Rosetta in the throat and she bled to death in my arms. I swore I would not live under such *el criminal tirania* (tyranny) and I said to myself, I must leave Spain."

A man sitting to his right asked; "Where are you going?"

"I am going to New Orleans; my brother Manuel has a bar and he wants me to work for him," he replied.

All went quiet for a while until Raul spoke again when he said, "Is anybody else going to New Orleans?"

No one responded, the dinner passed without any further verbal interaction. Abdel was last to rise and leave the dinner table and he walked out onto the fore castle to take in a breath of sea air. To his delight he spotted some bottle nose dolphins shadowing the ship. As they swam, they were leaping clear of the sea and seemed to be laughing, it seemed like they were performing for Abdel, it made him laugh out loud.

A voice came from behind him; "What makes you so happy?"

Abdel turned to see another passenger, who had been sitting next to him at dinner approaching.

"It's the dolphins they are having a good time I think, take a look."

The man who stood and gazed at the spectacle and was amazed," he said,

"I have never seen such a thing, these are dolphins, are they?"

"Oh yes, I have seen them before. They sometimes chase the ship and even swim under the bows of the ship when they get excited. It is said they bring good luck."

"I am sorry, my name is Scott Heller and I am on my way to New Orleans, I did not want to say that at dinner. I tend to keep my own council," he said.

"What is your own council? My understanding of English is not good," said Abdel.

"Oh, it means that I like to keep things like that to myself" he replied.

"Yes, I now understand, my name is Abdel Malik Rahman and I am pleased to meet you sir."

"Yes, I know you told us your name at dinner."

"I did yes, I forget these things sometimes. Do you live in America sir?"

"Yes, I was born in Winnsboro, Louisiana and you don't have to call me sir, its Scott."

"What does your father do Scott?"

"He is a farmer, we have a farm that grows crops including, corn, rice, soybeans and tabasco peppers. My grandfather came to America from Holland and he was one of the early settlers. My mother died ten years ago from consumption. I also have a younger brother Ted who is 16 now, he helps on the farm along with our farm labourers Henry and Frank. I got called up for the army in 1943 and I have seen action in North Africa and Italy with the 82nd Airborne Division."

"What's your story Abdel?"

Abdel went on to summarize his life so far and spoke of his hopes for the future. The two men continued to talk for some time until Abdel had realised that the dolphins had gone and said, "Our friends in the sea have left us Scott."

"They are sick of us talking I guess."

As the sun set in the sky, the two parted and returned to their cabins for the night. Abdel read a few more pages of his book before falling asleep. Abdel and Scott would often sit and talk on deck, sometimes Raul would join them. Three men that had endured war in different ways and were intent on living out their lives in a heuristic nature, that would encapsulate happiness hopefully, in a world without conflict.

The *Benedict* reached New Orleans on September 23rd 1945 and docked at 4.30pm. Luckily Scott was also bound for the railway station; they flagged a taxi to the station. Scott's train would be heading for Jackson, Mississippi and from there he would get the bus to Winnsboro. A journey of some 250 miles.

They arrived at the station at 5.55pm and went to get their respective tickets. Scott did not have long to wait, his train was due in at 6pm. Abdel had a longer wait for his San Francisco train, it was not due to leave until 8pm. They sat and talked and Scott gave Abdel his home address and asked him to write once he had established himself with his new life.

Abdel's kit bag intrigued Scott and he said, "What have you got in that bag partner?"

"I have all my possessions, I have my radio, the Noble Qur'an, my other books, camera, clothes and all my papers," he replied.

Then it dawned on Abdel, he should have a photograph of himself and Scott and said, "Can we have a photograph together Scott?"

"That is a great idea brother, I will ask somebody to take our picture, you get your camera out and I will pick someone."

Abdel got his camera out of his kit bag and Scott had picked on a very attractive blonde women who was passing and who was alone and she agreed. Abdel showed her how to operate the camera and she took the photo and handed the camera back to Abdel.

Scott could not resist an over the top thank you and said, "May I thank you and can I add that, how such a beautiful girl is travelling alone is a mystery."

"She smiled and said, "Your most welcome boys," and walked off to the ticket office.

"Abdel I am sure in love," he said as he followed her with his eyes all the way to the office.

"Do you know this woman?"

"Oh no, but boy, I would like to."

Once the girl had disappeared, normality returned to the scene. Then an announcement that Scott's train was ready to board was made. The two shook hands and Scott said, "A safe journey and don't forget to write you hear."

"I will do this I promise and I hope God guides you safely home."

"He surely will," and with that last statement, Scott was on his way to the platform.

At 7.50pm the announcement was made that the 8pm train bound for San Francisco was ready to board. Abdel joined the throng of people heading to the platform. He handed his ticket to the platform guard, who looked at it, then looked at Abdel, looked at the ticket again and then another curious look at Abdel, before saying,

"You got any papers and ID boy?"

Abdel got out all his ID and paperwork and the guard said, "Just step over here while I check these" and he motioned to Abdel to step aside.

He looked through the papers and said, "So you is going to San Francisco and then onto a ship, that right boy?"

"Yes sir, I am a merchant seaman sir," he replied.

The guard took another long look at Abdel before he waved him through and onto the platform. It made Abdel feel like an inconvenience and to be addressed as a boy agitated him. Then as he walked to the train and his carriage, he realised that he was the only passenger that was not white. Never before had this bothered him, until now and it troubled him. When he got to his carriage his demeanour improved when the train guard who was black took his kit bag and took him to his compartment.

When they arrived at his compartment the guard said, "You must be some rich nigger, to get a compartment on this train boy."

Abdel was shocked to hear such defamatory language from a man of colour like himself and said, "You must not say these things, you are a man of colour like me. God has made us all men in his image."

"Well, you aint seen enough of America yet brother, get used to it. You is on table seven for dinner at 9.00 o'clock and breakfast in the mornin."

"Thank you sir," and Abdel took his kit bag and laid it on the bed.

As the guard went to leave, he added; "You don't call me sir brother, I aint no one special."

When the guard had gone, Abdel sat on his bed and reflected on what had just occurred. It made him angry that a man could have little respect for himself. He had three days travel ahead across five states from Louisiana, Texas, New Mexico, Arizona and finally California. He washed and got into clean clothes for dinner and arrived on the hour and was greeted by a steward, again a black man who said, "I am sorry but you must have a tie for dinner."

Abdel was confused, the guard sensed this and pointed to a man sitting near wearing a shirt and tie. The penny dropped and Abdel said, "Oh I am sorry sir, I don't have one,"

"Do not worry, I will get a tie from laundry, just take your seat at your table."

Within two minutes the guard arrived with a blue tie, thankfully Abdel was wearing a white shirt with a collar. He put it on and the steward asked what he would like to drink.

"Could I have a glass of water sir?"

"Of course, I will bring you a jug of water while you decide on what it is you want to eat."

Abdel chose a chicken fricassee with vegetables and apple pie and cream. He was astonished how smooth the train was travelling and the view from his seat was very interesting as the train sped through Morgan City and Franklin. The steward returned with the water and introduced himself as William Collins and confirmed that he would be looking after Abdel for the journey to San Francisco.

"Thank you sir, my name is Abdel Malik Rahman."

"Yes, I know, your name is on my list, welcome to the Southern Pacific Union Railway. If you need anything, just ask me."

"Thank you, William sir."

"You do not have to call me sir, William will do."

Abdel thanked him, but that feeling that he was speaking to a subjugated person was evident again. When William returned with his meal, Abdel asked if he would like to talk after dinner was served. He said that any free time he had was around 10.30pm and he would meet him back in the restaurant car then. Abdel agreed and returned promptly at 10.30pm to find the restaurant car deserted. He sat at his table and within a few minutes William appeared.

The two men talked and expressed their feelings on many issues. Abdel was particularly interested in Williams family history and probed him about his parents and asked; "What do your parents do William?"

"I don't know, my mother died when I was born. My parents were cotton pickers in Louisiana and as black slaves they had only a wooden shack near Homer. My father was hanged when I was only five years old. They said he raped a white girl in Minden, I learned later that he was not even in Minden on the day she was raped. I was then taken in by my Aunt Bess who raised me. I never went to school, blacks never got education in Homer, so my aunt did her best getting me to read and write. She died when I was sixteen and I stayed and worked on the cotton plantations. One day a guy from the railway came to our farm and said that the Pacific Union were looking for workers on the trains, so I signed up and I have been here ever since."

"How old are you William?" asked Abdel.

"I am 32," he replied.

Abdel then told him about his life and why he was going to San Francisco. William then suggested that being at sea would be better than trying to make a life on terra firma when he said,

"People like us don't get nothing; we are still slaves. Even if we think we are part of the civilised world, we aint. We are still second-class subjects and still get ill-treated. One day I hope it will change and black kids can go to schools with white kids. And we get the vote without having to justify our citizenship and we stop the Klu Klux Klan killing black folks. I know you have seen bad things in your life and you will see more, but I guess being on a ship will give you some freedom from the abuse and hate in this world."

It was 11.15pm when Abdel returned to his berth. He prayed and read a few pages of his book before turning his bedside lamp off and drifting off to sleep to the sound of train rolling along the track towards Houston, Texas.

The journey was a scenic excursion through the south west with further stops at San Antonio, El Paso, Tucson, Phoenix, San Bernardino, Los Angeles and finally San Francisco. The train eased into the station in San Francisco at 10.20am on September 26th after a journey covering 1923 miles. Abdel made sure he said farewell to William and wished him health and happiness. He gave William $5 and thanked him for all his help during his time on the train.

CHAPTER FIFTEEN

Having left the train Abdel once again had his ticket checked on leaving the platform, this time without any further interrogation. He managed to hail a taxi and asked the driver to take him to Pier 24 at the port. The journey only took some 15 minutes and he was charged 1 dollar for the ride. It was a warm sunny day and the pier was a hive of activity, with trucks, wagons and people moving around in what seemed like a chaotic way. He made his way to an Office where men were coming and going. When he got there, he noticed a man with a board with the name Abdul Rahmoon daubed on it in red paint. He stood for some time and was unsure if that was his miss spelt name or another seaman's name.

Finally, he plucked up the courage and approached the man and said, "Is your name Mr Felix Danilo of the Santa Rita?"

"Yes, who wants to know?

"I think it is me you are waiting for sir; I am Abdel Malik Rahman and I am the new Deck Rating reporting for duty."

"I was beginning to think you were not turning up, I have been here an hour."

He produced Abdel's photograph, compared the likeness and said, "It looks like you, so let's get on board and I will give a quick tour of the ship and you can meet some of the crew."

The ship was docked some 200 yards away, it had a black hull with a green, white and black funnel and Abdel sensed it was the smallest ship he had ever been on. The Purser led him up the gangplank and onto the ship where they were greeted by the Deck Officer.

"Who have we got here Felix?"

"This is Abdul Rooman, our new deck rating Joseph."

"Abdul meet your Deck Officer, Mr Joseph Campbell."

"Welcome aboard young man, you have travelled some distance to take this job."

"Yes sir, I am happy to be here sir, but my name is Abdel not Abdul and my other name is Rahman sir."

"Mere errors in translation Abdel, not to worry. You are here and I will now show you to your mess and a short tour of the ship. Thank you, Felix, now you can go back to that shit hole you call your cabin."

Felix gave Joseph a look of disdain and stormed off to his berth.

"No love lost there, what do you say Abdel?"

"No sir, he is not very happy sir."

"To hell with him, let's get you settled in."

"Yes sir."

"My name is Joe or Joseph, no need for the sir. I have not been knighted by the King yet."

"Yes, thank you Joseph sir."

Joseph turned, laughed and said, "This sir thing, it is bloody obvious you use it all the time, is that so?"

"Yes sir."

He continued to laugh and said, "This will go down well with the rest of the crew, I am sure. I guess it's a sign of respect. I hope you don't expect me to call you sir, do you?"

"Only if you want to Joseph sir."

He turned and said, "Look Abdel, no more sir alright."

"Yes Joseph, if that is what you want?"

"It is, thank you."

They got to the aft accommodation on the poop deck and Joseph gave him his bunk. While there he introduced him to the crew that were present. In attendance were, Juan, Ernie, Gordon and Sean, the other deck ratings. Before they left for a short tour of the ship Joseph said, "Ernie, you and Gordon need to check the boats for any maintenance, I don't want any couplings rusting up. While you are on deck have a look at the Capstan and the Blake Slip, is that clear?"

"Will do Joe," replied Ernie.

"Right Abdel, lets show you the rest of the ship, because some of these poor bastards need rest, I don't know why. I have seen more life in a prisoner's blanket."

They both left to howls of derision from those present.

"I like to keep them on their toes."

"Yes sir, I mean Joe."

"That's better, I have heard that you have seen a lot of action during the war and lost a good few shipmates as well."

"Yes, I have seen many dreadful things and lost many friends."

"Us merchant men seem to have been forgotten when all the medals have been handed out, but that is no surprise."

The tour of the ship only took some 15 minutes, then Abdel had to go back to see the Purser and have his papers signed off and stored. While he was there, he was informed that he and another new crew member had to see the Port Doctor for a medical check tomorrow at 1pm. The ship would be leaving San Francisco the day after tomorrow on Friday, September 28th bound for Valparaiso, Chile. As he sat and took all this information, he noticed that the Pursers office was indeed a mess, stuff was just lying about. His desk was awash with documents and Abdel wondered if he would ever get his papers back.

The issue was playing on his mind and he had to say; "Will my papers be safe here Mr Danilo?"

The Purser looked at him, then scanned the room before saying, "I hope you don't think I am untidy; this is just how it looks. I can put my hand on anything I want and yes, your papers will be safe with me."

"Thank you, sir."

"You will get paid on the 3rd of each month and it will be in dollars, do you need any cash?

"No sir, I have money with me."

"Well, it is not a good idea to carry a lot of money around."

"Yes sir, I am always careful sir."

"That's everything sorted then, don't forget your appointment at the Doctors tomorrow, off you go now."

Abdel left the Purser's cabin and returned to his bunk. Three crew members were in the mess and they introduced themselves as Emile Castro from Mexico, Roberto Durando from Costa Rica and Sergio Genaro from Venezuela.

They were all Engineering Ratings or as Emile said, "We are all "greasers," in the engine room."

"We have two other greasers Jurado Salvador and our new shipmate Miguel Calada. He is being given some training down in the engine room by Jurado right now. As you can tell we are all Spanish speaking, Jurado and Miguel are from Honduras. We all speak English or "gringo" as we say on this boat."

As he finished speaking, Ernie and Gordon returned from their maintenance work on the bow deck and fell into their bunks.

Ernie spoke first and said, "So Abdul, you are our new recruit on the deck team. I hope you work harder than some of these lazy sons of bitches. Hey, I am Ernie Carlson," and he offered his hand, which Abdel accepted.

"My name is Abdel not Abdul and I work hard when I am asked to," he replied.

"That's you shot down in flames Ernie," said Gordon.

"It sure is brother, ok Abdel where you from boy?"

"I was born in Afghanistan but I lived in India after my father died. I worked for my uncle in Karachi."

The other two deck ratings, Juan and Sean joined their shipmates after their respective jobs were completed on deck. Ernie took the opportunity to formally introduce the new deck rating to the rest of the team, he stood up and said, "Now listen up you lot, can I give you the one and only Abdel not

Abdul, who is now a fully paid member of the Santa Rita deck crew."

Abdel just raised his hand and said, "Thank you, I am pleased to be here."

He was not totally enamoured by Ernie's approach and felt he was being less than genuine in his verbal repartee. Gordon rose to his feet and shook Abdel's hand and said, "Ignore this idiot, he is a New Yorker and he has the manners of a halfwit. I am Gordon Wallace from Inverness, Scotland. Pleased to make your acquaintance Abdel."

"Thank you, it is good to have friends on a ship," he replied.

Juan then welcomed Abdel saying, "It is good to have a new face on board; I am told you were attacked many times during the war. Tell us what it was like, we did not see any action on the west coast."

Abdel gave all present an edited version of his time on board the *Domelia* and the *Barat Star*. The audience listened intently and at the end, Ernie said, "Well, maybe I was little too quick trying to be the "big enchilada" Abdel. Sometimes I don't a give a rat's ass what I say and it don't mean horse shit man."

"I think that's the closest you are going to get to an apology Abdel," added Gordon.

Abdel just smiled, he did not fully understand what Ernie had said, but he gathered that it was sincere. An hour later, Joe told Abdel he would be paired up with Gordon and they were given their work rota prior to sailing. They were also given their watch duties Abdel would take the morning watch at 4am till 8am on the port, with Gordon having the same watch on the starboard.

The next day Abdel and the other new crew member Miguel left the ship for their medical inspection at the Doctors. The medical centre was on Pier 24 and not far from their anchorage. Abdel was called in first. He knew what to expect this time, but it did not make any easier to stand while the doctor examined his private parts for any infection. The rest of the examination was rudimentary in terms of just answering questions about his general health. After ten minutes it was all over and he was given his medical card stamped for acceptance. Miguel had to endure a longer inspection. Abdel sat outside the surgery and at one point he could hear the Doctor on the telephone. After twenty minutes Miguel appeared looking somewhat downcast.

"Is everything alright?" asked Abdel.

"Yes, but he did know of my condition," he replied.

Abdel was confused and said, "Did he stamp your medical card?"

"Yes, the Doctor did do that, but he wrote my condition on the card," he replied.

Abdel was reluctant to ask Miguel and he did not think he was going to say anything. Then Miguel said, "I have only one, how you say? Testicle."

Abdel did not know what to say but he whispered in Miguel's ear; "I will not speak of this to anyone Miguel, so God is my witness."

"Gracias Abdel, the Doctor said *"criar una familia"* how you say, I can have children, so it is good."

The Santa Rita left San Francisco at 8.30am on Friday September 28th, laden with a cargo of motor trucks, farm machinery and steel. Abdel had just finished his watch at 8am and stood on the forecastle as the ship sailed out into the Pacific on a cloudless sunny morning. The distance to Valparaiso is 5.800 miles and it would take 18 days, weather dependant on the Humboldt Current. This cold-water ocean current runs north from the tip of Chile up to the north of Peru, a distance of some 1.800 miles and it extends for 600 miles from the coast travelling at around 10 knots.

Having sailed for some twenty minutes a sea fog descended, a common occurrence in these waters in the summer. Once this had been negotiated the Santa Rita sailed on past Los Angeles, making good headway on a moderate sea and waves of 3 feet. By the time Abdel had started his watch at 4am the ship was west of San Diego.

The ship made good progress and after 4 days at sea she was due west of Acapulco, having sailed through the Tropic of Cancer. Below decks Abdel was in his bunk reading the last few pages of Dr Jekyll & Mr Hyde when Gordon walked into the mess.

"Have you seen the film Abdel?"

Abdel looked up at Gordon and said, "Film, what film is that Gordon?"

"*Dr Jekyll & Mr Hyde*, its great stuff. Frederick March got an Oscar for his part as Dr Jekyll. It was made in 1932, Miriam Hopkins was the femme fatale."

"Femme fatale, I don't understand," he said,

"You have a dictionary don't you, look it up," he replied.

"Yes, thank you I will do that now."

He quickly extricated his dictionary from his kit bag and thumbed through and finally said, "I have found it Gordon."

"Right, read it out then."

"An alluring or seductive woman who leads men into dangerous or difficult situations by her charm," he replied.

"Ah yes, Miriam Hopkin could lead me anywhere Abdel, if I was to be so lucky. There are not many like her in Inverness."

"Alluring Gordon, I have never heard this word."

"No, I doubt you have Abdel; it is like falling to the devil's temptation," he replied.

"God will guide me away from such women, I pray."

"Well, that may be so my son, but there is a woman out there for all of us, I guess. I have still to find her, but I know she is out there."

The conversation allowed Abdel to drift his thoughts to Maheera back in Karachi and he wondered if she was happy. Then there was Isabella in Malta, his only other "romantic" experience.

"Have you finished that book then?"

Abdel was still in this other world and did not respond to the question.

"Hey Abdel."

Abdel awoke from his mental excursion and said, "Yes Gordon, I am sorry, what did you ask?"

"I said have you finished reading that book yet?"

"Oh no, I have a few pages to go," he replied.

"I won't spoil it for you, but when you get the chance you must see the film."

Gordon noticed an Atlas on Abdel's bed among along with his Dictionary and the Noble Qur'an and asked; "Do you look at the atlas Abdel?"

Abdel lifted his head from his book and said, "Yes, it is good to see where we are going in this world. I like reading about places and where they are."

"Ah, but can you use a map reference to find a place on a map?"

Abdel looked puzzled and replied; "I just find the country and look until a find the place. I have found Karachi, Malta and Liverpool."

"There is an easier way bonny lad, let me show you."

Gordon picked up the Atlas and said, "Right we are going to find Inverness, my home town in Scotland."

He then went to the index at the back of the Atlas, found Inverness and then pointed out the page number 64 and the map reference of C3.

"So now we go to page 64, you find it for me."

Abdel found the required page and Gordon said, "Now, page 64 gives us Great Britain. If we look across the top of the page it gives us letters in alphabetical order. We want the letter C. Now if we look down the left-hand side of the page, we find the number 3, can you see what we have done?"

"Yes, I see that," he replied;

"So, by following the letter down and the number across we will find what we are looking for in that square on the map, can you now see Inverness?"

Abdel looked closely and spotted it saying, "Yes, I have found Inverness, here it is," and pointed it out to Gordon.

"There you go, that is how to use a map reference."

"This is good, I must practice this," he replied.

"Tell you what, I will write down some places and you can find them. How about that?"

"That would be very good Gordon, thank you."

"You finish your book and I will give you a list of places, pass your pen and notepad."

Abdel finished *Dr Jekyll & Mr Hyde* and set about finding a long list of places Gordon had written down.

"That will keep you busy for a while lad. But don't miss your watch or Joe will have your guts for garters," said Gordon.

Abdel spent the next two hours thumbing through his Atlas finding places including Glasgow, Mecca, London, Sydney, Wellington, Paris, Berlin, Cairo and many more besides.

In order to refuel with diesel, the Santa Rita had to dock at Guayaquil in Ecuador, before continuing her voyage to Valparaiso in Chile. The ship sailed into the port at Valparaiso on October 18th. The ship would unload its cargo and take on new cargo ready for sailing on October 24th, the Captain granted shore leave for 3 days. He allowed the crew to switch watch duties to enable seamen to get ashore. Abdel chose to take shore leave during the day and he sought the company of Miguel and Emile for these outings. It was convenient to have two Spanish speaking shipmates along, it made communicating with market sellers and shop owners, so much easier. He could not find a bookshop that sold English speaking books so he bought some clothes instead.

Aided by the Humboldt current the Santa Rita made good headway on her voyage back to San Francisco, arriving on Friday, November 9th. Since his somewhat sardonic quip at their first meeting Abdel and Ernie had formed a friendly bond and often spent time discussing all manner of things including their love of music. Ernie was a lover of the blues and enjoyed players like Robert Johnson, Sun House, and Mississippi John Hurt. Abdel liked what he heard on his radio and along with artists like Django Reinhardt he found an interest in what they were doing in a musical sense.

Ernie had promised to book tickets for them both if any of these artists were playing in and around San Francisco, as long as they were on shore leave at the time.

The Captain had given the crew a week's shore leave before their next voyage to Havana, Cuba. Ernie suggested that he, Abdel, Gordon and Emile should have a day in San Francisco and take in some of the sights. His fellow crew members were in agreement and on a warm Thursday, November 15th all four set off for the "city of hills." After a brief tour of Fisherman's Wharf and all its plethora of Italian restaurants they set out for the centre of town. They took a trip to the top of the Twin Peaks which are the central hub of the city. Then Market Street, Powel Street and a ride on a Street Car. Next was Grant Street and Chinatown.

Abdel was in awe at the sheer size of the buildings such as the State Building, the Library and the Legion of Honour Building, which is a replica of the building in Paris. He had his camera with him and he took many photographs as they toured the city. They managed to get to Golden Gate Park and went boating on one of the lakes. The itinerary also took in the Zoo and a walk around the Marina district to complete the tour. As they all sat in Torino's restaurant enjoying a meal, they chatted about what the future had in store.

Ernie said he had an apartment that he rented on Telegraph Hill from another merchant seaman who was an engineer on another of the Grace Line Ships, the Santa Clara. He also said that when he has had enough of the merchant navy, that he would settle in San Francisco.

"But you are from New York Ernie, have you not family there," said Emile.

"No, I was raised by my aunt in Brooklyn, my parents gave me up when I was 6 months old and went to Canada."

"Will you get married Ernie?" asked Gordon.

"Well buddy, I am 42 now. Not Sure if I want a wife, but you never know," he replied.

"Do you have a wife Emile?" said Abdel.

"Yes amigo, I have a wife Conchita and two boys, Carlos and Diego. We have a house in Mexico in a village called Puerto Vallarta on the coast. It is a beautiful village, my father was a fisherman, but he died last year."

Abdel took another photograph of his shipmates and asked a waiter to take a picture of the four of them before they departed and returned to the ship.

The Santa Rita continued to move passengers and cargo to Chile, Peru, Mexico, Costa Rica and Cuba. In the spring of 1947 two historic events occurred, one of which Abdel was privileged to witness. While on a voyage to Callao in Peru, the Santa Rita witnessed Thor Heyerdahl's Raft Kon Tiki setting sail for Polynesia. The ship the Guardian Rios was towing the raft some 50 miles out into the Pacific as the Santa Rita passed them one mile south west. The captain slowed the Santa Rita down to 9 knots and the crew waved the six men on for what was to be an incredible journey that would last some four months and cover some 4300 nautical miles.

On the other side of the world a momentous discovery was made, a shepherd boy called Muhammad adh-Dhib entered a cave in the cliffs at Khirbet Qumran 15 miles east of Jerusalem, looking for a lost sheep. What he found were the Dead Sea Scrolls, rolled up and inside large earthenware jars.

The world was changing, no more so, than in India. On August 15th 1947 the country was partitioned and the State of Pakistan was formed and India was given independence from the British Empire. As a result, Karachi was now in Pakistan. The change also brought conflict and the Indo - Pakistani War was fought over the states of Jammu and Kashmir. Hindu fought against Muslims and as a consequence Pakistan became a Muslim state.

In 1948 further conflict in the middle east resulted in the creation of the State of Israel on May 14th and in June tensions were rising in Berlin which would ultimately divide the country of Germany.

Change seemed to be the *"modus operandi"* and Grace Line were making changes of their own in terms of future routes by their ships, it was decided that the Santa Rita would switch to Vancouver and sail to Hawaii. Abdel was not sure this change was for the best and he sought advice from his shipmates, some of whom shared his concerns. Even Deck Officer Joe had reservations and was considering getting a transfer to another ship.

Fortunately, Abdel was nearing the end of his three-year contract and he could leave without any penalty being applied. He liked the San Francisco area and he had made a few trips to Sacramento with Ernie in the last two years. Ernie had friend a Brody, who had a Garage and a workshop in town, where he repaired cars, trucks and farm vehicles.

Every time Abdel went Brody offered him a job. This was now an attractive offer and he talked to Ernie at some length on this change in his life.

Ernie's approach was simple and he would say; "Life is too short Abdel, go with it. You are a good man and you work hard."

Abdel thought about what Syed would say and finally came to the conclusion that he would leave the Santa Rita and Grace Line and take up Brody's offer of employment. The only issue was that of gaining a Green Card, a Permanent Resident Visa. This allows foreign nationals to work and live in the USA.

With the help of Grace Line, Ernie and Brody, Abdel's application was granted. He got his Green Card at the State Building in San Francisco on September 15th 1948.

CHAPTER SIXTEEN

The following day he boarded the train for the 88-mile journey to Sacramento. A new chapter in his life had begun and like his first voyage on a ship, it excited him. He had telephoned both Hakim and Abdullah explaining his intentions. Hakim was not convinced it was the right thing to do and suggested that the change was too great. Abdullah was less reticent, but he suggested that if it did not work out, he would welcome him back to Karachi. Abdel had promised to send photographs of the people and places in his new life within the next few weeks.

After some twenty minutes on the train, he got out his Atlas from his kit bag. A woman sitting opposite watched Abdel work through the Atlas locating various places and said, "You obviously find maps very interesting young man."

Abdel looked up to see a woman who was very well dressed, she wore a small hat perched upon blonde curly hair and she was wearing a string of pearls around her neck.

"Yes, I have found reading maps very interesting," he replied.

"Do you read other books then."

"Oh Yes, I have read *War of The Worlds*, *Robinson Crusoe* and *Dr Jekyll & Mr Hyde*."

"My my, you have read some classics there, forgive me but you are not from these parts I guess."

"No, I was born in Afghanistan and my name is Abdel Malik Rahman and I am going to work for Mr Brody Miller, who has a garage on 10th Street near Capitol Park in Sacramento."

"Please to meet Abdel, my name is Caroline Wenzel and I am the senior Librarian at the City Library."

She offered her hand and Abdel delicately shook it and said, "You must have many books in your library."

"Oh yes, we have thousands of books, I do hope you will come and join the library, once you have settled in."

"I would like that very much, thank you."

"You must have an interesting story to tell, from Afghanistan to Sacramento."

Abdel then reprised his life from his trek to Karachi and his life at sea, the war and his subsequent arrival in Sacramento. Miss Wenzel was fascinated and after Abdel had captivated her for over an hour she said, "Well, I have heard many tales and experiences of life, but yours is truly inspiring Abdel. I hope you find happiness and prosperity from this day on. It has been a pleasure talking with you."

"Thank you Miss, I am sorry I forgot your name."

"Wenzel, Caroline," she replied.

"Within five minutes the train was pulling into the station and Abdel allowed Miss Wenzel to leave her seat before he too got up and made his way to the platform. There to meet him was Brody, he took Abdel's kit bag and said, "Great to see you, how was your trip?"

"It was very good Brody; I spoke with a very nice lady on the train. Her name was Miss Caroline Wessell I think."

"Wow, you aint just been talking to anybody there boy. That is some lady in this town and its Wenzel not Wessell. She is at the City Library and she is big in this here place," he replied.

The two men made their way to a waiting car. Brody got in the front next to the driver and Abdel got in the back with his kit bag.

"This here is Tom, he started to work for me in the garage two years ago, he is a good hand, say hello Tom," said Brody.

"How you doing man?" he said.

"Yes, I am pleased to meet you Tom," replied Abdel.

Tom was as black as pitch, with huge shoulders and his head was touching the inside of the car roof, suggesting he was a very big man.

"This guy is a gentle giant, but you don't want to cross him. That right Tom."

"Yes Boss, I aint no fighter though," Tom replied.

"I have got you some rooms off L Street Abdel it's a dollar a week. We will get you acquainted with the place, drop your bag off and we will get some chow' at the KI KI Café on 4th Street."

"What is chow, Brody?"

"It aint moose shit," joked Tom.

"It's food Abdel, you need to eat dontcha?" said Brody.

"Yes, I am hungry," he replied.

The car pulled up outside Abdel's new home, a ground floor abode with a bathroom, a bedroom, a parlour and a small back yard.

Brody gave Abdel a key for the front door, as Tom got his kit bag out of the car. Abdel let them in and Brody said, "Thelma cleans once a week, she charges 50 cents."

"Thelma, who is that Brody?" he replied.

"She knows you boy; she not coffee coloured like you, she is black like me. Don't cross her, she will scalp you with her yard brush," quipped Tom.

From there Tom dropped Brody and Abdel off at the KI KI Café for some food and refreshment. During the meal Brody explained Abdel's working shifts and what he will be paid saying, "You work six days a week Monday to Saturday, but sometimes if we get a breakdown on a Sunday. We are liable to get a call; you get $20 a week and any tips from customers are your own. There is me, Tom and Mike who work in the garage, you will meet Mike tomorrow morning. Any questions Abdel?"

"Tips, what are they?"

"Sometimes a customer will drop you extra money for good work."

"I was going to ask you if you are a church bible basher, but you are a Muslim, that right?"

"Yes, is there a mosque in town?"

"Nope, aint ever seen one."

"I will pray at my home, it is good. God is with us wherever we go."

"Well, I hope your right. I aint one for religion."

They finished their food and decide to walk back to Abdel's rooms on L Street. It was now 7pm and Brody left Abdel to settle in saying, "Don't forget, we start work at 7am, you aint got far to walk from here, see you in morning."

Abdel spent an hour putting his things away and then had a bath. He then laid his prayer mat on his bedroom floor and prayed for guidance and his new friends. He read from the Noble Qur'an and glanced through his atlas before climbing into his bed and quickly fell asleep.

He arrived at Brody's Garage prompt at 7am.

"Good start on time Abdel, how the hell do you know what time it is anyhow, you aint got a watch," said Brody.

"I have my radio, that tells me the time."

"You need to buy yourself a watch, you can't hump your radio around. We will have to have a visit to Myers Jewellery store on K Street and get you a cheap watch. We can do that at lunchtime, you happy with that?"

"Yes, but how much will this cost me?"

"How much have you got?"

"I have $15 left, is that enough?"

"Damn right, you don't want no expensive timepiece, it will maybe cost about $3 or $4."

"That is very good, thank you."

"You aint met Mike yet, Mike over hear and meet our new mechanic."

Mike appeared from behind a Station Wagon and said, "High their fella, I am Mike Ferrone, the best mechanic in Sacramento, pleased to meet you, Abdel is it?"

"Yes, I am very happy to meet you Mike," and shook Mike's hand.

"The guy who owns this heap of junk aint gonna be pleased to see me when I give him the bill for the work, I done," he joked.

Mike was a small guy, going bald and he had a horrendous scar across his jaw. Mike noticed Abdel looking and said,

"This hear scar was caused by a grinding disc flying out of the machine three years ago, that right Brody."

"Damn right, there was blood everywhere. We had to rush Mike to the Mercy Hospital on J Street."

"Yer, Mike was bleeding like stuck hogg," added Tom.

Abdel's first week would be all about watching and learning and that first day involved gaining knowledge of motor vehicles and how they work. He observed both Tom and Brody at work and as always asked many questions about engines and the tools and equipment. At 12.30pm he and Brody walked to Myers Jewellery Store and Abdel selected a Fero Swiss Mechanical Wristwatch with a leather strap, the cost $5.

While Abdel was paying for his watch another male customer who was looking at a selection of watches in the glass case under the counter, looked up and said, "Jesus Christ, what is this, a nigger that can read the time. What the hell is the world coming to, I despair I really do."

The word nigger sent shudders through Abdel, but before he could react Brody intervened and said, "Listen up you son of a bitch, this guy served in the war for the allies. Have some respect you arsehole, he's got balls, where are yours?"

"I aint causing any trouble buddy, just speaking my mind," he replied.

"Well do me a great big fat favour and keep your comments to yourself, you aint good enough to clean the shit of his boots."

The man abruptly stormed out of the store.

Abdel looked at Brody and before he could speak, Brody said, "Don't say nothin, just wait till he comes to me for help with his car, he aint gonna get any."

Mr Myers expressed his disgust at the departed potential customer, looked at Abdel and said, "Here in Sacramento we treat everyone the same, that guy does not represent the true folks of this town. You are welcome anytime and thank you Brody for your intercession sir."

Abdel's first week passed very quickly and he soon developed his practical skills, some of which he inherited from his work as a deck rating at sea. He showed particular aptitude in recognising simple problems with mechanical parts as the weeks drifted on in this new life. On September 23rd President Harry Truman spoke to a gathered crowd from the platform at the Southern Pacific Depot in Sacramento as part of his re-election campaign.

Abdel attended along with Mike and Brody and when he departed, Mike said, "He aint getting my vote boys, I don't trust him."

On October 15th Abdel was 30 years old, this was something he had not considered to be relevant in any way. His friends had other ideas and when he arrived for work that morning, he was surprised to see that the garage was closed. On the big wooden doors of the garage, there was a sign which read; "Please use the side door," and an arrow pointing to the left.

Abdel opened the door and a cheer went up as he stepped into the garage. Brody, Tom, Thelma and Mike burst into "Happy Birthday" and they all shook Abdel's hand.

"I am so happy that you have done this for me."

"That aint nothing, we aint doing no work this morning we are going for breakfast to celebrate your birthday at the Sutter Restaurant on K Street and I'm paying the bill," said Brody.

"How did you know it was my birthday Brody?"

"Don't forget, I have seen your papers remember."

"Oh yes, I understand."

Tom drove them all round to Sutter's Restaurant and a table was reserved for them. A white sealed envelope was sitting in the middle of the table with Abdel written on the front.

As they took their seats, Mike said, "Well Abdel, open that their envelope fella."

Abdel opened the envelope to find a card with a mountain scene featured on the front and happy birthday scrolled across the top. He opened the card and read, "Happy birthday to the new mechanic in town, from all your workmates." It had been signed by everyone including Ernie.

As if by magic, who should walk into the restaurant, but Ernie.

"Well, aint this just dandy, a birthday party," he announced as he grabbed Abdel and gave him a hug and shook his hand.

When everyone was seated Brody produced two parcels and presented them to Abdel saying, "We chipped in to get you these for your birthday."

Abdel opened the first to find a pair of overalls with his name sewn on the lapel. He was ecstatic and quickly opened the other parcel which revealed a book. It was *The Ship* by C.S. Forester. This rendered him speechless and on the point of crying, when Tom said, "You aint got time to read that at work, you got too many chores to do," and laughed.

Abdel managed to compose himself and said, "This is all very special my friends, I am very happy today."

They enjoyed a breakfast banquet of kedgeree, eggs, rye bread, pancakes, maple syrup and coffee.

During the breakfast Ernie announced that he had left the merchant navy and had picked up a job working as driver for a Fruit Wholesaler in San

Francisco and he had a lady friend called Donna, who worked for a local estate agency.

As always Abdel had his Kodak with him and many photographs were taken that morning. As they sat and talked Abdel said to Mike; "How do I join the City Library Mike?"

"You one for reading books then," he replied.

"Yes, I have read many books and I have met Miss Caroline Wenzel on the train, when I first came to Sacramento. She owns the Library I think."

Mike laughed and said, "I don't think she owns the Library Abdel, but she is a big fish over there, that's for sure. You can just turn up and register, but remember to take your ID papers and your green card."

"That is good, I will do this tomorrow," he replied.

The other topic of conversation around the table was about the removal of the streetcar tracks on 10th and K Streets. Opinion was divided on the subject with Brody all for it saying,

"Look, its gonna give us more work and that means more job security. Yes, it means more vehicles in the city, but this aint San Francisco."

"I think they got other plans Brody," added Mike.

"Well, it don't matter to me or Thelma, we aint drivers, that right girl," said Tom.

"Hallelujah to that," she said.

Breakfast lasted until 11.30am and Abdel was given the rest of the day off. He took the opportunity to get his ID and papers and walk to the City Library to register.

He felt a man in charge of his own destiny now and his new friends and his new job gave him a sense of independence. It also gave him a sense of achievement, that he could not say he enjoyed as a merchant seaman. His world was a good place to be and he had a zest for life. He now felt he wanted to share his happiness and he hoped that a romance might be forthcoming in the near future. There were many attractive lady's in Sacramento, he had noticed the young girl in the Ki Ki Café, the lady in serving in Myers Jewellery Store and a very pretty girl standing outside the Sacramento Hotel the other day.

He arrived at the City Library and stood and gazed at its magnificent façade. He felt overwhelmed by its grandeur and had doubts about continuing, then a voice behind him said, "You can go in you know, it's free."

He turned to see a young lady dressed in a pale blue suit and a wide brimmed hat. She paused beside him and said, "It looks like you are new to the Library, is that so?"

"Yes, that is right. I have come to join the Library. Miss Caroline Wenzel said I should join."

"Well, if she said that, then you must. Walk with me and I will see that you find the clerk who will complete your registration. Do you have your ID with you?"

"Yes, I have it all with me."

They walked into the building; Abdel was awe struck as he entered the main entrance. He was in state of wonderment as he followed his guide to a desk, where another young lady sat.

"This is Grace, she will help you with your registration, enjoy our library," as she turned to go Abdel said,

"Thank you very much miss,"

She smiled and said, "You are very welcome."

Then she was gone. Abdel turned to Grace and said,

"I did not know her name."

"That was Jessica, she is a librarian here."

"Do you know Miss Caroline Wenzel?"

Grace raised her head, looked surprised and said, "Indeed I do she is my boss in here, do you know her then?"

"Oh yes, we talked on the train into Sacramento not long ago."

Grace was a little unnerved by this revelation and after checking Abdel's papers she picked up the telephone and dialled a number, as Abdel waited patiently, she got a response at the other end of the line and said, "I have a gentleman here called Abdel M Rahman, he said that he knows you miss."

After hearing the response at the other end, she put the phone down and said, "I will process your application soon, if you would like to sit over there."

She pointed to a chair situated in the main entrance.

"Yes, thank you very much."

After only some three minutes, Miss Caroline Wenzel came striding up to Grace's desk and said, "Well, where is he?"

Grace pointed to where Abdel was sitting, Miss Wenzel turned and immediately recognised Abdel and strode over to him saying, "I am so glad that you found the time to come along to our library Abdel."

Abdel quickly rose to his feet and said, "Thank you very much, you have a wonderful library Miss Wenzel."

"Thank you, but call me Caroline please."

Grace stood gobsmacked by this spectacle and waved saying, "I have his library ticket, Miss Wenzel."

"Oh yes, we must have that."

And she took Abdel back to the desk to collect his papers and his library ticket.

"Thank you, Grace."

She then escorted Abdel away into the library.

Abdel was amazed at the number of books stacked on bookshelves that filled the various rooms within the building. Miss Wenzel gave him a full tour explaining the various sections and the subjects. When the tour was over, she bid him farewell saying, "Now don't forget, you can have up to six books at any one time. Remember to return them on time and I am sure I do not need to tell you this, but I will say it anyway; Please take care of the books you borrow and happy reading."

"Thank you very much Miss Wenzel"

She left Abdel to browse the shelves, he was in his element. He picked books and sat with them at one of the long reading tables and flicked through each one, then returned them to their designated place. At 5pm he had been there four hours and a librarian who had been watching him with some interest approached him and gently whispered; "We close in 30 minutes, if you would like to choose your books and have them stamped at the desk, thank you."

"Thank you, yes books I will choose them."

He had not chosen a book from the many he picked up and had not realised until he looked down at his wristwatch, how long he had been in library. He eventually chose *For Whom the Bell Tolls* by Ernest Hemmingway and *Tom Sawyer* by Mark Twain. He took them across to the lending desk where he had them stamped and the librarian said, "You need to return them on or before November 14th"

He watched the librarian stamp both books and he said, "Thank you very much Miss."

He left the Library full of self-confidence that he had achieved this challenge on his own. On his walk back to his apartment he took in the city and spent time observing the activities taking place and the people going about their business. He watched the traffic cop controlling the traffic and how so powerful he looked, one man against this tide of moving vehicles.

He spent the night listening to his radio and reading Tom Sawyer, until hies eyes grew tired and he fell asleep.

CHAPTER SEVENTEEN

Sacramento was growing into a strong independent cultural centre, having reaped the benefits from America's involvement in the second World War. Midway through the nineteenth century, Sacramento was famous for the discovery of gold at Sutter's Mill in 1848. As a consequence, the region was turned into a hectic and at times lawless territory. This resulted in the thousands of prospectors hoping to make a fortune. The Sacramento area was originally home to the Nisenan and Miwok Indians, whose presence went back some 4000 years. Their domination of the land would end with the arrival of the European settlers who brought diseases like smallpox and malaria, which in turn decimated the Native Indians. As more and more settlers came to the Sacramento valley, these indigenous native Americans were reduced to slaves for the new world settlers.

Despite the near extinction of these tribes, the Sacramento area developed into a melting pot of cultures. This was sustained and all ethnic groups mingled and sought to provide a homespun environment for all who lived and worked together. The city of Sacramento was and still is referred to as the "City of Trees." This is a reflective comparison, as trees come in many guises and spread their beauty and strength.

Changes were being made within its industrial and commercial milieu. Prior to 1945 Sacramento was dependant on farming, the railroad, the cannery and the Airforce base's at McClellan and Mather Field. These were the major employers and the economic lifeblood of the area. A great diversity of people came to Sacramento in the 1920's to work including Italians, Portuguese, Chinese, Japanese, Filipinos and Mexican Americans.

The city had a population of some 7000 Japanese Americans. Sadly, after the attack on Pearl Harbour and the declaration of war with Japan. It was decreed that all Japanese people were to be interned in camps for the duration of the war. They had to leave their homes and businesses, in some cases they rented out their homes to others to maintain a foothold. However, only 59 % returned to restart their lives after the war. To fill the void of their absence, the Bracero Programme was introduced and workers from Mexico were temporarily contracted in to work in the fields.

African Americans gradually moved into Sacramento during the Gold Rush and as the years advanced, their presence was enhanced with available work on the farms. During the war years, they were employed on armament contracts at McClennan. In general terms they were accepted as part of the infrastructure of Sacramento and racial tension was rarely evident in this period of Sacramento's history.

People of Sacramento were considered to be tolerant and understanding of each other's hopes and dreams. Abdel felt he was part of this culture and he was gaining in self-reliance. He was working hard at Brody Millers garage and learnt to drive under Mike's tutorage, resulting in a driving licence being awarded in February, 1949. He would often drive Tom back to his house in Oak Park after work and then he would go for a drive around the city.

His regular attendance at the City Library continued and he was becoming a familiar sight browsing the shelves.

On one such occasion he was asked by a woman for help locating a specific book within the historical section, when she asked; "Excuse me, could you tell me where I will find books on the Native American Indians?"

Abdel had seen a small section of books on this topic and said, "Yes, I will take you to that section, if you would like to follow me please."

He quickly located the shelf that housed the books saying, "Here is what you are looking for miss."

"Thank you and its Gretchen, pleased to meet you."

She extended her hand and Abdel did likewise and said, "I am pleased to meet you Gretchen, my name is Abdel Malik Rahman."

She was roughly about 5 feet 5 inches in height with long curly auburn hair swept back off her shoulders. She had light brown eyes and a very pretty smile.

"I am new to Sacramento; my family have moved here from Baton Rouge in Louisiana. I was born in Denmark and when I was five years old my parents moved to the USA."

"I will leave you to find a book. If you need any help, I will be sitting at the reading table over there" and pointed to the table in question.

"Thank you, Abdel, you are very kind."

Abdel left her to browse and walked over to the reading table, something just hit him about her, the attraction was immediate but he resisted the temptation to turn back to where she was standing and sat down with a copy of *The Way of Poetry* by John Drinkwater. He opened the book randomly opened at page 142.

As he began to read the second verse, he felt a presence. He looked around to see Gretchen standing over him. She felt embarrassed and said, "Oh sorry, I should have said something. It's just that you seemed so taken by the book."

Abdel sensed she was feeling a little awkward and said, "Do not worry, do you want to join me at the table?"

"That would be good, if that is alright?

"Please sit here," and he pulled out a chair for her.

She sat and opened her book, but seemed more interested in Abdel's book of poems.

"Do you like poetry Abdel?"

"Well, I have found some very difficult to understand. My English is not very good but I am getting better. I have a dictionary and I use it most of the time."

"You speak English very well Abdel, did you learn it at school?"

"Oh no, I have had no real schooling since I was eleven years old."

She was surprised and said, "Really, you speak very well. But I think like me, you were not born in America."

She thought Abdel was good looking, standing at 5' 9" with thick black hair. He had gained a good physique with the hard labour on board ship. He had a prominent chin that enhanced his features and pronounced mystic brown eyes, she was smitten.

Abdel then spent the next fifteen minutes telling her his life story. She was very attentive and never interrupted him as he revealed his life. She then told her story about her own life in the USA, her memory of Denmark was very vague. They had been talking for over thirty minutes when she looked at her wristwatch and said, "Oh no, my father will be waiting for me. He is outside in his car, I must go."

Abdel felt lost and wanted to see her again. The feeling was mutual, she wrote down her address on a slip of paper from her bag and gave it to him saying, "Please take this, it would be nice to meet again."

She smiled and departed to the desk to get her book stamped.

Abdel watched her until she was clear of the building. He was elated and sat and wondered how he should approach the possibility of another encounter.

After reading Shelley's *Loves Philosophy* another three times he took the book to the desk and had it stamped. He then left the library and headed home. He could not stop thinking about Gretchen and how to arrange another rendezvous. That night he tried to concentrate on reading Tom Sawyer, but Gretchen kept breaking into his thoughts. He gave up and fell asleep with her smile evoking a beguiling apparition.

After some two days of wondering how to contact Gretchen, he confided in Mike and sought help. At the end of their shift Abdel asked Mike if he would advise him on his predicament. Having availed Mike of the situation, his workmate said, "Ok buddy, so you have met a gal and you want to see her again, that is what you are telling me?

"Yes, but I do not know the best way to do this Mike, I have her address."

"What you gotta do is wait, don't rush in. Give her time to think, remember absence makes the heart grow fonder Abdel."

"Should I wait a week Mike?"

"Yip, good plan but don't go knocking on her screen door. Just put a note in an envelope with her name written on it and put it in their post box. That way no one is gonna see it but her. Be clever, just say in the note that you wanna see her and name a place, the day and time. You must put your name on it partner and your home address. You could put the garage phone number on, just in case she has a phone in her place. I am sure Brody won't mind on that, but mention it to him anyway."

"This is a good plan Mike, thank you. I will do this."

"Anyway, where does she live?" asked Mike.

Abdel rummaged around his dungarees and pulled out a piece of paper.

"Here it is," and read the address.

"She lives at 26 Haven Point. William Land Park. Sacramento."

"My, that is prime real estate brother, it's just south of Broadway. Her father must be a big hitter in town Abdel."

"I don't understand Mike, a big hitter?"

"It means he is an important guy, probably has a business or he works for local government maybe."

"This I do not know Mike."

"You will in a week's time I reckon," he said smiling.

Before Mike left Abdel, he informed him with a "must do" when he next meets Gretchen.

"Now Abdel, in order to curry favour from her and her mom and dad. When you meet her again, make sure you have a bunch of flowers for her and another bunch for her mother. That will make you the "cat's whiskers," buddy."

Again, Abdel did not fully comprehend this idiom and gave Mike a puzzled look.

"It means you will be very popular Abdel. That's another one for your dictionary."

Abdel had another five days to prepare and deliver his "billet doux." He planned to leave the note at her address after his shift at the garage on Friday, June 11$^{th.}$ He spent many hours writing his note and altering it repeatedly. Finally, he created a note that read:

"*To Gretchen,*

I enjoyed our talk in the library and I would like to see you again. I would be very happy if you could join me for a coffee and a walk in the park on Sunday, June 13th at 4pm. If you could leave me a note at my address or you can telephone me the garage where I work on 286346.

Thank you, Abdel Malik Rahman.
14 L Street.
Sacramento."

This final version was put in the family post box at the end of a large drive at 26 Haven Point at 5pm on June 11th. As Abdel dropped the sealed envelope into the box, he looked up the driveway, but no one was visible. He got back into the car and drove back to the garage where Brody was just in the process of locking up and said,

"You just made it Abdel," and handed him a dollar saying, "This is a tip from Chuck Davidson, he was impressed with your service. He came round half an hour ago."

"Thank you, Brody, and could I have a car on Sunday afternoon?"

"Yep, I reckon that is ok. You got a date then?"

Abdel felt a little embarrassed and he said, "Yes Brody, has Mike told you?"

"He didn't have to amigo; it is written all over your face. Just make sure you aint late in taking the lady home."

"Yes, thank you. I will be an honourable man Brody. I have given her the garage telephone number, to contact me. Is that alright with you?"

"Yip, as long as you aint losing time on your work," he replied.

On Saturday morning at 11.30am Gretchen rang the garage. Brody answered; "Millers garage how can we help?"

"Good morning, my name is Gretchen; could I speak to Abdel Rahman please?"

Brody shouted across the garage where Abdel was changing a wheel; "Hey Romeo Rahman, there is a gal on the phone for you."

Abdel dropped the wheel wrench and walked to Brody, who was holding the phone and had a great big smile on his face.

"There you go lover boy."

He handed him the phone and went to complete Abdel's wheel change.

Abdel was only on the phone a minute and only spoke to say; "Yes, that is good Gretchen, I will pick you up at 4pm goodbye."

When he put the phone back on the receiver, a loud cheer went up from all those present and then Mike said,

"Our boy is in love guys, it's in the bag."

At the end of the shift on Saturday, Brody told Abdel to put some gas in the car he was using for Sunday and said, "You got everything sorted for Sunday then?"

Tom who was sweeping the floor and chipped in with; "Am you going to sweep her off her feet then boss, you might need this here brush."

Mike laughed and added; "He is going up to William Land Park, there's money up there Brody. I reckon Abdel is going to buy you out." "Any more of that bullshit and I will make him second banana around here" joked Brody.

Abdel accepted all the leg pulling and said, "I am not worried, how you say? I call the shots."

"Well there is confidence for you, looks like he has got this gal on a lasso," said Mike.

Abdel washed up and bid everyone farewell, he was about to get into the car when it dawned on him. He turned around and addressed his workmates and said, "Where will I get flowers tomorrow?"

"Now then, good thing you remembered cowboy," said Brody.

"You will get em at Rosie's on K Street boss, what you gonna wear, you got smart clothes Abdel?" added Tom.

"Very good, thank you Tom, I have a suit I bought last week and a new shirt."

"You is gonna look like a movie star," he said.

Abdel got into the car and left for home, feeling so elated as he drove the short journey. Thelma had left him some homemade apple pie and he made himself a coffee and ate the pie with gusto. He put his radio on and Duke Ellington was playing, so he relaxed in his chair and picked up Tom Sawyer and read.

He awoke at 8am, prayed then ate a breakfast of rye bread and honey. Finished with a coffee and listened to Count Basie. He got his camera out and ensured he had a full film in his kodak. Having set out his clothes for the afternoon, he went out for the flowers at Rosie's on K Street.

When he got into the store, he was asked what kind of flowers he was looking floor. This created an air of confusion and stood contemplating until the assistant bailed him out by saying, "Are they for a lady then?"

"Oh yes, for two ladies please," he replied.

Now the assistant was confused and said, "Two ladies, are they sisters of yours perhaps?"

"No no, I am calling on a lady this afternoon, the flowers are for her and her mother."

"Ah, now I understand, do they have any special flowers that they like?"

"This I do not know, could you help me with this."

"Of course, let me see what we can arrange for you."

"My name is Charlotte; I work here at weekends only," and she smiled enthusiastically.

Abdel returned the gesture and said, "I am Abdel Malik Rahman and I work at Brody Millers garage."

"Yes, I know, I have seen you from time to time."

She then went to collect a range of flowers from a number of receptacles and returned. She explained what they were, providing a comprehensive breakdown of each example. The flowers included Pink Desert Willows, Orange California Fuchsias, Yellow Black-Eyed Susan and Red Coffeeberry. She arranged them into two bouquets and tied them up with pink ribbon, and when completed she said, "How do they look?"

"They are very good, how much will this cost please?"

"In total, this will cost you $2 and 20 cents."

Again, this was relayed with that ebullient smile.

Abdel handed over $3 and said, "Thank you very much Charlotte, goodbye" and turned to leave.

"Don't forget your change," she said holding out 80 cents.

"Please keep the change, you have been very kind."

"Why thank you indeed, have a nice day," she replied.

Abdel returned to his home and as recommended by Charlotte, he put the flowers in the sink and half-filled it. He then relaxed in the bath listening to the Tommy Dorsey Big Band on his radio.

It was a warm sunny afternoon as Abdel got in the car, a dark green 1940 Chevrolet KB Master 85 Coupe. He set off on the road to Gretchen's home, with the flowers and his camera sitting on the front passenger seat.

As if to spoil his plans for the day, the sky started to show big cumulus clouds and as Abdel rolled up outside Gretchen's home the heavens opened and it began to pour with rain. It was 3.55pm, he sat in the hope that the rain would subside. It did not and at 4pm he picked up the flowers and quickly extricated himself from the car and made his way up the driveway. There were two cars parked outside the house as he stepped up to front door and rang the bell.

He waited, he was just about to ring the bell again when the door opened and an older lady appeared and said, "So I guess you must be Abdul then?"

She looked at Abdel up and down as Abdel responded by saying, "Yes, but it is Abdel Mrs,"

It was then that he realised that he did know Gretchen's surname.

"It's Mrs Geersten. Abdel you say."

"Yes, I have brought you some Flowers," and handed both bouquets to her.

Abdel was hoping Gretchen would soon appear, because he was starting to panic.

"Why, all these are for me, my husband will surely be jealous."

Then Gretchen came to the rescue and appeared saying, "I believe one of these bouquets is for me Abdel, is that so?"

"I am only teasing him Gretchen. Please come in and welcome Abdel."

Abdel was ushered into a large sitting room and was introduced to Gretchen's father. A tall man in a pin striped suit, shirt and tie. He had grey hair cut short, a grey moustache and he wore wire rimmed round spectacles. He shook Abdel's hand and said, "Karsten B Geersten, please to meet you Abdel."

"Thank you and I am very pleased to meet you sir," he replied.

They all sat in comfortable lounge chairs, had homemade lemonade and made small talk until Gretchen thought it was time to vacate the scene and said, "Well Abdel, I am glad you have a car as this rain does not look like it is going to stop. Shall we change our plans about that walk in the park?"

"Yes, but we can still go for a coffee in town if you would like that," he replied.

"That sounds like a good idea, let's go."

"What time will you be back Gretchen?" asked her mother.

"How about 7pm Abdel, is that ok?"

"That is very good yes."

They rose to their feet and Abdel said, "Thank you both for inviting me into your home Mr and Mrs Geersten."

"You are most very welcome, and thank you for the flowers," Gretchen's mother replied.

They both dashed to the car as the rain poured down. Once inside Gretchen said, "That was not so bad was it, mother can be a bit of a pain."

"I felt a fool, not knowing your other name and giving all the flowers to your mother," he replied.

Gretchen smiled and said, "Yer, that was funny Abdel," and she gave him a broad smile.

They stopped outside the Mission Orange Coffee Shop on the corner of 10th and L Streets.

A table was located in a corner that afforded respectful privacy and they ordered coffee and cakes. Gretchen opened their conversation with; "When I first saw you, I thought you were a "*mestizo*," you have their colour."

Abdel was surprised by this and said, "I do not know this name, what does it mean?"

"It is someone of mixed race, often a father who is Portuguese or Spanish and a mother who is a Native Indian. We have many different nationalities here in Sacramento."

"Yes, I know this and sometimes it is hard to understand their language, but I am learning to understand."

"Your English is very good Abdel; I learnt my English from school here in Sacramento after we arrived from Denmark."

"Do you know the motto of this city Abdel?"

"No, this I do not."

"Every time you go to the Capitol Building you will see the words "*Urbs Indomita*" this is Latin for Indomitable City."

"This Latin, do you speak this language?"

"A little, I learnt it at school, it is a very ancient language used by the Romans. It has been replaced by many other forms of language like Italian, Greek, Spanish, French and German. What is your native language Abdel?"

"I speak Pashto, but I also know some Urdu and Hindi, from my years in Karachi. This used to be India, but know it is Pakistan after independence from the British Empire."

They talked and enjoyed their coffee and cake and without noticing, the time had evaporated. It was 6.30pm, and Gretchen said, "The time has gone so quickly, why don't we have another drink?

"Are you sure we might be late?"

"Oh yes, I will sweet talk my mother don't worry."

Abdel took the opportunity to ask the waitress to take a photograph of them. They ordered two soda's and at 6pm they left and returned to Oak Park at 6.15pm. When they parked, Gretchen reached across to Abdel and gave him a long kiss. Abdel put his arms around her and ensured it lasted as long as possible. They finally separated, both in need of air and a sense of composure.

As she turned to get out, she said, "You now know where I live, I have had a fine afternoon. We must do it again Abdel, if that is what you would like and thanks for the flowers."

"Yes, we must and I will speak with you soon."

She closed the car door and smiled before walking up the driveway. Half way up the drive she skipped and turned and smiled again waving her hand.

Abdel had a feeling he had never had before, a feeling of being wanted. The only comparison he could make would be Maheera, back in Karachi. But this was much more intoxicating, the thought someone had shown him genuine affection and trust. He drove the Chevy back to his place and parked it up.

He was feeling hungry, so he walked to Wilson's on K Street and had some fried chicken and salad. His mind was in a state of unbridled satiety and as he ate, he was oblivious to anything else that might be happening. The waitress asked him if he wanted another coffee, but he declined the offer.

His attention was drawn to a couple chatting on the next table. The man was commenting on a recent crime that was carried out in the Town & Country Shopping Village and said, "It seems this guy just produced a hand gun and demanded money from the till. He got away with $60 and pistol whipped a customer on the way out. I hope that Sherriff Brown and his men nail this son of a bitch damn soon Imelda."

"They will get him Arthur; I am sure of that," she replied.

The man looked up at Abdel, realised that he had blasphemed and said, "Sorry for my poor choice of language friend, but it aint good for business in these here places if you have a criminal like this running amok, that right?"

Abdel nodded in agreement and said, "Yes, this man must be stopped, I think it will worry people if he is not caught and punished."

"Damn right friend."

"Arthur, your language please," said Imelda.

"There I go again, forgive my wicked tongue sir."

Imelda had heard enough and at her request they paid their bill and as they left said goodbye to Abdel.

Abdel had not witnessed any criminal activity since his arrival in Sacramento, but it registered with him and he would be a little more vigilant around town from now on. He returned home and prayed for guidance and read from the Noble Qur'an before retiring to his bed for the night.

On arrival at work on Monday morning he got the third degree from his workmates with regard to his romantic liaison with Gretchen.

"I bet you was not happy when the rain fell Abdel, aint that right" joked Tom.

"My plans for a walk in the park, did not happen. So, we went into town and had soda's in the Mission Orange Coffee Shop," he replied.

"You surely know how to treat a lady," added Mike.

Brody poked his head from the office and said, "Aint you got work to do, time to drag ass fellas."

"Yes, sir boss, we is about to service this here Ford," said Tom.

Tom smiled at Abdel and they set about their task as Mike lifted the car on the hydraulic ramp.

Brody came out of the office with the day's copy of the Sacramento Bee and said to Mike; "Hey Mike, this guy who held up that store in the Town & Country Village, he has previous. He held up a store in Coloma, they even got his name and guess what? He is an ex-con."

"What's his name Brody?" asked Mike.

"This no-good excuse for a human being is called Walter J. Elman and he drives an old brown Dodge," he replied.

"Don't think he coming here for a service boss," said Tom.

"Just keep your eyes peeled boys, you never know," said Brody.

On Tuesday night Abdel and Gretchen went to the Senator cinema to see the Marx Brothers in the movie *Duck Soup*. They laughed for the duration of the film and Abdel was particularly smitten with the hilarity of it all. After the film, they went next door for a drink in the Moderne.

Gretchen told Abdel that she had got a part time job at the offices at McClellan Airforce Base and elaborated by saying, "My father did not want me to have a job. He said that I did not need to work, but I want a life of my own. He agreed, but only if I take a part time job."

"This job, what will you do?" he asked.

"It's just clerical work, filing documents, typing and answering telephones. I get a lift anyway; my father is a senior engineer on the base. He is very protective of me Abdel; I am the only child."

"I understand this Gretchen, your father is right."

"My father told me yesterday that a lot of Asian people were now in Sacramento to work at the base and in the farms. He said that they had come from Pakistan, China and Viet Nam."

"This is good, maybe I will meet with some of them. It will be good to speak my language."

"I will be at church this Sunday for holy communion at 10am, I have not been for two weeks and my mother insists that we all go."

"I do not have a mosque to pray in, so I just pray in my room."

"Maybe they will build a mosque soon, there will be more Muslims in Sacramento now."

"Yes, I hope this is so Gretchen."

Abdel drove her home, on this occasion he parked round the corner. This gave then some privacy to kiss and embrace each other. As he pulled up at the house, Gretchen's father was at the door, it was 9.30pm.

CHAPTER EIGHTEEN

Abdel and Gretchen maintained their romance and were regular patrons of the Senator Cinema, Tower Theatre, Alhambra Theatre and Edmonds Field to watch the Sacramento Solons baseball team. On July 16th 1949 the inevitable happened and they finally made love at Abdel's place after a jazz night at the Zanzibar Club. This would be repeated numerous times over the following weeks after nights out in town.

After a similar evening on August 26th Abdel was returning home having dropped off Gretchen. He decided to stop at an all-night store on Freeport Boulevard for some milk and bread, it was 9.25pm. He parked the Chevy next to a brown Dodge, as he passed it to go into the store, he noticed a man sitting in the driver's seat smoking a cigarette. Abdel found his milk and turned to get his bread as the man from the Dodge came through the door brandishing a Hand Gun.

"Don't you think about running nigger, if you do, I'll blow a hole in your god damned head. Hand over all the money you got."

Struck with fear, Abdel put the milk carton on the floor.

"Don't do nothing stupid nigger," and he pointed the gun close to Abdel's forehead. Abdel was shaking, but managed to extract all he had in cash from his pocket.

The man grabbed it out of his hands and said, "Seven dollars, that all you got?"

"Yes, sorry sir it is all I have,"

"You know who I am nigger?"

"No sir, I do not."

"I am Walter Elman and I aint to happy to see niggers with money."

He then struck Abdel across his face with his gun. Abdel fell to the floor and felt a surge of pain across his nose.

The assailant then turned his attention to the store owner who was motionless behind his counter.

"You better have more than seven dollars in that till or you are going to get more than this nigger got, do you hear me?"

The storekeeper nodded and opened his till and pulled out all the notes he had and laid them on the counter.

Abdel was in pain, but anger had replaced the fear and with blood pouring from his nose, he summoned up the energy to rise to his feet and in one motion threw himself at Elman. Both men crashed into a stand of canned fruit. Abdel's first thought was to somehow get the gun out of his hand. He was draped over him, but he managed to locate the guy's right hand which held the gun. Except the gun was not there, panic sent in. He must get the gun, the man started to get an advantage in the tussle that ensued and swung a fist into Abdel's abdomen.

Then he spotted the gun on the floor and made a grab for it. Abdel was quicker and despite the pain he was in, managed to get his hand on the gun. Unfortunately, Elman had matched Abdel's move and the pair were locked onto the gun as they struggled to gain possession. Elman somehow managed to get his finger on the trigger and tried to manipulate the gun in Abdel's direction. Abdel applied even more pressure and manoeuvred the gun to a vertical position. Elman was losing the battle and could feel his strength waning, but with one last effort manged to fire of a round.

At that same instance Abdel applied enough force to direct the gun so that the bullet passed through Elman's lower jaw, through his brain and out the top of his skull. Travelling at a speed of 1400 mph the round sped through Elman's head and ended up high in the wall behind them. Abdel's face was sprayed with his foe's blood and fragments of teeth and bone. Elman hit the floor, the combination of shock and exhaustion hit Abdel and he fell to his knees.

The storekeeper quickly attended to him saying, "My god man, are you alright?"

He lifted Abdel to his feet. Abdel could not speak and just stared at the sight before him. The storekeeper got him a chair and sat him behind the counter, then he rang the police. Three police cars were there within 3 minutes, Sherriff William T. Brown arrived a minute later. Abdel could still not speak, he sat and watched as the officers checked the body.

The store keeper was being interviewed by another officer and said, "I owe my life to this man," and pointed to Abdel. "Without fear of his own life he challenged this would be armed robber. The gun went off as they were grappling with each other."

When the Sherriff arrived, he said, "Get this man in a car and get him to the hospital, Officer's Ryan and Murdoch you take him and stay with him. Get a statement if you can, but don't worry if you don't get one, the guy is in shock."

As Abdel was led to the police car, he said, "I have killed a man; God have mercy on me."

As the car drove away officer Ryan asked Abdel; "Hey man, who is your next of kin?"

Abdel looked up and said, "I do not understand sir, next of kin what is that?"

"Have you got any family local?" he said.

"Oh no sir, just my friends Brody, Mike and Tom."

After further probing by the officer he managed to ascertain that Brody was his employer and he made arrangements for another car to go to Brody's address and bring him to Sutter Hospital.

Sherriff Brown was surveying the scene at the Store and asked the storekeeper; "So, Mr Gonzalez this man saved your life, that right?"

"Yes, sir he did so, this guy came in toting this gun and demanded money threatened to kill us both. He even pistol whipped that poor guy after he took seven dollars of him. He didn't mean for the guy to get shot; he was defending himself."

The Sherriff heard a commotion at the door and turned to see a reporter from the Sacramento Bee trying to get in the store and shouted; "Keep that hack out of here, he will get a statement soon enough."

"The people have a right to know if they are safe in this town," shouted the reporter.

The Sherriff halted his interview with the storekeeper and went to the door. He grabbed the reporter by the scruff of the neck, pulled him up close and said, "Listen here, unless you want hospital treatment, get the fuck out of here. I have told you I will provide a statement when I have all the facts. This is what I am trying to do right now, so meet me at my office in half an hour and I will give you an exclusive, is that clear?"

The reporter could not reply, due to the Sherriff having such a tight grip on his collar and just nodded in agreement. The Sherriff released his hold on him and the downcast reporter left the scene mumbling to the officer's present; "That's police brutality, that is."

Sherriff Brown returned to his interview with Mr Gonzalez.

"Ok, you say this guy came in after our hero that right?"

"Yip, I watched him come and pull out that revolver as this other guy was collecting a carton of milk. He said to him, "give me all your money or I will blow a hole in your head."

The mortuary team arrived and one of them said, "Can we bag this one Sherriff?"

He turned to see it was Bob Kowalski and replied; "Yep, bag him up Bob, this crime scene is secure."

"What about this gun Sherriff?

He turned to see the gun on the floor and shouted to the officer; "Hey numbnuts, aint you going to pick that fucking gun up and bag it for dusting?"

The officer replied "Ah, sorry Sherriff, yes sir err I am new sir. This is my first week on the job Sherriff."

"Christ, that's all I need a rookie, what's your name son?" he asked.

"It's Barney Casey Sherriff" he replied, as he carefully lifted the gun with a pencil and dropped into a clear plastic bag.

Just as Sherriff Brown was about to continue his chat with Gonzalez, Officer Casey said, "This here Beretta, is a 1938 Italian ex-military world war two model. It is a 380-calibre single action and it is need of a good clean."

The Sherriff was feeling just a little pissed off now and left Mr Gonzalez and walked over to Casey and said,

"So now you are a gun expert after a week on the job?"

"No Sherriff, it's just that I have a big interest in guns, my old man has a very big collection."

"Alright then, what information can you give me that will help me to exonerate that poor sucker that is on his way to hospital."

Officer Casey looked at the gun in the bag and said, "These hand guns like all guns need to be kept clean, they are prone to jam if they get too much dirt on the runners. This in turn can lead to the round jamming in the chamber. The trigger needs about 4lb – 5lb of pressure to activate firing, it's not a sensitive trigger."

"Well, I am truly over fucking whelmed son, is that it?"

"No Sherriff, the safety lock is off, which indicates this guy was prepared to shoot anyone who got in his way."

"Now that is more like it son, so get your arse in that car and get that gun down to the station."

"Yes Sherriff, I'm on my way."

Officer Casey, jumped in his car and sped off, forgetting his partner; who just looked at the Sherriff and said,

"How do I get back to the station Sherriff?"

The Sherriff just laughed and said, "In my car son, you got a real live one there. He is going to create some fun back at headquarters."

The Sherriff went back to Mr Gonzalez and continued with his interview until he had acquired enough information, he deemed necessary. He then drove back to the station with Casey's partner for company.

While Abdel was being treated for his injuries, Brody arrived and was allowed to see him but was informed that he must not ask any questions related to the incident by Officer Ryan. Still in shock, Abdel was cleaned up by a nurse and told that his nose was not broken.

Brody stood and watched Abdel slowly start to regain some sense of what had happened and said, "I have killed a man today Brody, what will become of me?"

"Look you need to try and calm down and I am sure all this will be ok Abdel. You are not a bad man and from what I have learned it was not your fault."

Officer Ryan interceded and said,

"No more questions please sir, he has not been formally interviewed yet."

"He aint been charged yet either, has he officer?"

"No sir, not yet."

On returning to his office, Sherriff Brown rang the District Attorney, it was 10.45pm and the DA was less than enthusiastic about the phone call and suggested that Abdel should spend the night at hospital and he will be formally interviewed tomorrow. The Sherriff agreed and he then rang the hospital with that request, which was complied with.

He then called in Officers Casey, Murdoch and the Station Sergeant Gregg Delgado into his office. He provided a breakdown of the events that had occurred at the store and said, "It looks like that poor guy at the hospital has been in the wrong place at the wrong time. This Elman has a rap sheet as long as my arm, he has done time in Alcatraz, San Quentin and Leavenworth, for armed robbery, grand theft auto, attempted murder and he is wanted in connection with a number of other unsolved crimes. This guy has had it coming and now he has a wooden overcoat. He aint no loss to society fellas so, this is what we are going to do."

"Looks like the same guy who held up that place at the Town & Country Village last week added Murdoch."

"Yep, looks like a match, but let's be sure. Get the incident report out Gregg. Casey, get me everything you have on our guy at the hospital. Make sure you get everything; personal details, relatives, friends, workmates, girlfriends and get his address. I don't think we are going to need a warrant, anything he has at home will be forthcoming I am sure, have you got that?"

"Yes Sherriff," he replied.

"Ok Murdoch, you will take the gun down to forensics, I want fingerprints and I want to know where that gun came from, it might be stolen. Then I want you to examine that Dodge, Christ knows what that might reveal. You alright with that?"

"Sure am Sherriff," said Murdoch.

"Right, I don't want any loose ends remember so disappear while I talk to the Sargent."

Casey and Murdoch left the office and the Sherriff said, "Take a load off Gregg and sit down. I reckon we got a five-star hero up there at Sutter Hospital. He must have been well pissed off after getting pistol whipped by Elman."

"How did the struggle pan out then Bill?"

"From what I leaned from Mr Gonzalez, Elman was hellbent on robbing both our hero and the storekeeper; even if it meant putting a bullet in both of them. After Elman had pistol whipped our hero, he threatened to shoot the storekeeper."

"As the storekeeper handed over the cash, our man threw himself at him and the struggle came to an end when the gun went off and discharged a round into Elman from close range killing him instantly."

"Where did the round hit Elman?"

"From what I gleamed from inspecting the body, the bullet went through his lower jaw and exploded out of the top of his skull. Blood and skull fragments were on the wall and on the face of our hero."

"Jesus, the guy must have been traumatised."

"He was Gregg, I sent him off to Sutter with Ryan and Murdoch."

"What do you want me to do Bill?"

"Well, you won't thank me for this, but I need you to get all you can on this Elman guy. I have his rap sheet here, but that don't tell the full story. He has done some real time this guy, he aint no angel. Check out a next of kin and any other relatives, somebody will have to bury this guy."

"Ok Bill, I will get on it. I have a brother - in - law who works in Alcatraz, he will have information on Elman I am sure and by the way, a reporter is outside waiting to speak to you."

"Shit, I forgot about him, call him in for me, will you?"

"Sure will," said Delgado, as he closed the office door with a wide grin on his face.

Back at Sutter Hospital, Abdel was informed that he would be spending the night for observation after his blow to the head. He was given a sedative to calm him and Officer Ryan would be staying as a security measure. Abdel was very withdrawn and Brody tried to lighten the mood with chit chat about all and nothing. Abdel fell asleep at 11.05pm and Brody decided to go home and return in the morning.

The Sacramento Bee crime reporter Paul Abrahams let himself into the Sherriff's office and before he could say anything, the Sherriff was on his feet extending a hand saying, "We did not get off to a good start, I'm William Brown Mr …. I didn't not get you name."

"It's Paul Abrahams Sherriff Brown, no need to apologise."

"I aint apologising son, just being polite."

The Sherriff was a long tall drink of water standing 6' 4" and he towered over Abrahams who stood looking up from a height of 5' 8", the intimidation was palpable. Sherriff Brown had been Sherriff for five years, after ten years on the force. He had seen three Captains come and go in that time. The City Manager had not found the right man for the job, which was vacant at the moment. Many thought Sherriff Brown was a shoe in for the post, he was well respected and got results.

He never broached the subject but privately, he knew he could do the job. He went on to give Paul Abrahams some important knowledge relating to police work.

"What you hacks must remember is that I need to get on and secure a crime scene quickly. In this way I can ascertain all the facts and then take the necessary action. For example, what would have been the outcome if the deceased had an accomplice sitting in another vehicle parked nearby and he wanted to exact revenge?"

"Well yes, I appreciate that Sherriff but there was no accomplice was there?"

"How in fucks name have you made that claim, based on what?

"He wasn't there Sherriff."

"Look Sherlock, you are obviously new to crime reporting. How long have you been a reporter with the Bee?"

"Not long, but we have to keep the public informed and its Paul."

"Ok, let's start, again shall we?"

Abrahams sighed and extracted his notebook and pen from his leather case.

"Right, you ask the questions and I will do my best to give you an accurate answer, how does that sound?"

"Fine Sherriff, who was murdered?"

"No one."

"But you have a cadaver with a gunshot wound to the head."

"Correct, you have been observant."

"I got that from Officer Ryan, Sherriff."

"There is your first mistake son, never release the names of your sources."

"Have you someone in custody?"

"Nope, we aint."

"Who was the man taken to Sutter Hospital then?"

"A patient."

"Come on Sherriff, you need to give me more than that."

"No, I don't son."

"Well, if you don't give me more, I will get it from Mr Gonzalez."

"No, you won't, because I will charge you with interfering with a witness and I will also charge Gonzalez with perjury for giving false testimony."

"Was there a racial motive here Sherriff? We Americans are not dealing with the issues regarding racial awareness in this city, perhaps this guy was racially motivated."

"Ok, I will stop you there. "We Americans, where the hell does that come from? The only true Americans are up on the reservations at Hoopa Valley and Round Valley. My grandparents were Scottish and I guess with a name like Abrahams, you have a Jewish ancestry am I correct?"

"Yes, my grandparents left Lithuania as the pogroms were beginning to eradicate Jewish communities."

"Alright let's not hang our hat on any racial link to this crime. Look, why don't I give you a statement of facts and we can all move on."

"Ok Sherriff, can I print this verbatim?"

"Yes, son you can."

Being called son was starting to annoy Abrahams, but he guessed that was the Sherriff's bit of browbeating psychology, to gain the advantage and he would have to live with it.

"Here we go then, at approximately 9.45pm today, the Sacramento Police Department received a telephone call from a storekeeper on Newport Boulevard saying that a violent crime had occurred on the premises. On arrival the Police discovered a deceased male lying on the floor with a single gunshot wound to the head. It appears that he was in the process of committing armed robbery. This is an ongoing investigation and we are speaking to a number of people in connection with this incident. We are unable to divulge any names at this delicate stage of the investigation. Any further information will be provided as soon as it is prudent to do so."

"No names then Sherriff?"

"Nope, within the next half hour I will be speaking to an individual in relation to this fatality, but that is all I can say at the moment. Hopefully, I will be in a better position tomorrow to give an update on progress with this case. One further thing Mr Abrahams, please do not follow me when I leave this station. In order to enhance your story, I am willing to give you an exclusive at some stage tomorrow when I have collected the requisite details and I am confident of the outcome with regard to any subsequent police action. How does that sound young man?"

"That is a fair result Sherriff, I look forward to our next chat."

Paul Abrahams left the office and Sherriff Brown soon followed and made his way to Sutter Hospital; it was now 11.50pm.

Abdel was just beginning to wake from a much-needed sleep, when Sherriff Brown entered the hospital. On arrival at the ward where Abdel was being treated, Officer Ryan was sitting outside Abdel's side room. He asked Ryan to accompany him to an empty office and said, "Now Ryan, how long have you been on the force here in Sacramento?"

"Three years Sherriff."

"What is a vital element in maintaining crime scene confidentiality?"

Officer Ryan thought and finally said, "To observe and stay focussed."

"Now that is not a bad answer Ryan, however what you failed to do was to ensure the crime scene was not compromised. In general terms you arsehole, you went and blabbed to that fucking reporter, did you not?"

Officer Ryan was now aware of his failings and said, "Sorry boss, that guy was getting on my nerves with his questions."

"That is his fucking job Ryan, you could well have compromised this investigation you idiot. From now on keep your mouth shut. If it happens again, I will put you on traffic control, do you understand?"

"Yes boss."

"Now then, what have you learned so far about Wyatt Earp in there?"

"Not a great deal, his employer Brody Miller has been in to see him. But the guy just sits and mopes about killing someone. He is a Muslim, and he keeps asking God to show him mercy. They gave him a sedative two hours ago after they treated him for his injuries."

"If that reporter turns up, cuff him and put him in your car."

"Ok Sherriff."

"I am going in to see Abdul is it?"

"It's Abdel boss and his English is good."

Sherriff Brown quietly opened the door to the side room. A nurse was checking Abdel's temperature and his blood pressure. He was awake, if not quite fully *compos mentis*.

Abdel looked up to see the Sherriff standing in the corner of the room, waiting for the nurse to complete her checks. On completion of her work she turned to the Sherriff and said, "He is still in a state of mild trauma Sherriff, please be responsive to his state of mind. If you could limit your talk to ten minutes, it would be most appreciated."

"No problems nurse, sorry I didn't get your name."

"Nurse Gena Salvador Sherriff."

"Sherriff William T. Brown and I will be as quick as I can, thank you."

He closed the door as the nurse left the room and pulled up a chair alongside Abdel's bed.

"Hey Abdel, I am Sherriff Brown of the Sacramento Police Department, you are quite the hero round these parts my boy."

"What have I done Sherriff? God will not show me mercy for this crime," said Abdel.

"Abdel, I want you to listen to me very carefully, then you can ask me anything you like. Do you understand?

"Yes sir, I understand sir."

"Firstly, you do not need to call me sir, Sherriff will do fine."

Abdel nodded in agreement.

"Ok, let me put your mind at rest. You have not committed a crime. It is very important that you remember that. Tell me you understand this."

Abdel looked confused and said, "But I have killed a man Sherriff sir."

"No, you have not. You did not pull the trigger on that gun. The man that you challenged was an evil criminal and it was his finger that pressed the trigger. All you did was to stop him killing you, it's called self-defence. To add to that, if you had not challenged this man, it is very likely that he would have killed both you and the storekeeper. He would have done this to make sure there were no witnesses to his crime. This man was wanted in three states for many serious crimes Abdel, you have done society a favour. You must not carry the burden of this man's death, you have nothing to answer for, this I can assure you."

Abdel sat and tried to digest what the Sherriff had told him and finally said,

"What will this man's family think of me Sherriff?"

"You are a devout Muslim are you not Abdel?"

"Yes Sherriff."

"Well, the Noble Qur'an tells you that you must not carry out sins and evil deeds. What you have done is rid the world of an evil man who had being doing evil deeds most of his adult life. God will not punish you; he has forgiven you and I am sure he is with you at this troubled time in your life. You now need to be strong and think of your family, your friends and remember, had it not been for you; Mr Gonzalez the storekeeper would not be alive today. I am going to leave you to get some rest. I will speak with you again tomorrow, so get a good night's sleep my boy."

The Sherriff rose put his chair back in the corner of the room and moved to leave the room. As he opened the door to leave Abdel said, "Thank you for your kind words Sherriff Sir."

"You get some sleep, goodnight," he replied and closed the door behind him.

Once outside the room Sherriff Brown reminded Ryan not to let the Sacramento reporter in and said, "Any problems, you can get me at home remember. Who is relieving you at 2am?"

"It's Officer Avella Sherriff."

"Give him the same instructions."

"Yes Sherriff."

With that the Sherriff left the hospital and went home, it was 12.50am.

At 7am the next morning Brody Miller was sat in his office in the garage waiting for Mike and Tom to turn in. Within ten minutes Mike arrived, as he went to put his overalls on Brody said, "Hey Mike, don't bother with them, you aint going to need them today brother."

Before he could explain Tom arrived. He told them about what happened at the store on Newport Boulevard and why Abdel was in hospital.

"Jesus, is he ok boss?" asked Mike.

"Well, this guy pistol whipped him and his face is a bit of a mess. It's his mental state that I am worried about, when I left him, he was in a hell of a state."

"I heard something on the radio about it, but it didn't give any names," added Mike.

"Holy Moses, well that man with the gun, he got what was coming to him boss I reckon," said Tom.

"Ok, so I aint opening the garage today boys, Mike can you put a sign on the door saying that we are not open for business today due to an emergency."

"Sure thing boss."

"What we gonna do boss?" asked Tom.

"We are all going to Sutter Hospital to see our workmate Tom. But first I must ring Gretchen and let her know, I got her phone number round here somewhere."

"Yes boss, you will be doing right there, that's for sure."

Mike fashioned a sign and hung it on the door as Brody went to use the phone.

"Who is he on the phone to Tom?" asked Mike

"He be ringing Abdel's girl Gretchen."

"Shit, she is in for a shock Tom."

"Damn right, he was with her last night. I think they went to the Jazz Club."

Brody made the call and Gretchen's mother answered the phone.

"Good morning, my name is Brody Miller. Is it convenient to speak to Gretchen please?"

"Yes, I will give her call, please hold the line."

"Hello, this is Gretchen, how can I help?"

"It's Brody Miller, I employ Abdel in my garage."

"Oh yes Mr Miller, is there something wrong?"

Brody then imparted the information relating to the events of last night on Newport Boulevard. She was understandably shocked and her first words were; "How is Abdel, where is he and I need to see him."

Brody enlightened her on his well-being and where he currently was. He could tell she was in tears and he did his best to reassure her that he was in good spirits. She said that she would get her father to take her to the hospital as soon as possible. Brody added that he, Mike and Tom would soon be setting of for Sutter Hospital and said, "If you get there before us, don't be too worried about his injuries. They look worse than they are. See you soon," and he put the phone down.

Sherriff Brown was back at his desk for 7.30am.

On arrival the duty officer Don Porcini said, "Your early boss, not sleeping again?"

The Sherriff's insomnia was well-known in the department.

"As usual Don, this job will be my downfall. Any news of our guy in Sutter?"

"Nope, all quiet except for that hack from the Bee wanting his exclusive. He has been on the phone four times already."

"Damn it, that guy must have worse insomnia than I have. When Casey, Delgado and Murdoch arrive send them to my office Don."

"For sure boss."

Sherriff Brown poured himself a cup of black coffee and sat at his desk. He went over the incident of last night and started to piece together how it played out, looking for anything that would change his assumptions on the resulting outcome. He would have to put this in perspective for the DA and sign it off. The alternatives that he mulled over were; were Abdel and Elman in it together and Elman went too far, so had Abdel put a stop to it. Did Elman have another accomplice and are there any witnesses?

There were the results of the forensics on the gun and the Dodge, what would they throw up? Most of this conjecture would be put to bed once his subordinates had gathered their evidence. That would only become available mid - morning at the earliest.

In the meantime, some food would be a good idea. He went back to the duty desk and said, "Hey Don, have we got a gofer in hear?" I need some food; pancakes would be good. "

Don turned and shouted; "George, get your butt in here. You got a big mission on for the Sherriff."

George was the new recruit and keen as mustard and he came bouncing through the open doorway saying, "Her I am, a slave to justice" not realising that the Sherriff was standing at the desk.

"Oh jeeps, Sherriff I didn't think, I mean I thought."

"George, my slave to justice. I want food, so go and get me some pancakes with maple syrup. What about you Don, want to join me?"

"No thanks, I will take a rain check on that Sherriff Brown."

George was handed $4 and off he went.

"So, Bill, this guy in the hospital, is he kosha then?"

"Yep, I believe he is Don, unless something jumps out that we haven't seen. I will know that after the boys have given me their findings."

Sherriff Brown returned to his office and was only sat for a minute when Gregg Delgado came in with what info he had on Elman.

"Morning Gregg, you got anything for me?"

"Yip, got a good pen picture of this Elman guy from my brother in law boss. As well as what is on the system. As yet no contact with any family. He has a brother in Springfield, Ohio. Aint no reply to a number I've got for him, but will try again when I am done here."

"Ok show me what you got on this miscreant."

"He was in Alcatraz for a 5 to 10 stretch for armed robbery, he did 6 years. That was in 1931. He then got time for Grand Theft Auto with aggravated assault on two police officers in Topeka, Kansas that was 1938. Did 4 years in Leavenworth for that misdemeanour. His last prison time at the behest of the criminal justice system was in San Quentin in 1943 for attempted murder of a barman in San Francisco, he did only 5 years."

"Hang on, only 5 years for attempted murder."

"Well, he turned in some states evidence that led to the arrest of a gang who took down a score on an armoured truck in San Diego."

"My word a serial criminal with a social conscience, what is this world coming to?"

"Ernie my brother in law, said he was a real handful in Alcatraz. He left a fellow inmate with a nasty scar after he cut him during dinner in the canteen over some argument about baseball. This guy is no loss to the world, that's for sure boss."

"Is there a chance he has an accomplice Gregg?"

"His previous suggests otherwise Bill, a loner so to speak. He doesn't like sharing this guy."

"Ok Gregg that's great thanks, can you draft that up for me and put on my desk. Let me know if you uncover anything else and don't forget that brother in Ohio."

"Sure thing boss."

Just as his stomach was beginning to churn and grumble, in walked George with his pancakes.

"There you go Sherriff, as you ordered" and laid his meal on the desk and started to walk out of the office.

"Hey, what about the change George?"

"Ah yes forgot, it was $2. 25 cents Sherriff, here is your change."

"It's ok, I am feeling generous, keep it."

"Gee thanks boss."

Sherriff Brown was thinking; lets gets this eaten before Casey and Murdoch show up. Their timing was perfect, he had just finished devouring the last pancake when in walked Casey.

"Do you want me to come back Sherriff," noticing that his boss was eating.

"No, it's fine, I am finished. Come in show me what you got."

"This guy Abdel is a war hero boss. He has served in the Merchant Navy and he has been torpedoed three times during the war. His papers are sound, he got his green card in 1945 and he has an Indian passport. He was born in Afghanistan, but moved to Karachi in 1929. He has no rap sheet and he has a clean driving license and a Library Card here in Sacramento. He works at Millers Garage as a vehicle mechanic. He has a girl called Gretchen Geersten who lives on Land Park.

"He has a brother in South Africa and a cousin back in Karachi. He is squeaky clean boss and apparently an all-round good guy. I even got a testimonial from none other than Caroline E. Wenzel of the California State Library."

That's great Casey; this guy is gonna become a local hero alright, whether he is up for that I am not sure. He is a reserved individual who is a devout Muslim and still believes he did the wrong thing in making this nefarious hoodlum history. Can you write this up for me Officer Casey and put it on my desk as soon as?"

"Yes Sherriff, on its way."

As if the department was running like a finely oiled machine, in walked in Murdoch.

"I could get used to this atmosphere of zealous endeavour," enthused the Sherriff.

Murdoch looked perplexed and said, "Is there a problem Boss?"

"Only if this meticulousness does not continue Officer Murdoch"

Murdoch was lost for words and the Sherriff rescued him from the situation and said, "It is fine Murdoch, what have you come up with? But I warn you, your colleagues have been very efficient so far. Can you match their exactitude?"

"I have established that Casey was correct about the gun Sherriff. It is an Italian Army Beretta Gardone dated from 1938. A single shot pistol of 380 calibre and the safety catch was off. The prints on the trigger were the deceased however, we have not taken prints of Abdel Rahman yet."

"The gun was stolen from a collector in San Bernardino in March this year and he would like it back. There were another 4 rounds in the clip, but it is amazing that the gun released any bullets, it was very dirty inside and it is surprising it didn't jam. The Dodge was stolen in April from a parking lot in"

"Don't tell me let me guess, Los Angeles."

"Nope, Salt Lake City."

"Well, I will sleep on my mother's porch; this guy liked to travel, that's 400 miles away."

"No real evidence in the Dodge other than fingerprints, some clothes, cigarette packets and empty beer cans. I have circulated the details of the Beretta and the Dodge to other police forces in the west, just in case they can provide any more information."

"Good work Murdoch, it may be that another police force might like him for any unsolved crimes. We aint gonna takes prints from Abdel Rahman, no need he aint no criminal. Alright, and can you write that up for me and have it on my desk as soon as possible?"

"Yes Sherriff"

Sherriff Brown sat back and put his feet on his desk feeling quite satisfied with the morning's achievements. The next focus would be to talk with Abdel again along with his girlfriend and work colleagues. Then there was his duty to the wider public and a statement to the media including Paul Abrahams of the Sacramento Bee.

It was now 8.05am and he rose from his chair and as he passed Don on the duty desk he said, "If our reporter rings tell him to meet me at the Sutter Hospital at 9.00am for his exclusive and ring the DA and ask him to get here for a resume of our progress at 10.00am."

"Ok Sherriff, pancakes meet with your approval, did they?"

"They sure did Don, see you in a while."

"I may not be here when you get back Sherriff, change of shift remember."

"Of course, rest up well buddy"

He parked up and walked into the hospital straight into Paul Abrahams.

"Aint you got a bed to sleep in son," he said.

"I am responsible to the public, just as you are Sherriff."

"No, you are beholding to your editor. I am accountable to the DA, the public and the Sacramento Police Force."

"Walk with me and lets us show a united front, police and journalist together."

"Sounds like you have had a productive morning Sherriff."

"You could say that, it's down to my excellent police officers who have worked tirelessly on this case over the past twelve hours."

As they walked Sherriff Brown detailed how this get-together with Abdel Rahman would pan out.

He made particular attention to the fact that he is still a patient of the hospital and both he and anyone else in attendance at this briefing must adhere to the wishes of both Abdel and the medics in attendance. Abrahams supported this directive and said, "From what I gather, this guy is the local hero Sherriff, that right?"

"Just don't go overboard with that, he still feels guilty about how this has turned out. I need to reassure him again and this is where your newspaper can help."

"Meaning, we promote him as a shining light as a justifiable vigilante."

"There you go again, don't go down that road. He aint no vigilante, he is guy trying to stay alive along with that of an innocent storekeeper."

As they walked into the ward, they were met by Brody, Mike, Tom, and Gretchen. No one had had the chance to see him yet, he was still sleeping. The Sherriff took the opportunity to talk to the Doctor who said that Abdel had not had a good night and his blood pressure was too high.

Sherriff Brown then escorted everyone into a rest room and introduced himself to those present.

Gretchen asked the Doctor;

"Is he going to be alright?"

"Yes, he has just had a very traumatic experience, one he will never ever forget. His physical injuries will heal quickly. However, it will take some time for him to accept what he has been through. He will need the support of friends to get him through this. I believe he has no family in the US, is that so Sherriff?"

"Yes, that is correct Doctor."

"I am going to wake him now and do some checks on his blood pressure, temperature and his general health. I will then ask you to see him, but not all at once. I believe you would like to see him first Miss Geersten, is that so?"

"Yes, Doctor please, I am so worried for him."

The Doctor spent fifteen minutes attending to Abdel and then came along to take Gretchen in to see him. As she was led to his room, Sherriff Brown told the Officer on duty to return to the station.

Gretchen walked into Abdel's room and her first reaction was one of shock. He looked unrecognisable, his nose was severely swollen, he had stitches on the left side of his cheek and his left eye was badly bruised and closed.

She wanted to put her arms round him, but just kissed him. He was so glad to see her and tears poured from his eyes. This was quickly reciprocated by Gretchen, they held hands for a short while without speaking. Abdel was the first to speak and said,

"I am very glad to see you Gretchen, I have been worried about you."

"You need not worry about me Abdel; my God look at you."

"They have been very good looking after me here. I can remember everything and the Doctor has told me it will take some time to get well. The Sherriff has spoken to me and he has said I do not need to worry, this man I killed was very bad and he would have killed me and the storekeeper if I had not stopped him."

"What you have done is a very brave thing Abdel, I am so proud of you."

They talked for a little while until Gretchen thought that he may be getting tired and she said,

"I am going to leave you now and return home, but I will be back later Abdel. I think the Sherriff wants to talk to you again."

She kissed him and wiping away the tears, she left his room.

The Sherriff was briefing Paul Abrahams prior to going into see Abdel.

"It is vital that you listen objectively with a sympathetic ear. This guy believes he has committed a crime, I have already told him he has not. However, I have to go through the whole incident with him to get his version of what happened. I am not telling you your job but, and I know you need to inform your readers, but can you do that with a sense of compassion. Is that a reasonable request?"

"Yes, I am happy with that. We could do with a photograph Sherriff."

"That aint happening son, you can print his name but no pictures."

"Ok amigo, I gather you will be asking all the questions Sherriff?"

"Oh yes, don't even think about chipping in with your own questions."

The two men entered Abdel's room and were greeted with a smile from the patient.

"Thank you for seeing me again Abdel, this is Mr Abrahams. He is a reporter from the *Sacramento Bee*, our local newspaper. He is going to listen to what you say and make notes, is that alright with you Abdel?"

"Yes Sherriff, pleased to meet you Mr Abrahams," he replied.

"Thanks for allowing me to sit here with the Sherriff Mr Rahman," said Abrahams.

"Abdel, I want you to tell me what happened last night when you went into the store on Newport Boulevard. Tell me everything you saw and what exactly you did while you were there. Is that alright with you?"

"Yes Sherriff, I will try and remember everything I can."

"Ok off you go and take your time."

"I was going back to my house in the car and I thought I would stop at the store for some milk and bread. I parked the car and I noticed the Dodge and a man inside smoking a cigarette.

"I went into the store; I do not think there was anybody else in the store except the storekeeper. I picked up a carton of milk and I turned round to see this man pointing a gun at me. He said "don't do nothing stupid nigger," and he said to give him all my money. I gave him seven dollars, that is all I had. He was not happy and he said, do you know who I am? He said he was Walter Elman and then he hit me with his gun. I fell to the floor; my face was hurting badly.

"He then pointed the gun at the storekeeper and told him to get all the money out of the register, I thought he was going to shoot at the storekeeper. I do not know why, but I was angry and I charged at the man. We both fell to the floor and we struggled to our feet and he struck me in the stomach. I tried to get the gun of him, but he was strong and I got it pointing up at the roof and he pressed the trigger and the gun went off in his face. It was terrible,

"I did not mean for him to be killed Sherriff."

"Ok Abdel, did you see anyone else in the Dodge or in the store?"

"No sir Sherriff, I did not see any other people."

"That's fine, I have heard enough and I can formally tell you that you will not be charged for any offence in regard to this unfortunate incident. On behalf of the Sacramento Police Department I would like to thank you for your bravery in disarming this dangerous criminal, we are all in your debt. Can I also tell you that your hospital bill will be covered by the Local Authority and the District Attorney would like to thank you personally when you are well enough?"

Abdel was unsure what to say and looked at the two men, then said,

"I have seen death many times, in Afghanistan and at sea during the war. I never ever thought I would kill another person, but I have and you say he was an evil man Sherriff."

"Yes, he was and this could have ended with you being killed along with the storekeeper at the hands of this man Abdel. Do you have a question for Abdel Mr Abrahams?"

Abrahams was surprised by the Sherriff's offer he had not expected a chance to put a question to Abdel, but after a few seconds he said, "Abdel, if the same were to happen tomorrow, would you do the same again?"

Sherriff turned and looked at Abrahams, his face spoke volumes. "That

I do not know Mr Abrahams, but I am glad that I am alive to speak of this terrible thing, that is all I can say."

"Right amigo, you have some friends that want to see you. We will leave and let them see you," said the Sherriff.

They both left the room and the Sherriff waved Brody, Mike and Tom over to go in and see their friend.

He then turned to Abrahams and said, "I do not believe you, what an arse you are. Remember what I said about compassion and a sympathetic approach?"

"Look Sherriff I am a reporter, sometimes we are sitting on the other side of the fence, that's the way it is."

"Well, I trust your exclusive will capture the moment and give an accurate account of what this poor man has been subjected to. Because if it does not, I promise you I will hound you and make your fucking life a misery."

"It's great to witness a senior public servant giving the press so much adulation."

Sherriff Brown just looked down at Abrahams and said, "Son, if brains were made of goose fat, you would not have enough to oil the spring in my fucking watch."

Abrahams turned and made an abrupt exit, as he walked away, he lifted his middle finger in the air.

"William T. Brown just smiled and shouted; "You have a nice day now son."

Sherriff Brown returned to the station, to be informed that the DA was on his way.

William Brown sat in his office and young George provided a black coffee. Thankfully, Casey, Murdoch and Delgado had written up their reports and they were sitting in a file on his desk.

The DA breezed into the office holding a cup of coffee.

"Well Bill, what we got?"

"We got an all action Wyatt Earp up at Sutter Hospital, that's what we got Jeff."

Jeff Conrad was the new kid on the Justice Block. He had been promoted to his present job two years ago, on the back of some great work in the San Diego Police Department. He was slim, good looking, intelligent and he knew it.

"Have a look at that Jeff and then I will give you my appraisal of the whole ball game."

The DA read the file and because he could, he used his pen to highlight any grammatical errors within the reports.

After reading the reports he said, "Well, Bill what's your take on all this?"

"I have seen and spoken to this guy up at Sutter's Hospital. The guy is in bits, he is wrecked mentally by this and he is pretty banged up. He is a bona fide God damn hero Jeff. This Elman guy was the real deal, he would have killed them both if Abdel had not shown incredible bravery in tackling this bastard. He is a devout Muslim Jeff and he can't reconcile that he has played a part in Elman's death. Can we get our hands on an Imam? We need a cleric to come and speak with him to reassure he has done no wrong."

"You really think there's is no connection between this guy in the hospital and Walter Elman Bill?"

"Hell no, Elman was a loner. I got some background on him from his time in Alcatraz. He was a bad guy and he was wanted in three states for violent crimes including armed robbery. We have sent details onto other Police Department in Ohio, Texas, Arizona and Nevada, this guy has been busy and he may well be linked to a number of unsolved crimes including first degree murder."

"What about any racial motivation on the part of Elman. We have a coloured and a Hispanic as the victims of this robbery."

"No way; yes, he called him a nigger but Elman was just a bad egg Jeff."

"Of course, there is the capacity for expediency, we could use this incident to our advantage here Bill."

"Where are you going with this Jeff?"

"Look, we have had racial tension in this city in recent times Bill. This gives us an opportunity to bring the community together and enhance the profile of good race relations."

"Jeff, we live in a city of cultural diversity. We have Hispanics, Jews, Italians, Japanese, Chinese, Filipinos, Portuguese, Native and African Americans. There will always be tension because there is no equality and you know what I am saying. Let us not jump on that cart and try to travel down that road to gain political points. I have already had a similar conversation with our hack from the Bee."

"Well, I just thought we could win some much-needed credibility, that's all." Anyway, are you confident about how this has turned out?"

"Yep, I am sure as I ever will be Jeff."

"Ok Bill, I will run with you on this one, you have called it right I'm sure. I just hope nothing crops up that will bite us in the arse. It's one less troublesome arsehole to worry about, I guess. I will see what I can do about getting that Imam, is our hero still in hospital?"

"Yes, he is but I don't know if the Doc is going to let him go yet. He is worried about his mental state."

"We need to gain some political points on this one Bill, how have the press handled it?"

"I have had one of the Bee's new boys following me like a lap dog for 24 hours, he has been a pain in the butt at times, However, he has seen a story that hits the right notes and it will give us some much-needed respect and sensitivity."

"Wow, that would be good. How about me getting on the local network with this hero Abdul and publicly congratulating him for his bravery?"

"Not sure, we don't want a media circus Jeff, I don't think our hero will be up for that. It's Abdel not Abdul by the way."

"We can limit the exposure, just a photo of me visiting him in hospital along with the mayor. It will be good for moral and a scoop for the press. I will go on the radio and express our gratitude to this Abdel for his bravery. I am sure there is an award we can present to him, leave it with me."

"Ok Jeff, but try and be tactful."

"Tact and diplomacy are my watchwords Bill, you know that."

Casey came into the office and said, "We have had a call from Elman's brother in Springfield, Ohio. He wants nothing to do with his deceased brother. He hasn't seen him for 20 years. However, he did say he would pay for any burial. Not sure I would, but it's one less problem for us I guess."

"It's a done deal then Bill, I will be in touch," said Jeff.

The DA strolled out the Sherriff's office and back to his bolt hole in the Federal Building.

Abdel was visited by Gretchen and her mother around lunchtime. The DA had set up the press for a photo opportunity with Abdel, himself and the Mayor for 5pm at his bedside. Prior to that, he had arranged for an Imam from San Francisco to sit with Abdel. At the hospital Abdel was presented with a bravery award as part of the honouring of his courage by the Mayor of Sacramento.

The following day Abdel was discharged from Sutter Hospital, there was a small gathering of reporters at the main entrance as he made his way to Brody's car.

"Why are these people here Brody?"

"You are news Abdel, what you did has created quite a stir around this here town and even further. You made news in San Francisco amigo."

As Brody drove them away, he said, "I don't understand Brody, a man is dead because of me."

"No, that aint right Abdel, your courage saved lives, including your own buddy."

"Brody drove to his place, a house in Coloma Heights."

"Why are we here?" asked Abdel.

"You are going to stay here for a few days, just to get some peace and quiet. You are going to meet my wife Martha and she is sure looking forward to meeting you."

Brody parked on his driveway and they got out the car.

"This is a very grand house Brody," said Abdel.

"The fruits of my labour Abdel" he replied.

Martha was standing waiting on the porch as they climbed the three steps.

"Well, so this is who everyone wants to meet. Pleased to make your acquaintance Abdel."

She put her arms round him and said, "It's great to have a real man about this house, come on in."

Brody shook his head and said, "Now Martha, give the guy some peace" as he trudged behind carrying Abdel's bag.

"Pay no mind to him son, he is just the hired help round here, that right Brody"

"Yes dear, I will put his things in the spare room."

Martha took Abdel into the living room, sat him down and then went into the kitchen and returned with a dish of homemade pecan pie and cream.

"There you go, have some of this. There aint no finer pecan pie, this side of the Sacramento River."

"Thank you, Mrs Miller, you are very kind."

"It's Martha when you are in this house Abdel. Now enjoy and make yourself comfortable."

Brody returned and sat down and said,

"A few folks are coming to see you later Abdel, around six o'clock today. But you can just relax and get settled. Your face is getting better, those stitches should be coming out soon I guess."

Abdel spent two day's with Brody and Martha and returned to his house on a wet September 2nd 1949. His facial injuries had improved greatly and he attended the hospital later that afternoon to have the stitches removed. He had received some mail while he was staying at Brody's. He had a letter from Abdullah in Karachi and another from Hakim in Durban, saying he was now a father of a baby daughter, called Mina. He also had a letter from Mr Gonzalez, the storekeeper and it read:

Mr Rahman, I want to express with heartfelt thanks for your actions on August 26th. What you did was very courageous and I thank you on behalf

of myself and my family. If you could find the time, I would like you to return to my store so that I thank you in person. If you would rather not do this then please feel free to visit my home at any time. I leave my address and telephone number as a means of contact. I hope to hear from you soon.
Regards Mr Juan Gonzalez.

*12. Oak Park Avenue. Sacramento.
Tel: 5636826.*

CHAPTER NINETEEN

Abdel was at a personal crossroads in his life. He longed to tell both Abdullah and Hakim what has happened to him here in America. He wanted to speak of the pleasing things in his life and sadly what befell him at the store. He could telephone, but that would not be a good experience because both would want him to join them back in Karachi or Durban. He had to face this challenge himself, the talk with the Imam had helped him come to terms with what had happened at the store.

His relationship with Gretchen had waned, not because of any reluctance on their part. Her father had not been too impressed with the incident at the store and suggested to Gretchen that perhaps that Abdel did not offer secure prospects for his daughter. This she rightly questioned as she truly believed that they loved each other. But as the month's past, it was clear that Gretchen was put under tremendous pressure to curtail her involvement with Abdel.

Their meetings and nights out became very infrequent and on a cold snowy night in January she broke off their affair. Abdel was upset, as was Gretchen but they knew deep down that they had to move on.

Abdel also felt that he needed to make a change in his life that would determine his future and was contemplating going back to sea and re-joining the Merchant Navy. On February 3rd 1950 Abdel contacted the Merchant Navy Shipping Register and enquired about a job as a Deck Rating. He was given a number of possible jobs, which he received in writing to consider.

He had talked to Brody about this and although Brody was disappointed, he accepted that this was something Abdel had considered for some time and supported him and said he would provide an excellent testimonial. Among the offers of work was a posting on board a freighter sailing from New Orleans to Havana, Cuba and then onto London, England. The company was the Constantine Shipping Co Ltd.

He telephoned the company and provided his details and job history. The company asked him to apply in writing to their New Orleans office. This he did and the same day he informed Brody of his intentions. Brody sent a testimonial to the same address, the following day, February 18th

Five days later Abdel received confirmation by telegram that he was required to be in New Orleans no later than Saturday, March 4th 1950 at 11.00am and report to the Purser aboard the freighter the Avonwood.

He had not made contact with Mr Gonzalez after receiving his letter. He could not face going back to the store. But he did want to speak to him, now that he would be leaving Sacramento. He rang him at home and arranged to go to his house on February 27th at 7pm.

Unknown to Abdel, Brody had organised a farewell party at his house for February 28th.

Abdel found his last week at work in Brody's garage difficult at times, knowing he would be leaving Sacramento and never see Tom, Mike and Brody again. The night before he met with Mr Gonzalez he wrote letters to both Hakim and Abdullah, explaining that he would be going back to sea. He did not mention the incident in the store and felt it would be better if he spoke in person over the phone. This he would do on his first shore leave after sailing with the Avonwood.

The next night he drove to the home of Mr Gonzalez, arriving five minutes late. He was welcomed by Mr Gonzalez at the front door.

"I am so happy that you have come to my home Mr Rahman, please come in and meet my family."

Abdel was guided into the house and the into the main living room. There waiting were the family, all seven of them.

"This is my dear wife Maria and all my children."

Maria stepped forward and put her arms round Abdel and said, "Senor Rahman, I am in your debt. You are so brave and I thank you for saving my husband."

All the children stepped forward and one by one they each shook his hand. The introduction was given by Maria giving each child's name.

Abdel was overwhelmed, for the first time since that night he felt that what he did was the right thing to do and said, "You all very kind, thank you. What I did that night will live with me all my life but I can see that if I had not stopped this man, so many people would have suffered. And I am sorry Mr Gonzalez, but I do not know your first name."

"My name is Julio, and we would be happy for you to join us for *"la comida"* a meal with my family please."

"Thank you very much Julio, I would be very happy to join your family for a meal," he replied.

Abdel enjoyed the evening and Julio and his family made him very welcome and he felt such genuine respect and honesty. It made think of what he was leaving behind, but it also redefined his life and he wanted to remember all the fine things that he experienced here in America. Before he said goodbye, Julio got all his family together and said, "Abdel Rahman, I want thank you for all you have done" and he handed Abdel an envelope.

"Your thanks are more than enough Julio, please you do need to give me anything."

As he attempted to hand Julio the envelope, Maria rushed forward hugged Abdel and said, "Please take our gift, you saved my husband and I am so happy that I am not a widow."

Abdel felt humbled and before he could say anything, the whole family held up their hands and in unison said,

'tener exito en la vida, el amor el respeto."

He gazed at Julio with a look of mystification and Julio just held out his arms and said, "We wish you well for the future."

He opened the envelope to find $50 and a photograph of Mr Gonzalez and his family.

'This is very kind and I will frame this photograph, thank you all for your kindness. '

He said goodnight to the Gonzalez family and drove back to his rooms. It was s stormy night and snow was steadily falling as he parked the Chevy. When inside, he got out his prayer mat and thanked God for his mercy and guidance and prayed for the Gonzalez family. He had a sense of adventure again and wondered what the world had to offer him.

The following day back at Brody's garage, all the talk was about who was going to replace Abdel in the garage. Mike laboured the point and said, "Where are you going to get a talented amigo like Abdel Brody? This guy is the big noise round here cowboy, he is the talk of the town, being a hero and all."

"Yip, he is difficult to replace, we have never had so much publicity in my time, that's for sure," he replied.

Tom chipped in with his take on the matter and added; "Am thinking, this man is set for bigger things. He is good looking, he can change a wheel in 3 minutes and he is braver than a wolverine, what you say boss?"

"Can't argue with that Tom, you are on the money, he is a straight arrow alright," replied Brody.

Abdel laughed and said: "I think you want me to stay, is that right?"

"You will be a big loss, who is going to get our pancakes from the Ki Ki Café," joked Mike.

Much of the day was filled with anecdotes about Abdel's time working in the garage. No mention of the party that Abdel would be attending at Brody's place. At 3pm Brody told Abdel to wash up and go home and get changed ready to be picked up by Tom at 6pm.

"Where I am going Brody? he asked.

"Martha said I had to feed you before you set off tomorrow, so I just do as I am told. So be ready for tom at 7pm."

"Your wife is very kind Brody."

"Oh yes, but I pay her well."

Abdel grinned and replied; "You are a funny man Brody, but yes, I will be ready."

Tom arrived at 6.40pm and Abdel jumped into the Chevy alongside Tom.

"I hope you is hungry brother. I bet the food is going to be good, man I wish I was joining you," said Tom.

Abdel noticed that Tom was well dressed unlike his normal attire and said, "Are you out tonight Tom?"

Tom was caught out, but managed to maintain the ruse by saying, "Yes sir, I is going to the Zanzibar Club for some swing jazz with my brother Ben."

"Who is playing tonight?" asked Abdel.

Tom was now struggling to think of an answer and said, "I aint sure, some band from Phoenix."

In order to deflect any further questions Tom changed the subject and said, "You got your camera, that right boss?"

"Yes, I have it with me Tom."

As they drove up to the house Abdel noticed that the house seemed to be in darkness.

"You sure Brody is at home Tom? I can't see any lights on."

"He be saving his money on the electric if I know Brody," replied Tom.

Tom parked and Abdel got out, saying, "Thank you for the lift Tom, enjoy the jazz."

"Sure will brother."

Tom drove away and Abdel was a little unsure about there being anybody at home. He knocked on the door and waited. Within a matter of seconds, the door swung open and the house lit up.

Brody stood at the door smiling and behind him a great cheer went up, then a shout from Tom, who had parked the car.

"Hey don't lock me out I aint going to no jazz club," said Tom.

Both men were invited in to great merriment. Abdel was so surprised and said, "You have kept this secret I think."

"It's your last night in Sacramento Abdel, so we wanted to give you a big send-off," said Brody.

Abdel looked around at all those present, Mike, Thelma, Martha, Brody, Tom, Julio Gonzalez, Sherriff Brown,

Nurse Gena Salvador and to his amazement Ernie Carlson. After coming to terms with what was going on, he said, "This is wonderful, I thank God that I have so many friends and I am very sad to leave you all tomorrow."

Martha took him by the hand and walked him into the dining room saying, "I hope you are hungry my boy."

Abdel was dumbstruck at the sight before him and tears filled his eyes. He was unable to speak and Martha just grabbed him and give him a great big hug saying, "You have enriched all our lives; this is our thanks."

"Give me your camera Abdel, I will take the photographs," said Ernie.

Brody put some Tommy Dorsey on his phonogram and the party started. Abdel mingled with all his guests and everyone was encouraged to dig in to the magnificent banquet that Martha had provided.

At around 9.30pm Sherriff Brown asked everyone for a moment of quiet and raising his glass of beer said, "A toast for our departing Sacramento hero, Abdel. We wish you health and happiness for the future and maybe one day you will come back and see us all. Raise your glasses everyone to Abdel Malik Rahman."

Abdel lifted his cup of tea and said, "I have been treated like a true friend by everyone hear. God has helped me and shown me mercy and I want to thank you all very much." And in Pashto he added;

> "Khwshala yam aw ghwaram che manana tashakor aw ze yam hamesha taso tasi malgaray."

"I have never heard you speak in your native tongue Abdel," said Brody."

A voice from the doorway said, "Oh, but I have."

Abdel turned to see Gretchen with a great big smile on her face. He was so full of emotion, he just stood staring at her. Before he could say anything, she walked to him, hugged him and kissed him.

"Well, raise my rent, aint that just something folks," said Tom.

After mingling with those gathered, Abdel and Gretchen found a quiet corner to chat. She wished him well for the future and hoped he would find love and happiness. He wished the same for her, as they chatted, the Sherriff spoke and said he had an announcement to make.

"I guess you should be the first to know that from tomorrow, I will be the new Captain of the Sacramento Police Department. I will do my best to ensure Sacramento continues to be a fine place to live and grow and I will do my utmost to make this indomitable city a safe haven for all."

A round of enthusiastic applause was given and Mike added; "I reckon that was your acceptance speech right there Sherriff."

"Well, you aint far wrong on that one," he replied.

The night passed so quickly and before he knew it, he was saying goodbye to Gretchen and as she kissed him for the last time she said, "Abdel be strong and do not be a prisoner of the past, you have so much to give."

"I wish you happiness Gretchen and may God protect you." She left and although Abdel felt an impulse to chase after her, he just turned back to his remaining friends who were conscious of his feelings.

Tom broke the silence and said, "I have something for Abdel."

From behind his back he produced a wrapped parcel and said, "This here present is from all of us, even the Sherriff chipped in," he joked.

Abdel opened his present to find a leather-bound photograph album.

"Now that is for all your photo's Abdel, I know you have got plenty," said Mike.

"Damn right, he has hundreds of them," added Ernie.

"You have been so kind, thank you very much my friends."

"Come on then, tell us what you said after the Sherriff's speech amigo," asked Julio Gonzalez.

"I just said that I was very thankful and I will always be your friend," he replied.

The festivities ended around 11.00pm and Abdel said his goodbye's and thanked everyone in person and left with Tom, who took him home.

Abdel had to be at the station for 10.30am the next day. He spent an hour getting everything he needed in his suitcase, which was a gift from Mike. It proved to be a huge benefit as he would not have got all his clothes, radio, camera, prayer mat and books in his kit bag.

His last avocation for the night was to pray and then at 12.15am he fell asleep for the last time in Sacramento.

Having rose at 8am, Abdel was out his home within half an hour. His plan was to walk to the station. This was his chance to say farewell to Sacramento, one last sojourn in the indomitable city. He stopped for a coffee at the Ki Ki Café on his walk-through town on a cool morning with dappled sunlight breaking through the trees on route.

He arrived at the station in good time at 10.00 am. He got to the platform for the New Orleans train and there they were; Brody, Mike, Tom and Ernie.

"Did you think we wouldn't give you a send-off?" said Brody.

"You should all be at work my friends, what do you always say Brody? Time is money," replied Abdel.

"I will live with this break of tradition, just for you buddy," he replied.

"I have brought my camera, we need a photograph of all of us, you got all the pictures, so we need our own," added Mike.

He got a station porter to take a snap of all five of them. They all sat on a platform seat waiting for the train. Brody reminded Abdel to keep in touch and said, "Now listen up cowboy, you have our number at the garage, my home number and my address. So, no excuses for not keeping in touch ok."

"Yes, I will tell you of my life my friends."

"You is truly a man of the world Abdel. I aint been nowhere not even Lake Tahoe and that's spittin distance from here," said Tom.

"Well, there is a challenge, when we get some time the three of us will go to Lake Tahoe and we will raise a jar to Abdel. What do you say fellas?" said Brody

"Yip, that is a good idea Brody," added Mike.

They sat in the sunshine and reflected on Abdel's time in Sacramento. The train pulled in bang on time and Abdel embraced his friends in turn and boarded the train. He found his birth and sat at the window to give a final wave to his friends. He had a feeling of sadness, but also one of excitement as the train eased out of the station and the waving hands of his friends grew smaller and smaller.

Abdel sat for some time just admiring the view as he travelled through California. He was just past San Jose when he realised that he was hungry. He remembered about a tie for the dining car and extricated it from his case and left his compartment for the dining car. As he entered a voice behind him said, "Well, if that don't beat all."

He turned to see a set of big gleaming white teeth; it was William Collins.

"I know the face, but can't recall the name boss," said William.

Abdel smiled offered his hand and said, "It's Abdel Malik Rahman, it was two years ago that we met on the train to San Francisco. I believe it is William, I am correct?"

"You most certainly are, it's good to see you again. It looks like California has been good to you, aint that something?"

William showed him to his table and chatted for a while before taking his dinner order. Before he left Abdel, he said, "I get off at 10.30pm, how about me and you have a good talk here in the dining car?"

Abdel agreed and as William wandered down the dining car, a couple on the opposite table made a comment that Abdel had heard many times, but as ever he chose to ignore it. However, the man persisted with his acerbic comments and said, "It is little wonder that this country of ours is on its knees. To allow these spades to mix with us white folks."

The woman sitting next to him suggested that he had gone too far saying, "Now Wilbur, that is quite enough."

Abdel thought about ignoring him, as he has done in the past but something urged him to react and he replied;

"Sir, and I call you sir because I am giving you respect. You know nothing of who I am or what I have done. The colour of a man's skin does not give you the right to speak with so much hate. I feel sorry for you, if all you can think of, is to abuse a man that looks different to you."

Both the man and the women were quite surprised at Abdel's considered retort and were speechless. An awkward silence descended and they never spoke for some time, not even to each other. Abdel felt good that he had responded to the slander and thankful he had enhanced his use of the English language.

He sat and enjoyed his rump steak smothered in onions followed by his favourite, pecan pie and cream. The couple opposite had eaten and gone by the time he asked William for a coffee.

At 10.30pm William joined him at his table and the two talked well past midnight. Abdel felt comfortable in confiding in him with his life in Sacramento and William was illuminated with Abdel's account of the misfortune he underwent in the store and said, "You must have been mad as hell to do what you did brother. I hope I don't get on the wrong side of you boy."

Abdel smiled and replied; "I never thought anything of it, I was just angry that this evil man would kill both of us even if he robbed the store. I think it was fear that made me act the way I did William."

"Well, that guy had it coming I reckon, and you is still here talking to old William."

The journey to New Orleans was made much more bearable with William to talk to and he asked another steward to take their photograph for his burgeoning album.

The train pulled into New Orleans at 8.30am on Saturday, March 4th. He hailed a cab at the station and arrived at the port office to ascertain where the Avonwood was docked. The port supervisor pointed to a vessel docked about 300 yards away and said,

"That's her with the red funnel with a black top and band, they are the Constantine Shipping Company colours."

As Abdel approached the ship a shout came from the port bow; "Hey Abdel, are you lost my boy?"

Abdel looked up but the sun was blocking his view, so moved a short distance closer to the ship. Then he realised who it was, a laughing Jack Rowley. Abdel was elated to see a familiar face and raced up the gang plank.

"Take your time shipmate, don't be in such a hurry," said Jack.

They embraced and Abdel said, "I can't believe that you are on this ship, after all these years Jack."

"You can't keep a good man down, once a sailor always a sailor. My, you have grown into a fine figure of a man. I heard you got a commission on the *Domelia*?"

"Yes, I have a lot to tell you Jack."

"Well, that will have to wait, you need to see the Purser and I have got to get into the engine room."

With that Jack took Abdel to the Purser's cabin and went below decks.

Abdel knocked on the door and was invited in. Frank Allen was the Purser on the Avonwood and he had been in that role for some three years. He was a small man with intense brown eyes, thick black hair parted down the centre. He looked over his wire rimmed spectacles and said, "You must be our new deck rating, Abdul Rahman?"

"No sir, its Abdel Malik Rahman."

The Purser looked down at the paperwork on his desk and said, "Oh yes Abdel, sorry for that slip up, welcome to the Avonwood. Have you got all your documents?"

"I have sir," and Abdel handed over his paperwork.

He stood as the Purser meticulously inspected his documentation. As Abdel waited, he was drawn to a framed quotation on the wall behind the Purser, it read;

"God moves in a mysterious way
His wonders to perform;
He plants his footsteps in the sea,
And rides upon the storm.
William Cowper

The Purser completed his scrutiny of Abdel's documents and looked up to see Abdel looking at the quotation. "You enjoy poetry and verse then do you?"

"Yes sir, I like reading all manner of books," he replied.

"Well, fell free to help yourself to my collection behind you."

Abdel turned to see a well-stocked bookshelf and replied; "That is kind of you sir, I will when I have finished my latest book."

"What is it your reading?"

"It's *Kon Tiki* by Thor Heyerdahl' he replied

"I am sure I have a copy of that, it's the blue one on the second shelf, I think."

Abdel turned looked at the shelf and said,

"Yes sir, it is the same book."

"You do not need to refer to me as sir, Frank will be fine. Here are your papers, there are all in order. You will need to see the Doctor before I sign you off, is that alright?"

"Yes Frank. Where do I go?"

"I have arranged an appointment for later today at 4.30pm. The Doctor will examine you next door in the medical room. I have asked your Deck Officer to meet you here, he should be with us soon, so take a seat."

Abdel sat and after five minutes, there was a knock at the door.

"Come in Peter," said the Purser.

Peter Wraith was a man of medium build standing at around 5' 9" with short cropped black hair with a Clark Gable pencil moustache.

"This is your new Deck Rating, Abdel Malik Rahman."

Abdel stood and offered his hand and said, "Pleased to meet you sir."

Peter shook his hand and replied; "Great to have on board Abdel, I have just been talking to Jack and he tells me you two go back a long way."

"Oh yes, Jack gave me my sea legs when I was much younger, on the City of Venice."

"Alright. Let's get you billeted and you can meet some of your shipmates."

Both men left the Purser's cabin and made their way to the poop deck accommodation.

As they walked Peter said, "I hear you saw a lot of action during the war?"

"Yes, I lost many friends."

"Me too, it's a bloody tragedy that so many men were lost and not enough gratitude has been attributed to all those brave souls."

"You have an accent like Jack," said Abdel.

"Oh, I lad, were both proud Yorkshiremen, he is from Barnsley and I am from York."

In the accommodation mess there were five seamen, three lying in their bunks and two more playing cards at a table.

"Now then you horrible set of sea dogs, this is your new shipmate, make him welcome. This is your bunk here and you have the second dog watch at 6-8pm Abdel."

Peter Wraith left Abdel to get acquainted with his fellow seafarers.

"Hello me old son," said one of the card players. A small man with a full set of ginger hair and beard, who went on to introduce those present.

"I am deck rating, Henry Dobson, my card playing shipmate here is Eric Horncastle, another deck rating. The three lazy buggers on their bunks are engineering ratings, Wally Robinson, Norman McCormack and our Spanish matador Enrico Orta."

Abdel introduced himself saying, "I am happy to be your shipmates and I look forward to working with you all."

"Your English is very good," said Enrico.

"Yes, thank you I have worked hard in reading and writing," he replied.

"Aint much need of that here," added Wally sarcastically.

"Ignore our ignorant yank, he is as thick as a builder's sandwich" joked Eric.

Wally raised his middle finger and said, "Up yours, you degenerate limey."

Abdel sorted his possessions and put his stuff in the designated locker. Once that was done, he sat and talked with Enrico about the all things maritime. He asked Enrico where the other crew members were and he replied; "Chino and Tico the other two deck ratings, are on shore leave along with Monty, Zahrani and Federico, who are engineering ratings."

"Chino and Tico, I know those names," said Abdel.

"You well might, if you have been on the City of Venice," added Eric

"It will be good to see them again," said Abdel.

"Can you remember Bill Hawkins, the Engineering Officer on that ship?" asked Enrico.

"Yes, I can remember him."

"He is our Engineering Officer on this ship now" he added.

"Yer, damn right and what a son of a bitch he is. He aint worth spit in my book," said Wally.

"You can tell that Wally, has no great affection for Mr Hawkins," said Henry.

General banter continued until Abdel had to go for his medical appointment with the Doctor at 4.30pm. He arrived at the medical room on time to find the Doctor waiting. The usual examination was given relating to blood pressure, temperature, weight, eyesight and the obligatory examination of genitalia. He was given a clean bill of health and he took his medical report to the Purser who logged it and returned it to him.

He was now very hungry and at 5pm he enjoyed a healthy portion of chicken and rice, followed by a good helping of pink blancmange. Wally had another name for this desert and said, "You are a better man than me for eating that "ballerina shit" it is fucking poison."

"You know what Wally; you are the most miserable arsehole I have ever had the misfortune to meet," said Henry.

"It's because he is a greaser with a brain the size of seagull's dick" joked Eric.

No verbal response from Wally, who again just raised his middle finger.

"Does anyone know when we are sailing tomorrow? "asked Norman.

"Hello, the sweaty sock is alive, he has spoken," said Eric.

"I have heard it could be 9am if the tide is up," said Wally.

"Where are we sailing to?" asked Abdel.

"We are off to Cuba my boy, we are taking soya beans, wheat, fruit and nuts; as well as ten passengers to Havana," replied Henry.

"And how do you know all this?" asked Wally.

"I overheard the skipper talking to Frank Allen," he replied.

"We will have to get some rum when we are there, if the skipper gives some shore leave," added Eric.

"We are bound to be there at least three days; we will take on cargo for England. We will be laden with sugar, rum and cigars, that's for sure," said Norman.

Peter Wraith returned and said, "Right Abdel, I will give you a breakdown of your watch, come with me."

Peter Wraith took him to the bow of the ship and said,

"Ok your watch is here on the foc'sle, are you alright with this?"

"Yes, it is a watch I have done many times. During the war I used to spot for U Boats and mines," replied Abdel.

"Oh well, you are tailor made for this watch. Some hate it, because when the weather is rough you tend to get hammered."

"It is not a problem sir,"

"It's Peter Abdel, I have not yet been knighted," he joked.

Abdel returned to the mess for another twenty minutes before his watch began.

As Abdel took to his bunk Wally raised the issue of watch duty and said, "Why the hell we have to do watch duty, when we are anchored up in port beats the shit out of me. Other tubs I have been on never put you on watch while in port."

"You must have been on some shit tubs then Wally," replied Eric.

Unknown to anyone in the mess, Jack Rowley was just outside the mess and heard the discussion. He entered and said, "I see you are debating our watch system on the ship, if I can join in this conversation and put some reasoning behind our system. Can I firstly address Wally, our resident knucklehead? The watch is required to maintain safety and security on board. We get split watches and an Officer must be in attendance. Some skippers will relax this task while in port but they must have an officer on watch and place a gangway lookout on duty. Our Captain maintains a more disciplined approach and not to post any watch keeper would be breaking maritime law. Any further queries gentlemen?"

"I think we get the drift thanks Jack," replied Norman.

"Can we have a special plaque mounted in the mess that signifies that Wally is our resident knucklehead Jack?" joked Henry amid much hilarity.

"Now now boys, Wally is our top greaser, regardless of his lack of moral fibre," replied Jack.

Abdel enjoyed the banter and felt at home in this environment. He completed his split watch at 8pm and returned to the mess to find Peter Wraith explaining the ships sailing time and destinations.

He paused as Abdel took to his bunk and then said, "As Abdel has just come in, I will start again. So, we will be leaving New Orleans at around 9am tomorrow. We have a cargo of wheat, soya beans, barley, cotton, fruit, nuts and whisky. In addition to the cargo, we have nine passengers."

"We are bound for Havana, Cuba and our arrival time in Cuba should be on March 5th at approximately 17.00 hours. We will unload cargo and take on new cargo for England. Shore leave will be granted as follows; a 48 hour shore leave will be granted to all hands except the Captain, the Navigation Officer and the Engineering Officer. The Captain will organise a rota for shore leave to enable all officers to get ashore. A reminder that on no account will any females be allowed on board at any time. All officers and ratings must be back on board by 23.00 hours, when the gangway will be lifted. Any questions gentlemen?"

"Can you ask our mad Mexican Juan the Cook not to serve up any more shithouse flap valves Peter. My arse is still trying to recover, it's as sore as a cobbler's thumb," said Norman.

Raucous laughter broke out and Abdel asked Henry; "What are shithouse flap valves?"

Still trying to control his laughter Henry replied; "Its slang for hamburgers, well that's what they are supposed to be. My advice is to avoid them like the plague. It would be better to starve to death."

Abdel said, "I will follow your advice then, but I do not eat ham it is unclean and against my religion to eat the flesh of that animal."

"I doubt there is anything resembling meat within the ingredients Abdel. But I suppose it's best not knowing anyway," added Henry.

After Peter had finished his declamation, Abdel met up with Chino and Tico again. They exchanged tales of their time at sea and agreed to visit Havana together when shore leave is granted.

The Avonwood left New Orleans at 9.15am and headed out into the Gulf of Mexico for the three-day trip to Cuba. The weather was warm and only a moderate swell, with waves of 4 feet. The ship had a top speed of 10 knots and the 454 feet long steam driven freighter made good headway on her 800-mile journey.

Abdel met up with Bill Hawkins again when he came on deck from the engine room to see the Captain.

"Well now then shipmate, you have changed from that youth that sailed on the City of Venice," said Bill.

"Yes, I have seen many things since that trip to the Persian Gulf" he replied.

"I bet you have; well this is a good boat and the Captain is a good man.

He is tough but fair Abdel, and I am sure you will be fine on this ship. Are you still reading your books?"

"I am and my English is so much better now. It has helped that I have lived in America for two years."

"Really, where in America were you then?"

"I lived and worked in Sacramento, California."

"That is great; look, I have to go to see the Captain, but we will have another talk soon."

CHAPTER TWENTY

The Avonwood docked in Havana on March 8th at 15.00 hours and the Captain granted shore leave at 18.00 hours. Abdel, Chino and Tico made their way down the gangway onto the wharf and left the port. Abdel had his camera with him and began to take photographs of some of the buildings within minutes of entering the city. The shipmates walked along Avenida Del Puerto and into the old city along Santa Clara, it was a very warm evening with a temperature of 24 degrees Celsius. They stopped for a Cuban coffee and took in the atmosphere. Chino enjoyed a cigar and ordered a rum to compliment the ambience of the moment. Abdel took many photographs and asked a waiter at the café where they enjoyed their coffee to take a photo of all of them together.

Havana was a bustling city with many bars, restaurants, clubs, café's, cinema's and Abdel felt at ease. The American influence was everywhere; in particular the plethora of American automobiles. English was used by many Cubans and this in turn enhanced communication. After their coffee they walked on and saw the Capital Building, which was built in 1929. They had a meal of fish salad and at a restaurant on Muralla, before returning to the ship at 10pm.

When they returned to the mess Abdel put his radio on, and to his surprise he was able to get many American radio stations. He found a station playing jazz and blues, the Spade Cooley Band was playing.

"You like that music Abdel?" asked Tico.

"Yes, I heard a lot of jazz in Sacramento and I saw Tommy Dorsey at the Zanzibar Club," he replied.

"It's just noise to me," said Monty Railton, who was lying on his bunk smoking and blowing smoke rings in the air.

"So, Monty, what music to you like then?" said Henry.

"I aint a music lover of any kind really" he replied.

"These fucking yanks are so wrapped up in their own world, they forget how to enjoy themselves," said Eric, as he poured out a set of dominoes out onto the table.

"Ok limey, let's see how good you are at dominoes, anyone else up for it?" said Monty.

"Yes, I will play," added Abdel

"Go on then, I will join you," said Henry.

Zahrani asked if he could play, saying,

"I would like to play, but I am not very good."

"That's fine we will just take your money anyway" joked Henry.

"It's 10 cents a round boys, you happy with that you tight arsed limey's?"

added Monty.

"Kiss my arse, just get your money on the table," replied Eric.

The game went on until it was time for Eric's watch at midnight. Abdel had acquired a sum of $2. 30cents from the game. Zahrani had gained 60 cents in his first game of dominoes, largely due to advice given by Abdel. Monty had lost $1. 75cents and he returned to his bunk saying,

"I fucking hate dominoes," resulting in much laughter from his shipmates.

The Avonwood took on board its cargo of sugar, rum, bananas, cigars along with 8 passengers and left Havana for London on March 10th. The journey would cover some 2.600 nautical miles, taking around 11 days.

Abdel was looking forward to his first visit to London, he had heard so much about the city and its history. He took the time to write to Abdullah, Hakim and Brody as the ship sailed across the Atlantic. He informed Hakim and Abdullah of the incident in Sacramento and where he was heading; now that he was a merchant seaman again. He would get to post these letters once he arrived in London.

During the voyage he found time to have long conversation's with Bill Hawkins and Jack Rowley about his past and what lies ahead for the future. While talking to Eric, Henry and Peter Wraith he began to think that England may well be the place to set down his roots. He listened to the BBC World Service on his radio and looked forward to docking in London, it evoked a zealous desire within in his consciousness.

The voyage was uneventful, other than three crew members going down with jelly belly after four days at sea. Wally, Norman and Federico suffered, having consumed copious amounts of the cook's Vindaloo, aptly named *"ring stinger."* Jack Rowley was not best pleased, as this put three of his engine ratings out of commission for 48 hours.

The ship entered the Thames and dropped anchor at the Canada dock at 15.45 hours on a cold afternoon on March 21st.

After the cargo had been taken off the Captain summoned the officers to his mess for a briefing. He informed those present that the ship would be in port for one week. Before any new cargo was taken on board, the ship would be fumigated and cleaned. As a consequence of this able seamen would be given four days of shore leave.

Officers would be granted three days, which would be staggered to ensure two officers would be on board at any given time. The Captain indicated he would be taking two days to go home and see his wife and family in Dorset.

While sitting in the mess and waiting for the green light to go ashore,

Zahrani asked Abdel if he wanted to join him in London saying, "I have a brother in Camberwell who will put us up for a few days and we can also visit the Mosque for prayers. I can also show you the sights of London."

"That is very kind Zahrani, will your brother be alright about us staying in his house?

"Oh yes, Hasan has a very big house. He is a Doctor and works at St. Thomas's Hospital. He has a wife Soraya and a son called Ahmed; he has been in London since 1945."

Abdel and Zahrani walked down the gangway at 18.30 hours and Zahrani rang his brother's house from a public telephone. His wife answered the phone saying Hasan was at work, but she said they would be pleased to have both of them for a few days.

Zahrani put the phone down and said, "We have a home for a few days Abdel, shall we get on a bus and go into London?"

"I need to post these two letters to India and South Africa. Mr Allen the Purser has given me the correct stamps."

"Well, look over there. That red post box will take your letters Abdel."

He dropped them in the post box and they sought advice from a policeman on what bus to catch, within 15 minutes they were in central London. Armed with his camera Abdel took numerous photographs of Buckingham Palace, Westminster Bridge, the Houses of Parliament, St Paul's and Westminster Abbey. They curtailed their sightseeing at 8pm and got the bus to Camberwell. When they got to Hasan's house it had just started to get dark and the street lights were just coming on.

Hasan was at home having finished his shift at the hospital at 7pm and welcomed them at the door and said, "My dear long-lost seafaring brother Zahrani and also his friend who is,"

"Abdel Malik Rahman sir, pleased to meet you."

"Please come in, you are most welcome and praise be to God, the most merciful for your safe journey.

As they entered the hallway of the house Hasan's wife and son greeted them.

Hasan said, "This is Soraya my wife and my son Ahmed"

"Abdel Malik Rahman, and I am happy to meet you both," he replied.

Abdel was shown to his room by Zahrani and at 9pm they all enjoyed a Beef Biryani.

When Ahmed was put to bed, they chatted about all manner of things for more than an hour, then Zahrani suggested that they retire for the night. As Abdel climbed the stairs to the first floor, he said to Zahrani; "This house is very big, even bigger than my brother's house in Durban"

"It has six bedrooms Abdel, sometimes our parents come and stay for a few weeks in the summer."

"Where in Egypt do your parents live Zahrani? "asked Abdel.

"They live in Dike, about 20 miles from Alexandria on the coast. My father is also a Doctor there."

"When did you last see them."

"It was over a year ago, I was docked in Alexandria for five days with my last ship."

They bid each other goodnight and Abdel prayed before getting into bed. As he lay, he started to think of all the people he has known in his life, he thought of his own parents, his brother and cousin. At 32 years of age he had experienced so much in life. He had encountered; fear, anger, hatred, sorrow, desolation, happiness, friendship and love. He now hoped he could begin a new chapter in his life that would enable him to explore and discover his destiny. He fell asleep as the rain began to fall on the window of his room.

The next day, the two shipmates went to see the Marx Brothers at the Lyceum Theatre and when they left, they were both unable to have a coherent conversation without laughing.

Their short break in London ended with a visit to the Tower of London and prayers at the Brick Lane Mosque in Spitalfields; before returning to the ship. Abdel had taken many photographs and he was contemplating buying another album on his next trip ashore, wherever that may be.

The Avonwood had been fumigated and cleaned and was now being loaded with cargo for the return voyage to Cuba. The cargo consisted of timber, steel, agricultural machinery and paint. The ship left the Canada dock on March 31st for a 10-day return journey to Havana. The Avonwood continued to make return cargo voyages to and from Cuba. Occasionally the ship would make other port destinations such as, Colon in Panama, Kingston in Jamaica and Barranquilla in Columbia. In 1952 Abdel made a decision that would change his life forever.

While in Tilbury Dock, London; Peter Wraith Deck Officer of the Avonwood was appointed Captain of the British Pilgrim, a general cargo vessel. He asked Jack Rowley to join him as Chief Engineering Officer, which he accepted.

Peter also asked Abdel if he would like to "jump ship" and join the crew. After a lot of soul searching and discussion, he decided to accept the commission. The ship was being refitted in Glasgow and would be ready in three weeks. While this refit was being carried out Peter, Jack and Abdel would be put up in a hotel in Glasgow. The owners of the British Pilgrim were the Macleod Steamship Company based in Glasgow and they arranged for the transfer of the all three crew members.

Within two days, Peter, Jack and Abdel were on a train from London bound for Glasgow. The company had booked them into the Grand Central Hotel on Gordon Street, a short walk from the station.

When Abdel saw the hotel he just stared in awe and said, "Are you sure the company are paying for our stay Peter?"

Peter laughed and replied; "Don't worry shipmate all expenses have been covered, let's get checked in. I have a meeting with the owners in an hour."

On June 11th 1952, Peter, Jack and Abdel arrived at the King George V dock at Shieldhall at 9am. The rest of the crew were told to report from 12.00 noon and no later than 6pm. The British Pilgrim is a 8.870-ton freighter, built in 1938 and it is fitted with 2 screws with a top speed of 14 knots and can accommodate up to 12 passengers. Cargo would be loaded in three days' time and this would enable the new skipper to familiarise himself with his crew. The crew started to drift on board from midday and Abdel welcomed the ratings as they returned to their bunks.

He introduced himself and as he was looking through his Photo album, he heard a familiar voice saying, "I don't believe it, that can't be Abdel can it?"

Abdel looked up to see the unforgettable face of Gordon Wallace a former crew member of the Santa Rita.

"Well, I'll be blowed, what the hell are you doing on this tub wee man?" said the big Scotsman.

"This is my new ship Gordon," Abdel replied.

"So, you have finally made it to God's country, bonny Scotland me old shipmate. I thought you was in America with Ernie Carlson."

"Yes, I was there for two years, but the sea called me back."

They sat and talked as other ratings came into the mess. After some twenty minutes, Gordon introduced them to Abdel saying, "Noo hear this boys, this wee man here is Abdel Rahman and he is an old shipmate of mine. So, I would like you all to give him your respect."

"I hear we have a new skipper, is that so?"

"Yes, it's Peter Wraith, he was my Deck Officer on my last ship, the Avonwood," said Abdel.

"What's he like, is he a good man?" asked Gordon.

"He is a good man Gordon; he will make a good Captain I think," he replied.

"That's good enough for this big ugly Scotsman, sure enough."

All the Officers were on board by 16.00 hours and Peter Wraith gathered them all in his cabin for a get together and to introduce himself and Jack Rowley. Those present were the Purser, Engineering Officer, Navigation Officer, Steward, Deck Officer and Medical Officer. Having asked them all to take a seat he said, "Welcome gentlemen, thank you for your punctual return to the ship. This is my first commission as a Captain and I do hope we can work together in order to maintain a safe and reliable merchant navy vessel for our employers."

He went on to ask each Officer to introduce himself and to give a resume of their respective careers. This done he went on to say; "Well gentlemen, we have a refitted vessel that can now accommodate a diverse cargo and 10 passengers. Our first voyage will be across the English Channel to Dieppe in France with a cargo of timber, coal, iron ore and steel. In addition, we have five passengers to accommodate."

"We set sale in four days' time on the morning tide and we should reach our destination on June 16th around 22.00 hours. After the ship has been cleaned below decks, we will sail to Newcastle Upon Tyne with a cargo of pit props, fruit and vegetables. Any questions so far men?"

"I will need to undertake a medical inspection of all new crew members Captain," said Richard Jobson, the Medical Officer.

"That's fine you can start with me and then Jack and Abdel our new deck rating. Have we any other new crew members Andrew?

"Yes Captain, a new engine rating called Harry Bond," he replied

"Can I leave you to liaison with Richard on that issue then Andrew?"

"Yes, Captain will do."

"Any further questions men?"

"There is one issue you should be aware of Captain," added Trevor Norris, the Deck Officer.

"Alright Trevor, what is it?"

"Two crew members were involved in a violent confrontation on our last voyage and the general feeling was that they should have been let go."

"What action was taken then Trevor?"

"None Captain."

"Well, let's have their names then."

"Deck Rating Steven Bryant and Engine Rating Bill Watling Captain."

A sense of unease was very evident within the room, with some shuffling around in chairs. The obvious tension was exasperated when Andrew Collings said, "They both have a history of drunkenness on board Captain, but the last Captain chose to take a lenient approach to this."

"Ah, now we are getting somewhere. Right then, I want them here as soon as both of them have returned to the ship. I will not tolerate violence and drunkenness and if I have any doubts about them after I have seen them, then they are history gentlemen. However, If I do let them go, we will be two men down and it's too late to get replacements, so we will have to wait until we get back to Newcastle. If we need two more able seamen, can you wire the company as soon as possible Andrew?"

"Yes Captain."

"Well, this has been an education, it does not reflect on my determination to have a cohesive crew on board this vessel and I am confident that will be achieved, thank you gentlemen."

Having dismissed his officers Peter Wraith sat back in his chair and contemplated his next course of action. He did not have to wait too long to formulate a reaction, in this his first major decision as Captain.

Within fifteen minutes both protagonists stood outside his cabin, along with the Purser Andrew Collings.

He called all three men into his cabin and asked them to take a seat.

"Good afternoon gentlemen, its Steven and Bill I believe. Is that correct?"

"Yes skipper," they both answered.

"I would prefer Captain gentlemen, if you don't mind," he replied.

The two men just looked at each other and Bill Watling said, "The other skipper didn't give a fuck, about what you called him."

"Well, there lies the problem. However, you have the great honour to have me, Captain Peter Wraith as your superior officer on this ship. Now it seems that both of you have a little bit of history as "agent provocateurs," have you not?"

Both men, were obviously in a state of perplexity and Steven Bryant said, "I haven't got a clue what you mean."

"Let me clarify then, it appears that you both have been involved in drunkenness and violence aboard this vessel in recent times, is that correct?"

"So, it does you good to let off steam skipper," said Watling.

"There you go again Bill; you have not responded to my earlier wish to be called Captain."

"Don't give a toss really."

"Mr Collings sir, would you gather Bills papers and have him escorted from this ship immediately," said the Captain.

Whereupon Watling rose to his feet and threw a punch at the Captain. Peter Wraith was a fit athletic man and easily avoided the blow and then crashed an uppercut on Watkins chin, that would have impressed Jake La Motta. The punch sent Watling flying backward over his chair and into the cabin door. He slid down the door in a semi-conscious state. Both the Purser and Bryant were dumbstruck.

"Now get that malignant, braindead, halfwit of my ship."

"Jesus Christ, that was some punch," said Bryant.

"Oh yes, you're also looking for another job, goodbye," added the Captain.

The Purser and Bryant lifted Watling up still in a dazed condition and carried him out of the Captain's cabin.

As Watling was helped down the gangway by Bryant, a puzzled Jack Crowley asked the Purser; "What the hell happened there?"

"Let's just say the Captain has a new name,"

"What's that?"

"*One punch Wraith*," replied Andrew Collings.

He then told Jack Crowley all about the Captain's "*coup de grace*" with Watling and how he has to try and get two able seamen to join the ship when they dock in Newcastle.

"I have taken a shine to our skipper, after his positive action today Jack," said Andrew.

"Well, I have to say, I am not surprised. He does not suffer fools gladly. By all accounts we are better off without those two firebrands "*ecce homo*."

"Behold the man indeed, it means you're a man down until we get to Geordie land."

"We will survive Andrew."

The British Pilgrim sailed out of Glasgow on June 15th and reached Dieppe at 21.30 hours. The ship anchored offshore until the next morning when the Pilot boarded and she docked at 8.45 am. The holds were cleaned and the new cargo was loaded the following day and the ship sailed out into the English Channel bound for Newcastle upon Tyne on June 18th. The 380-mile voyage would take some 27 hours.

The British Pilgrim docked at The Albert Edward Dock on the north bank of the Tyne. The Captain decided not to speak to the whole crew until the events of his encounter with Watling and Bryant had circulated around the ship. Prior to announcing shore leave he gathered the Officers in his cabin.

Jack Rowley maintained authority on deck as the meeting took place, he was briefed by Peter beforehand.

The officers gathered and the Captain began; "Thanks gentlemen, well our first sojourn to France and back here to Newcastle has been eventful. Thanks to both Jack in his absence and Trevor for having to sail a man short."

"Now then, the circumstances behind able seamen Watling and Bryant's removal from the ship. I gave them the opportunity to explain their recent inappropriate behaviour on this ship. Sadly, they were somewhat reluctant to engage in any constructive debate on this subject and let us just say that more positive reinforcement was needed to get my point across. This was the case with Mr Watling, who seemed to take a negative approach that required intervention from yours truly."

"Yes Captain, we have a condensed version and it appears that you acquired a nickname in that regard," said Trevor.

"Really, you do surprise me. Can I ask what this nickname is?"

"One punch Wraith," quipped the Navigation Officer, Jim Anderson.

The Captain laughed and added; "To be honest gentlemen, I just thought; bollocks I am not having this and lamped him one."

"He had it coming skipper, oops Captain sorry," said Trevor.

The Captain laughed again and said, "Skipper is fine, I just wanted to see how those two idiots would react."

Laughter permeated around the room and the Captain gave details of their stay on the Tyne and discussed the engineering and maintenance schedules while in port. Shore leave would be a maximum 24-hour hiatus. Watch duties would be designated by Trevor and Jack Rowley and at least two Officers would need to be on board at all times, along with the Captain.

Abdel decided to stay on board and volunteered for watch duty along with Gordon, Mohammed and the new engine rating Harry Bond.

Mohammed had been with the ship for five years, he joined as a deck rating at 16 and his home was in Basra, Iraq. He was pleased that he had another Muslim to talk to and often spoke of his country and how conflict between Sunni and Shia sects caused so much unrest. Like Abdel he was a Sunni Muslim, but he never considered there to be any great difference. Islam is Islam, he often said. He envied Abdel, having made the pilgrimage to Mecca for the Haji.

They shared the first watch that night and Mohammed spoke of a cousin, who lived in South Shields across the river and said, "My cousin Nawab has been in England for three years and he is to be married soon."

"What does your cousin do for employment?" asked Abdel.

"He works in the shipyard at South Shields."

"If we are to visit the north east again, I will take you to his house."

"That would be very good," said Abdel.

"I am thinking back to when I was in the war. I met a soldier from South Shields. I think his name was Peterkin, he was going to Italy; I hope he survived."

"The north east is a very nice place, but the way they speak up here is very different Abdel."

"If it is like Liverpool, I will not understand them I think."
"They are called Sandancers."
"Oh yes, I know this Mohammed.
"Do they have a special dance?"
"Don't know, I think it is because the town has sandy beaches. My cousin likes it in South Shields and many people of our colour live in the town. There are Somalia's, Indians and Arabs in the town, they were sailors like you who settled in the town and married local girls."

The British Pilgrim sustained a continuous schedule of sailing around the British Isles and northern Europe for another year. In August 1953 the ship was in dry dock in Middlesbrough for major repairs. The repairs would take some 12 weeks to complete and as a consequence the crew were given accommodation in lodging houses near the port.

Abdel and Mohammed were set up in such a lodging house in South Bank, Middlesbrough.

The lodging house was owned by Mr & Mrs Snaith. Mr Snaith was a sea going engineer and was at sea most of the year. Abdel and Mohammed shared a room, they also shared a bathroom and the rooms were always kept clean. The Macleod Steamship Company paid the rent for all its seamen while the ship was in dry dock. They had accumulated a number of boarding houses in the South Bank area for the crew.

As the weeks went by it was very evident that the landlady Doreen Snaith had taken a liking to Abdel. He was very aware of this and tried to avoid any contact with her. This was not lost on Mohammed and on a quiet Saturday afternoon as they both sat and listened to Abdel's radio he said, "Abdel, I think Doreen likes you very much."

"Yes, this is not good Mohammed, she is a married woman."

Doreen Snaith was indeed an attractive woman of 32. She had long blonde her that she usually kept in a pony tail, she was slim and had bright blue eyes that magnified her engaging smile.

"Abdel, she is very pretty and her husband is thousands of miles away."

"Mohammed, you think I have no honour. You think I should go with this woman and lie with her at night. You think little of me, that I would do such a thing."

"Abdel, you like her, is that true?"

"Yes, she is very pretty Mohammed."

The conversation ended abruptly, but Mohammed was correct she was very attractive and he was indeed smitten by her. However, the die was cast and on a rainy afternoon in October it happened.

Mohammed had decided to go to South Shields by train to see his cousin, he left at 8am and he would not be returning until late the next day. Abdel got up at 9am and went downstairs for breakfast. Doreen was at the cooker frying eggs.

"Good morning Abdel, have you slept well?" she said.

"Yes, Doreen I have; my bed is very comfortable thank you."

As soon as he said it, he knew that would then encourage Doreen to embellish the point. She did not let him down and replied; "That's good, my bed is the same but when you are alone it can be difficult to sleep."

She turned away from the cooker and gave him such an infectious smile that was so bewitching he felt helpless and he struggled to gain his composure. She recognised he was in a state of arousal and moved close to him, leaned over and gave him a sensitive long kiss.

At the end of the kiss, he tried to speak but she just placed her finger over his lips, smiled and said, "I have wanted to do that for weeks Abdel, please don't take offence."

"Please Doreen, I think this is not right."

She pulled another chair alongside him and said, "When two people are attracted to each other, then something has to happen. You find me attractive, don't you?"

"Yes, I do but…"

She stood up took his hand and they walked up the stairs to her bedroom. He felt guilt beginning to question his morals, his heart was pounding but he wanted so badly to make love to her.

They entered her room, she closed the curtains and returned to him, then another long kiss signalled a passionate embrace. They made love and fell asleep in each other's arms.

The *affaire d"amour* continued and with only three days left, they were again in each other's arms in her bed. It was a warm afternoon and Doreen rose to open the window slightly. Then she saw her husband walking down the street, he was some 300 yards away and she said, "Oh my God, it's my husband, he is in the street Abdel. Quick, get your clothes on while I get changed. Panic ensued; Abdel fell out of the bed in his eagerness to get ready. He grabbed all his clothes and made a swift exit back to his room and shut the door.

Mohammed was sitting reading and got a shock to see Abdel naked holding his clothes and said, "What has happened Abdel?"

"Oh God forgive me; her husband has returned," he replied.

Within three minutes they heard the front door open and a shout of; "Doreen, it's me the man of your dreams."

Doreen had changed clothes and composed herself enough to meet her husband at the foot of the stairs saying, "How I have missed you my darling, are you hungry love?"

"Just for you," and he wrapped his arms around her and kissed her.

Abdel and Mohammed listened intently to the conversation and Mohammed said with a wry smile on his face; "Well I am hungry Abdel, you must be hungry also, after all the exercise you have had today."

Abdel just gave him a look of indignation and replied; "You go and eat; I will stay here and listen to my radio."

The remaining two days were a challenge for Abdel, this was exasperated by Mohammed's insistence on being present at all times and occasionally throwing in a comment that put Abdel and Doreen on the defensive.

On the last day of their stay Doreen managed to get rid of her husband to spend a short time alone with Abdel. As he was packing his stuff away to re-join the ship, she sat with him in his room. Mohammed was banished to the lounge downstairs.

She sat on his bed with him held his hand and said, "Abdel you have made me feel like a woman again. I am very fond of you, but you and I both know that this affair was always going to be short. Can I tell you that you are a gentle, loving man and some girl is going to be very lucky one day? Please do not feel that you have been used, what happened was wonderful. Remember me, because I will never ever forget you, that is a promise"

She kissed him for the last time and left the room.

Abdel felt his self-esteem had been undermined. His naivety had affected his reality and as he sat wondering what might have been. The realisation being, he was never going to run off with Doreen, where would they go? She was very content to be married, so it seemed and had she done this before? He then began to analyse the validity of the whole experience and finished packing as Mohammed returned full of questions.

"What is happening Abdel. Are you going to run off with her?"

"Mohammed, we are going back to our ship, so finish packing. The taxi will be here soon."

"But Abdel…"

"Do not speak of this anymore, do you understand?"

Mohammed stared at Abdel, thinking about what had been said and replied; "If that is your wish."

"Yes, it is, thank you."

Their taxi back to the ship arrived and the two shipmates climbed into the back. As the car drove away Doreen appeared at the window and waved, Abdel returned the gesture and smiled.

CHAPTER TWENTY-ONE

The British Pilgrim sailed out of the River Tees bound for Belfast with a cargo of timber, steel and aluminium, on November 13th. After that trip they were back in Newcastle and the opportunity to visit South Shields was taken and the two men travelled across the Tyne on the Ferry, The Northumbria. Mohammed's cousin lived in a house on Commercial Road, which was a short walk from the Ferry Landing.

Being a Saturday, Mohammed's cousin was at home with his family. Ramadan was due to end a day later and Nawab Hussain and his family were preparing for the feast to celebrate it. Abdel was pleasantly surprised at the number of Arab and Asian people living in the area known as Windmill Hill.

They stayed with Nawab for two days and in that time, Abdel saw much of the town. He spent time walking on the beach and went to Marsden Rock. They visited various friends of Nawab and prayed in the community Mosque on Smith Street, the building used to be a public house. It was converted into a Mosque in 1928 by the Arab community and it included a bathing area that was once the cellar of the pub.

They returned to their ship on November 31st and the visit to South Shields had generated an ebullient curiosity in Abdel. Having settled back into his bunk he said to Mohammed; "South Shields is a good town Mohammed and I felt safe and the people were very friendly."

"Yes, I like the town and there is lots of work if you do not want to go to sea."

This sparked Abdel's fascination and for a number of days' it remained a constant diversion. He thought off jumping ship and getting a job on one of the many Colliers hauling coal from the Tyne.

The next trip at sea involved another sailing to Dieppe in France and returning to Newcastle on December 21st. Abdel had broached the subject of leaving the merchant navy and settling in South Shields with Mohammed. While sailing to Dieppe he again confided in Mohammed and said, "Do you think I should leave the British Pilgrim and find work in South Shields Mohammed?"

"Do you mean jump ship Abdel?"

"No, but I can ask the Purser if he could contact the company and ask them if they would cancel my contract."

"Well my friend, they might do this thing; but they will need another sailor first I think."

The ship docked in Dieppe on December 6th and Abdel went to see Andrew Collings with his enquiry. The purser was a little surprised by the request and said, "This is a bit of a revelation Abdel, is it the ship or the crew that has created this wish to leave?

"No, it is not anything like that Mr Collings. I am 35 years old and I want to settle down and hopefully have a family."

"So, where do you want to settle down then Abdel?"

"I think South Shields would be a good place."

"Well, I will inform the company of your request Abdel. I can't promise it will happen, but you have a first-class record in the Merchant Navy and you have given 20 years of excellent service. Leave it with me, I will telephone the company office in Glasgow. What are you going to do for work?"

"I will try and get on a Collier taking coals from Newcastle sir."

"That might be difficult, but I will mention that to the company."

"Thank you, Mr Collings."

The ship was delayed in Dieppe for engineering repairs and would not be returning to Newcastle until January 2nd 1954. Andrew Collings asked to see Abdel on December 9th and said, "Well, able seaman Abdel Malik Rahman, it seems that the company have agreed to your request and you can follow your destiny and leave McCloud & Company."

Abdel could not hide his elation and rose to his feet and shook the Purser's hand saying, "This is wonderful news Mr Collings, I thank you very much. I am so happy sir."

"Hang on a moment, before you get carried away and run down the gangway. We need a replacement before you can leave and if you want to settle in South Shields, you will have to wait until we sail."

"Oh yes sir, I understand."

"Have you got somewhere to live in South Shields?"

"Mohammed has a cousin who lives there and I will ask him if he can put me up until I find a job and somewhere to live."

"Right then, I will sign you off when we get to the Tyne, your replacement will be joining the ship at the Albert Edward Dock. The company have given me a contact for you with regard to employment on the Colliers to the Tyne. It is the Readhead Company of Newcastle and they have a post on the Highlander. If you would like me to contact them for you, I can do this today."

"That would be very kind of you sir."

When Abdel returned to the mess, he found that Mohammed was on watch. So, his news would have to wait a few more hours. The Chief Officer Jack Rowley appeared and asked Abdel to check on the Joining Shackles on the forward starboard side. As Abdel jumped off his bunk and Jack said, "A little bird has told me that you are leaving us Abdel."

Abdel felt a pang of guilt and replied; "Yes, that is so sir. I am going to live in the north east and work on a Collier."

"Have you got somewhere to live then?"

"Yes, I hope that Mohammed's cousin can give me a bed until I find a place to live."

"I hope he does; you don't want to be sleeping rough, its bloody cold up there in winter."

"That is right sir, it is very cold. It reminds of when I was a boy in Afghanistan, when I lived in the mountains. "

"Can I say it has been a pleasure to know and work with you Abdel and I wish you all the best for the future. If you ever get to York, come and see me shipmate."

"Thank you, Jack sir, you have been a good friend. I will always remember that first voyage on the City of Venice"

"God, that seems a long time ago shipmate."

Abdel did his chores and returned to the accommodation mess to find Mohammed asleep in his bunk. He woke him, much to Mohammed's chagrin; "Mohammed, I have a new job. I am leaving the ship; I need your help my friend."

Mohammed was still half asleep and said, "Wait Abdel, you are leaving now?"

"No, I have been released by the company and I will leave the ship when we dock in Newcastle. I need you to ask your cousin if he can give me a bed until I get a lodging house."

"Where will you work Abdel?"

"I hope to have a job with a company shipping coals to France. Mr Collings is doing this for me."

"I will need to telephone my cousin Nawab, I can do this now if you want to come with me. We will ask for a ship to shore call from Mr Collings cabin, you might have to pay for it Abdel."

"This is good, I will pay Mohammed."

Both men went to the Purser's cabin and Mr Collings was just coming out.

"Now then what can I do for you boys?"

"Mr Collings sir, would I be able to telephone my cousin in England. It is important, I need to ask him if he has a room for Abdel; Abdel will pay for the call sir."

"I am off for a meeting with Captain boys, but if you came back in an hour, I will organise it for you."

"Thank you, Mr Collings sir," said Abdel.

It was 9pm when they returned and Mr Collings was in his cabin. He made the call for them and Mohammed spoke with his cousin. Nawab said that he would be happy to give Abdel a room until he found himself a place.

"How much do I pay for the call Mr Collings?"

"Nothing, accept it as a farewell gift from me."

"You are very kind sir, thank you," replied Abdel.

Abdel returned to his bunk and began to write letters to Hakim and Abdullah telling them of his plans. The British Pilgrim sailed for Newcastle on New Year's Day and docked the next day. The Captain Peter Wraith was on deck to say farewell to Abdel along with the crew who gave him a grand send off with three raucous cheers as he walked down the gangway. Mr Collings had sorted out his papers and he was given a letter of acceptance from his new employer Readhead & Co Ltd as a deck hand on the Highlander.

It was a very cold day and Abdel was well wrapped up in a heavy coat, scarfe and balaclava as he boarded the ferry Northumbria at North Shields.

He arrived at Nawab's house on Commercial Road at 6.30pm. Nawab welcomed him into the house and his wife Meenah gave him a hot cup of tea to warm him up and said, "How do like the weather in South Shields?"

"It is very cold Mrs Hussain."

"Please you are a guest in our home, call me Meenah" she replied.

"Thank you very much."

She turned to her husband and said, "I think he will have no trouble finding a lady friend here in South Shields Nawab."

"Do not listen to my wife Abdel, she thinks she is a matchmaker," said Nawab.

"I would like to go to the Mosque and pray tonight Nawab," said Abdel.

"Of course, we can go after you have eaten; Meenah has made a Beef Madras curry for us all." Abdel sat down with Nawab and his family and enjoyed an excellent meal. He found the accent of the children to be very different form their parents and he struggled to understand some of the things they said.

It reminded him of Gordon Wallace and his Scottish articulation with phrases including, *ye alreet, whey aye, howay, garn yem* and *what ye deeyin*.

Having eaten, Abdel and Nawab went to the Mosque on Smith Street. Abdel was made welcome and met many men who had moved to South Shields over the years and had raised their families in the town.

His letter from his new employers indicated that he had to be at Dunstan Staithes at 2pm on January 5th and report to the Captain of the Highlander, Mr Donald Dewar.

Nawab provided instructions on how to get to the ship via public transport and Abdel arrived at Dunstan Staithes at 1.45pm.

He met a crew member who directed him to the Captain's cabin.

He knocked on the Captain's door and a voice said, "Enter at your peril."

Abdel opened the door and said, "I am Abdel Malik Rahman Captain, the new deck hand sir."

"Oh yes, come in and sit-down son. Have you got your papers?"

"Yes Captain, here they are," and he handed them over.

The Captain scanned Abdel's documents and then said,

"Well son, you have certainly got lots of experience. However, you haven't worked on one of these tubs, have you?"

"No sir, I have not."

"I am sure you will be fine, but its dirty work lumping coal all over Gods creation. We sail on January 7th bound for London. I will now send you to see the 1st Mate, his name is Larry Henson and he will show you your bunk."

Abdel left the Captain's cabin and found the 1st Mate after asking another crew member of his whereabouts.

"Mr Larry Henson sir, pleased to meet you. I am Abdel Malik Rahman sir, the new deck hand."

"Ah, wondered when you was going to show up. You seen the skipper yet?"

"Yes sir, I have met the Captain," he replied.

"Very good, I will show you your bunk. We have a few of you fellas on board, Where you from then?" He asked.

"I was born in Afghanistan sir, but I lived in India before I went to sea. Then I lived in America for two years."

"Did you see action during the war then?"

"Yes, I did and lost many friends on the convoys."

"Yip, those bastard U Boats did for us merchant seamen."

Abdel was shown his bunk and introduced to three crew members who were relaxing in the mess.

"Alright you three lazy sod's, this is Abdul Rahman our new deck hand. Make him welcome fellas."

Larry Henson then left those gathered to get acquainted.

"My name is Abdel not Abdul. Pleased to meet you all."

All three were men of colour and the first to introduce himself was a man sitting reading the Noble Qur'an.

"Good to see you Abdel, my name is Abdul and I am from Aden."

He then introduced the other two, and pointing to a man on the top bunk opposite said, "That is Jamal, he is from Libya, say hello Jamal."

"Hello my friend welcome to the dirtiest ship on the high seas."

Abdul then said, "This sleepy lascar above me in his bunk is Majid."

Majid replied; "I am fully awake thank you and I am pleased to meet you Abdel, now we have four Muslim's on board. You are a Muslim Abdel; am I right?"

"Yes, I am and like Abu Bakr the father in law of the Prophet, I am a Sunni Muslim."

"We are all Sunni's Abdel, God be praised," said Jamal.

They talked for some time exchanging tales of their seafaring adventures for over an hour. Then the 1st Mate returned to inform them they would be leaving the staithes in an hours' time at 4pm, bound for London.

Four more seamen arrived in the mess and introduced themselves. Geordie and Stan were local men from Gateshead. Nazim was from Lebanon and a Coptic Christian and Thorsen was from Norway, all four were engine ratings.

The weather was very poor with visibility down to 100 yards as the Highlander left the Tyne and headed out into the North Sea. It was a rough sea with waves of some 10 feet crashing into the bows. It was raining heavily and as the ship sailed south east into a Head Sea, the rain turned into snow and sleet. The ship entered the relative safety of the Thames Estuary the next day at 9pm. She anchored there until the London Pilot came aboard at 7.30am and she docked at 8.15am.

Abdel formed a strong friendship with Nazim and they would often play dominoes together. Nazim was well educated having attended a private school in his home city of Bscharreh in the Qadischa Valley in the North of Lebanon. He could speak French, Hebrew, Arabic and English, which was very good. Like Abdel he enjoyed reading and had many books in his locker.

The months passed by and Abdel had managed to get himself a flat in Corstorphine Town. This is an area of South Shields that had back to back terraced flats, some of which were split into an upstairs and downstairs tenancies.

His new home was number 26 Garwood Street, an upstairs two roomed flat with an outside toilet. There was a small kitchen at the top of the rear stairs which had a sink with cold running water.

He rented the flat from a Mr Mubarak for £1 and 5 shillings per week. When not at sea, he would bathe at the Mosque in Smith Street. On October 2nd, he was on his way back to his flat when he came to the aid of a woman in H.S Edward Street, which ran adjacent to his own street. The woman had been attacked and robbed, a man had pushed her to the ground and stolen her purse. She was badly shaken and Abdel helped her into her home some

30 yards way. He sat her down and made her a cup of sweet tea for the shock.

After giving her the tea, he asked her; "Did you know this man, have you seen him before?"

Slowly sipping her tea with shaking hands, she replied; "No, I have never seen him around here, thank you Mr…"

"I am Abdel Malik Rahman and I just live round the corner."

"Thank you so much for your help Abdel, my name is Rose Thornton."

"I should telephone the police, there is a telephone near here I think," said Abdel.

"If you go to the corner shop Mrs James will ring the police, if you don't mind. My purse had all my money in it, I have nothing," she replied.

Abdel went along to the shop and the police were called. Abdel retuned to Rose's house and within five minutes a police constable arrived. Abdel let him in and the constable introduced himself as Constable John Fenwick and said, "Firstly are you injured in any way and do you need hospital treatment Rose?"

"No, I am alright just shaken," she replied.

He took down the details of the robbery along with a description of her assailant and when that was completed, he said, "Right, I have a pretty good idea who the culprit is, this is the fourth robbery in this area this week. We now him, but he is a crafty individual. But be rest assured we will apprehend him."

He took Abdel's details and left. Abdel asked Rose if she needed some cash, but she refused saying, "No, that is very kind of you. I have a sister who lives in Eldon Street, I will go along to see her. Can I ask another favour of you?"

"Yes of course what is it?"

"I still feel a little frightened, would you walk round to my sister's house with me?

"Yes, I would be glad to do this."

The walk to her sister's house only took some ten minutes and as Rose went inside Abdel said, "If there is anything I can do, please call on me, I live in Garwood Street, number 26."

"You have been very helpful Abdel, thank you."

Abdel returned home and made himself something to eat and listened to his radio before going to bed. He was awoken at 8am the next morning with a knock at his door. He quickly put some clothes on, descended the stairs and opened the door to find Rose and another woman.

"Good morning Abdel, sorry if I woke you."

"It is alright Rose"

"This is my sister Jane."

Jane moved forward and shook Abdel's hand and said, "Thank you for helping Rose yesterday, it was very good of you."

"It was nothing really," he replied.

"We would like to invite you for tea later today, as a thank you for your help."

"That is very kind, are you sure?"

"Oh yes, can you come along to my house in H.S Edward Street at 5pm; its number 16."

"I would very happy to come along, thank you Rose."

The two women said goodbye and Abdel watched them as they walked down his street and as they were rounding the corner Rose turned, smiled and waved. Abdel returned the gesture, closed his door and climbed the stairs back to his flat.

He sat and pondered the events of the last 24 hours. Rose was very attractive and perhaps he had been a little too zealous in accepting her invitation, was she married too? However, the invitation was from both of them, not just Rose. He began to doubt his decision to accept the invite.

Around mid-morning he left his flat to get some provisions from the local shop. Mrs James was full of questions about Rose and the thief, as Abdel was paying for his groceries she asked; "Well, did they get that waster that robbed that poor girl?"

"I do not know Mrs James, but she came to my flat this morning to thank me for helping her."

"Poor thing, she must have been terrified bless her. Is she a friend of yours then?"

"Well, I only met her yesterday Mrs James."

"Oh, I see, well I hope they catch the bugger and cut his hands off," she replied.

Abdel returned home to find the postman had been and two envelopes were on the floor. One from South Africa and the other from Pakistan. He read Hakim's letter first, which detailed how well his brother was doing in Durban. He had started another two business ventures a General Food Store and a Fishmongers. He hoped that Abdel would make a trip to South Africa again and he also hoped Abdel would soon take a wife and have his own children.

Abdullah was more diplomatic and gave a general synopsis of progress back at Rahman's Chandlers. The business had grown and he now had three vehicles for transporting his goods. He also said he would be soon married and hoped Abdel could come to the wedding.

Reading the letters made him reminisce about his life in Karachi and how things were changing everywhere. He went to the Mosque where he prayed and bathed, he returned home for 4pm. He changed into his two-piece suit and a clean white shirt and at 4.55pm he walked the short distance to Rose's flat.

Jane opened the door and said, "Hello Abdel, glad you came come in, Rose is inside."

He sat on an armchair in the front room and Rose came in and said, "How are you today Abdel?"

"I am very well, thank you."

"They found my purse yesterday; it was in the back lane of Eldon Street. Sadly, all the money was gone. That policeman came back and told me they hoped to get the bloke who robbed me sometime today."

"Mrs James was asking me today about it," said Abdel.

Jane said, "that woman is a real gossip, be careful what you tell her. It will be all around Corstorphine Town before you know it. When she is not fishing, she is mending her nets."

Rose laughed and said, "Jane will be going soon she has to go to work, is that right Jane?"

Jane gave Rose a quick smile and replied;

"Some of us have to go to work, I've still got ten minutes before the bus comes."

"Where do you work? asked Abdel.

"I work as a barmaid in the Stags Head on Fowler Street" she replied.

"So, Abdel, what do you do for a living," asked Rose.

"I am a Merchant Seaman and I work for the Readhead Shipping Company of Newcastle. I am a Deck Rating on the Collier the Highlander at the moment. I will be back at sea in two days' time."

"Oh, all the ladies love a sailor," quipped Jane.

"I am sure your bus is due Jane," said Rose as she stared at Jane.

Jane took the hint and as she put her coat on, she said, "Well you two have a good time, don't do anything I wouldn't do and goodbye Abdel; I hope to see you again." She smiled and left.

Rose invited Abdel into her dining room, where she had set a table for two and had provided a plethora of home cooked food. There were pasties, corned beef squares, sandwiches, scone and cakes.

As Abdel took his place at the table she said, "This is a thank you for looking after me the other day."

"This is very good of you, you did not need to do this Rose," he replied.

As they sat and ate, Abdel talked of his life and for the first time he spoke of the armed robbery in Sacramento. Rose was captivated and only spoke to clarify some aspects of his life. Rose was an attractive woman she was around 5' 4" in height with iridescent brown eyes. Her thick brown hair was bound up in a bob. She had a radiant smile that enhanced her allure. She wore a printed dress with a floral design that hung just above the knee. She was not wearing a wedding ring, but on her right wrist she had a silver bracelet.

After Abdel had given a resume of his life, Rose enlightened him on her past. She was the youngest of three children. She had an older brother Jack, who was killed in Italy and her sister Jane who was two years older. Rose was 29 years old but looked much younger. She worked in a Solicitors office as a clerical assistant in the centre of town.

She had been engaged to be married, but her would be husband abandoned her for another woman, that was three years ago. Her mother was still alive, but her father passed away a year ago. She was born in Stocksfield in Northumberland. The family moved to South Shields when she was four years old, so that her father could get work in the shipyard.

Having consumed copious amounts of food and drank what seemed a great amount of tea, they retired to the front room. They continued their confabulation for another couple of hours, along with more cups of tea.

Finally, Abdel said, "This has been very good of you to invite me into your home and I have enjoyed this very much."

"As I said, this a thank you for helping me. Folks in this town remember when people who do good deeds Abdel," she replied.

The feelings that they harboured were mutual and Abdel said, "Would you like to go to the cinema tomorrow Rose?"

"That would be nice, do you know what is showing?"

"I do not, I don't even know where the cinema is."

"Ah well, you better leave it with me then. I will drop a note in to your flat with the place and time before I go to work, is that ok?"

"That is very good, thank you Rose"

"No thank you, I have had a great time here today."

It was now 10pm and Abdel said he would go home. As he opened the front door he turned and said goodnight. Rose kissed him on the cheek and said, "Thank you again, see you tomorrow."

Abdel returned home and that feeling he had for Maheera and Gretchen surfaced again and he wondered if this could be the woman that he will share the rest of his life with.

He put his radio on and listened to some late-night jazz from Bix Beiderbecke. All the food he had eaten left him with indigestion and he did not fall asleep until well after midnight.

The next day Rose pushed a note through Abdel's letterbox it read;

> *"Abdel, the Savoy on Ocean Road is showing The Glenn Miller Story at 7pm. Can you pick me up at 6.15pm please? Rose."*

This would allow Abdel to have time go to the Mosque to pray and bathe. He knocked on Rose's door promptly at 6.15pm.

"Come in and grab a seat while I just put some make up on," she said.

Abdel was filled with adoration when he saw her and said, "You look beautiful tonight Rose."

She blushed and said, "Thank you, I can't remember the last time anyone said that to me, just give me a minute."

They got the bus from Eldon Street to the Market Square and had a leisurely walk down King Street to Ocean Road. It was a Friday night and the town was busy with people going in and out of pubs. As they passed the Golden Lion, a couple came out and the women instantly recognised Rose and said, "Rose Thornton, well I never, how are you?"

"I am fine Karen, how are you?"

"Great thanks, this is Bob my husband."

"This is Abdel, we are on our first date," said Rose.

The two men shook hands and exchanged pleasantries.

"You still at that solicitors then?" asked Karen?

"Yes, I am, been there two years now."

The banter continued until Bob said, "Come on love, we are meeting John and Denise in the Vaults in ten minutes."

They said their goodbyes and Abdel and Rose continued down King Street.

Rose said, "so, is this a proper date then Abdel?"

"Yes, I believe it is Rose," he replied.

They enjoyed the film, Abdel especially delighted in the music. He bought ice creams at the interval and when the film was over, they had a bag of chips from the Red Hut Fish & Chip Shop. Abdel took Rose home and they kissed at her front door. This was something Rose insisted upon, to limit the gossip from the curtain twitcher's in the street.

Abdel went home with a spring in his step and he felt he was in a good place right now. But it was back to sea tomorrow and he would not be back for another three weeks. He reported back at the Highlander the next day and was told that it would be four weeks before they docked back in Newcastle. They had cargo for Rotterdam, Zeebrugge and Cork before a return trip from London to Newcastle.

It was October 6th 1954 and four weeks seemed a long way off for Abdel. He used some of his time to send a letter to Rose, in the hope that she would not get to disheartened by his absence. Thankfully he had his books and radio to keep him occupied, along with regular games of dominoes with Nazim.

On his return to South Shields on November 7th, he dropped his kitbag off at home and went round to see Rose, it was 8.30pm.

He knocked on the door, but no answer. He knocked again, no answer. He turned to go back home then he saw her coming down the street with a big smile on her face. As she got closer, she ran and jumped into his arms and said,

"Sorry, I have been to see my mother she has not been well. It's great that you home again"

Then she gave him a long passionate kiss and they went inside. Once inside Abdel said, "I hope your Mother gets well soon Rose."

"Mmm well, she is not at all well Abdel, it looks like she has cancer in her bowel. She goes into hospital on Monday."

"I am sorry for this Rose; can I help in any way?"

"You're so kind Abdel but no, it's alright. She will be in the best place at hospital. By the way they caught that man who stole my purse. They locked him up, but he had to pay me and three other women damages for what he did," she added.

They chatted and Rose made a chicken supper for them. They arranged another night at the cinema to see *Shane*. In addition, they would go for long walks around the town and beyond, their treks included Westoe, Cleadon Hills, Whitburn, Simonside and Boldon. Their courtship was sustained despite Abdel's trips away to sea. They had not made love prior to Abdel returning to the Highlander on November 14th. That would change on his shore leave on December 20th.

He got back home around 9pm that night and went to Rose's house after a brief stop at his place. A long kiss when they met led to the inevitable and they made love for the first time. A truly lustful happening for both of them and for the first time Abdel stayed the night.

Tragedy struck on December 23rd when Rose's mother succumbed to her illness in hospital, she was 69. Due to the Christmas holiday she could not be buried until January 3rd. Abdel had to report back to his ship on January 2nd, therefore he could not be with Rose to support her, on that sad day.

Back on the Highlander, Abdel began 1955 with a sense of discontentment, his lengthy absence away from Rose was having a negative influence on him and he was seriously thinking about leaving the Merchant

Navy. But what would he do? He confided in his shipmate Nazim and he suggested work on the River Tyne. They discussed this prospect one morning as they sat in their bunks and Nazim said, "There are many jobs on the river Abdel, there are the ferries, pilot boats, tugs, fishing boats and shipyards. They will all give you more time at home my friend."

The idea activated a desire to investigate the possibilities and he replied; "Would you help with this Nazim?"

"If I can, but how Abdel?"

"You could come back to South Shields with me when we get our next leave. You can stay at my house and we can both go and find work on the river."

Nazim was a little hesitant and said, "I am not sure Abdel; the wages may not be as good."

"Yes, I know but if you do not want to accept the work you can always go back to the ship Nazim. But it will help me to have a friend with me to guide me," he replied.

"Yes, I will do this Abdel; you are a good friend. With Gods guidance, we shall prevail."

Abdel wrote a letter to Rose informing her of his plans and that he would be back in South Shields on February 12th. The two shipmates wrote down what they planned and sought advice from any crew members that may have contacts on the river. The crew were not forthcoming with a great deal of relevant information and Abdel was reluctant to let the Purser know of his intentions. They would have to do their own exploration of future employment prospects, when they got back to South Shields. As planned, they arrived back in South Shields on February 12th and Abdel managed to accommodate Nazim's sleeping arrangements with a folding bed supplied by his landlord Mr Mubarak.

CHAPTER TWENTY-TWO

Abdel took Nazim to meet Rose and he informed Rose of his intentions regarding future job prospects. In his absence she had done a little research of her own and Jane her sister gave her the name of a man who was a 1st Mate on a Tug Boat and she said to Abdel;

"I have a name for you that Jane gave me. It's a man who works on a Tug on the river. He often goes into the Stag's Head for a drink and Jane asked him about any positions."

She handed Abdel the note with the man's name on it.

"That is very kind of your sister, you must thank her for me Rose," he replied.

The name on the note was, Mr Fred G. Younger with a telephone number.

Abdel and Nazim stayed at Rose's for lunch and then made their way to the Mill Dam where most of the Tugs were moored. They spoke to a number of men who all said that they worked for Lawson-Batey Tugs, but didn't know who to contact. They found a telephone box on Commercial Road and rang Mr Younger. He said that they would need to complete an application form, which was available from the office on the Mill Dam. They returned to the Mill Dam and found the office. They were given application forms by a woman in the office and asked to return them with all their merchant navy paperwork.

While in the area, they enquired at the shipyards of John Readhead and Hepple & Co Ltd. and were told to complete more application forms. They then decided to return to Abdel's house and complete their respective application forms before venturing further in their quest for work. They spent every day looking for work, they travelled to Sunderland and enquired about work at Austin & Pickersgill on the Wear, the Naval Yard at Wallsend, R.B. Harrisons at Bill Quay and Hawthorn Leslie's of Hebburn. The Tyne Pilots were also contacted.

On February 17th a letter arrived at Abdel's address inviting both him and Nazim for an interview at the Mill Dam offices of Lawson-Batey Tugs the following day at 3pm. Nazim did not have a suit to wear but he was able to borrow a black suit from a Mr Alli Khan at the Mosque. They arrived at the Companies Mill Dam office at 2.45pm and Abdel was interviewed first by Mr D.W. Purvis. He enquired about his previous jobs and experience and checked his paperwork. The interview lasted for some fifteen minutes, then Nazim underwent his interview. After another fifteen minutes Mr Purvis invited them both back into his office and offered them jobs as Deck Hands on the Tug *Homer*. They would start on March 8th 1955. Their wage would be £7. 10 shillings per week.

They both thanked Mr Purvis and left the Mill Dam in a jubilant mood. They had now had to break the news to Readhead & Co Ltd of their change of employment.

Abdel had the telephone number and they used a public telephone on South Eldon Street to ring the company. The woman who answered the call said, she would take the details and pass them onto the accounts department and she would contact the Captain of the Highlander. She checked the schedule for the ship and told Abdel that the next voyage would commence on February 27th bound for London. However, both he and Nazim would have their contract terminated in a weeks' time on February 25th. She informed them that all monies due to Abdel would be posted to his home address and that Nazim would have to attend the office in Newcastle to receive his final pay.

After the phone call Abdel and Nazim called on Rose and gave her the news. She had hoped that Abdel could find work that would enable them to see more of each other and on hearing the good news she said, "This is great news Abdel; I am so pleased."

"Yes, I am very happy now. I feel that I have found a home here in South Shields."

Nazim brought up the issue of somewhere to live and said,

"I will need to find a place to live Abdel, I can't stay at your house."

"I will see Mr Mubarak, he might have somewhere for you Nazim," he replied.

Rose added; "If not, there are private estate agents like Moody's. They have houses and flats to rent."

Abdel's life was taking another direction, one that he had envisaged. A life that gives him some control of his future, he felt empowered. He had that same feeling when he was in Sacramento, but circumstances dictated otherwise. His feelings for Rose were unequivocal, they had been courting for six months now and he could see himself spending the rest of his life with her.

That night Rose cooked a celebration meal of Mince and Dumplings, served with vegetables. She invited her sister Jane round to join in the celebrations. They put the radio on and listened to music by Fats Waller, Nat King Cole and Bing Crosby. Jane dropped a few hints on the future of Abdel and Rose, that were greeted with disdain from Rose, who was quick to change the subject. For the first time Abdel had brought his camera and he took photographs as the night wore on. He also ensured that Nazim took a photo of both him and Rose.

The next evening Abdel and Rose went for a walk-in town and he took her to the Golden Lion in King Street for a drink. As always in these situations Abdel had a soft drink of lime and lemon. In a quiet corner they sat and talked of their future and she said, "Abdel, it is time for me to tell you how I feel about you."

He was in a state of trepidation and his stomach was churning up inside hoping that this was not "*I like you but ...*"

Abdel Malik Rahman, I have never met a man with so much honesty and love. I yearn for the day we can be together; I love you so much."

A tear slowly descended down her cheek as she gently squeezed his hand.

Abdel felt his heart was going to burst and at first, he struggled to speak, eventually he said, "Rose, I am so very happy and I love you very much. I am glad you feel the same and I want to protect and care for you for the rest of my days, God willing."

She leaned across the table and kissed him gently on the cheek. The moment was one of consummate unconditional desire and their own "coup *de foudre.*"

They had another drink, Rose had a second glass of white wine and said, "After my failed engagement, I assumed love was just like spit in the rain. Something that is so easily washed away. I thought I would never meet someone like you Abdel. That day I was robbed was a turning point in my life, you were there."

"God has not forsaken me Rose, he has been my guardian in so many difficult times and I want to be part of your life and you part of mine."

They finished their drinks and strolled on down to the coast and walked along the sea front. The weather was quite warm for March, with a slight breeze blowing of the North Sea. They got back to Rose's place and for the first time he spent the night. After they made love Rose said, "Well, this will give the neighbours something to talk about. They will be thinking we are "*living over the brush"* Abdel."

Abdel had not heard this idiom before and replied; *"Over the brush"* what does this mean Rose?"

With a smile on her face she said,

"It's nothing to worry about, you will find out in time no doubt."

"I have one thing to ask you Rose."

"Oh, that sounds worrying" she joked.

"Have you ever thought about the colour of my skin and what that means?"

"Abdel, I am surprised you even mentioned it. The colour of a man's skin does not tell me about who that man is. We live in a world of many millions of people, if we can't treat each other the same; there is no hope for mankind."

"I never doubted you at all, I am sorry. It's just that I have been called many things over the years and it upsets me that some people have no respect for someone who is different in colour to them."

"Those people are no great loss to humanity Abdel."

The following week was centred on sorting out Nazim's accommodation, gathering all the paperwork for their new employers and meeting their new shipmates. In addition, both Nazim and Abdel required further training relating to the safe working practices while on board the Tug. All this was achieved and on March 8th they arrived at the dock where the Homer was berthed. The weather was particularly bad with winds touching 50 mph and persistent rain.

The Master Mr Rueben Morgan had been informed that no vessels were in need of a tow into or out of the river. Abdel and Nazim had the opportunity to meet the rest of the crew and spend some time getting to know them. The 1st Mate and Chief Engineer was Harry Finlayson, the other two Deck Hands were Sam Lowery and Ronnie Nesbitt. They all sat in the dock cabin and exchanged banter.

The 1st Mate Harry enquired about Abdel's previous merchant navy experience and said, "Abdel you have 20 years' service, that right son?"

"Yes, that is true Harry; I have worked on ships before and during the war. I was in the Atlantic and survived a U Boat attack and again in the Mediterranean," he said.

"Christ that must have been scary," added Sam.

"I was very scared, but you just have to pray that God is with you and you do your best to stay alive," replied Abdel.

As the banter continued, it was somewhat difficult for Abdel and Nazim to understand some of the conversation due to the dialect. And although Abdel was learning to adapt, some of the colloquial verbalisation left him and Nazim bewildered.

An example of this was when Ronnie said, *"Ah daynt nar how yee lived through arl that, I woulda shit me sell."*

Nazim just looked at Abdel, hoping for a translation; that was not forthcoming. Harry noticed the confusion from the two new crew members and said,

"Our new shipmates will have to learn how to '*tark like Sandancers,"* Ronnie.

"Ya not rang there Harry," he replied.

"You must be used to the Geordie lingo now boys, you have worked on a Collier on the Tyne, that right?" added Sam.

"Yes, we have, but we still find it hard to understand sometimes," said Nazim.

"Well, we will *ave te larn ya then*," said Ronnie.

"Here we go then," said Sam

"When you go somewhere, *you say I am garn.*"

"If you are going home, you say *I am garn yem.*"

"Now say I am *garn yem.*"

Abdel grinned and said it first, much laughter ensued. It created a bigger sense of hilarity when Nazim tried to emulate the phrase.

He ended up saying "*Um I goon yum.*"

After the laughter had subsided Harry addressed Sam and Ronnie and said, "Well shipmates, we are gonna have some laughs with these two fellas."

The conversation went onto talk of where everyone lived, their families, girlfriends, previous jobs and entertainment. At 12.30pm Harry, Sam and Ronnie got their lunch out along with their flasks of hot tea. Harry quickly realised that neither Abdel or Nazim had any lunch with them and said, "It looks like our new shipmates have no food fellas."

"We never thought about it Harry," replied Abdel.

"Never mind, come on fellas. Give them a sarnie each."

"No, it is very kind of you, we will find somewhere to eat thank you," said Nazim.

"Not round here you won't so dig in, and you will both need to buy a flask and a sandwich box. You have to eat boys," said Harry.

"We carl them Bait Boxes rooned here" joked Ronnie.

Their first day at work was a bit of an anti-climax, but it enabled them to familiarise themselves with the rest of the crew and the weather was due to improve overnight. This would then entail some movement on the river.

Before heading back to Garwood Street, Abdel and Nazim went to Woolworths in King Street and bought their flasks and sandwich boxes. When they got home an envelope was on the floor behind the front door. It was from Mr Mubarak, inside was a key. The note read;

> *"Abdel, I have a place for your friend. It is number 28 South Eldon Street. The key will get you in the front door. It is a 2 roomed downstairs flat. Toilet is outside in the yard. Rent is £1. 15 shillings a week. Can you please fill in the rental form, it is on the bench in the kitchen?*
> *Mr Mubarak."*

"Now you have your own home Nazim," said Abdel.

"Let's go and see it now Abdel," he replied.
"Yes, but I want to call on Rose and give her the news of our first day."
"This is good, I am so happy not to be a burden on you anymore."
"You have never been a burden on me, you would do the same for me."
"Yes, I would do this for you."

They called to see Rose and she was pleased to hear that Nazim had his own place. From there they went to Nazim's flat. It required a good clean and the furniture amounted to a single bed, an electric cooker, a sink, a kitchen table, kitchen benches, a wardrobe in the bedroom and a tin bath.

"It is much like your flat Abdel," said Nazim.

"It is, your kitchen is bigger than mine and you have a tin bath. You will need to buy some things Nazim, but you could be settled in by the weekend."

Rose had told them to go back to her house for some food when they had looked at Nazim's flat. She had been baking and they enjoyed some home-made bread, broth and suet dumplings.

When Abdel and Nazim returned to Garwood Street, Abdel told Nazim of his intentions to marry Rose and he planned to buy a ring and propose to her. He will go to Turnbull's in Laygate Lane and select a ring. Nazim was delighted for his friend and said,

"This is wonderful Abdel; I am so happy for you and Rose is a very nice lady. Do you know what size she is?"

Abdel was confused and replied; "Size, what do you mean Nazim?"

"Abdel not all woman's fingers are the same size."

"Oh yes, that is correct. But how will I find this information?"

"If you do not want Rose to find out and you want to keep the proposal a surprise, then someone will have to find out for you."

"Jane, she could do this. I will ask her Nazim."

"Will she be able to keep a secret Abdel?"

"Yes, I am sure she will."

Within a week, Abdel had manged to see Jane for a brief moment when she was at Rose's house. She was very excited and said she would somehow think of a plan to get a size for an engagement ring. It took another week for Jane to get the required size and she dropped a note through Abdel's letterbox which read;

"This was hard work, but I got her size after she tried my dress ring on. The size that Rose needs is the letter K. Do not spend a fortune on this ring Abdel, it's just an engagement ring. Jane."

Abdel went to Turnbull's on a Saturday, April 2nd after he had been to the Mosque. He got to the counter and Mr Turnbull said, "How can I help sir?"

"I would like to buy an engagement ring please."

"Yes well, we have a tray of rings you might want to look at sir, how much do you want to spend?"

"I don't know yet, but her size is K," replied Abdel.

"Ah, a man who has done his research, a wise policy sir. Let me select a number of rings that you may like. They are not all size K, but we can alter any ring very easily."

Abdel scanned the velvet tray of rings and chose two, they were simple bands with a simple engraving on each.

"Good choice sir, they are both American Gold and both rings are sized K."

Abdel looked at him, smiled and said, "I lived in America for two years."

"Is that so, well sir what a fitting tribute for your bride to be."

Abdel settled on one and asked the price.

"For this ring the cash price is £12 sir, however we can take an initial payment of £6 and then you can pay the balance within 14 days. If your fiancé does not like the ring for any reason, then we will exchange it for another at the same price. If for some reason the ring does not fit her finger to her liking, then we will alter the sizing for a small fee."

Abdel considered the arrangement and said, "I am happy with this arrangement sir, and I would like to pay the £6 today please."

"That is excellent Mr…"

"Rahman, Abdel Malik," he replied.

"Splendid Mr Rahman sir, let me box this up for you and get you your receipt."

Abdel paid his £6 and carefully placed the small box in his pocket along with receipt and said, "Thank you sir."

"Your welcome Mr Rahman and all the very best to you sir."

Abdel felt this was a huge turning point in his life and only hoped Rose would except his proposal of marriage. He now had to decide where and when to do it. Three days later they had arranged to go for a walk along the Leas, this was a long stretch of clifftop expanse that ran from the Marsden Grotto to the New Crown Hotel. It was a Wednesday and Abdel had the day off, having completed two long 14 hour shifts that week. He called upon Rose at 5pm and the weather was warm for April with a slight breeze.

When he arrived, Jane was sitting in the front room and with Rose in the kitchen she said quietly; "Have you got the ring, is it tonight?"

Abdel just smiled and nodded, then Rose appeared and said, "Anyone for a cup of tea?"

"No thanks Rose, I am off to meet a few friends in the Eldon Arms," said

Jane.

"What, the Eldon Arms at 5 o'clock in the afternoon," replied Rose.

"Well, the bar is not open. We are meeting to organise a trip to the races."

Rose gave her a quizzical look and said, "Didn't know you were keen on the races Jane."

"It's a day out, something different I suppose," she replied.

As she said goodbye Jane glanced at Abdel, winked and said, "You two have a nice night."

"She is a funny one my sister, I never know what she is thinking half the time," quipped Rose.

They sat and chatted drinking their tea and Abdel said, "So, are we having a nice walk along the Leas tonight then Rose?"

"To be honest Abdel, I am a little tired tonight" she replied.

Abdel was in a predicament; does he push it any further or does he accept he will have to organise another opportunity. He responded by saying, "Oh, I was looking forward to a nice walk to take in the sea air."

"Well, I suppose it will do me good to get out and get some fresh air," she replied.

"Thank God," Abdel said to himself as Rose went to get changed.

He checked that the little box and ring were safely located in his inside pocket of his jacket. They left her house at 5.20pm and headed for the sea front. They walked along Eldon Street to Laygate, past the Town Hall, along Beach Road, Bents Park Road and finally the Leas. He was conscious of selecting the right time as they strolled along the cliff path.

He changed his mind on four occasions until finally he chose a quiet spot overlooking the sea. He took the box from his inside pocket and as she gazed at the view out to sea he said, "Rose, I want to ask you something."

She turned and said, "Yes, what is it?"

Then he presented the box to her and said,

"Rose, will you marry me and spend the rest of your life with me."

She threw herself at him and with tears in her eyes replied; "Yes, oh yes Abdel; I was afraid you were never going to ask me. This has made me so very happy."

He gave her the box, she opened it and the emotion was too much for her and she just sobbed in his arms.

"You should be happy and not crying Rose," he said.

"I am so happy Abdel and to think I didn't want to go for a walk," she joked.

She composed herself and looked at the ring and put it straight on saying, "This is beautiful Abdel; a piece of string would have done," and she gave him a long kiss.

"I could get it changed if you like, what colour string would you like?" he joked.

She laughed and replied; "Not on your life, you have got me now."

They stood holding each other gazing out to sea and she said, "Abdel, we must take care of each other, love each other and remember this day. We will have days when things get us down, but together we must cherish what we have."

"I promise to do all I can to make you happy Rose. I have found someone who loves me for who I am."

"Right then, when do we get married?" she asked;

"Remember, I have been engaged before Abdel," she added;

"This I understand Rose, we must sit down and look at what is best for both of us," he replied.

Over the next few weeks, they discussed where and when they should be married. Abdel was happy to married in a Registry Office. Rose would also be happy to have a marriage ceremony in the Mosque as well as the Registry Office. They agreed to do both and chose Saturday, August 20th for both ceremonies. They went back to Turnbull's and chose the wedding ring, which cost £20. They booked a room in Golden Lion in King Street for a wedding reception.

Abdel rang both Hakim and Abdullah and gave them the good news and they both said they would attend. Rose would invite some of her family including two Uncles and three cousins, along with wives or girlfriends. In addition, she would have two guests from work and Jane would be her bridesmaid.

Nazim would be Abdel's best man and other guests would include Hakim, Abdullah and their wives and Mr & Mrs Hussain. Abdel also invited Harry, Sam and Ronnie and their wives or girlfriends. In total there would be 25 guests at the wedding.

Abdel rang Brody in Sacramento and told him the good news, but sadly he could not attend as he had already planned a holiday with Martha in Florida on August 15th. He sent his best wishes and he would let everyone know back in Sacramento.

The marriage at the Registry Office would be at 10am, followed by the Nikah in the Mosque at 11am. Hakim had agreed to do a reading from the Qur'an like his brother did for him in South Africa.

It was a bright, sunny and very warm day on August 20th and both ceremonies were performed without any hitches. Brody sent a telegram congratulating them on their happy day. The reception included the cutting of a wedding cake that Jane had organised. In addition, an impromptu musical interlude was performed by Sam on his Larry Adler Harmonica, who played a selection of favourites. Nazim was charged with taking photographs with Abdel's camera and a small finger buffet was provided by the manager of Golden Lion.

At 4pm the reception was over and family members were invited back to H.S Edward Street, now the home of both Abdel and Rose Rahman. Life from then on was an odyssey of self-recognition and a sharing of achievable goals. Abdel had established himself as a reliable and component Deck Hand on the Homer. Rose was a trusted and skilled administrator in her position as a legal secretary for her employers. They came to the decision that the downstairs flat in H.S. Edward Street was not big enough to raise a family and they sought a bigger house to rent. Council housing was now well established in South Shields with estates in Simonside, Laygate, Whiteleas, Biddick Hall, Marsden and Cleadon. They put their names on the council list for a three bedroomed semi-detached house. They also left details of their requirements with local estate agents for any rental properties that become available.

"In April 1956, they were given a three bedroomed semi- detached house in Simonside. The timing could not have been better, Rose was three months pregnant.

They went to view the house and on arriving, they felt that they had achieved a huge landmark in their search for a secure and happy future together. As they gazed out onto the garden at the rear of the house in Airey Avenue, Abdel said, "Rose this is what we have been looking for, it is a home for a family."

"Yes, it is, and it's ours Abdel."

They moved into their new home on May 3rd, Nazim and Jane helped them move on the day. Nazim had helped Abdel to decorate the rooms, in the two weeks leading up to the move. The house had coal fires in both the front and rear downstairs living rooms. The kitchen had a coal burning Rayburn Stove which heated the water.

Rose's pregnancy was generally without incident, other than Abdel's insistence that she rests at every opportunity. She worked as long as she could, her final day at work being on June 27th 1956. Jane made herself available when Abdel was on a long shift through the night. On September 12th Rose's waters broke, Abdel was on the Homer nearing the mouth of the Tyne. It was 2am in the morning and Jane raced to a nearby telephone box and rang for an ambulance. It arrived after some twenty minutes with Rose's contractions becoming more and more frequent. While in the ambulance

Jane said, "Just hang on Rose, it won't be long now."

"Just hang on, bloody hell Jane; no one can prepare you for this. I wish my mother was here."

At 3.37am Rose gave birth to a baby girl weighing 6lb 7oz. Jane immediately rang the dock office of Lawson – Batey, luckily Bob the night watchman picked up the phone and took the message. At 4.45am the Homer docked and Abdel and his shipmates got to the dock cabin just as the heavens opened and the rain came tumbling down. Bob gave Abdel a note and it read;

"Abdel you are a father, you have a daughter, born at 3.37am weighing 6lb 7oz."

Abdel stood and for a moment, he could not comprehend what he was reading and then the penny dropped and he exploded into a joyful rapture saying, "Friends I have a child, a daughter. God has smiled upon my wife and I."

Nazim was delighted and began dancing around with his hands in the air before grabbing Abdel and the pair of them continued this madcap dance around the cabin.

The tears began to well in his eyes as Sam shook his hand, laughed and said, "You will be looking for permanent nightshift now shipmate."

Ronnie embraced him and in his own inimitable way added; *"Whey I man, you can forget sleep noo bonny lad."*

Harry was much more pragmatic and said, "Well, Abdel Malik Rahman, you are now a father and your responsibilities have just increased dramatically, but congratulations son," and he too shook Abdel's hand.

"Well, I suppose you want to go and see your wife and your daughter now, so off you go Abdel. I will clear it with the Master Rueben. Bob take my car and get him to hospital; I am not sure they will let you see them yet. You might have to wait a few hours for that, but get yourself away son."

Bob drove Abdel to Harton Hospital and when he got to the ward Jane was there. They embraced each other and Jane said, "Congratulations Abdel, you're a daddy now. It was a close shave; I thought the ambulance was never going to turn up. They are both sleeping so we will have to wait to see them."

It was not until 6am that Abdel got to see his wife and baby. Rose was sitting up breast feeding their daughter, when Abdel walked into the ward. A nurse pulled the curtain round as Abdel sat next to Rose's bed. He leaned over to kiss Rose, then he kissed his daughter and said, "My life will never know a more precious moment as this Rose."

He sat and gazed at this tiny person in his wife's arms and Rose said, "Sorry I could not hold on Abdel until you got home."

"You must not be sorry Rose; we have a beautiful daughter. There are three of us now and we have not talked about a name for her yet," he replied.

"I will be in hospital for another three days at least, so we have plenty of time to come up with a name" she added.

Abdel spent an hour with his wife and daughter and then he was politely informed that he would have to leave. He could return at 2pm with one other visitor.

He then asked the nurse if Rose's sister could just see the baby for a few minutes.

The nurse was reluctant to allow this but said, "Alright, sister is not on the ward, so five minutes only please."

Abdel kissed his wife and daughter, left the ward and told Jane she had five minutes to see them. In the end Jane was there ten minutes before the nurse had to insist, she left. When she returned to Abdel in the waiting room, she said, "Abdel she is beautiful; she has your eyes and lots of dark hair. Have you got a name for her yet?"

"No, not yet Jane," he replied.

As they walked back home Jane bombarded Abdel with names for his daughter.

"I like Emma, Helen, Nancy, Greta, Karen and Rose of course, I also like Samantha, Elizabeth, Annabel and...."

Abdel interceded and said, "Jane, they are all very nice names but we haven't thought about it yet. We will decide in the next few days."

"Sorry, yes, it's just that I am so excited for you both. I am going to celebrate tonight with a few friends. I am an Aunty now and I will spoil that child rotten, I promise you that."

Abdel returned to the hospital at 2pm and carrying a bunch of flowers he arrived to find his daughter in a crib next to Rose's bed. Abdel kissed his wife and handed her the flowers and said, "For you Rose, but they are not Roses I am afraid."

"Thank you, Abdel, I will get the nurse to put them in a vase for me. She has been very good; she is always ready to help me in any way. Her parents are from Italy and her name is Ariana, she was born here. Her parents are from Sorrento and they came to England before the war in 1935 and she was born a year later. I really like her name Abdel; do you think we could call our daughter Ariana Rose Rahman? Ariana means very holy in Italian and her birth flower is the Aster."

"How do you know these things Rose?"

"Ariana told me Abdel; hear she comes."

"How are we feeling Rose, can I get you anything?" asked Ariana.

"No, I am fine thanks. I was telling my husband about your name."
"Oh yes, how are you Mr Rahman? You have a beautiful daughter."
"Thank you for all you have done," he replied.
Ariana went to attend another patient on the ward and Rose said,
"Well, do you like the name Abdel?"
"Yes, it is a very good name Rose and we shall name her Ariana Rose Rahman."
"Abdel, you are very quick to agree with most things we talk about: are you sure?
"Yes Rose, I am very happy with that name, if I was not, I would say so."
"Have you got some time off from work Abdel?"
"I am back at work tonight at 7pm and it could be a 12-hour shift Rose. When will they let you come home?" he asked.
"I think it may be tomorrow, but probably Friday. You must have had very little sleep Abdel; you must get some sleep before you go back tonight."
"Yes, I will get some sleep when I get home today."
"That will only be four hours sleep Abdel, that's not enough."
"I will be fine Rose; we might get some time on the Homer where I can get a short nap," he replied.
"You might be able to get the birth certificate tomorrow afternoon Abdel."
"Oh yes, I need to go to the Registry Office is that right?"
"I will write down the details for you; the time, date, place and full name and you might get there tomorrow. If not, it doesn't matter, we have plenty of time to register her birth."
"The baby stirred in her crib and Rose said, "Now is your chance to hold your daughter for the first time Abdel," and she asked Ariana who was approaching; "Could you please lift her up for me and let her Father hold his daughter,"
"Yes of course" and she carefully picked the baby up and handed her to Abdel and said, "There you go Daddy."
Abdel cradled her in his arms and she immediately began to cry and he said,
"Oh, what have I done?"
"You will get a lot more of that Daddy, she is probably hungry quipped Ariana."
The baby settled and Abdel felt so proud and said, "We have got a name for her."
"Great what are you going to call her?" asked Ariana.
Abdel looked at Rose, smiled and said, "You can tell her Rose."

"We have decided to name her after you, Ariana Rose Rahman."

"Oh my, this is a surprise and I am very honoured that you have you done this, thank you."

"You are welcome," added Abdel.

Rose and the baby were allowed to go home on Friday; Abdel had registered the birth, bought a cot for Ariana and arranged for Jane to stay for a few days. Abdel managed to facilitate some hours with Rose during the day, having agreed some flexible hours with the company. After three weeks Rose had to revert to bottle feeding, in order to keep Ariana sustained with milk.

As time passed, Ariana settled into a steady sleep pattern and with Jane's help they got into a routine. Abdel made full use of his camera and took many photographs. When Ariana was six months old, she was baptised at Trinity Church on Sunday March 25th, 1957 with Abdel's full support. He would not instil his religious beliefs on his child and he was very happy for her to be baptised as a Christian in the Church of England. Nazim and Nawab Hussain were her Godfathers, with Jane and Rose's friend Jenny Snell as Godmothers.

Life continued with Abdel working on the Homer and Rose a devoted mother. Abdel took a keen interest in gardening and planted a good crop of vegetables to sustain the family. On occasion Rose and Abdel would go to the cinema and Jane would babysit for them. Money was a little tight with Rose not working, but they made the best of it. When Ariana was two years old Rose managed to get some part time work at the Solicitors, again Jane would look after Ariana.

Jane was in a relationship with a local policeman Stan Martin from Bill Quay. They were married in 1960 and a year later Jane gave birth to a baby boy and they named him David Jack Martin. Nazim had also found romance and he too was married in the same year to a girl from Whiteleas called Hazel Davidson. She was a Civil Servant based at Longbenton and a keen artist. In 1961 Ariana began her education at Garnett Infants School in Bainbridge Avenue, Simonside.

Along with his love of gardening and music, Abdel liked to gamble on horse racing and on Saturday's he liked a flutter. Rose conceded to this diversion as long as it was within their financial remit. The problem was that Abdel was a sore loser and when his bet did not produce the correct result, he would drift into a morose demeanour.

Rose would always drag him out of it by saying something that would engage his interest. She had a knack of hitting the right note in her appreciation of her husband's feelings. In April 1962, Rose learnt she was pregnant again and gave Abdel the news as he returned from work. His reaction was one of great excitement and he said, "This is wonderful news Rose; a brother or sister for Ariana, I am so happy."

Rose was somewhat unsure what his response was going to be, but fell into his arms and replied; "I am so glad Abdel; I didn't know if you would be pleased or not."

"Of course, I am Rose; we will manage and we have the spare bedroom remember."

Rose laughed and added; "It's more than just the spare bedroom Abdel, we are not a wealthy couple; We will have to tighten our belts a little, where money is concerned."

"Yes, this is so, but we will be alright I am sure; with Gods help and guidance."

Abdel informed Hakim, Abdullah and Brody by telephone of the good news and soon set about decorating the spare bedroom ready for the new arrival. They had thought about getting a television for some time and Rose said, "We might not be able to get a television now Abdel, with a baby now on the way. We can't afford to splash out £70." "Well, Nazim has a television, he is renting it from Radio Rentals, I think. I will ask him how much this will cost when I see him tomorrow" he replied.

The outcome led to Abdel renting a television from Radio Rentals for 5 shillings per week. They spent the first week watching the TV at every opportunity. Ariana was particularly fascinated and her favourites were, Andy Pandy, Animal Magic and Popeye. The expense incurred by the TV didn't create any financial burden as Rose was very adept at ensuring the bills were paid and money was carefully designated for food and household items on a weekly basis.

Ariana would often sit and talk with her father and ask many things about his life. Abdel would only talk of things that he deemed important and concentrated upon his childhood in Azaw, his family and the people he regarded as good people. He would tell her stories about his trek to Karachi and meeting the *Kuchi*, his fishing trips with Osman and his adventures as a seaman.

CHAPTER TWENTY-THREE

On November 28th, 1962 Rose gave birth to a son weighing 7lbs 4oz. The birth was particularly difficult and at one stage the Midwifery Team were contemplating a Caesarean Section. Eighteen hours after being admitted to the maternity ward the baby was delivered, Rose did need a blood transfusion.

Rose was given a side room in which to recover and it was another 24 hours before Abdel could see her and on seeing Abdel she said, "Abdel I thought I was going to die; we will not be having any more children; do you understand?"

"Yes Rose, and kissed his wife."

"Now go and see your son, I need more sleep."

Abdel left his wife and sought out his son, who was being fed with bottled milk by a nurse and as he appeared, she said, "Ah, the father, perfect timing" and she handed Abdel his son.

Abdel cradled his son and gently gave him the milk from the small feeding bottle.

"Have you got a name for him yet?" asked the nurse.

"Not yet nurse," he replied.

"Well he gave his mother some grief today, I will tell you."

"Yes, how is Rose? She looks very unwell."

"She will need rest; she has lost a lot of blood and she is completely exhausted" she said.

Rose spent a week in hospital with her baby and on the day, she was allowed to go, Abdel arranged a taxi to take them all home where Ariana was waiting to see her brother for the first time. On the drive to Simonside, Abdel talked of a name for their son and said, "I would like our son"s middle name to be Syed, are you happy with this name Rose?"

"Yes Abdel, I know how much Syed meant to you. I would like our son's first name to be Jacob."

"I knew a great man called Jacob Levi; it would be a noble thing to give our son this fine name," he replied.

The Rahman family thrived and both children flourished. Rose returned to her position at the Solicitors when both children were at school. Abdel continued as a deck hand on the Homer, but by 1970 he was finding the work a little demanding and he actively sought another job. In September of that year Abdel received the tragic news that his brother Hakim had died after a stroke.

Abdel wanted to attend his brother's funeral, but it was not financially feasible and as a mark of respect for his brother; he organised a service in the Mosque. On November 3rd Abdel suffered a heart attack as he walked from the Lawson - Batey dock at South Shields. He had noticed that he was getting pains in his chest and said to Nazim;

"I think have a little indigestion Nazim" and before Nazim could reply Abdel fell to the ground. Nazim shouted for Harry to help and put him in the recovery position.

He was conscious but in a distressed state and unable to speak. An ambulance arrived within ten minutes. He spent a week in Harton Hospital and was told by the Doctors that he needed to look for a job that would not put too much strain on his heart. The cardiologist was definitive when he told Abdel; "You have survived this heart attack, but it may well be that you will not survive another. The condition of your heart can be stabilised with medication, and with a reduction in the physical aspect of your work, you can sustain a reasonably normal lifestyle."

Abdel was prescribed medication for his high blood pressure and told to rest and take some time off. Rose was adamant that Abdel would not be going back on the Homer and during his period of time off she encouraged him to look elsewhere for another job, Abdel was still only 52 and she was positive that he could gain a suitable job with less physical activity. In the weeks that followed Rose and Abdel spent many hours talking of their hopes and aspirations for the future.

Abdel would get melancholy at times and reflect upon his past. On one such occasion, he talked of his life at sea and how the horrors of the war and the loss of good friends was very painful. And how he became so single minded in his determination to survive and said to Rose; "I have seen many terrible things Rose, and God has shown mercy on me. I have lost many friends who were good men and I have witnessed death and destruction. I have killed another man Rose; this is an evil thing to do and yet here I am."

Rose was very emotive for her husband and said, "Abdel, you have nothing to feel remorseful about. You are a brave and honest man who has survived many life-threatening experiences."

"As a merchant seaman you helped keep this country going and what happened in Sacramento, could have happened to anyone. However, it was your courage that meant that evil man would not take a life that day in the store. You do not need God's forgiveness Abdel; your bravery was recognised by the law and you were commended for it remember."

"Yes, that is true Rose; sometimes I think could I have done something else. But I acted the only way I could at the time, I did not think this man would die."

"It is better that he died so you could live Abdel. If it had been you that had died that day; I would never had met you, loved you and I would not have this wonderful home and family."

After some three weeks of convalescing, Abdel was recommended for a post at the Ferry Landing in South Shields as a Night Watchman by the Master of the Homer, Rueben Morgan. Mr Morgan provided an excellent reference for Abdel and he attended an interview on December 21st with a Mr J. L. Stevenson.

Abdel arrived for the interview on time and was asked to complete an application form detailing his previous experience. He spent some 30 minutes completing the form and asked for more paper in order to finish his work resume.

Mr Stevenson sat opposite Abdel behind a fine oak desk and carefully read Abdel's submission. He was a small bald man with glasses that perched on a badly broken nose. He constantly adjusted them as he read, thus preventing them from slipping off his nose.

Having read the application form he removed his glasses saying, "I am I glad to take them off, glasses are a necessity I am afraid. But having my nose broken in two places by a cricket ball some years ago; does not help in keeping my glasses on my face. Well, you have extensive experience Abdul.

"It is Abdel sir, not Abdul," he replied.

"Sorry, forgive my ignorance Abdel."

They talked very informally and it allowed Abdel to relax and generally be himself. Mr Stevenson provided details of the job including; working conditions, contract, pay, sickness benefit, pension, holidays and duties of the Night Watchman. Abdel was confident in talking of his past and Mr Stevenson encouraged him to talk of his family and any interests. After another 30 minutes, Abdel was offered the job; which he gladly accepted and shook Mr Stevenson's hand saying,

"Thank you very much Mr Stevenson sir."

"Please, call me Jack. The Queen has not yet given me a Knighthood" and smiled adding; "I hope you enjoy working for the company Abdel and it has been a pleasure to offer you this position, good luck."

Abdel began his new job on January 5th 1971 at the South Shields Ferry Landing. The man he was replacing was Frank Kennedy and for the first week before his retirement he worked alongside Abdel and he demonstrated the duties that had to be undertaken. Frank was 65 and looking forward to his retirement and spending more time with his family. Abdel's shift began at 10pm after the last crossing from North Shields. The ferry was the Northumbrian, a passenger and car ferry under the auspices of the Tyne & Wear Passenger Transport Executive. The prospect of nightshift did not phase Abdel, as he was used to working long hours at night. The work itself was fairly repetitive, with general maintenance and security issues related to the vessel and the surrounding ferry landing. He had a small cabin that was furnished with a heater and simple appliances like a kettle and a fridge, along with a telephone. He took his radio and after doing his essential checks he would sit and listen to jazz. He would inspect the ferry and landing every two hours as a matter of routine.

On the odd occasion he would have to divert people away if they had missed the last ferry and much to their annoyance, were faced with an expensive taxi ride back to North Shields.

Ariana was enjoying school at Westoe Secondary Girls and was a keen netball and hockey player. She excelled in English Language and Literature, History and Geography. Like Ariana, Jacob attended Simonside Junior School and he enjoyed his sport with a particular passion for football and athletics. Life for the Rahman family had a symmetry and dignity about it and Abdel's new job had allowed him to regain some self-respect and a sense of responsibility.

In July 1972, the Al – Azhar Mosque was opened in Laygate and Abdel was present for the opening. A new building to welcome worshippers from the Muslim community. Abdel still used his prayer mat at home for prayers, if he could not get to the mosque. Abdel never influenced his children with his religion. Quite often he, Jacob and Ariana would talk of Islam and Christianity as equal theologies of spiritual importance. Abdel's employers had changed and Nexus were the organisation that now controlled the Cross Tyne Ferries. Rose had extended her working hours with her employers and money within the household was as good as it had ever been. This led to annual holiday's in Scotland, Malta and in 1973 they enjoyed a two-week holiday in Rimini, Italy.

During their stay Abdel wanted to visit the Commonwealth War Grave cemetery in Gradara. He was astonished at the sheer scale of the cemetery and as they walked along the rows of gravestones, he read the memorials of fallen soldiers, airmen and seamen.

Suddenly he stopped and he realised what was before him and said, "Rose, I met this man on board my ship during the war," and with tears cascading down his face he said,

"This man was from South Shields and he was on his way to Italy; Corporal James Peterkin, I talked with this man. "He then read the inscription on the memorial;

"In memory of Corporal James Frederick Peterkin. 4466854, 5th Battalion., Sherwood Foresters (Notts and Derby Regiment) who died

aged 32 on 15th September 1944.
Husband of Catherine Peterkin of South Shields, Co. Durham.
Remembered with honour."

Abdel fell to his knees in tears and Rose, Ariana and Jacob rushed to embrace him.

As he knelt over the grave Rose said, "War is so evil Abdel and hear are the remains of a man from my home town and I suspect his poor wife has never even been able to put flowers on his grave."

As she looked at the sea of gravestones she added; "All the families that have been torn apart in the name of freedom; it is so very sad."

Both Ariana and Jacob hugged their parents and Jacob said, "Why do we have wars Dad?"

Abdel turned to his son and said, "It is because the world has men who are tyrants and these men use their power to enslave and cause men's hearts to be hardened. "

They left the cemetery and caught the train back to Rimini. As they rose to leave their carriage at Rimini, Abdel noticed a nun struggling to carry her bags. He politely indicated that he would carry one of her bags for her. She smiled and said;

"Grazie figlio mio, Dio sia con te"

Having put her bag on the platform Ariana said, "What did she say Dad?"

Abdel looked at Rose for guidance, who replied; "I think she said, thank you Ariana."

Abdel continued to communicate with Hakim's widow Rahmina in Durban and Abdullah in Karachi via telephone, but they became less frequent as time moved on. On July 13th 1975, Abdullah died after a long battle with lung cancer. Abdel was saddened by this news and felt helpless, being so far away. He sent a telegram to Abdullah's family expressing his deepest sympathy for their loss. The people that were instrumental in his early life had gone and Abdel sought solace with his own family and valued their love and compassion.

Ariana like her namesake, began her training as a student nurse in September 1975. Jacob was a pupil at Harton Comprehensive School and his skills in sport had been quickly recognised. He was a junior member of South Shields Harriers and played football for his school, South Shields Schoolboys and County Durham. In 1976 he had trials for Darlington, Newcastle, Sunderland and Burnley. All the clubs were interested in signing him on schoolboy forms but he declined these offers to concentrate on completing his education. He was particularly adept in Geography, History, Science and

Technology and planned to go onto do "A Levels at the local South Shields Marine & Technical College. His other great interest was the Sea Scouts and he had an affinity with all things maritime. Abdel did not discourage him but would sit and talk of his past in the merchant navy. This only seemed to engage Jacob even more and rather than deflect his enthusiasm, it enhanced it. Rose was not so keen to see her only son sail off into the sunset and tried her best to dissuade him from this vocation.

In January 1977, Ariana fell pregnant to her fiancé Eric Hawkins. Eric was an only child and he was just coming to the end of his apprenticeship as an Electrical Engineer at Reyrolles in Hebburn. They were married in May of the same year and in September Ariana gave birth to a baby girl whom they named Molly Jane. Ariana was able to complete her nurse training with the help of Rose who reduced her hours at the solicitors in order to look after Molly. Abdel and Rose were delighted grandparents and at 15 years of age Jacob was now an uncle.

Jacob's first reaction to this news was to say;

"There is no way that I will be babysitting."

"Now Jacob, this is your niece and you are her only uncle. You may be called upon sometimes," said Rose.

"But I am still a child myself mam," he joked.

CHAPTER TWENTY-FOUR

Abdel was now 59 and looking forward to an early retirement. He had his Merchant Navy Ratings Pension due in a years' time and he would receive his state pension in 1983.

His general health was starting to decline, he found it difficult to shake of a cold and often it would lead to bronchitis. The harsh winter nights at the ferry landing were starting to have an adverse effect on his health.

Ariana had two more children in 1979 and 1980, another girl Grace Emma and a son Eric Abdel. Jacob finished his "A 'Levels getting excellent grades and began a degree in Mechanical Engineering at Newcastle University.

The winter of 1980 would be a defining period in Abdel's life. On the bitterly cold evening of December 17th he set off for work as usual at 9.45pm. He past the Ferry Tavern and noticed that a party was in full swing in the lounge.

Two "ladies of the night" were standing outside enjoying a cigarette and as he walked past, one of them said,

"How about a quickie love, round the back."

It wasn't the first time this had occurred and Abdel replied; "Thank you dear, but not tonight," and proceeded to the ferry landing.

Due to the inclement weather the ferry had stopped for the night and a sign had been hung on the entrance gates saying,

NEXT FERRY NOT UNTIL 7.30am - TOMORROW DECEMBER 18th

Abdel made his way to his cabin and dropped his bag off before speaking to the crew who were just tying off the ferry Freda Cunningham and securing her to the dock. After chatting to the crew, he returned to his cabin and put his heater on. As the snow began to fall, the crew waved goodnight to Abdel as they left the landing. Just before midnight as Abdel was carrying out his first inspection, a man approached the landing. He was obviously drunk as he swayed from side to side struggling to maintain his equilibrium.

Abdel had had various examples of revellers looking to catch the last ferry and said, "Can I help you sir?"

"I need the ferry mate, where is it?"

"I am sorry but there are no more ferries until 7.30am in the morning."

The man looked about 6'2" in height and big across his shoulders, he had close cropped hair and he probably weighed something like 17 stone. He was wearing a blue denim Levi jacket and matching jeans. He looked to be in his mid-thirty's and he carried a prominent scar on his left cheek. Abdel chose not to get to close and kept a good distance between him and the man and said, "I think you will need to book a taxi sir."

"Fuck off, I'm not paying for any fucking Taxi you black bastard."

His response was not unusual and Abdel had over the years, experienced similar aggressive reactions by people who had missed the last ferry. On this occasion he felt he was back in Sacramento standing in that store. He feared violence would be coming his way, and wondered how this was going be resolved and said, "I am asking you to leave the ferry landing sir, or I will have to ring for the police."

The man turned and wandered out of the landing cursing as he went.

Abdel felt relieved that the situation had not escalated into a violent confrontation. He watched as the man disappeared into the market square. Abdel completed his inspection and returned to his cabin and picked up his latest read *"Bury My Heart at Wounded Knee"* by Dee Brown, an account of the native Indians of the American West and their compelling story of how their land and culture were taken away. Abdel felt a resonance with the Indians and found the narrative a sad commentary on man's inhumanity to his fellow man.

He looked out of his cabin window, the snowfall had stopped and he returned to his book. As he turned a page to chapter eleven, he heard something and raised his head to see a figure standing a short distance from his cabin.

The man who half an hour earlier, had abused Abdel had returned. Abdel had no time to react as the man hurled a 3-foot-long, 2-inch diameter iron bar through the cabin window. The bar struck Abdel on the bridge of his nose and sent him flying into the cabin wall behind him. The impact knocked him unconscious, the man fled leaving Abdel badly injured.

Abdel stirred and slowly began to come to terms with what had happened. His eyesight was blurred, but he managed to find the telephone and dial 999. He was in a bad way and again fell unconscious after making the call. His nose was badly broken, he had lacerations to his face, neck and hands from the flying glass. The police and ambulance were on the scene within five minutes and he was rushed to Harton Hospital. He had lost a lot of blood and he was still unconscious when he was admitted to A&E.

Rose was informed of the assault on her husband when the police arrived at 1.45am. Both her and Jacob were taken to the hospital in the police car. When they got to A&E Abdel was still unconscious, he was being examined for internal injuries and treated for the numerous cuts and abrasions to his head. When she saw him lying on the bed, she barley recognised him and she broke down.

Jacob held his mother tight and with tears in his eyes said, "Don't worry mam, Dad is made of strong stuff; he will get over this," and added; "I will ring Ariana and tell her what has happened" and off he went to use the hospitals public telephone.

The police were in attendance, waiting for Abdel to regain consciousness, so they could gain some information as to the assailant.

When Jacob returned, a Doctor asked both Rose and Jacob to join him in an adjoining room. He invited them to sit down and said, "Hello Mrs Rahman, my name is Doctor John Fitzgerald. Your husband has sustained serious trauma to his head Mrs Rahman. We are treating him for blood loss and monitoring his vital signs including temperature, blood pressure, heart rate, breathing and we are currently checking for any fractures and internal injuries. We are hoping he will regain consciousness soon but he is in a stable condition as we speak, have you any questions at this stage?"

Rose was still in a state of shock and she was finding it difficult to converse and Jacob asked; "What damage has he sustained to his head Doctor?"

"Well, he has suffered a very powerful blow that has certainly resulted in some kind of trauma. What that trauma reveals will be available after we have an x-ray, which we will be carrying out very soon. All I can say is that the sooner he awakes the better, it will enable us to gleam more information in that regard," he replied.

"Has he spoken since he was admitted?" asked Jacob.

"No, I am afraid not. But that is quite normal, in these cases. He is on pain relief and medication to guard against infection," added the Doctor.

Both Rose and Jacob thanked him and the Doctor left to return to his patient. As he left two police officers came in and introduced themselves as constables Dennis Ringwood and Peter Sloanes. Constable Ringwood spoke first and said, "We have been assigned to this case Mrs Rahman and I promise you we will apprehend the perpetrator of this cowardly crime. Do you have any questions for us?"

Rose was now coming to terms with what had occurred and said, "Were you there after it happened?"

"Yes, we were first on the scene; just before the ambulance arrived."

"Was Abdel conscious when you got there?" She asked.

"No, I am afraid he was not; however, he must have been lucid at some stage because he managed to dial 999 and we were on the scene within five minutes," replied constable Sloanes.

Constable Ringwood went onto say, "Had Abdel spoke of any recent trouble at the ferry landing regarding threats or unruly behaviour Mrs Rahman?"

"He has always had the odd guy who was drunk who had missed the last ferry, but no threats of violence or anything like that really," she replied.

"Well thank you for that and we will be able to find this individual once we have spoken to Abdel, when hopefully he can give us a description of his attacker," said Sloanes.

Rose and Jacob remained in the side room and within fifteen minutes Ariana arrived. She hugged both her mother and brother and tearfully asked;

"How is Dad, can I see him?"

"He is in a stable condition Ariana, but you won't recognise him. He is in one hell of a state," said Jacob.

"Oh my God, he should not be left alone on that ferry landing. There all sorts of nutters down there when the pubs are emptying, when did it happen? she replied.

"We think about 12.30am," said Jacob.

"Is he awake then?"

"No, he did ring 999 after it happened; but he has not regained consciousness since the ambulance brought him in," added Rose.

"Have they got the swine who did this?"

"No, not yet. They are hoping that Dad will be able to give the police a description when he wakes up," replied Jacob.

At 1.45am Abdel underwent a brain scan and thankfully there was no evidence of any bleeding in the brain or skull fracture. At 2am Doctor Fitzgerald spoke to Rose, Jacob and Ariana again saying, "I am pleased to say that Abdel has not sustained any brain injuries and skull fractures after we have x – rayed within the last half hour, that's the good news. However, we need him to wake soon to assess his cognitive reactions. His vital signs are encouraging, his heart rate is good and he has been taken off the ventilator. It's now a waiting game I'm afraid."

As she sat in the side room Rose said, "That's it, he is not going back to that job after this, he will have to take early retirement."

As they discussed the implications of Abdel's retirement a man walked into the room and said, "I am so sorry about this tragic event. I believe it's Rose is it not" and he stepped forward to shake her hand.

"My name is Robert Wainwright and I am a Senior Executive of Nexus, your husband's employer."

"Thank you," replied Rose.

"If there is anything I can do, please let me know. I assure you that we will be doing everything we can to ensure the person that is responsible for this heinous crime is brought to justice. If you need anything please let me or my staff know and in the short term, we will cover the cost of any transport for your family to and from the hospital. I had the pleasure of meeting Abdel some weeks ago before he left the ferry landing to go home. I must say he impressed me with his honesty and dedication to his work and I have to admit I felt humbled in his company. I do hope he makes a speedy recovery."

"Thank you for your kind words," replied Rose.

At 4am in the morning Abdel woke up from his enforced dormancy. As he started to take in the surroundings pain began to hit him with great intensity. The nurse by his bedside quickly called the Doctor who came and ascertained where the pain was and administered the subsequent morphine.

As the pain relief began to work the Doctor asked Abdel if he could talk for a short while, Abdel said, "I think I can, where am I?"

"You are in Harton Hospital Abdel Rahman, my name is Doctor John Fitzgerald. Can you remember what happened to you last night?"

Abdel looked at the Doctor and said, "I can remember snow falling."

"Yes, that is true it did snow last night. What else can you remember?"

Abdel's brain was conjuring up all kinds of mental imagery and then he replied; "A man, a saw a man and blood and glass."

"Anything else Abdel?"

"Telephone, the telephone I think I rang…"

"That is correct you dialled for an ambulance and you were brought here."

Panic gripped Abdel and he said, "My wife and family, I must see them."

"Yes Abdel, they are here. But before I bring them in, I need you to see Philippa our Psychiatric Nurse. Is that alright, it won't take long?"

Philippa came in and sat by Abdel's bed and said, "Hello Abdel, you have sustained quite a few injuries. I just want to ask you a few questions, is that ok?"

Abdel nodded and asked; "Will it take long; I need to see may family; they will be worried about me."

"Oh no, this will not take long at all," and she said,

"Firstly, how old are you Abdel?"

"I am 62" he replied.

"What is your date of birth?"

He gave this a little thought and said, "October 15th 1918."

"What was your mother's name?"

"Fatima," he answered.

"Do you take any medication and if so, what is it for?"

"I take pills for high blood pressure."

"Last question Abdel, can you give me the names of your children?"

"Ariana and Jacob."

"That's great Abdel thank you."

She then went to collect Rose, Jacob and Ariana. Before taking them to see Abdel Philippa said,

"Please I know you are desperate to see him, but be aware that he has been through a traumatic experience and can you limit your time with him. This will allow us to carry out further checks on his physical injuries and his mobility."

"What about the police, they want to speak to him about the assault," added Jacob.

"I am sorry, but they will have to wait, possibly tomorrow. Your father is still in a fragile state of mind."

They thanked the nurse and went to see Abdel. Rose wanted to hold him so much, but just held his hand as she sat on a chair next to his bed. Jacob and Ariana pulled two chairs to the other side of his bed. Abdel could not speak at first, the emotion was too much and the tears just cascaded down his face. Rose spoke first and said, "Abdel oh Abdel, I am so happy that you have woken. This has been terrible, but you will get better. We are all going to take care of you."

"I thank God that I have you all with me, mercy has been shown to me again."

"Are you in pain Dad," asked Ariana.

"No, not really Ariana. But I think they have given me pain killers."

"What can you remember about last night Dad?" asked Jacob

"I do not remember much at all, but little things are slowly coming back to me Jacob."

"Don't worry about that, you get well first," added Rose.

They sat with Abdel for fifteen minutes; then Doctor Fitzgerald and Philippa the Physiocratic Nurse returned, the Doctor then said,

"I know this is tough for you all right now, but we need to give your father some rest. He is in good hands here and he has made significant progress already. I will give you my diagnosis in twenty minutes, if you would like to return to the side room."

As promised the Doctor met with Rose, Jacob and Ariana and gave his diagnosis and care plan saying, "We have established that there is no evidence of any brain damage; that's great news because in cases like this it is a major concern. Let's tell you what his injuries are and we can take it from there. Firstly, his nose is broken in two places and that needs surgery. Secondly, he has numerous lacerations to his face and head, some will leave scarring. Thirdly, he has a dislocated left shoulder and three broken fingers on his left hand. Finally, there is a concern about the amount of fluid on his lungs. All these issues can and will be treated while he is in hospital.

"In addition, there is the physiological aspect of his condition. He can remember some elements of what occurred, but it may well be that he will never be able to regain his memory of what actually happened. That is the dilemma, but it has not created any physiological trauma. That may well occur when he reflects on the incident. What I will say is this; Abdel has a remarkable knack of overcoming physical and mental pain. I have read his medical report and this man has been through a number of life-threatening experiences, as no doubt you are aware. I am sure he will overcome adversity once again and with your love and devotion, he will be fine. Do you have any questions for me?"

"The police will want to talk to my Dad soon," said Jacob.

"Well, I understand their need for information; but I will only allow that to happen, when I feel your father is ready to impart any relevant facts."

They thanked the Doctor for his candour and at 5am they spent a few minutes saying goodbye to Abdel, before jumping in a taxi. Nexus picked up the tab for the car. After spending Christmas in hospital Abdel went home on January 3rd, having spent 16 days recovering. He still carried the scars of the assault and his mobility was weakened, he needed to be helped in and out of the taxi. Rose could see that the attack on her husband had made him fragile and he seemed withdrawn.

The police had arrested the man responsible for the assault. After the violence he rained down on Abdel, he flagged a taxi to take him home to North Shields. Police interviewed all taxi drivers who were working in the area that night and one driver identified the man and provided his address. Ironically, he was a merchant seaman by the name of Brian Colin Hamilton aged 37. He pleaded not guilty, but he was found guilty of Grievous Bodily Harm and was given the maximum sentence of 5 years imprisonment. Abdel did not attend the trial at Newcastle Crown Court, but Rose did and told Abdel she just wanted to *"look this coward in the eye."*

Abdel did not return to work, NEXUS gave him an early retirement package on the grounds of ill health, he was 62. It took some time before he adjusted to sleeping at night and he often had nightmares of his attack. As the months past he grew stronger and got back to spending time in the garden.

He had regular visitors including Nazim, Harry and Sam. In addition, family were always visiting and he looked forward to see his grandchildren who kept him amused with their relentless energy. In May 1981, he received the sad news that Brody had died after a long battle with stomach cancer. It was at this time that Rose began to complain of headaches but just put it down to migraine and lack of sleep. On one occasion Ariana asked her to go to the Doctors saying, "Mam, you need to get it checked out."

"Yes, I will I suppose."

She didn't and after another month the headaches had intensified and became unbearable. She relented and went to the Doctors with Ariana. The Doctor immediately sent her for an x – ray, the prognosis was not good. Rose had a tumour on her brain. She was devastated and she was informed that it was inoperable and she would have to undergo a course of chemotherapy. The consultant could not give a timeline but said that the tumour was particularly aggressive. He added that the chemotherapy drugs may slow down the growth of the tumour, but the cancer was terminal.

Abdel took the news badly and broke down uncontrollably. Rose tried to appease him by saying,

"Hey, I am not dead yet, lets us make the most of this time together. We should have a trip away somewhere."

"What am I to do without you Rose, you are my life."

"Abdel, you must think of yourself and our family. You have to be strong" she replied.

"God has forsaken me Rose."

"No, he has not, your God wants you to be the man you have always been. You must not let me down now, I want what time I have left to be happy for us both and something for you to cherish, as I will."

In August 1981, Abdel and Rose spent a week in Scotland staying in Inverness and Oban. It was a time of reflection and devotion. Abdel took his camera and recorded the moments and got the odd stranger to capture them both on film. They enjoyed the highlands and openly talked about what the future held. At times it was too emotional for Abdel, but Rose was strong and pleaded with him to look forward. The tumour was unrelenting; the drugs were not having any great effect and Rose was regularly taking strong painkillers during their stay. On their return Rose was admitted to South Shields General Hospital and after a courageous battle she died at 4.15pm on September 15th.

Abdel was at her bedside when she he quietly fell asleep for the last time. He could not control his sadness and despair and he asked the ward sister to telephone Ariana and give her the news. Within twenty minutes, Ariana arrived with Jacob and Jane and all four were entwined in sorrow and grief. Having gained, a modicum of composure Abdel said, "Your mam did not deserve this, I always thought I would die first. Why has God done this to us?"

"Dad, we all have to go sometime, who knows how long mam has had this cancer. I had to take her to the Doctor's in the end, but it was probably too late then," added Ariana. The Doctor joined them and gave his condolences, he turned to Abdel and said, "It is no consolation I know, but your wife did not suffer at the end. She just slowly drifted into a deep sleep and passed away, and I am so sorry for your loss."

The desolation in Abdel's eyes was palpable and he sank his head in anguish. As they left the hospital, Abdel looked up to the heavens. An incandescent red glow had appeared in the eastern sky, it seemed to tell Abdel that his beloved Rose was at rest and in God's hands.

Ariana suggested that her father should stay with her for a few days saying, "Dad, I think you should come and spend some time with us."

"That is a good idea Abdel, you need your family around at this time," added Jane.

"Thank you Ariana, but I must go home; I need time to pray and be at home for visitors to call and give their respects to your mother."

Jacob gave Ariana a quick glance and raised his eyebrows and said,

"Dad, just go for one night; mam would have wanted it that way."

Abdel paused and looked at Ariana and said, "Yes, I will do this; but I must go to the Mosque first. Can you take me there?"

"Yes Dad, come on jump in the car," replied Jacob.

Abdel spent two days with Ariana, Eric and his grandchildren and then returned home. He did his best to come to terms with the solitude and with regular visits from family and friends the feeling of isolation was diluted. Then Rose's funeral had to ne endured. She was buried in Harton Cemetery on September 22nd after a short service at All Saints Church on Boldon Lane. Jacob did a reading and the eulogy for his mother, highlighting how her love for all the family and his Dad was all consuming.

Jacob, Eric, Nazim and Nawab Hussain carried her coffin out of the church followed by Abdel arm in arm with Ariana. It was a warm late summer day as she was laid to rest in a family plot that Abdel had procured. The wake was held in the Old Ship in Harton Village. Abdel was doing his best to remain dignified and composed, but as the time moved on, he became downcast by the reality of his loss. Jacob had noticed this and suggested his father should go home accompanied by close family and Nazim, who was at his friends side throughout. Taxi 's were organised and Ariana, Jacob, and Nazim returned to Simonside with Abdel.

Back in his home Abdel sat and began to reflect on his life. He began with his devotion to Rose and rekindled their first meeting and how it led to their romance and marriage. Although his children had heard snippets of their early married life, both Jacob and Ariana enjoyed their father's recollections. This personal appraisal of their parents was cherished and at times Ariana's emotions got the better of her and she openly wept.

As Abdel went further back to his childhood and his life in Karachi, he recalled many experiences his children were not aware of and Jacob said, "Did mam know of your life back then Dad?"

"Oh yes, my son; your mother knew everything about me. It is a wonder to me she still married me," he joked.

They sat and listened intently and Ariana made numerous pots of tea, as the tales unfolded.

Nazim voiced his thoughts and said,

"You could write a book about your life Abdel."

"It would not be me, but someone could Nazim," he replied.

Time had seemed to evaporate and at 10pm Ariana said, "Dad we have been sitting here for five hours, where has the time gone?

"I must get back to my family," added Nazim.

"Yes, mine too," said Ariana and looking at her brother added.

"Anyway Jacob, when are you going to give Dad another grandchild?"

"When I find the woman of my dreams," he replied.

Nazim grinned and said, "What does this woman look like then?"

"I will tell you when I find her," he replied.

"She will need the patience of Job, that is for sure" quipped Ariana.

"Now then children, patience is a virtue is it not," said Abdel.

"Yes Dad, but its Jacob we are talking about here" she joked.

"Are you going to be alright tonight Dad?" asked Ariana.

"Yes, I will be fine. I am going to listen to some of my records, before I go to bed Ariana" he replied. They all bid goodnight and as he hugged his father Jacob said,

"Just ring if you want anything Dad."

"Go, I will be fine son and take care of your sister," he added.

Abdel sat and reflected upon what was left of his life and although overcome with sorrow, he somehow felt a need to restore his faith in God. He got his prayer mat out and asked God for his help with his dilemma. He then put his Hot Club of Paris LP on his record player and listened to the magic of Django Reinhardt and Stephane Grappelli. After ten minutes he fell asleep and awoke at 3am in the morning. He could not sleep and sat and watched as the late September sun slowly rose in the eastern sky.

Being the only occupier of the house, the local council had a policy of re – housing widows or widowers to enable families to be accommodated in a more suitable residence. Ariana had ensured that he would be allocated a good alternative and she made herself a bit of a tyrant with the housing office, until she was satisfied with the final outcome. Her father would be given a bungalow in Winskill Road, not too far from Airey Avenue.

With the help of both Jacob and Ariana, Abdel moved into his two-bedroom bungalow on February 12th 1982. Jacob stayed with his father for two days to soften the blow of leaving a home that had so many happy memories. Later that year Jacob graduated from Durham University and Ariana, Jane and Abdel were there to see him receive his degree in Engineering.

In January 1983 year Jacob married his girlfriend Michelle and, in the December of 1983, she gave birth to a boy whom they named Adam Hakim Rahman. He was christened at All Saints Church in Boldon Lane on Sunday, April 29th 1984.

Abdel had grown weaker and he was now taking regular medication for his blood pressure and bronchitis. He still made his weekly visit to the Mosque and his family were constant visitors to his bungalow. He had help with his cleaning from the council's home help department.

He spent much of his time watching TV, playing videos of films such as The Godfather, Ben Hur, The Old Man and The Sea, Laurel and Hardy and the Marx Brothers. He maintained his passion for reading and his current book was *Seven Men at Daybreak* by Anthony Burgess. His general health would not cope with any physical work, therefore his enthusiasm relating to gardening was reduced to a few potted plants.

He still received letters from Karachi, Durban and Sacramento. He enjoyed reading how his friends were getting on with their lives. Over the years Abdel had taken many photographs and he had a number of albums filled with visual recollections of his life. He was quite independent and always managed to provide meals for himself and would often create his own curries using a variety of new spices. It was the loneliness that proved to be the greatest challenge for him and he began to opt out of his regular visit to the Mosque. Both Ariana and Jacob had discussed this and felt a little helpless. Jacob suggested a short break to Scotland or the Lake District, but Ariana thought that would be too much for her Father. On June 17th they called on their father and sat with him to try and get him to spend some time with Ariana and his grandchildren.

After a few games of dominoes his demeanour improved and he reluctantly agreed but added; "I do not want to be a burden on my family, but I will come to your house and see my grandchildren again."

Abdel enjoyed this short break and spent many hours talking to his grandchildren about his life and the many people he had met. He reminisced about his trek to Karachi, his first voyage on the City of Venice, his life during the war, South Africa and Sacramento. In July 1985 Abdel was admitted to hospital with severe breathing difficulties and spent time on the cardiac ward. His condition improved and he was allowed to go home after six days of treatment and convalescence.

Having a telephone enabled him to speak to his family, it also allowed Jacob and Ariana to make regular calls to check on his health and well-being. As autumn turned to winter the cold weather had an adverse effect on Abdel's condition. He was a virtual prisoner in his own home.

Ariana and Jacob made regular trips to see him and fulfil his wants and needs. On December 8th Nora his home help was cleaning his kitchen when she heard him coughing and then a heavy thud. She dashed into the sitting room to see Abdel on the floor. She crouched down and called to him; "Abdel can you hear me?"

There was no response, she could see that he was breathing, but very languid. She rang 999 and within five minutes an ambulance arrived, shortly followed by a police car with two officers. The ambulance crew managed to get him stabilised and he was rushed to South Shields General Hospital at 2.36pm.

After he had been whisked away the two officers spoke to Nora and asked what had occurred. Having taken the details one officer asked; "What was he doing when you were in the kitchen?"

She pointed to the photo album on the floor and said, "He was looking through his photo's, he always liked to reminisce" and added.

"You must inform his family, there phone numbers are on the table next to the phone."

Ariana and Jacob arrived at the hospital at 3.05pm. Their father was in A&E and on a life support machine. He was still unconscious, but on a ventilator. A Doctor asked to speak with them and they went and sat in a side room. The doctor introduced himself as Dr Robin Higham and said,

"Your father is very ill and I am afraid his prognosis is critical. He is on a ventilator but he has already had two heart failures since he was admitted. We have resuscitated him, but his heart will not withstand another trauma. All we can do is hope and pray that he somehow gains enough strength to breath independently. I am sorry to give you this sad news but I have to be perfectly honest with you."

Ariana wept openly and Jacob cradled his sister and asked; "Will he ever regain consciousness Doctor?"

"It is possible, but highly unlikely. If he does; he will be able to hear you, but he cannot speak." he replied.

Ariana and Jacob sat either side of their father's bed.

"He looks so peaceful Jacob," said Ariana.

"Yes, he must have some inner strength to be able to be revived after two more heart attacks Ariana," added Jacob.

Jacob had barely finished speaking when suddenly Abdel opened his eyes. Ariana sat up and although shocked said,

"Jacob he is awake, Dad is awake."

A nurse heard Ariana and called the Doctor.

Abdel looked at Ariana and then turned to look at Jacob.

"Dad, its Ariana and Jacob, thank God your alive," said his daughter, as the tears cascaded down her face.

She held his hand and Abdel's eyes filled up. As quickly as they had opened, they closed for the last time and the monitor above his bed gave out a constant buzz. The Doctor and nurse rushed in and checked his vital signs. Ariana and Jacob stood at the end of the bed holding each other. Abdel was pronounced dead at 5.13am. His lungs had been unable to function with so much fluid and his heart had stopped for the third and last time. Resuscitation would have been futile and Abdel Malik Rahman entered paradise on December 9th 1985, aged 67.

Abdel was buried in the Muslim section of Harton Cemetery on December 12th. It was a very cold morning and Abdel had requested that the local Imam should conduct the burial. The temperature read -10 and the soil surrounding his grave was solid with ice. Jacob read a quotation over his father's grave, first penned by Napoleon Hill in 1938.

> *"The first duty of every human being is to himself. Every person owes himself the duty of finding how to live a full and happy life. A life that is lived with fullness of peace of mind, contentment and happiness always divests itself of everything it does not want. Will you be guided by faith? Or will you allow fear to overtake you?"*

Up in the higher reaches of the Paropamisus Mountains a red star shone in the moonlight. The star was not in the sky, but emblazoned on the wreckage of a Soviet Mi-24 Hind Helicopter. Afghanistan was in violent turmoil once more. A snow leopard pays little attention to the crumpled wreckage as she searches for pray. Her soft feet are silent as she moves through the sagebrush looking to catch an unsuspecting markhor. Her cubs are in need of sustenance. She freezes as she senses movement and then sees her quarry some 20 feet above her on a snow lined ridge.

BIBILOGRAPHY

The Way of Poetry by John Drinkwater. Collins. London. 1919.
The Second Great War. Volume 5. Amalgamated Press Ltd. London. 1949.
Poems for Speaking by Richard Church. J.M. Dent & Sons Ltd. London. 1950.
The Kon-Tiki Expedition by Thor Heyerhahl. Allen & Unwin. London. 1952.
The Ship by C.S. Forester. Michael Joseph Ltd. London. 1952.
The Holy Bible – King James Version. Harper Collins Publishing. London. 1957.
The Observers Book of Ships by Frank E. Dodman. Frank Warne & Co Ltd. London. 1958.
Nor They Understand by L.B. Winter. Jacaranda Press PTY Ltd. Brisbane. 1966.
Afghanistan – Land of the High Flags by Rosanne Klass. Robert Hale Ltd. London. 1968.
Traveller Extraordinary – The Life of James Bruce of Kinnaird by J.M. Ried. The History Book Club. London. 1968.
The War at Sea 1939–1945. Book Club Associates. Hutchinson Publishing Group Ltd. London. 1974.
The Battle of the Atlantic – World War II by Barrie Pitt. Time Life Books. New Jersey. 1977.
Sea and River Pilots by Nancy Martin. Terrence Dalton Ltd. Lavenham. 1977.
Twenty Singing Seamen by Ronald Hope. The Marine Society. London. 1979.
Secrets of The Sea by Carl Proujan. Readers Digest Association. London. 1979.
The Hardware of World War II by E. Grove, C. Chant, D. Lyon & H. Lyon. Orbis Publishing Ltd. London. 1984.
Bury My Heart at Wounded Knee by Dee Brown. Vintage. 1991.
The Oxford Book of the Sea by Jonathan Raban. Oxford University Press. Oxford. 1992.
Robinson Crusoe by Daniel Defoe. Alfred A. Knopf. New York. 1992.
High Fronts & Low Backs by Alan Norris. The Professional Authors & Publishers Association. London. 1994.
From Ta'izz To Tyneside by Richard I. Lawless. University of Exeter Press. Exeter. 1995.
Geographical Atlas of The World. Tiger Books International PLC. London. 1995.

The Noble Qur'an. Darussalam Publishing. Riyadh. 1996.
The Peoples History – South Shields, by John & Joyce Carlson. The Peoples History. Seaham. 1998.
Sailors Luck by Rear Admiral Geoffrey Hall. The Memoir Club. South Shields. 1999.
The Worlds Merchant Fleets 1939 by Roger Jordan. Chatham Publishing. London. 1999.
Illustrated Dictionary of Sailing Ships, Boats & Steamers by Scott Robertson. Nexus Special Interests Ltd. Swanley. 2000.
Afghanistan – A Short History of its People & Politics by Martin Ewans. Harper Collins Publishers Inc. New York. 2002.
Battleship by H.P. Willmott. Cassell. London. 2002.
The Quiet Heroes by Bernard Edwards. Leo Cooper. Barnsley. 2003.
Sacramento – Indomitable City by Steven M. Avella. Arcadia Publishing. Charleston. USA. 2003.
World Travel Atlas. Highway Columbus Publishing. Swanley. 2003.
The Road to Oxiana by Robert Byron. Pimlico. London. 2004.
Royal Navy Handbook 1939-1945 by David Wragg. Sutton Publishing Ltd. Stroud. 2005.
Into the Minefields, British Destroyer Minelaying 1916-1960 by Peter C. Smith. Pen & Sword Maritime. Barnsley. 2005.
Humour Across Frontiers by Richard D. Lewis. Transceen Publications. Warnford. 2005.
Tales from the Tyne by Dick Keys & Ken Smith. Tyne Bridge Publishing. Newcastle Upon Tyne. 2006.
Afghanistan: A Brief History by Shaista Wahab and Barry Youngerman. Infobase Publishing. London. 2007.
Naval Accidents by Malcolm Maclean. Maritime Books. Liskeard. 2008.
Lessons from The Qur'an by Mahmood Jawaid. Ta – Ha Publishers. London.
Nautical Curiosities by Terry Breverton. Quercus Publishing. London. 2010.
Remembering Sacramento by James Scott and Tom Tolley. Turner Publishing Company. USA. 2010.
Afghanistan – A Cultural & Political History by Thomas Barfield. Princeton University Press. Princeton. 2010.
The Sea by John Mack. Reaktion Books Ltd. London. 2011.
Engineers of Victory by Paul Kennedy. Penguin Books Ltd. London. 2013.
Down to The Sea In Ships by Horatio Clare. Chatto & Windus. London. 2014.

Hitler's Gateway to the Atlantic by Lars Hellwinkell. Seaforth Publishing. Barnsley. 2014.
The Naked Shore by Tom Blass. Bloomsbury Publishing. London. 2015.
Ocean by DK Publishing. London. 2015.
The Seaman's Pocket Book. June 1943. Osprey Publishing. London. 2015.
The Making of India by Kartar Lalvani. Bloomsbury Publishing Plc. London. 2016.
Inside the Soul of Islam by Mamoon Yusaf. Hay House UK Ltd. London. 2017.
Pashto – Dictionary & Phrasebook by Nicholas Awde & Asmatullah. Hippocrene Books Inc. New York. 2017.
Off the Deep End by Nic Compton. Bloomsbury Publishing Ltd. London. 2017.
A Short History of South Africa by Gail Nattrass. Biteback Publishing Ltd. London. 2017.
First History of Sacramento City by Dr John F. Morse. Sacramento County Collectors Book Club. USA. 2018.
Cargo Liners & Tramps by Mark Lee Inman. Amberley Publishing. Stroud. 2018.
The War for The Seas by Evan Mawdsley. Yale University Press. London. 2019.
A Short History of Seafaring by Brain Lavery. Dorling Kindersley Ltd. London. 2019.

QUOTATIONS

The Noble Qur'an
Be grateful and God will give you more
Dear believers, seek help through resilience and prayer. Indeed, God is with the resilient`
In the name of Allah
Fight in the way of Allah
Oh God, bless this couple

St. James Bible
Psalm 55: 4-6
Psalm 117:2

The Corsair by Lord Byron
O the glad waters of the dark blue sea

Robert Burns
Till a` the seas gang dry

Bernard Edwards
As always, their spirit was indomitable

William Cowper
God moves in a mysterious way

Napoleon Hill
The first duty of every human being